The Warhammer world is founded upon the exploits of brave heroes, and the rise and fall of powerful enemies. Now for the first time the tales of these mythical events have been brought to life in a new range of books. Divided into a series of trilogies, each brings you hitherto untold details of the lives and times of the most legendary of all Warhammer heroes and villains. Combined together, they will reveal some of the hidden connections that underpin the history of the Warhammer world.

—❮ THE BLACK PLAGUE ❯—

The tale of an Empire divided, its heroic defenders and the enemies who endeavour to destroy it with the deadliest plague ever loosed upon the world of man. This series begins with *Dead Winter* and continues in *Blighted Empire*.

—❮ THE WAR OF VENGEANCE ❯—

The ancient races of elf and dwarf clash in a devastating war that will decide not only their fates, but that of the entire Old World. The first novel in this series is *The Great Betrayal*, and is followed by *Master of Dragons*.

—❮ BLOOD OF NAGASH ❯—

The first vampires, tainted children of Nagash, spread across the world and plot to gain power over the kingdoms of men. This series starts in *Neferata*, and carries on with *Master of Death*.

Keep up to date with the latest information from the **Time of Legends** at *www.blacklibrary.com*

TIME OF LEGENDS™

Book Two of the Blood of Nagash

MASTER OF DEATH

The Blood of Nagash

Josh Reynolds

BLACK LIBRARY

For Noah

A BLACK LIBRARY PUBLICATION

First published in Great Britain in 2013 by
Black Library,
Games Workshop Ltd.,
Willow Road, Nottingham,
NG7 2WS, UK

10 9 8 7 6 5 4 3 2 1

Cover illustration by Stefan Kopinski.
Map by Nuala Kennedy.

See Black Library on the internet at
www.blacklibrary.com

Find out more about Games Workshop
and the world of Warhammer at
www.games-workshop.com

Printed and bound by CPI Group (UK) Ltd, Croydon, CR0 4YY

It is a Time of Legends.

Nagash the Usurper is dead, but his last revenge has devastated the once-mighty kingdoms of Nehekhara. As the city-states turn to dust and their kings moulder in their graves awaiting their promised rebirth, a new power rises.

Before the fall, in the city of Lahmia, Queen Neferata and her inner circle learned the secrets of eternal life from Nagash's unholy tomes, becoming the first of a brand new race – the vampires. Thirsty for blood and power in equal measure, each of these powerful creatures pursues their own goals with single-minded fervour.

Neferata, proud and vain, seeks to re-establish her empire and once again reign as queen. W'soran, master of the magical arts, desires power over life and death.

Abhorash, a warrior born, battles to slake his bloodthirst and regain his lost honour.

But for all their plots and schemes, the vampires are nothing more than pawns in another, much larger, game – Nagash's influence weighs heavily upon all those of his blood, and one day, he will return...

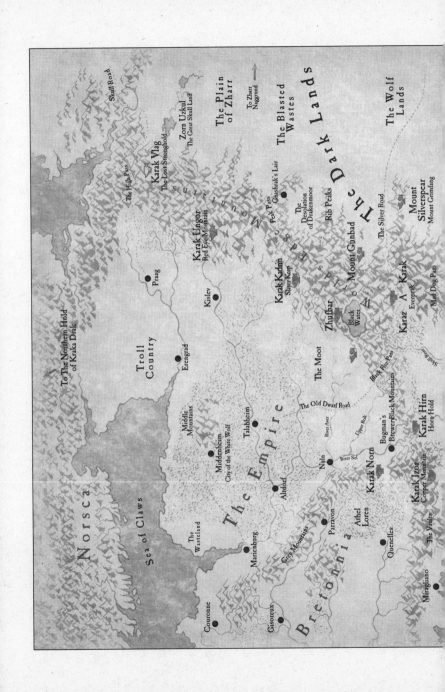

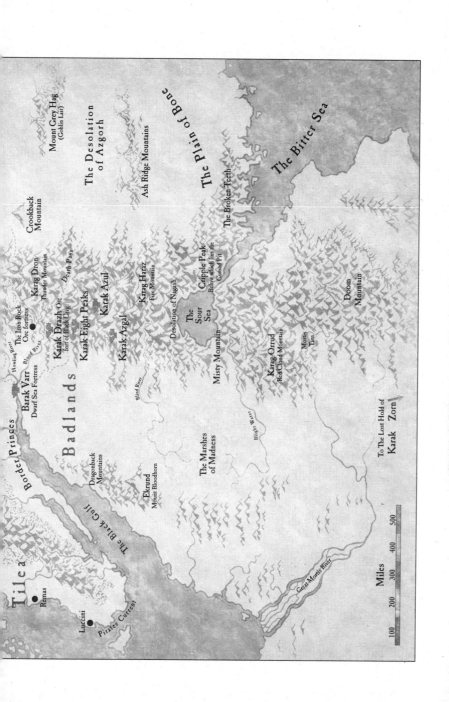

─◄ PROLOGUE ►─

The Worlds Edge Mountains,
(Year -223 Imperial Calendar)

W'soran awoke slowly, reluctantly. Eyelids as thin as parchment peeled back from dull orbs – one a grisly yellow, the other milky white and blind – even as thin, desiccated lips retreated from the thicket of needle fangs that occupied his mouth. The twin leathery slashes that were his nostrils flared, taking in the air instinctively. He smelled the effluvium of age, the cold, harsh stink of rock and the faintest odour of long-ago spilled blood.

The latter brought memories scrambling to the surface of his mind. This place had, once upon a time, belonged to a particularly tenacious mountain tribe: hairy savages who had, nonetheless, managed to wrest some form of civilised dwelling from the mountains. They had built a fastness on a fang-like crag, piling stones upon ancient foundations that

9

W'soran suspected had once belonged to one of the elder races. It had been an impressive feat, given their relative brutishness.

W'soran had butchered the lot in a single night, glutting himself on their blood in an uncharacteristic display of excess. The memory of it, of their screams and cries, of the taste of their rough throats, warmed him. His narrow chest expanded like a pig's bladder filled with water as he sucked in the phantom scent, luxuriating in the thought.

With it came more memories, shaken loose from a stagnant brain. Names, faces, events flowed thinly at first and then came in a flood, a deluge, crashing and smashing through the cobwebs that clung to W'soran's mind. He remembered his name, his purpose, his fate and more besides.

He remembered Mahrak, the City of Hope, and how he had been driven from the city of his birth by jealous rivals. He remembered Lahmia, the City of the Dawn, and how it had burned. He remembered Neferata, prideful, spiteful, savage Neferata and the gift she had grudgingly given him. Had given all of them – the gift of vampirism.

That gift had been tainted, he now knew. It had taken him centuries to puzzle it out, to understand the dark joke that had been played on all of them – Abhorash, Ushoran, himself and yes, even Neferata. A joke played by Nagash; Nagash the Usurper, Nagash the Great Necromancer.

Nagash, the Master of Death.

Thirst prickled at the back of his throat, not for water or wine, but for the copper tang of blood. Not even moments after awakening, the blood-lust returned in full. No matter how much he drank, how many screaming, squirming bags of flesh and bone he wrung dry, it never dimmed or dulled. That was Neferata's gift, eternal thirst to go with eternal life, forever in thrall to base need.

But then, he was no stranger to need. Even now, even after everything that had happened he still felt it, burning in his gut like a slow poison. The need, not for blood or to feel the life of squirming prey ebb from twitching meat, but for – what? – respect, perhaps? Acknowledgement, certainly; the admission of his superiority by those who dared call themselves his peers. For was he not their superior in every way that mattered? Did he not control the charnel winds that gave life to the lifeless and made the black blood of all of those gifted with vampirism quicken in their crooked veins? Was he not as much master as Nagash, as much a king as Neferata was a queen, as much a warrior as Abhorash? But it was not in the nature of their kind to recognise superiority, even when it was proven. He had wasted many years trying to do just that, before recognising the futility of such endeavours.

He gave a disgusted grunt and pushed the thought aside. There was a strange smell on the air. Something had awakened him before his time. His unfinished calculations quivered in his head like beheaded serpents. Irritation washed through him, billowing into anger. He had felt the feather-light touch of another mind, through the link of shared blood; an avenue of contact only open to those upon whom he had bestowed his blood-kiss, those whom he called his apprentices.

'I was not to be disturbed,' W'soran croaked, long-dormant vocal cords quivering to life as he forced musty air through them. 'There are calculations yet to be made.'

No reply was forthcoming. That was not unexpected given the proclivities of his apprentices. They were not social creatures, too much given to introspection and meditation, even as he was. Then, he had earned that right. They had not.

The braziers that encircled him had long since gone cold, and the torches on their wall-brackets were doused. The surge of anger, as cold as a deep mountain stream, overflowed its banks. They should have been in attendance, and braziers and torches lit. That was their duty after all: to watch over him as he meditated and to record his calculations and utterances.

He scanned the room, seeing the piles of parchment and the ratty tomes, bound in human hair and tanned skin, piled haphazardly about him like offerings to some primitive god. Even these had been left unattended. That was perhaps the least of their sins. For W'soran, the grimoires and scrolls were merely tools to be used, absorbed and discarded. It was a lesson he despaired of teaching his followers, many of whom treated the decaying tomes as a mother might a child. It was the nature of the savage to graft import to the inanimate, and, regrettably, most of his followers were little better than the rock-dwelling primitives he had butchered to make this lair.

'Urdek,' he rasped, naming the most senior of his current crop of apprentices. That could have changed, he knew. He encouraged a certain bloody-minded initiative amongst his disciples, though he'd thought Urdek was made of sterner stuff than that.

Then again, it wouldn't be the first time he'd been wrong about that sort of thing. In the spirit of practicality, he called out the name of the next most senior apprentice, 'Kung?'

His pointed, conch-whorl ears twitched as he caught the faintest whisper of sound. A pallid tongue, as dry as the desert lands that had once been his home, flickered out through the nest of fangs, tasting the air. W'soran's yellow eye narrowed and the dim lantern light in its depths suddenly flared into brilliance as he recognised both scent and sound. 'Ah. Hello, boy. Come to say hello to your master?' His fanged mouth quirked in a sly smile and he added, 'Perhaps to... beg forgiveness for old sins?'

'Do I require it, old monster?' the visitor snarled in reply as his hunched, beast-like shape circled W'soran in the darkness, padding about him like a wolf hugging the edge of the firelight. Then, the newcomer had always fancied himself as something of a predator. 'Maybe it is you who should ask *my* forgiveness.'

'Rank impertinence,' W'soran said, almost gently. 'I will forgive it, just this once.' His withered frame twitched in the circle of long-cold braziers. He was still sitting cross-legged, his taloned fingers clutching his bony knees. With some degree of academic interest and not a little bit of sweet pain, he began flexing each muscle cluster in turn, forcing his body to remember how it felt to move. His dust-stiffened robes crackled as he shifted position. 'Why are you here, my son?'

'Not your son, old monster,' the visitor snapped.

'Tch, such anger, Melkhior,' W'soran said. 'And to think, you were once my favourite, and beloved above all others.' He lifted his hand and curled his fingers, watching the play of the black veins beneath the parchment skin. He was reminded for a moment of the mummies of the Great Land, whose internment into eternity he had overseen in once-beauteous Mahrak.

That had been before Lahmia. His fingers tightened into a fist and his talons gouged his palm. 'Such anger,' he repeated. His one good eye narrowed and he unfolded his limbs like an awkward spider as he rose to his feet. 'Such disrespect for one who has given you nothing less than eternity,' he said, stretching slowly, in increments. Muscles pulled and bones popped in a symphony of fleshly shackles that seemed to grow ever weightier even as his frame dwindled, shedding its unnecessary bulk across the centuries. He gestured and the torches sprang to life as one, driving back the shadows all in a rush.

Melkhior jerked back, surprised, his flat, black eyes gleaming in the sudden blaze of light and his monstrous features writhing in consternation. Melkhior looked akin to nothing so much as one of the great bats of the deep dark, squeezed and twisted into a mockery of human shape. His quivering spear-blade nose flexed wetly as he exposed his scythe-like fangs in a hiss. 'As handsome as ever, my son,' W'soran said.

'Don't call me that,' Melkhior growled, turning his face away from the light.

'Why? It is what I have always called you – it is what you are. Blood of my blood, flesh of my flesh, did I not raise you up as unto a god? And what is a god, but a father writ large?' W'soran spread his gangly arms. 'I have forgiven you, my son.'

'Have you, old monster?' Melkhior asked, looking at him sidelong. 'If so, that would be a first – you nurse grudges like infants, W'soran.'

W'soran folded his arms. 'Hurtful words, such hurtful words. But you are right. I am tempted to pluck out your heart and eat it, my boy. Even the long years cannot dampen that fire you stirred in me. You know this; why have you come so rudely to my sanctum?'

'Not much of a sanctum,' Melkhior said, pulling his ragged cloak more tightly about his malformed body. 'How the mighty have fallen.'

'Lest we forget, you did have a hand in that,' W'soran said. He eyed Melkhior, studying the changes time had wrought in his once-student. The once muscular frame had withered into the semi-hunched simian shape that all of W'soran's followers assumed over time, like something equal parts sun-spoiled corpse and mangy animal. He had been a warrior once, one of the *ajals* of Strigos, a proud, tall war-leader of Mourkain. W'soran found a great deal of pleasure in his former student's degeneration. He smiled, and Melkhior's eyes narrowed.

'Even now, you laugh at me,' Melkhior said bitterly.

'Because you amuse me, Ajal Melkhior,' W'soran said as he stepped out of the circle of braziers. Melkhior flinched back and W'soran's smile grew. 'As I recall, the last time I saw you, you were driving a knife into my back. Come to try it again, my son?' He extended a hand, and a sour green balefire sprouted from his fingers, crackling and snapping hungrily. 'I am not distracted now. I can give you my full, undivided attention. Isn't that what you've always wanted?' W'soran purred.

He was not a warrior, as Melkhior had been, though he had played one often enough. Nonetheless, a hunger for conflict roiled within him, as great as his thirst for knowledge. He could not recall whether it had first come with the blood-hunger of vampirism, or whether it was something more innate, a holdover from the man he had been, back along the black line of centuries. To fight, to kill, was a pleasure as sweet as the nectar of human life to W'soran – he had overindulged in it more than once, and to his detriment.

For a moment, he thought Melkhior might try his hand. He could practically smell the urge for violence seething in the other vampire's gizzards. Melkhior tensed, but then relaxed. Melkhior had always been sensible despite a few notable exceptions, W'soran reflected, curling his fingers and snuffing the eldritch fires that had engulfed his hand. 'Why are you here?'

'To warn you,' Melkhior said.

W'soran guffawed. Bats stirred in the high reaches of his

sanctum and tittered fearfully as the sound of it curled upwards. 'And why would you do that? Does some small affection for poor, old W'soran yet linger in that sour heart, my son?'

'Stop calling me that,' Melkhior snarled, his eyes flashing. 'And you are not half as crippled as you pretend, old monster.' He pointed a claw at W'soran. 'Even now I can smell the dark magic festering in your carcass.'

W'soran snorted and let his claws drift up to play with the amulets dangling from his scrawny neck. There were half a dozen of them. Some were crafted after the fashion of the reptilian masters of the far Southlands, while others were the tangled devising of Cathayan craftsmen. All reeked of power to one degree or another, as did everything in this chamber, from the tomes to the wide-mouthed clay jars that crowded the corners.

It was the former that attracted his attention. Some were missing. He knew each scroll and tome by look, scent and position in relation to his circle. A momentary flare of avaricious panic sliced through him, as he realised just which ones were missing, before recalling that those particular volumes were sealed away in a vault of his own devising. He always sealed them away before meditating – they were too dangerous to be left out, unguarded. If his apprentices had free access to them, to the secrets within them, they would massacre one another within a fortnight. Perhaps they had done just that.

All of this occurred to him in the span of seconds. He

realised that Melkhior was still talking. 'Our enemies draw close, W'soran,' Melkhior said. 'Even now they may already have penetrated the defences of this draughty pile you call a sanctum.'

'Well, one has, at any rate,' W'soran said, stalking towards the bone-decorated archway that marked the exit to the chamber. Skulls had been stuffed into the many nooks and crannies of the archway, and as he passed, he stroked the closest. Never one to waste raw materials, he had decorated his new residence with the remains of the former occupiers – those that he hadn't raised to serve him in other capacities.

'I do not deny it, but this time, I have come to aid you,' Melkhior said, hurrying after him.

Outside the chamber was a corridor that curled around the slope of the crag that the crude fastness clung to like a limpet. W'soran frowned. There should have been guards on duty. Paranoia, honed to a killing point by centuries of experience, flared. Where were his apprentices? Why had they not responded to his calls? Had they attempted to stop Melkhior? He shoved the questions aside as unimportant. He had to get to those tomes. Everything else was replaceable, unnecessary.

'I doubt that, Melkhior,' he said, stalking onwards. The vault was buried in the rock of the mountain like a cavity in a tooth. It had taken him a year to carve it with the proper tools and weave the proper spells to render it invisible to all but him. 'Did you kill them? Urdek and the others, I mean.

You always were a murderous one in regards to your fellow students.'

'Are you listening to me, old monster?' Melkhior said. 'I said that *our* enemies are gathering – yours *and* mine. He has found you, W'soran. *He* is coming.'

W'soran stopped, but did not turn. Through a large gap in the wall, he could see the peaks and crags of the mountains, and the silvery glare of the moon overhead. 'Is he now?' he said, softly. 'And how would you know this, Melkhior?'

'You are not his only prey,' Melkhior said.

W'soran closed his eyes. 'Neferata,' he hissed, hatred oozing from every syllable. 'So that's where you went... afterwards.' He opened his eyes. 'I looked for you, you know. But you ran too quickly, and hid too well.'

'I learned from the best,' Melkhior spat. W'soran smiled. It stung his old apprentice, the thought of cowardice. So prideful, the Strigoi people; they were all brainless, barbarian bullies for the most part. Only a rare few had possessed even a modicum of talent. Melkhior was one, and Morath as well... his smile slipped as he thought of the treacherous necromancer. He had never accepted W'soran's gift of immortality. He had too much pride, though of a different sort than that of Melkhior. He had had too much pride to follow his master, the being who had made him, into exile, instead remaining to serve his mad king...

'Do you understand me, W'soran?' Melkhior hissed, drawing closer. 'He is coming for you – for *us*!'

A chill sliced through W'soran. 'Ushoran,' he said. He shook himself and said, 'How soon?'

'Soon,' Melkhior said.

'Why warn me?'

Melkhior was silent. W'soran snorted. 'She spurned you then, eh? Turned you out and sent you running, your tail between your legs?' He chuckled and then, more quickly than Melkhior's eyes could follow, spun about, backhanding his former apprentice against the wall. As Melkhior reeled, W'soran sprang on him, digging his claws into his throat. W'soran swung Melkhior towards the gap in the wall and thrust him out through it. Melkhior's eyes bugged out as he grasped at W'soran's thin wrist. His feet kicked helplessly over the abyss below.

'She rejected you and you came scurrying back to me, like a whipped dog,' W'soran said. 'Treachery for the treacherous, eh?' He cocked his head. 'I should drop you. You'd make a very satisfying noise upon landing, I think.'

'You – you need me,' Melkhior gurgled. 'I-I can help you!'

'Could you? Somehow, I doubt that.' W'soran smiled thinly, but the smile was wiped from his face as he caught the scrape of flesh on stone. He whirled, dragging Melkhior back inside even as a blade looped out of the darkness.

Melkhior squalled as the blade chopped into his back. W'soran dropped him and lunged over his falling body, burying his meat-hook talons into the face of the owner of the sword. The swordsman screamed as W'soran tore the face from his skull in one jerky motion, and staggered back, clutching at his mangled features.

W'soran snarled in anger as he caught the foul scent of the bloody mess in his grasp. It stank of death and grave-mould. His attacker was a vampire. He made to finish his would-be killer, but a shadow passed across the gap in the wall, and he smelled the stink of old blood, bear fat and weapon oil. He twisted bonelessly as a second vampire sprang through the gap in the wall with a guttural roar. W'soran slithered around the blow and caught the attacker's scalp-lock in his hands. With a curse he drove the latter's face into the opposite wall hard enough to crack the stone.

Strigoi, he realised. They were Strigoi. Melkhior hadn't been lying after all.

Still holding tight to the attacker's scalp-lock, he turned back to the gap, dragged the dazed vampire around and flung him out through the hole. Then he turned back to the one whose face he'd flayed off.

The Strigoi rose to his feet, eyes blazing with equal parts agony and battle-lust in his now fleshless face. With a gurgling snarl he lunged. His hands scrabbled for W'soran's neck, and his fangs clashed frenziedly as he dipped his head, biting at the other vampire's throat.

Then his head was bouncing free, along down the corridor. W'soran shoved the headless body aside and looked at Melkhior, who had somehow managed to prise the sword from his back and decapitate the Strigoi. 'There will be more of them,' Melkhior said, gesturing with the sword.

'Irrelevant. I have forces enough here to see off a few piti-ful assassins,' W'soran said, pushing aside the blade of the sword.

'Then where are they, these forces, eh?' Melkhior said. His eyes glittered. 'Where are your worshipful disciples, your bony legions?'

W'soran hesitated. Then he shrugged. 'It is no matter to me. As you said, I have power enough,' he said as he made to stride past Melkhior. 'If this fastness is compromised, I shall find another.'

'Is that your answer then? Run?'

'Well – yes,' W'soran said, striding down the corridor. 'I am not a warrior, as past experience has made clear. So I will run and I will hide. Let Neferata duel with Ushoran for these peaks if she wishes. There is a wide world out there, and I have an eternity to explore it.'

'Where are you going?' Melkhior asked, following him. He still clutched the sword, W'soran noted. His former appren-tice had always been more comfortable with a weapon in his hands. He snorted in derision.

'A better question – why are you still here, eh? You have delivered your warning. Scamper off,' W'soran gestured with-out turning or stopping. He kept moving, leading Melkhior through the crude, sloping corridors that connected the numerous large chambers that honeycombed the crag. The whole mountain was structured like a stony wasp's nest. W'soran thought that it had, at one time, been akin to one of the fire-mountains of the eastern wastes which occasionally spewed flame and ash into the sky. It was long cold now, its fire having gone out at some time in the dim past. It had been ready-made for shaping into a fastness, as its previous owners could have easily attested, had he left any of them alive.

'Were you not listening? Ushoran knows where you are, old monster! He is closing in on you – his hand is at your throat, though you see it not!'

W'soran ignored him and ducked through the archway that marked the end of the corridor. It opened out onto a large, vaulted chamber. Heavy support columns had been shaped from the stone of the walls and stretched from the rough floor to the uppermost reaches. Several columns had fallen and shattered in some long ago cataclysm and he had had his minions roll them aside when he'd made the place his. Skulls bound in nets of human hairs hung from the great stone stanchions that lined the circumference of the space. Their eye-sockets were empty of the balefires that should have lit them, and they were not screaming in alarm, as he expected, given that he had ensorcelled them to do so. W'soran did not pause. Someone had obviously dispelled his magics and rendered his alarms useless. That explained the lack of guards as well. But where were his apprentices? He grunted in annoyance as suspicions began to percolate. He glanced over his shoulder, considering. Melkhior was still following him, moving quickly.

'Where are you going? We must make a stand against him. Together, we might be able to–' Melkhior began.

'Together? I see you've found a sense of humour in our time apart, my son,' W'soran said.

'I am not your son, and it is no joke,' Melkhior almost screamed. 'We are running out of time. We – look out!'

His claws snatched at W'soran's robes, hauling him back as something bestial hurtled down from above. Claws cracked the stone as W'soran reeled back, off-balance. The Strigoi was all muscle and fang, a gargoyle-shape that lunged and clawed with lightning speed. Three more dropped down; W'soran realised that they'd been clinging to the upper reaches of the chamber like bats. How many of them had infiltrated his sanctum, he wondered as they crouched before him, crimson gazes blazing in the darkness.

When he'd fled Mourkain, few Strigoi had been able to mould their shapes beyond sprouting claws. Things had obviously changed in his absence. The creatures that spread out around him were more beast than man, clad in crude cuirasses and stinking furs, their faces shredded by gnashing tusks and oversized jaws. One gave a bay of triumph and sprang for him, drawing a sword.

W'soran spat a deplorable word and the Strigoi's roar became a shocked scream as his flesh withered and dropped from his bones and he came apart at the seams. W'soran stepped back as the pile of dust and bones crashed to the floor before him. 'Next?' he asked, his yellow eye bulging as dark magics crackled the length of his arms and swirled about his spread fingers.

They came in a rush, crimson-eyed and snarling. Black fire rippled from W'soran's fingers, coiling about the first, burning him to nothing in moments. He realised that Melkhior was beside him a moment later when the latter caught a sword meant for W'soran's skull on his own blade. Melkhior roared and forced the Strigoi back, trading blows. W'soran laughed and turned to the remaining Strigoi, who circled him warily.

'Did Ushoran really think that he could overcome me this way, with simple brute force? Has his famous guile deserted him?' he cackled, knowing even as he said it that there was something he was missing. It nagged at him. What was he not seeing? If Melkhior had wanted him dead, why not simply let the assassins kill him while he meditated? Why wake him up?

The Strigoi came at him from either side, confident in their strength. W'soran killed them both with a gesture, his magics flaying the meat from their bones before they could so much as scream. Overconfidence was a persistent weakness of their kind, a predatory surety which served as a crude population control. He had noted it early on in his studies. The only cure was age. Age brought cunning to temper the ferocity. Age brought wisdom, the wisdom to hide his strength, and his secrets; that was why he had built his vault. Nagash had been too trusting with his secrets, or perhaps simply too arrogant to consider that anyone might covet them more than they feared him.

'Master of Death,' he murmured, 'Master of Fools, more like.' He turned as a heavy body crashed to the ground.

Melkhior raised the sword and brought it down, lopping off the twitching Strigoi's head. His former apprentice kicked the head aside and looked at him. 'Do you still doubt me, old monster?' he growled.

'I never doubted you,' W'soran said smoothly. He gestured. 'I knew, here in my heart, that you would come to your senses eventually and return to me.'

Melkhior gave a grunt of bitter laughter. 'Where are we going?'

'I am going to collect something very valuable and then I am going to flee,' W'soran said. Melkhior could prove useful, though only in the short term.

'The books, you mean,' Melkhior said softly.

W'soran's good eye narrowed. Melkhior shook his head. 'I know you,' he said. 'You prize Nagash's scrawling even over your own life.' His eyes flashed. 'How many of them do you possess now... two, perhaps three?'

Before W'soran could answer, the sound of monstrous shrieks echoed through the forecourt. More than three, or four or even five of them this time, he realised. It sounded like a dozen or more, and all of them looking to take his head. 'They are coming,' Melkhior said, backing away. 'We must go!'

'Not without those books,' W'soran snarled, shoving him aside. 'I require them for a bit longer yet.'

'Then we had better hurry,' Melkhior said. They moved swiftly, robes flapping. They sped across the forecourt and through another archway. W'soran led the way, running smoothly despite the fact that he'd been as stiff as a corpse earlier.

The vault lay at the juncture where the fastness gave way to solid rock. W'soran had devised it in such a way that even if his sanctum was wiped from the side of the crag, his vault, and the precious artefacts and tomes within, would remain untouched. Rock walls rose around them and over them in a rough, curved tunnel, braced by heavy wooden beams set into place by dead hands. It was as wide as a plaza and a force of men could pass through it easily. There was no light, for they needed none. They'd left the howls of their pursuers behind, but W'soran knew they would be on them soon enough. The Strigoi could be relentless in pursuit of prey.

At the end of the tunnel sat the vault. It was a simple enough thing… a great wedge of stone, set into a gap like a cork into a bottle. Hundreds of chains, coated in dust and rust in equal measure, lay before it, connected to the wedge by a massive iron ring. As W'soran approached, he saw that the dust on the floor, and on the chains, had been disturbed. He smiled crookedly. Melkhior stood behind him, casting nervous glances back up the corridor.

'How do you get in?' Melkhior asked. 'I see no lock, no handle, save those chains.'

'The chains are the handle,' W'soran said. Then, he spoke a single word. It hummed through the air and the stone of the walls and link by link, the chains began to rattle. Melkhior stepped back with an oath, as the chains rose to the height of a man and in the wide space before the stone, motes of pale light appeared and blossomed into ragged phantoms. Men, women and children, their hazy features twisted with incomprehensible agony. They moaned and screamed in silence, writhing beneath the weight of the chains. 'I forged them in the blood of the former inhabitants of this place as well as my own,' W'soran explained, 'and bound their shrivelled little souls to the links… and to me. Only my voice can awaken them. Only my will can make them open the vault.'

Even as he said it, the ghosts began to move forward, straining against the wedge, pulling the chains. Melkhior watched in awe and, W'soran was pleased to note, not a little fear. To bind the dead to their own corpses was a parlour trick compared to this. W'soran preened slightly as the wedge groaned in its housing and began to pull free of the hole, releasing a burst of foul air. It was a ponderous affair, and with every step, the ghosts flickered and twitched in mute agony. That they still felt the weight and pain of their last moments was, to W'soran's mind, of the utmost delight. They had dared set themselves against him, tried to prevent him from taking what was his, and now they would suffer for eternity for that hubris.

After long moments, the vault was open and the spirits slumped or sank to their knees, as if they were still prone to the fatigue that might cripple living flesh. 'Only my will,' W'soran said again. He turned with a nasty smile on his face. At a single twitch of his fingers, the spirits rose as one, screaming silently as their ghostly forms were caught up in a maelstrom and flung together, causing the chains to clash and rattle thunderously. The spirits were smashed against one another, and they merged, still shrieking, into a colossal figure, a giant made of writhing shapes and weeping faces that gathered up the chains and then drove one heaving, squirming shoulder into the vault door. The vault was slammed shut with a roar and the phantoms vanished. The chains fell, and the stone echoed loudly with the sound. Melkhior gaped, uncomprehending. 'That was why Urdek and the others couldn't open it, of course,' W'soran said, examining his talons.

Melkhior froze. W'soran nodded in satisfaction. 'No bodies. No hint of them. What happened to them, I wonder?' His smile became sharp and feral. 'Did you eat them? I recall that's what you did to that one young fellow, the ajal with the golden hair... did you crack Urdek's thick skull open and eat the sweetness within when you realised he couldn't aid you? Maybe your Strigoi friends helped you, hmm? How long have you lot squatted here, in my lair, trying to get at my secrets while I slumbered unawares?' He exposed his fangs. 'And then, when you could not, you decided to wake me up and play me for a fool, yes, with staged attacks to harry me and confuse me? Oh Melkhior, you are too clever by half, my sweet boy,' W'soran said. Black fire crackled between his fingers and he held up a hand. Melkhior glanced back. W'soran clucked his tongue. 'They won't get here in time to help you,' he said.

'Actually, we are already here,' a feminine voice said. W'soran glanced up in shock as a lithe shape dropped from the ceiling and a blade flashed. Pain tore through him as one of his hands was removed at the wrist and he yowled, releasing the deadly magics contained in the other at the pale shape of his attacker.

Laughing, she sprang to the wall and nimbly leapt over the coruscating lance of black flame. 'Now, Melkhior,' she howled. 'Take him!'

Melkhior charged forward, bat-face split in a roar of pure hatred. He brought the sword down on W'soran's shoulder, driving the blade down through bone and muscle in a burst of inhuman strength. W'soran staggered and nearly fell. Shrieking, he slapped Melkhior away with his bloody stump and faced his other attacker. His good eye widened in shock. 'You,' he hissed.

'Me,' the Lahmian said, 'I warned you, old beast. And now, you are done.'

With that, the Lahmian danced forward, impossibly quick, her Cathayan blade moving like quicksilver as it cut ribbons from his unprotected hide. He screamed and reeled as stinking smoke rose from the wounds. The blade was edged with silver and every cut was agony. Clutching his wounded wrist to his chest, he tried to fend her off, spitting cursed syllables with desperate rapidity, his mind racing as he unleashed spell after spell. She avoided every one, her sinuous shape curling and sliding through the air like a leaf or a plume of smoke, drawing ever closer to him, until at last her blade bit deep into his belly. 'Die,' she purred into his ear as she forced the blade into him. 'Die, in the name of my sisters, W'soran.

Die, in the name of the Queen of Mysteries.'

'I've already done that once, witch,' W'soran rasped, black blood filling his mouth. 'I'll not do it again!' His good hand shot forward and spidery talons wrapped themselves around the Lahmian's neck. Her eyes widened as his claws tightened. He would pop her head from her neck.

But before he could do so, saw-edged fangs sank into the side of his throat, and claws into his scalp. He released the Lahmian and clawed wildly at Melkhior, who savaged his throat unheeding. Remora-like, his former apprentice dug his bestial snout into the wound his teeth had made and gulped the ancient blood that spurted forth. W'soran stumbled and sank to his knees. Melkhior hunched over him, ripping and tearing with a terrible fury.

W'soran fell forward, and Melkhior staggered back, covered in black blood, his eyes wide with madness. W'soran tried to push himself up, but he was too weak. 'No,' he gurgled, clawing at the stone floor. Through a red haze, he saw Melkhior pad forward, deadly intent writ in his movement. There was a hunger in his former apprentice's eyes that chilled him, a terrible monstrous hunger that he recognised, and feared. 'Not like this,' he croaked.

Melkhior crouched over him and his animal features were alight with hideous joy. 'I have waited centuries for this, old monster,' he whispered. W'soran's fading vision was filled by that ravenous maw dipping towards him, his blood still wet upon the serrated fangs that lined it.

Then, he saw nothing but darkness.

─◄ CHAPTER ONE ►─

Lahmia, the City of the Dawn
(Year -1200 Imperial Calendar)

The first thing he saw upon awakening was Ushoran. Given that the last thing he'd seen had been Neferata, her beauteous features contorted in an animal snarl as she thrust a jagged chunk of wood into his heart, it was an improvement, though not by much.

The Lord of Masks drew back, the damnable splinter of wood in his grip. He was as W'soran remembered him, the dull glamour masking the bestial shape within, a mask within a mask. Which was the true Ushoran? W'soran knew that he could find out easily enough, but he didn't particularly care. He never had, in truth. Let Ushoran play his silly games, and hide his crimes in double-talk and feigned innocence. W'soran had never feared consequence or result, for opportunity was born in both.

'W'soran,' Ushoran said, softly, as if he were afraid to awaken the other vampire.

'Ushoran,' W'soran replied. He was lying on the floor of the temple cellar. She hadn't bothered to move him very far. He felt a glimmer of insult – had she even considered that someone might attempt to find him? Then again, no one had. Maybe she was smarter than he'd given her credit for. Or perhaps she was simply more paranoid. He thought he knew which was more likely.

'It's been–' Ushoran began hesitantly.

'Twenty-two years,' W'soran cut him off. 'Twenty-two years folded up and crammed into a jar,' he said, letting only a hint of the bitterness he felt seep into his words. It gnawed at his guts, to have been so close, only to be ripped away at the moment of enlightenment. He raised his arm and felt for the already healing place where Neferata had rammed the stake that had pierced his heart. And for what – spite? Or perhaps jealousy; she had never been one to share power. It all came down to power in the end. And hers was as nothing compared to that which he had touched in those brief, beautiful black moments before she had consigned him to spiteful oblivion.

Nonetheless, he could still feel it, echoing in his bones. The ritual had been a success, more so than he had dared to even hope. He had cracked the bones of the world and touched divinity itself. Not one of the old, weak gods of the Great Land, but a vibrant god, a new god. The Undying King himself, his eyes blazing like baleful suns, had graced W'soran with a moment of his attentions. The Great Necromancer had answered his call, and in that moment, Nagash, the Master of Death, had claimed a new servant in W'soran of Mahrak.

He could feel the pressure now, in his head. He had always felt it, since Neferata had given him the blood-kiss, but only now did he recognise it for what it was. The others did not see it. They would never see it. Nobility were blind to any powers that were not their own, but W'soran, who had always served, recognised the hand of a master easily enough. Nagash's hand was at their throats and his blood was in their veins. And soon enough, he would join his true master.

But first...'I take it I'm forgiven. No, don't bother. Something's gone wrong, hasn't it?'

'I see two decades of pickling has only sharpened your tongue,' another voice intruded.

W'soran didn't bother to look. He recognised the voice easily enough. No one else sounded that petulant. 'Hello, Ankhat,' he said, slowly sitting up. 'Still clinging to Neferata's hem?'

'Put the stake back in him,' Ankhat snarled. 'Put him back where we found him. Lahmia will survive without him.' The nobleman had never liked him, W'soran recalled. Indeed, he had even helped Neferata disrupt W'soran's ceremony. He had tattled like a child hoping for a reward. More jealousy, more narrow-minded spite, and as with Ushoran, perhaps a touch of fear; only a few among the Lahmian Court did not fear W'soran in some small way, though it was a fear born of shallow assumption rather than true understanding, and for that he hated them. For all that he despised her of, W'soran knew that Neferata feared nothing. She could not conceive of defeat, or of submission to another.

Perhaps he would bring Nagash her head, as a gift.

'Neferata has commanded that we free him,' Ushoran said smoothly, not taking his eyes from W'soran, as if he'd heard the *other vampire's thoughts. Maybe he had. Neferata's blood had awakened strange talents in each of them. W'soran idly wondered if such abilities were transferable between vampires. What part of Ushoran's brain would he have to excise in order to do so?*

Ushoran continued, 'And so we have. Let the consequences be on her head.'

'Why?' W'soran asked. 'Why would she do such a thing?' But he already knew. He had foreseen it the moment he had learned that the petulant prince of Rasetra had escaped.

'Alcadizzar,' Ushoran said.

The Dark Lands
(Year -326 Imperial Calendar)

The cavern was immense. Its inhabitants had worn the stones of the floor smooth, generation by generation, and the walls had been bolstered by supports crafted haphazardly from both stone and wood even as it had grown, its circumference increasing with the population of the mountain. Great, crude chimneys were driven into the curve of the roof, carrying out smoke and bringing in fresh air, as well as allowing for the ingress and egress of the more agile inhabitants. Irrigation canals had been carved into the rock walls and slithered across the floor, creating a weird pattern of filthy, sluggish water that seemed to be going nowhere in particular. Vast, primitive portcullises crafted from badly forged metal were embedded in the walls at irregular intervals, marking hundreds of exits and entrances, leading up into the heights and down into the depths.

From each of these, bipedal rats poured into the cavern, and it seethed with their numbers. Rat-things squirmed forward with a frenzied murderousness not usually found in vermin, unless they were cornered. Which, W'soran suspected, these very much counted as, given the situation. This was a bastion under siege, and its defenders fought with tooth, claw and spear to hold it against the silent ranks of the invaders. Wave after wave of screaming, chittering rat-men broke against skeletal phalanxes composed of dead men stripped of flesh and feeling alike. The walking dead fought without frenzy or fear, moving remorselessly forward at the behest of the minds of their masters, and their masters' master.

Despite their advantages, the dead didn't have it all their own way. The rat-things had weapons aplenty. One such, a grotesque giant rat-like behemoth that was all bulging flesh and exposed muscle, a tube of stitched meat that wailed from a dozen snapping mouths, raced towards the ranks of skeletal warriors, urged on by its verminous handlers, who clung precariously to the rickety howdah strapped to its undulating spine.

'Kill it with fire!' W'soran howled as he gestured towards the lumbering abomination which was waddling speedily towards his position. Its thunderous squeals buffeted his ears as it clambered across the cavern floor, its dozens of legs lending it ungainly speed. The rat-things had lashed and bolted the contraption on the monster's very bone, and ballistae had been mounted atop it. One fired even as W'soran spoke, and the great, crude bolt crashed through the ranks, crushing dozens in its flight. Smaller shapes, neither wolf nor rat but some foul amalgamation of both, loped to either side of the titanic monstrosity, uttering high-pitched bays of hunger. There were hundreds of them, W'soran realised, even as he knew that this was only the first line of the enemy's defence.

The rat-things who occupied this hole called themselves skaven. The mountain was riddled with them and their foul warrens, from the crags to the roots; it would take months, if not years, to cleanse it of their presence. If the mountain hadn't overlooked one of the largest passes through the mountains, Vorag likely wouldn't have bothered. As it was, it had been easy to convince the Bloodytooth – as his followers called him – to attack, especially after a number of black-clad skaven had attempted to assassinate the renegade Strigoi vampire.

The skaven had made the mistake of trying to warn Vorag off from dallying in their territory overlong, and had attempted to murder him in his tent. W'soran couldn't blame them, though he did fault their methodology. The assassination attempt had been swift, savage and, sadly, futile. Vorag had survived, and, for all that he was a brute and savage, but he was nothing if not courageous. An attempt on his life was practically an invitation for retaliation. A crude, curved knife in his pillow and soon enough,

Vorag's rag-tag horde of Strigoi exiles – and W'soran and his small coterie with them – was besieging the fastness that the skaven called Crookback Mountain.

Granted, Vorag had set his eyes on the mountain from the start. It commanded the passes of the north-eastern edge of the Strigoi Empire, and trade, such as it was, flowed steadily through those passes to the east. After Vorag's disastrous attempt at usurping the throne from Ushoran, and the resultant civil war between rival factions of Strigoi – supporters of Ushoran on one side and everyone else on the other – the Bloodytooth and his followers had fled Mourkain and the Strigoi Empire, to regroup and plan anew. The mountain, with its command of the region, would be an ideal citadel from which to strike at their enemies, and to rebuff any attempt by said enemies to collect the scalps and fangs Ushoran demanded in recompense for Vorag's betrayal. In time, it might even rival Mourkain, and a new empire would grow about it, with Vorag on the throne, and W'soran behind him, whispering in his ear. But first, they had to deal with the skaven.

W'soran had fought them before, in the cramped dark beneath Nagashizzar centuries earlier, and his knowledge had only increased in the interim. They had caught captives early and often, the beasts being more inclined to flee or surrender than fight when their numbers were limited. Nagash had never bothered to learn more than the most rudimentary secrets of the skaven during the long war for the *abn-i-khat* mines, but W'soran recognised that there was some power in even the most inconsequential bit of trivia. After a few weeks with the flensing knives he knew their pestilential race inside and out, everything from the subtleties of their tittering language to the way certain glands squirted an acrid musk when they were frightened.

They had entered the mountain easily enough through the great clefts and labyrinthine tunnels worn into the rock millennia earlier by long-since vanished rivers. The skaven had crafted hidden gates and barbicans in those tunnels, but the defenders, used to the half-hearted assaults by the savage greenskin tribes of the region, had been unprepared for the speed and inexorable momentum of the initial undead attack. Vampires had rooted the ratkin out of their dead-drops and hidey-holes, flinging them squealing from the heights down onto the spears held aloft by bony hands. Even the multitude of deadly traps – deadfalls and unstable tunnels, among others – had done little to discourage the invaders. The dead were nothing if not durable, and failing that, easily replaceable.

It had been a simple enough matter to draw the slaughtered skaven to their feet and send the bodies forward to lead the invasion of their own lair. W'soran thought that there was poetry in it. The vile little things were as treacherous as they were disease-riddled, and coups came to the living skaven as naturally as breathing. Why should their dead be any different?

Battle had become a constant as they pushed deeper into the mountain. Vorag's army had divided into dozens of smaller forces, each one led by one of his chosen warriors. Including this one, led by an idiotic Strigoi brawler called Rudek. W'soran seethed, but privately. Vorag did not trust him, despite the fact that it was W'soran's magic that ensured that he had an army in the first place. But that would change, and sooner rather than later, if he had anything to say about it.

W'soran stood, surrounded by his acolytes, on an armoured palanquin, held aloft by the barbaric shapes of a dozen massive ghouls who were chained to it. He had bred the beasts himself in Mourkain, weaning them on vampiric blood and flesh. As a consequence, they had grown to elephantine proportions, each one a match for twenty lesser foes. They were armoured as well, bolted into heavy iron cuirasses, gorgets and greaves to protect them from stray missiles. Their malformed simian skulls were encased in leather and brass muzzles, to keep them from biting any of his acolytes who wandered too close to the edges of the palanquin. Fed on vampiric juices as they had been, the brutes now craved it with an addict's frenzy. The ghouls bellowed and shifted in place, eager for the coming fray.

W'soran snarled and gestured. 'I said burn it,' he snapped. His acolytes flung out their hands as one and spoke with him as the sorcerous incantation left his withered lips. The air grew hot and began to smell of boiled meat as the spell rushed through the musty air of the great cavern and struck the monster. The abomination reared up with a shriek that shivered the stalactites from the upper reaches of the cavern as weird green flames crawled across its pustule-ridden frame. It screeched again and again, thrashing in agony. Its claws flailed, crushing wolf-rats and uprooting stalagmites as it hurled itself down and rolled over, trying to snuff the eldritch flames.

As he'd hoped, the howdah, with its complement of artillery, was crushed beneath the thing's weight. As the abomination regained its feet, he saw that the contraption had been swept off it entirely, tearing great wounds in its back in the process. It hunched and mewled in pain, its screams setting his teeth on edge.

Strigoi warriors bounded forward with howls of glee. Inhuman muscles bunched beneath their armour as the vampires hurled themselves on the wounded beast, stabbing it with swords and spears and tearing at it with claws. Vorag had been profligate in gifting those who had followed him into the wilderness with the blessings of undeath. Too, years of battle had seen his forces slowly but surely shed the living in favour of the dead the way a snake shed its skin. There were no living men left in the army of the Bloodytooth – only the silent dead. Blocks of skeletal infantry moved forward, carrying spears or bows, and more vampires loped through their ranks. There were more ethereal components to the besiegers' force as well: spectral maelstroms, composed of hundreds of moaning, gibbering spirits bound to W'soran's will, surging forward towards the army marching to meet them.

Black-furred skaven wearing heavy, red-daubed armour

marched in semi-orderly blocks, hefting cruel-looking halberds. Ahead of them, untold masses of scrawny slave-soldiers scurried forward. At the back of the army, bellowing rat ogres shook the chains that bound them to the massive war machine they hauled into position, as shrieking overseers snapped whips over their blunt skulls. The machine was shaped something like an overlarge ballista: a weird amalgamation of wood and metal crafted like no engine that W'soran was familiar with, and somewhere amidst that confusion was the commander of the skaven forces facing them. The longer he examined the war machine, however, the more the shape of it put him in mind of the dragon staves that dead Lahmia had once used in war. Which had unpleasant implications, should the skaven ever actually use it.

The abomination gave a final scream and collapsed, its flabby shape crumpling. The Strigoi crouched on it, howling and whooping. The front ranks of the skaven hesitated, but their masters drove them on with chittering curses and snapping whips and the slaves started forward. The dead moved to meet them, marching in silent unison. As one, the front ranks of the skeletal spearmen lowered their weapons and locked shields. In life, they had been as disciplined as the barbaric Strigoi could get, and that had not changed in death.

W'soran watched, awaiting the impact of bone on flesh, when a slender shape suddenly landed on the palanquin, startling him. He spun about with a hiss, hands raised and an invocation on his lips. He swallowed the words as he realised who it was. 'Rudek,' he said. 'Shouldn't you be leading a heedless assault of some sort?'

'And shouldn't you be hiding, sorcerer?' Rudek countered, his red eyes narrowing. 'That is what you're best at, after all.' He was handsome, as the Strigoi judged such things, with sharp features and dark hair bound in the customary scalp-lock. Slim and long-limbed, with the grace of a born swordsman and the agility of a cat, Rudek was one of the more devious of Vorag's pets. W'soran despised him.

'Watch your tongue, Rudek,' one of W'soran's acolytes growled. Melkhior threw back the hood of his robe, revealing his animalistic sneer, and slapped a claw to the sword sheathed on his hip.

Rudek turned with a lazy smile. 'Ah, the coward speaks up.'

'I'm no coward,' Melkhior snarled, his flat, black eyes pulsing with anger.

'Then why are you here with these thin-blooded graverobbers and not out there with the rest of us, cousin?' Rudek hissed, flashing his fangs. The hair on the back of his neck had stiffened like the quills of a porcupine and he hunched forward, arms spread. Melkhior's round maw split to reveal his own impressive nest of teeth, and his sword-hilt creaked in his grip.

W'soran watched the confrontation in amusement. He'd forgotten that Melkhior was related by blood to many of Vorag's followers. The nobles of the Strigoi, whether living or undead, were interrelated to a degree that even a Nehekharan found to be ridiculous. It made such confrontations rather more heated than they would have been otherwise, as well as more amusing.

He clapped his hands together before either vampire could make a move. 'Why are you bothering me, Rudek? I have spells to cast,' he said.

Rudek turned back to W'soran, his sneer returning. 'Yes, and at my command, necromancer,' he said. 'We are to smash the vermin here and hold our position. Lord Vorag wishes to make a final push into the heart of this nest. He believes that the vermin are retreating here from throughout the mountain, thanks to our valiant efforts.'

W'soran turned away, scanning the cavern. It was by far the largest such space they had yet encountered, as well as the most built up. The upper reaches were strung with rickety walkways, and strange towers and balconies had been grafted onto the larger stalactites like barnacles; the walls of the cavern had quite obviously been hollowed out, and rough stairways curved in and out of them in places. Strange metal globes of enormous size, full of burning incense, had been strung up here and they cast a milky pall over the whole of the cavern. It reminded him of similar open areas he had seen in the depths of Nagashizzar, that had heralded the entrances to the deep burrows and breeding pits of the skaven.

He was forced to admit that it made sense, though he doubted Vorag had arrived at the conclusion through any studied process of consideration. Rather, it was the instinct of a jackal hunting a rodent and knowing that its prey will seek shelter. He glanced back at Rudek. 'And how would you suggest we go about holding this place, Rudek? We have barely a third of the army here, and we're likely sitting right on top of the main nest of the ratkin. There'll be millions of them in here with us before long.'

'Then we shall have a chance to see just how effective your magics are, sorcerer,' Rudek said, grinning. 'I will lead the attack, and you will join me.'

W'soran hesitated. Idly, he stroked his dead eye and the scar that crossed it. 'And if I refuse?'

'Then I will butcher you here and now,' Rudek said with a shrug. 'Your choice.'

I'd like to see you try, you preening ape, W'soran thought. What he said, however, was, 'I shall join you. It would be my pleasure.'

'I thought you might see it that way,' Rudek said, laughing. 'Do not tarry, W'soran. There is blood to be spilt and rats to be spitted!' A moment later he was gone, bounding from the palanquin and racing away towards the forefront of the battle. Other Strigoi joined him as he moved, like wolves being summoned to the hunt by the pack-leader.

W'soran grunted. It was an inconvenience, but one he could easily turn to his advantage, if he were quick about it. He turned to Melkhior. 'Stay here and oversee our works. Keep the dead on their feet and the rats off our flanks.'

'I will come with you,' Melkhior said, drawing his sword. 'You will need my help, master.'

'Melkhior, the day I need your help to murder a cousin of

yours is the day they roll me into a crypt and shut the door,' W'soran said. Melkhior blinked.

'What?'

'Why else do you think I agreed to his idiotic demand? I'm going to kill him,' W'soran said, bluntly. 'Do you have a problem with that, my son?'

Melkhior looked at him. 'He's not a close cousin,' he said, after a moment.

'I'm simply overjoyed to hear it,' W'soran said as he moved to the edge of the palanquin. Quickly, he flung off his cloak, revealing the curved and scalloped plates of the Strigoi cuirass he wore beneath. Cruelly hooked pauldrons protected his skinny shoulders and a flaring gorget encased his throat like the crest of some great Southland saurian. Bracers decorated with intricately wrought sigils covered his forearms and greaves of similar design protected his shins. He drew the Arabyan scimitar from its wolf-skin sheath on his hip and leapt from the palanquin.

He could feel Melkhior's glare on his back even as he moved after Rudek and the Strigoi. Whether he was angry about being left behind or about W'soran's plans the latter couldn't say. Nor did he particularly care. Let him stew. Melkhior was entirely too fixated on hierarchy; so much so that he spent the bulk of his time machinating against his perceived rivals rather than on his studies.

W'soran shook his head in disgust as he threaded his way through the ranks of the dead. If only Morath hadn't been so blinded by his petty fealties, he might have joined W'soran in his self-imposed exile. That one was a student worth the name. His grasp of the darkling magics that rode the winds of death was instinctual, equal even to W'soran's own. In time, he might have even been a match for his master. Not now, however. For now, he was Ushoran's plaything, a slave to a slave.

Then, are you any different, playing loyal servant to Vorag? a treacherous part of his mind whispered. Irritated, he swatted the head off an unoffending skeleton. It bounced away across the rocks, joining the bones and bodies that littered the ground between the two forces. The skaven had pulled back after their initial clash, retreating in a wave of fear-stink. Their lines pulsed and squirmed as the overseers within their ranks tried to whip the survivors into some form of martial order. W'soran paused to watch, interested.

The skaven were a stable mutation, likely the result of excess exposure to the warping effects of abn-i-khat at some point centuries ago. He had seen and studied other such mutations in his time – the beastmen of the northern mountains, for instance, were of similar origins, though they were far less stable. He had dabbled in recreating the effects himself, in his experiments in Mourkain. He smiled as he thought of the vast, hidden crypts he'd left behind in the bowels of the mountain the city rested on, and the dozens of sealed stone sarcophagi in those crypts. Each sarcophagus contained a Strigoi who, despite receiving Ushoran's blood-kiss, for want of influence or friendship or simply common sense, had lost favour with their master and been turned over to W'soran to do with as he wished, when he himself had had the master of Mourkain's trust. Those sarcophagi had been crafted with veins of abn-i-khat, which was easy enough to find the further north you went, running through them. He shivered in pleasure as he imagined the changes that must have been wrought in those captive vampires. It was too bad he would likely never find out.

Unless he could find a way to recreate those experiments in peace and privacy; for that, however, he'd need a secluded hideaway. A mountain fortress, for instance... W'soran grinned and continued on. Plans, plots and schemes tumbled through his crooked brain, and he forced them aside. He had to concentrate on the here and now. Things could still go wrong. The Strigoi – Vorag – had to trust him. And to trust him, they first had to respect him. But savages respected only physical might, and that meant getting his hands dirty.

He swung the scimitar experimentally as he approached the gathered Strigoi, re-familiarising himself with its weight and balance. He'd learned the art of the blade in his youth, when duels were still common amongst the priesthood of Mahrak. Since then, he'd fought in hundreds of conflicts, wielding both sorcery and sword with equal intent.

'You almost look as if you know how to use that thing,' Rudek said. The Strigoi with him laughed at the perceived witticism. W'soran sneered.

'I learned the ways of the blade before you gnawed your first teat, Rudek.'

Rudek frowned and turned away. 'We'll see about that,

sorcerer. The skaven have yet to deploy their war machine. I think it would be wise to see that they never get that opportunity.'

'I follow your lead gladly, my lord,' W'soran purred, bowing shallowly. 'If they hold true to form, that is where this rabble's commanders will be as well. If we kill them, this lot will flee.'

'I forget that you have fought them before,' Rudek said. 'Is it hard for you, then?'

'What, my lord?' W'soran asked.

'To fight creatures you so obviously share a kinship with,' Rudek said. Before W'soran could reply, Rudek drew his blade and thrust it into the air. 'For Strigos and the Bloody-tooth,' he roared, and sprang forward into a dead sprint. The others followed suit, and W'soran, slowly, reluctantly, followed them. Behind the vampiric spear-point came the skeletal ranks, marching steadily, if much more slowly than their bloodthirsty masters.

It was a by-now familiar tactic – the Strigoi had a fondness for the close-in, red wet work of war. Lines, columns, ranks: all of that irritated a people whose first, last and only instinct was to charge. It had taken Neferata and Abhorash, once-champion of Lahmia and now lickspittle of Mourkain, centuries to mould the army of Strigos into a disciplined fighting force equal to any that had ever marched across the dry sands of the Great Land. Needless to say, the nobility, forever frozen at the height of their barbarity like insects in amber by immortality, often forgot those lessons. That could be dangerous, given the persistence and numbers of the skaven. W'soran almost laughed. It would be easy enough to see to Rudek, in the battle.

On the flanks, W'soran heard the howls of those forces he had brought with him into his exile – mobs of so-called 'crypt horrors' as the Strigoi had taken to calling them. It had taken him decades to perfect the process of their creation, and they were the perfect shock troops. The bloated, gigantic ghouls lumbered forward, swinging mauls, clubs and other outsize weapons as they loped ponderously towards the skaven. They were followed by packs of normal-sized ghouls, their grey flesh marked by W'soran's brand. Through blood and black sorcery he had bound several clans of the corpse-eaters to himself, and they raced ahead to join the Strigoi, caterwauling and shrieking, propelled by his will.

Sizzling bursts of magic streaked overhead to crash against the skaven lines. Melkhior might be unhappy with his lot, but he was effective regardless. W'soran ran swiftly, ignoring the barrage of sling stones that were loosed from the ranks of the ratkin to patter against the armour of the vampires. Occasionally there were crackles of green lightning from the looming war machines, and the smell of burning abn-i-khat grew stronger the closer they got. W'soran snorted; the vermin used the stone for everything, from lighting fires to powering their mechanical constructs to foodstuffs. He thought that was likely why the war machines hadn't been put to use yet – the stone took coaxing to release its strange essence, and even then it was highly volatile.

More sling stones flew, and then the Strigoi were upon the front ranks. W'soran narrowly avoided a spear-thrust and swept his scimitar across the throats of three skaven. Rudek had leapt high, avoiding the front ranks altogether, and crashed down amongst the back rows. His formerly handsome visage had twisted into an inhuman mockery, all teeth and eyes. He savaged the ratkin, slaughtering them with abandon, ripping them open and tossing them into the air. The others followed suit, tearing holes in the semi-orderly ranks of the skaven.

W'soran did his best to keep up. He did not relish combat in the same way, though pain and the expressions thereof were like the sweetest nectar to him. The screams of the skaven filled his ears as he carved his own path. Spears drove at him from all sides, the points skidding off his armour. He snarled and hacked through the spears and the hands that wielded them. Limbs and blood spilled to the ground. In moments, the skaven broke and began to flee, stampeding backwards to escape the rampaging vampires. The larger, black-furred skaven moved forward, heedlessly trampling the survivors in their efforts to reach the Strigoi. W'soran saw no reason to engage in any more pointless combat. His blade and armour were doused in the foul blood of the ratkin; more than enough, in fact, to impress upon the Strigoi his courage.

As the armoured skaven approached, he extended a hand and a dark mist coalesced before him and slithered towards the enemy. The mist billowed and spread as it moved, and swept over the ratkin with predatory intent. They screeched and clawed at themselves as it seeped into their mouths, noses and eyes. Heavy, muscular bodies withered and crumpled like drained wineskins as the mist drew out their lives like an ethereal leech.

W'soran laughed as the armoured ranks melted away before him. It was so much more satisfying to kill with a gesture than with the swing of a sword. He stepped over the bodies without a backward glance. Behind him, he could hear the tread of bony feet as the army pressed forward.

More skaven boiled out of concealed holes and tunnels, racing to the defence. Rudek and the other Strigoi pounced on them, butchering them. W'soran ignored them, and headed for the war-engine. The skaven had dragged it from the wide, gaping mouth of a tunnel and set it up facing the undead. Slaves and overseers scurried and clambered over the engine, doing what W'soran couldn't say. Even as he loped towards the closest, he saw that a massive chunk of abn-i-khat had been mounted inside its brass and iron frame. On the platform that the weapon was mounted on, a group of skaven stood, watching the approaching undead with a disturbing lack of concern.

The air suddenly took on a greasy feel and W'soran's hackles bristled. A trio of Strigoi bounded past him. The war-engine shuddered like a dying beast as lightning squirmed across its hull, and suddenly W'soran had the unpleasant feeling that the whole battle so far had merely been a distraction, to ensure that the skaven got their toys positioned properly.

Light burst from the stone and a crackling bolt was spat from the copper tip of the engine. The Strigoi ceased to exist a moment later, their bodies rent asunder by the bolt of sickly green energy. W'soran was thrown from his feet by the force of the explosion. More bolts were fired as the engine shuddered and vomited death on the approaching undead. Whole ranks of skeletal warriors vanished into dust and screaming ghouls were sent tumbling into the air, their flesh peeling and blackened. Green smoke obscured the destruction a moment later.

W'soran staggered to his feet, momentarily stunned by the sudden display of raw power. Thus, he did not detect the pad of heavy paws until too late. Alerted at the last moment, he spun about, only to be seized in an iron grip and wrenched from his feet as the snarling maw of a rat ogre gaped hungrily before him. He struggled, but to no avail. With a hungry bellow, it hauled him towards its open jaws.

━◄ CHAPTER TWO ►━

Lahmia, the City of the Dawn
(Year -1200 Imperial Calendar)

The catapult stone tore through the gatehouse. Stone and timber exploded inwards from the force of the impact, and W'soran was hurled backwards, the precious tomes and scrolls tumbling from his grip. He cursed as a heavy stone crashed down atop his legs, pinning him against the remaining wall. There was no pain; panic, however, filled him. Despite the pantomime of bravery he'd put on for Ushoran and Ankhat, his time in the jar had been pure torment. To be trapped, unable to move, to escape, had been almost more than he could bear. A few more years of being folded up in that clay prison and he might have gone insane.

Frantically, he shoved at the rock, trying to free himself. Another stone struck the gatehouse, showering him with splintered wood and powdered stone. Desperate now, he beat on his captor with his fists. The stone cracked and popped and he jerked his legs free even as a third catapult stone took out one side of the gatehouse. The structure groaned and what was left of the floor buckled. W'soran scrambled to his feet, snatched up the tomes and papyri and bounded down the quivering stairwell to the ground. People were running in all directions; a sea of humanity heaved and pulsed and W'soran's blood quickened at the sight of it.

His lean shape was given a wide berth, covered as he was in blood and dust. He hugged the grimoires to his chest. He had to get them out of the city. Nothing else mattered. Lahmia was done; even if Neferata somehow managed to win this battle, the city was doomed to fall. The other cities had been roused against them now and they would not return to their own demesnes without something to show for it.

Suddenly, the crowd heaved itself like a single organism, retreating. W'soran paused, wondering if Alcadizzar's forces had somehow already reached the city. The great western gates of Lahmia swung wide, admitting a ragged band of infantry and several riders. He spotted Ankhat and his personal guard – the once haughty noble had a look of panic on his face as he and his men lashed out at the tide of humanity that could not help but find itself in their path. 'Move,' he roared, 'Make way for the Queen! Move or die!'

W'soran's good eye widened as he caught sight of the large figure mounted on the horse behind Ankhat – Abhorash. The champion looked as if he had bathed in blood, and his long arms held a limp figure that W'soran realised was Neferata. He felt a moment of gloating triumph that was quickly washed aside by understanding.

If Neferata had fallen, the city was indeed doomed.

It was time to go; but where?

North, maybe… instinctively, he looked. He could not see the mountains from where he was, but he knew they were there nonetheless. He could feel them pulling him. There was a lodestone in his blood, and he felt drawn towards the mountains beyond the Sour Sea. To a mountain, wreathed in an unholy greenish light, which belched smoke; a mountain surmounted by a fortress as cruel-looking as it was foul. In his head was a word: Nagashizzar. And in his mind's eye, he saw again the skull-faced giant of his two decade-old vision: a giant clad in brutal armour, wreathed in sorcerous flames, and in his hand, a jagged metal crown.

Nagash.

The Undying King, the Great Necromancer… master of the power he so desired. Decided, W'soran turned, hoping to blend into the mass of humanity before either Ankhat or Abhorash spotted him.

There was nothing holding him to Lahmia. The city had never been his home, not really. But there was a place waiting for him, he knew.

He just had to get there in one piece.

The city was already alight by the time he made it to the northern gate. The soldiers of the other cities were spilling into the streets of Lahmia, looting and pillaging. W'soran, his robes pulled tight over the burden he carried and a cowl over his head, moved with the steady tide of would-be escapees seeking to flee the city.

Just before he reached the gate, however, the sound of hoofbeats filled the air. People began to scream and push and trample each

*other as the horsemen burst into the forecourt before the gate,
riding hard towards the crowd with whoops and cries of triumph.
W'soran growled in frustration as people shoved against him. Losing patience, he lashed out, breaking bones and ripping flesh with
a single flailing blow. The crowd gave way before him, dispersing.
W'soran was alone in moments and out in the open as the riders
closed in.*

*With a snarl, he threw aside his cloak and flung out a hand.
Dark energies rippled from it, and men died...*

The Dark Lands
(Year -326 Imperial Calendar)

The rat ogre drew him towards its maw. W'soran had
dropped his blade, so he grabbed the creature's snout, one
hand on each jaw. The rat ogre's grip tightened and his
cuirass creaked. W'soran hissed and his withered muscles
bulged as he tore the top of the monster's head loose by its
upper jaw in a spray of gore. The beast toppled, releasing
him as it fell. He hit the ground hard and sprang to his feet,
snatching up his blade as he moved.

More rat ogres closed in, driven from behind the ranked
war machines by the whips of their masters. The brutes had
been freed from their chains and even now most of them
were running headlong towards what remained of the front
ranks of the undead army. W'soran dashed past them, avoiding a casual swipe from one of the closest.

Even as he moved, W'soran saw the skaven war-engine fire again. Crackling green light burst into being and washed over the undead ranks, dissolving bone and melting ancient armour to slag. The advantage had been taken from them in an instant. W'soran saw Rudek and the other Strigoi loping towards the party of skaven on the nearest machine's platform. Rudek was no fool, despite his swaggering manner. He knew as well as W'soran that that weapon signified a quick defeat for the Strigoi, unless they could put it out of commission.

W'soran moved quickly after the Strigoi. Possibilities and potentialities rushed through his head as he ran. Among the skaven on that platform was one whose fur was not brown or black but a filthy off-white, and W'soran knew enough to know what that implied. The Strigoi reached the platform and bounded across it. Two heavy-bodied rat ogres, who stood to either side of the group of skaven, lumbered forward to meet the vampires with massive mattocks clutched in their paws. Unlike the scarred and chained brutes he had just avoided, these were well-fed and armoured. They were likely bodyguards or pets of some description.

The Strigoi closed with the beasts, looking like hounds going after bears. Rudek dived past them, heading for the skaven. W'soran cleared the edge of the engine platform even as Rudek removed a burly skaven's head with a casual backhand. More black-furred creatures closed in, striking at the Strigoi with halberds. Rudek weaved around the blows, and his sword looped out, repaying them in kind.

The white-furred ratkin watched the Strigoi butcher its
guards with visible disdain. It was a tall creature, and clad
in colourful, if filthy, robes. Heavy horns curled from either
side of its skull, and its eyes glowed with a terrible, easily
recognisable green hue. By all rights, the creature should
have fled by now, W'soran thought – instead, it seemed to
be eager for the confrontation. Almost languidly, the skaven
raised a paw and gestured.

Green fire boiled from its palm and seared a black scar
across Rudek's shoulder. He screamed and flopped over
backwards, clutching at the smoking wound. W'soran
stabbed his scimitar into the slimy wood of the platform
and laughed. The skaven turned, energy leaking from its eyes
and mouth. One hand was full of abn-i-khat, which it hur-
riedly shoved into its mouth as he approached.

'Yes,' he murmured, 'I expected as much. They eat it, you
know.' He directed the last towards Rudek, who hissed
at him. W'soran gestured absently, his eyes on the white
skaven. 'Oh yes, my yes, they eat it, they secrete, and bathe
in it for all I know. It provides them with the energy for their
magics as well, even as it dissolves them from the inside.
Foolish little beasts…'

The skaven snarled and gestured sharply. Green fire
washed towards W'soran and he slashed his arms out,
dispersing it with barely a twinge of effort. 'They are quite
powerful, though, in the right circumstances. Facing an
unprepared opponent, for instance,' W'soran continued,
stepping between Rudek and the skaven.

More green flame, darker this time, and hotter. Green foam bubbled from the creature's mouth, and its eyes bulged as it thrust both hands forward. Its claws had blackened and its flesh was peeling. Thin cracks of green had appeared in its skin, showing easily through its patchy fur.

It was powerful, but not so much that it was a threat. Another shrieking burst and W'soran's own magics deflected the energy, sending it curling towards the Strigoi and the rat ogres. All died, consumed by the weird flames. W'soran chuckled. 'Yes, quite strong. It'll be dead soon though. You can always tell when their skin begins to crack and flake like that. It's burning up from the inside out.'

The war-engine shuddered. W'soran's eye flicked upwards. The massive chunk of abn-i-khat mounted in the weapon seemed to be reacting with the white skaven's magics. The stone was unstable at the best of times, but right now it was smoking and sparking. The dull internal glow that it always seemed to have had brightened to an almost blinding degree.

Calculations rattled through his skull. The simplest solution was invariably the best. He lunged forward through green fire and wrapped his claws in the skaven's robes. It squealed in fear for the first time as W'soran swung it easily into the air. Its stunted body radiated a strange, unnerving heat, and his flesh puckered and steamed as he drew the creature over his head. He met its wide-eyed gaze and exposed his fangs. 'I have a theory. Let us test it together, eh?'

Then he hurled the screaming skaven towards the glowing chunk of stone.

The explosion, when it occurred, was far from disappointing. The top of the war-engine erupted in a gout of fiery emerald. The upper mechanisms toppled, smoking, and smashed into those of the next engine in line. Further explosions ran down through its frame in a massive chain reaction, torn apart by the very thing they had used to deal destruction. Fire washed past him without touching him. W'soran watched in satisfaction as blistering, emerald smoke filled the cavern, thrown up by the explosion. He could hear the rumble of collapsing stone and the squeals of the skaven as their victory was snatched from them. He turned to Rudek. 'I see you still live,' he said.

Rudek grimaced and made to sit up. He was healing slowly. The touch of the abn-i-khat was deadly even to a vampire. 'I suppose you have proven your use yet again, sorcerer.' He grinned weakly. 'Vorag's concubine will be displeased.'

'Will she now?' W'soran said mildly. Inwardly, however, he was seething. That damnable witch! Lupa Stregga – one of Neferata's harlots – clung to Vorag's cloak, whispering in his ear and guiding him. She had done so since before the Bloodytooth had decided to remove himself from Mourkain; indeed, W'soran suspected that she was the reason for Vorag's rebellion against Ushoran. As ever, when something went wrong, Neferata could be found at the heart of it. A queen-spider, crouching in her web, weaving plots and schemes to trap all the little flies... but there were flies, and then there were flies. She'd bitten off more than she could chew with Ushoran.

For a moment, he was again back in the black pyramid of Kadon, around which the city of Mourkain had sprouted like gangrene in a wound. He was again in that moment, that split-second moment when the ghost of Alcadizzar, the last Prince of Rasetra, had been drawn from his ignoble tomb by sorcerous hooks and forced to relinquish the black crown he held to Ushoran. He saw it all, like a phantom pantomime occurring across the surface of his mind. Mourkain had been built on Alcadizzar's bones and the ghost of the crown – Nagash's crown – had drawn them all there. All of them – Ushoran, Abhorash, Neferata and even he himself – had felt its malevolent pull. It spoke to them, whispered sweet nothings into their skulls and promised eternity.

But it had spoken to Ushoran strongest of all, apparently. And now, the crown had him. It rode him the way the Strigoi rode their stubby mountain ponies, filling his crooked mind with Nagash's thoughts and his twisted frame with Nagash's power.

In that moment, that brief flicker of time, W'soran had craved that power for himself. But Neferata had been quicker. And what had that gotten her, but abuse, humiliation and enslavement? She had been swatted like a fly by the darkling thing Ushoran was becoming. And he was becoming something – he was a chrysalis, a worm on his way to becoming... what? Something terrifying. W'soran thought that it was a fate that had, perhaps, been intended for him. Might still be intended for him…

'She wanted us to kill you, you know,' Rudek said as he heaved himself up. His skin was blistered and peeling. Cracks of green mingled with the veins of black in his flesh, as the lingering traces of abn-i-khat spread through him. 'From the very minute you caught up with us, your ragged little pack of tomb-robbers at your back and Abhorash on your trail, she wanted you dead. Said we could buy a few months grace from Ushoran's wrath with your head. Vorag caught on and disciplined her. I think she rather enjoyed it. The Bloodytooth thinks we need you, that we need your magics. He is frightened of Ushoran…'

'And you, Rudek, what do you think?' W'soran said carefully. Thoughts of fate and the past faded, obscured by plans for the future.

'I think you have betrayed more than one master, old monster. And you will betray more before your sands are run out,' Rudek said.

'You are wise, in your time,' W'soran said. He reached out and pressed a finger to the still bubbling wound in Rudek's shoulder. 'Too wise, I fear. Goodbye, Rudek, your cousin sends his regards.'

The green cracks suddenly widened. Rudek's flesh ripped and split, and the vampire made to scream. It was childishly easy to agitate the lingering residue in the wound, and return it to volatility. Abn-i-khat reacted strongly to the merest whisper of the winds of magic. The green cracks spread, tunnelling through Rudek's flesh. He tried to jerk back from W'soran's fingertips, but was held in place by the curling magics that shuddered through him. Steam belched from his open jaws and his eyes went from red to pink to the ugly white of a badly boiled egg.

With a sound like meat sliding off the bone, Rudek toppled over, a burnt-out husk. W'soran flicked bits of cooked flesh from his fingers and stepped over the body to reclaim his scimitar. The smoke from the explosion was clearing as he dropped off the wrecked engine and strode back towards the battle. Skaven fled past him, scurrying for their holes. This army was broken. Skeletons, some blackened and burnt, tromped past in pursuit. Several Strigoi were with them. None of them so much as looked at W'soran, which suited him. There'd be questions, in time, but not until well after the fact. And none of them could challenge him.

The tread of heavy feet caught his attention. The crypt horrors and their burden approached through the smoke. The palanquin was undamaged, though its occupants could not say the same. Several were missing, and W'soran wondered whether Melkhior had followed his example and put paid to a few perceived obstacles. He grinned at the thought, amused. Melkhior was hard on his fellow apprentices. Then, he was a barbarian, and barbarians knew only one way to climb in status.

The barbarian in question crouched on the edge of the palanquin, leaning on his sword. He peered down at W'soran.

'The battle is won, my master,' Melkhior said.

'So it is. Your cousin has had an accident, I'm afraid.'

'He was always very clumsy,' Melkhior said. 'Vorag has arrived.'

'Good,' W'soran said. He jerked his chin at the palanquin. 'You saw battle, then?'

Melkhior shifted uncomfortably. 'Olgik and Yuri fell to the spears of the ratkin– fixed through the heart, the both of them.'

'Then pull the spears out and wake them up,' W'soran said.

'The ghouls trod on them afterwards. I'm afraid there wasn't much to save,' Melkhior said. 'And the rats got what was left.' He motioned to the ground. Thousands of black rats squirmed and squealed across the battleground. They came with the skaven, but rarely left with them. The vermin tore and fought over the dead, stripping the flesh from bone in moments. W'soran eyed the rats for a moment, and flicked away one that got too close with the tip of his blade. He looked up at Melkhior.

'The rats,' he said.

'The rats, yes,' Melkhior said.

'I trust you recovered their papyri and tomes from their bodies?' All of his apprentices travelled with their own copies of the lore that W'soran, and they themselves, had accumulated. They fought over the scraps of his knowledge in much the same manner as the rats. As such, every one of them had secrets the others did not – bits of sorcerous lore he'd given them as a reward for some small task.

Melkhior hesitated, and then nodded. 'Yes,' he said.

W'soran laughed. 'Good. Then the loss is minimal.'

'Trust you to think that way, beast,' a woman's voice said.

W'soran turned. He restrained a snarl as the tall, Amazonian form of Lupa Stregga stalked towards him across the carpet of rats and bodies, her sword-arm wet to the elbow with blood and her face equally smeared. 'Where is Rudek?' Stregga asked.

'Dead,' W'soran said.

'Why am I not surprised?' she said harshly. She glanced at the palanquin. 'Hello, Melkhior. Have you begun to regret accompanying the old leech from Mourkain yet?'

Melkhior stood. 'Watch your tongue, she-wolf, or I'll–'

'Or you'll what, coward?' a voice bellowed from above.

W'soran stepped back as the great shape landed heavily between the palanquin and Stregga. Where it had come from, whether it had been clinging to the roof of the cavern or squatting nearby, he couldn't say. The rock cracked beneath its weight and the rats fled as it rose from its crouch. It was a brute-shape, all muscle and hair. Great, cavernous jaws snapped at the air as hot eyes blazed at Melkhior.

A greased scalp lock snapped like a whip as the monstrosity spun about to face W'soran. A curved talon pointed at him. 'Keep your curs on a leash, W'soran, or I'll crack their skulls and suck their bones dry myself,' Vorag Bloodytooth roared.

He had changed much in the years since he'd fled Mourkain at the head of a rebel army. Where once he'd been a man, bigger than most perhaps, he was now as frightful as Melkhior, with the bloated musculature and savage claws and fangs of an animal; his once proud beard had become a tangled mess and hair grew in lank patches from his burly form, bursting through the rents in his badly-kept armour. Only his scalp-lock remained pristine, though whether out of his vanity or Stregga's attentions, W'soran didn't know. Behind the hair, his face was a nightmare of devilish ridges and bony growths. Inevitably, such a physical ruination seemed to be the lot of every person gifted with Ushoran's tainted blood-kiss, though the beast had always been close to the skin in Vorag. He'd been one of the first Strigoi turned when Ushoran had assumed the throne. Vorag had pledged his sword to the new king with a rapidity that was still spoken of with some awe in the snake-pit court of Mourkain.

But Timagal Vorag had grown dissatisfied all too quickly with his new master. And he'd found a co-conspirator of sorts in Neferata when she arrived at last, looking to worm her way into Ushoran's good graces. Together, those two had caused much trouble. Separated from Neferata, Vorag was no less dangerous, especially with a creature like Stregga whispering in his ear. Neferata might have been smashed into subservience by Ushoran, but she had not ceased weaving webs.

'Of course, Lord Vorag,' W'soran said, spreading his arms and bowing low. Melkhior had done the same, as had his other apprentices. Vorag grunted and turned away, to survey the aftermath of the battle.

As he rose, W'soran saw a familiar shape behind Stregga. His robes were stained with blood and other substances and the heavy iron gauntlets covering his withered talons were splotched with rust and scorch marks. Zoar inclined his head to his master, his skeletal features twisted in a smile. W'soran smirked; Zoar was, of all of his remaining followers, one of the most capable, besides Melkhior.

He glanced at the latter. Melkhior's face was hard to read, given the extent of its deformity, but W'soran knew him well enough to know he was angry. Melkhior hated Zoar. Zoar, for his part, pretended not to notice Melkhior at all. Zoar was the last of the Yaghur, the primitive fen-dwellers that Nagash had made his own when he'd raised Nagashizzar from the mountain and made it his citadel. W'soran had seen his intelligence, and claimed him. He had claimed many; few of Nagash's followers had been interested in self-aware servants.

Zoar, as such, felt himself privileged over all others. W'soran had never had to discipline him, as he had Melkhior or Morath. The Yaghur knew his place, and was content with it. Or such was the impression he gave.

'Where is Rudek?' Vorag growled, stroking his ratty beard. He'd calmed slightly. W'soran could see that blood matted his hairy arms up to his shoulders. He'd seen hard fighting in the tunnels. So had the other Strigoi – there were more than a dozen of them, all seasoned campaigners.

Of them, W'soran's closest rival was Sanzak. The brute-faced Strigoi was covered in the scars he'd acquired in life, before Vorag had turned him. Of all the Strigoi not under W'soran's thumb, he was one of the closest to understanding how to manipulate the winds of death, thanks to the efforts of Zoar. W'soran pretended not to know, as such a liaison had provided him with more useful information than a host of spies. Despite that, and despite the fact that Sanzak looked like the losing end of a fight, W'soran recognised the scarred brute's cunning. Even without Zoar's influence, he had, in his centuries, begun to study things which did not concern him. And, most distressingly, to teach others, which meant he was dangerous.

'Dead,' Stregga said, responding before W'soran could.

Vorag's eyes swivelled to W'soran. 'How did he die?'

'The skaven were accompanied by a sorcerer.' W'soran gestured to the ruptured and still-smoking war machine with his scimitar. 'I dealt with it when he proved himself inadequate to the task.'

The other Strigoi bristled visibly. Vorag merely grunted. 'I seem to lose more of my followers that way. Were they all inadequate, then?'

'I make no judgements,' W'soran said.

Stregga gave a sharp laugh. W'soran glared at her. Vorag raised a talon, silencing them. As the battle-fury faded, Vorag became more human looking. W'soran watched the change with interest. He had long theorised that the bestial nature of the Strigoi was as much the result of their close proximity to Nagash's crown as it was to their inexplicable love of the foul-tasting blood of ghouls. A little less of Vorag the man returned after each battle, a little more of the beast remained.

'Dead is dead,' Vorag grunted. 'The rats are beaten. We have driven them into the depths.'

'They are not beaten,' W'soran said, peering about him at the thousand and one holes and shafts that decorated the walls and floor of the cavern. 'They are merely taking stock of their situation.'

'And how would you know that?' Sanzak barked.

'I have fought them before, as you well know,' W'soran said. 'There are millions of them, scurrying in these walls, watching us even now. We will have to uproot this mountain and tear it inside out to fully cleanse it.'

'And why would we want to bother?' Stregga asked, reaching out to tear a strip from Zoar's robe. The vampire frowned, but fell silent at W'soran's look. Stregga cleaned her blade with the already-filthy cloth and tossed it aside with a grimace of disgust. 'There is nothing for us here, my love.' She directed the latter at Vorag, who was studying the remains of the war-engine, seemingly taking no notice of the discussion going on around him.

'Nothing but a ready-built fortress, should we choose to capitalise on it,' W'soran said mildly.

'There is a fortress waiting for us to the north,' Stregga said.

'Ah, yes, so you say,' W'soran spat, 'but we have yet to hear from your mistress. For all we know, she's failed, and the Silver Pinnacle has resisted Ushoran's attempt to annex it. Or perhaps she's chosen to embrace her new life of servitude, and decided against her mad plan of convincing Ushoran to take the hold.' He leered at Stregga and spread his hands. 'Or maybe she's dead, her head decorating a spike in the halls of the dwarfs, eh?'

'You shut your filthy mouth,' Stregga growled, lifting her sword.

'Quiet,' Vorag rumbled. He turned, glaring at them both. 'What is that machine, sorcerer?'

'A skaven weapon,' W'soran said. 'They are a clever species.' He looked at Vorag, gauging his mood. 'There are likely more such, far below.'

'What does it do?'

'It fires lightning,' W'soran said.

'Lightning,' Vorag repeated. His face scrunched up in an expression of consideration. 'Such a weapon would prove useful, in the coming war.'

'Indeed it would, most puissant lord,' Zoar said, sidling towards Vorag. 'And my master is just the man to learn the secrets of these engines for you, oh wise Vorag.' W'soran hid his smile. He had placed Zoar close to Vorag in order to counteract Stregga's whispers. Zoar's ingratiating manner and practiced unctuousness appealed to Vorag.

'We do not need such things,' Stregga said. Several of the Strigoi growled in agreement.

Vorag turned. 'What we need and do not need is not for you to say, she-wolf,' he snarled, the sound ripping through the cavern. Stregga didn't flinch. Vorag's molten gaze fell on W'soran. 'How long would you require, sorcerer?'

'Several months, at least,' W'soran said, sheathing his scimitar. 'I will need a working one, of course. We'll have to delve deeper into the ratkin warrens.'

'Which means we will need to fortify this place,' Vorag said, looking around. 'We shall need a citadel with which to push against our foes. A bulwark against attack...' Even as he said it, W'soran knew that the Bloodytooth wasn't talking just about the skaven. Vorag was frightened. There was a shadow growing in the north, and even simple brutes like Vorag could see it. It was a shadow that W'soran had helped to unleash. And that, given enough time, he thought he could control.

The only question was whether it would consume him before he got that chance.

⫷ CHAPTER THREE ⫸

Nagashizzar
(Year -1168 Imperial Calendar)

'How dare you,' W'soran snarled, fangs exposed and claws extended. 'What are you doing in here, liche?' The chambers were in shambles, scrolls and papyri scattered about the stone floor and the bodies of his apprentices amongst them. Most lived; one, at least, was dead, his torso a smoking ruin. That one would not be punished for his failure to stop the intruder, but the others... 'Answer me,' W'soran snapped. 'What are you doing in here?'

'Whatever I like,' Arkhan the Black said, turning. His voice was a hollow rasp, and it seemed to echo in W'soran's mind rather than in his ears. In one bony hand, he held the throat of the strongest of W'soran's apprentices, Zoar. The barbarian still struggled, albeit feebly, his claws scoring the bone of Arkhan's fingers. 'These were my chambers, after all.'

'You weren't using them,' W'soran said. 'Release my property.'

He had claimed the chambers soon after arriving in Nagashizzar, several decades before. Nagashizzar had once rung with
the sounds of living men, hundreds of them, if not thousands;
whole tribes and clans of the savage barbarians from the eastern
marshes. Now, it was eerily silent, save for the scrape of bone
on metal. Only the dead resided in the mountain fortress of the
Undying King now, and of the dead, only a few dozen were self-
aware enough to interact to any great degree. Most were wights,
or liches like Arkhan; the corridors rang with the sounds of the
internal battles that served to occupy their time when they were
not about Nagash's business. W'soran had won his chambers in
one such struggle, early after his arrival. His powers had grown
by leaps and bounds under Nagash's tutelage, even as his blind
devotion to the being he had seen as a god began to dim.

'Oh.' Arkhan glanced down at the weakly struggling vampire.
'Is this yours?'

'Release him, liche, or–'

'Or what, leech, you'll finally strike openly at me?' Arkhan said,
letting Zoar slide from his grip. 'The assassins you sent to kill me
in the deep mines failed, W'soran, as you can see.' He turned and
spread his arms. 'Do you have the courage to attempt it yourself?'

'I sent no assassins,' W'soran said. 'Perhaps you have more
enemies than you know.' It was the truth, as far as it went. He had
ordered no attack on Arkhan; no, his target of late had been one
of the liche's comrades, Mahtep. The latter was prone to hiding his
decayed features behind a mask of human flesh and wore heavy
armour in imitation of their master, Nagash. He was also a stupid
creature, prone to challenging his betters whenever Nagash fell

into one of his contemplative moods and removed himself to his throne to ponder upon the Great Work. While the Undying King communicated with whatever dark spirits drove him, his minions squabbled amongst themselves, lashing out at one another openly. Mahtep had decided that this year, it was W'soran's turn to suffer the annoyance of his attentions.

Mahtep had sent scuttling creations of bone and sinew, their carven fangs loaded with poison, to kill W'soran as he meditated. W'soran had returned the favour with the gift of a bellicose serpent-thing composed of a hundred human spinal columns and the head of Mahtep's favourite skeletal steed. Mahtep had been dragged into the northern barrows by the thing; no one had seen him come back up yet. W'soran wasn't concerned. If he survived, he'd know better than to try again. And if he didn't, well, surely Nagash would thank him for removing a weak link amongst his disciples.

'Something stinking of grave-mould and whatever bastard elixir you call blood attacked me in the mines,' Arkhan said, striding towards W'soran. 'It nearly tore my head off.'

'Perhaps it was a singularly ferocious ghoul,' W'soran said, raising an eyebrow.

'Or perhaps it was one of these jackals you call apprentices,' Arkhan rasped.

'Or maybe it is something else,' W'soran said. He paused, considering. 'Several of the others have reported that there is a – ah – "stirring" in the warrens of the corpse-eaters below us. They're growing bold, without Nagash's will to hold them in check, and attacking the corpses in the mines, feasting on them.'

'Then we will slaughter them,' Arkhan said. He was silent for a moment. Then, 'What do you suspect, blood-drinker?'

'I think someone – something – is plotting to take Nagashizzar by force.'

'The skaven,' Arkhan said.

W'soran shook his head. 'No. It's something else, something more cunning than any ratkin. If Nagash were paying attention, I do not think it would dare...'

'But he is not,' Arkhan said. His empty eye sockets flared suddenly with a weird light.

'No,' W'soran said. He smiled crookedly. 'But we are.'

Crookback Mountain
(Year -325 Imperial Calendar)

'Drive them back!' Vorag roared. With a bellow worthy of a bull-ape, he wrenched the rat ogre's head from its massive shoulders and sent it sailing back into the mass of skaven that sought to push the undead out of the cramped and crooked tunnel. The two forces met and fought beneath the light of the large, eerily glowing green censer spheres that had been strung from the roof of the tunnel. The skaven had fortified the tunnel and were in the process of sealing it off when Vorag's forces had attacked.

The Bloodytooth was at the forefront, as always. He disdained the use of weapons, relying instead on his own claws, fangs and strength to carry him through. At his side, Stregga screeched like an angry wildcat and beheaded a spear-wielding skaven with a single fluid movement. Together, the two of them formed the point of the spear. The tunnel was barely wide enough for a dozen men to move shoulder-to-shoulder, and it was up to the Strigoi to dismantle the crude barricades that the skaven had constructed.

W'soran watched it all from a safe distance. There were ten ranks of skeletal troops between him and the Strigoi, marching forward blindly. He followed them, shrouded in his robes, Melkhior to one side and Zoar to the other. 'The skaven are falling back,' Zoar murmured.

'You doubted it?' Melkhior snorted.

'I was merely making an observation,' Zoar said mildly. 'It seemed strange, given their persistence earlier...' He looked at his rival with a hooded gaze. Zoar had made a game of provoking his fellow disciple. Melkhior, for his part, rose to the bait every time. It was yet another reason that W'soran despaired of the Strigoi ever achieving his full potential. There was too much pride there. Melkhior would never be anything more than what he was. Neither would Zoar, but the Yaghur had had longer to get used to the fact, and his ambition was ashes and embers. Melkhior's blazed like fire.

'Maybe they simply know when they are beaten,' Melkhior said.

'Unlike some people,' Zoar said.

Melkhior rounded on him with a snarl. 'What is that supposed to mean?'

'I thought you were supposed to be intelligent, Strigoi. Figure it out.'

Melkhior leaned close to Zoar and growled. Zoar yawned into his face. W'soran ignored them, and instead concentrated on the shard of abn-i-khat balanced on his palm. The wyrdstone, as the Strigoi had taken to calling it, had a particular resonance; each piece called to its fellows, growing warmer as it drew closer if one exerted the slightest touch of magic to it. W'soran had several more shards slung around his neck, and each glowed with a strange light. He was using the lot as lodestones, trying to find the quickest, most direct route to the main warren of their enemy, or at the very least, wherever it was that they were keeping their store of the stone and constructing their weapons. Sanzak and the other Strigoi were leading similar assaults in the tunnels running parallel to the one they found themselves in, pressing the skaven back on multiple fronts. They were accompanied by W'soran's other apprentices. With the dead from the previous battles added to their ranks and the discovery of the food stores, consisting mainly of the stacked and gnawed bodies of skaven and greenskins, in the upper reaches, Vorag's army had swelled to a significant size.

Nonetheless, it had taken almost a year to reach this point. Months had been wasted, crashing through pits and hidden caverns, burning and slaughtering the seemingly numberless creatures. They had faced only one more war-engine in that time, and the skaven, with prescience that was as frustrating as it was startling, had destroyed it when they realised that the vampires were after it. The vermin had been retreating steadily since then, squirming deeper and deeper into the darkness, fighting only to delay or harry the undead, rather than defeat them. They had even taken to collecting their dead, or burning them, in an attempt to wage a war of attrition.

Vorag roared and heaved the body of the rat ogre towards the barricades, shattering them and sending skaven tumbling. The vampire vaulted the still-twitching body and fell upon the fleeing ratkin. Stregga was right behind him, as were his personal guard. The vampires moved so quickly, they outpaced the dead marching behind them. W'soran snorted in disgust. Foolishness... why bother with an army if you were going to abandon them at the first whiff of blood?

His eye caught a quick, furtive movement from above. W'soran looked up, and his good eye widened. 'Usirian's jowls,' he snarled, throwing up a hand bristling with necromantic power. 'They're above us!'

There were dozens of stunted, black-clad bodies clinging to the roof of the tunnel. Their black rags were covered in cave-dusts and their fur was slick with something vile that W'soran knew had served to kill their scent. Each was armed with a bandolier of clay flasks. Even as W'soran raised his hand, one of the skaven plunged its claw into its rags and extracted a handful of flat, metal disks.

The disks hissed as the ratkin sent them spinning through the air. They sank home into W'soran's palm and forearm, eliciting a shriek of anger as his spell was disrupted. He staggered back, clutching his arm. 'Kill them!' he snapped.

Zoar and Melkhior reacted swiftly, unleashing a barrage of deadly magics. Skaven fell, screaming and burning. But not all of them, and not quickly enough – W'soran saw it all in an instant. The plan was obvious, in retrospect, and he cursed himself for not seeing it sooner. The skaven had drawn them in, drawn them deeper into the cramped tunnels, and now they were going to be made to pay. The surviving skaven tore off their bandoliers and hurled them towards the ground.

The ground erupted in green flame and the rock of the tunnel groaned and shifted as the flasks exploded, ripping the heart out of the tunnel. The skaven had used the wyrd-stone for explosives. The tunnel was tearing itself apart, cracks running through the walls and floor. Skeleton warriors were consumed in the explosion or crushed by the falling rocks, or swallowed by the gaping floor. As the tunnel collapsed, the skaven, as trapped as W'soran and the others by what the latter now realised had been a suicide mission, leapt down, blades at the ready. A sword chopped into his raised arm, and he felt the sizzle of something smeared on the blade. With a scream, he smashed the skaven into the wall, even as the floor gave out from beneath him.

He heard Melkhior and Zoar scream as they all fell into darkness. Furry bodies slammed into him, squealing curses in their own chittering tongue as they hacked and chopped at him. He could smell something seeping from them; a poison perhaps, or a drug designed to remove their natural tendency towards cowardice. That was the only explanation he could find for their persistence. W'soran struck rock, bounced and spun, tumbling. His fingers found a hairy throat and he tore it open. Incisors sank into his shoulder and he hissed and reached backwards.

More rocks struck him. The explosion had caused a chain reaction. It was collapsing the tunnel and those below, ripping a wedge straight through the network of frail corridors like a knife through a wasp's nest. Fleshy tails wrapped around him, squeezing and pulling. He couldn't reach his sword. He caught a blade, breaking it and stabbing at its wielder.

W'soran grunted as he struck an outcropping. A normal man, especially the man he had been, would have been pulped a few moments after the explosion. As a vampire, short of being completely mashed into a fine paste, he had no doubt he would survive it. The skaven must have been desperate. Why else would they risk destroying their own fortress?

What if that was their intent? To gut the mountain and bring all of its glacial weight down on the invaders, entombing them forever. The thought chilled him – he had been buried before. For the first time in a long time, panic surged through him. Suddenly, survival was something to be feared. In animal terror of the great weight closing in around him, he flailed about and his claws dug into the rock. He could smell the fear-musk of the skaven now, and their writhing bodies tumbled past. He couldn't see Melkhior or Zoar.

He scrambled up, trying to pull himself to safety. The fear

grew, sweeping him up into its embrace and sucking him down. How long would he persist, buried in the darkness – centuries, possibly or even millennia; his experiments in that regard had not been forthcoming. He thought again of the vampires he'd left in the dark of Mourkain and he cowered, waiting for the collapse to end.

Stones crashed down around him, and dust swirled, obscuring his vision. As the last rock bounced away, W'soran shoved himself quickly into a crouch. He was unable to rise any further. His armour was cracked and hanging from his thin frame in ragged strips. His robes were torn and his flesh was streaked with black blood. He'd lost his blade. He didn't bother to call out for his apprentices. If they had survived, they would find him. If they had not, they would be of little use.

The tunnel was little more than a half filled-in grave. There was little room to move and if he'd still been a breathing man, he'd likely have suffocated in minutes. But he wasn't breathing and he could move. 'Small mercies,' he grunted. The rock swallowed his voice.

He looked up. Part of the tunnel had fallen in, across two sections of the wall, creating a small air pocket. Beyond the pocket, the rest of the tunnel was probably buried. He could see the crushed and pulverised remains of a number of skaven caught between the rocks.

Panic teased his thoughts. Suddenly, he was back in his jar beneath the temple, unable to move, to blink the spiders from his eyes or pluck the beetles from his flesh. He wouldn't be buried again – he couldn't! He closed his eyes and clamped down on the fear. 'Why should you fear?' he whispered to himself. 'You *are* fear. You have been trapped before. Think. Think!' He clutched at the abn-i-khat amulets dangling from his neck and squeezed them.

Abruptly he opened his eyes. He looked down, and the panic fled like a morning mist. 'Haaaa,' he breathed. The amulets glowed and trembled in his fingers. He held them up to his mouth and blew on them, expelling a lungful of sorcerous breath. The glow grew, and he felt the sickly warmth of the stones on his palm. Gathering his legs under him, he wrenched one of the amulets loose.

He hesitated. He had never dared take that step in imitation of Nagash. There was no telling what the eating of the stone would do to a being like him, or whether it would even have any effect whatsoever. But if it did... it was concentrated magic. Eating it had made Nagash more powerful than any other necromancer. Eating it empowered the skaven as well. And he needed power. He looked at it, looked at the way it seemed to suck in the darkness around it. The wyrdstone ate light and darkness alike, and the shadows seemed to be dragged towards the nooks and crannies of the amulet, as if grasped by invisible talons.

Even so, the worry was there. Nagash had consumed it and been consumed by it. He had been made both more and less than a man by a lifetime's consumption of the soft, powdery stone. He had become addicted, requiring more and more of it to empower his spells.

Then, power was a stronger drug than any W'soran had ever heard of. The only thing it was good for was gaining more power. That was what creatures like Neferata and Ushoran had never understood – power was an end in itself, to be hoarded and increased, as the skaven did with their wyrdstone.

The weapons, the secrets of the skaven, would give him that power. They would give him the power to stare down the mad, phantom soul that rode poor, pathetic Ushoran towards oblivion, and to add its power to his own. 'You think you're safe, old liche?' he murmured, examining the abn-i-khat. 'You think your secrets are safe, hiding in that iron circlet? You think to devour me, hollow me out like a mummy and slip inside to ride me into the dark, far future, my master? You're wrong, as you were wrong about Alcadiz-zar. I will be the one to devour you. I will swallow the carrion remnant of your tattered soul, Nagash, and I will be a true master of death.'

W'soran opened his jaws and his tongue, the colour of a leech flush after a feeding, unrolled and extended upwards like the questing tendril of a squid, rising past his thicket of fangs. The tip of his tongue brushed against the amulet, exploring the rough facets. A surge of power rippled through him and he shivered in anticipation. Then, with a grunt, he dropped the amulet into his mouth.

Even as his fangs sank into the soft stone, his body shuddered. He felt as if he had bitten into a lightning bolt, as if he were burning up from within. Swallowing the small chunks of stone, he flung out his hands and spat words of power. Dark magic coursed through him, and he felt it more strongly than ever before. A sorcerous blast struck the rocks and the rough stone bubbled and slopped like mud. W'soran scuttled forward, unleashing blast after blast, carving a path to freedom. The remaining amulets grew warmer, and he was tempted to eat another, but resisted the urge.

He continued forward for what felt like minutes, but might have been hours. The abn-i-khat pulsed in his long-dried veins, and his mind felt as if it were full of quicksilver; his thoughts rattled in his head like hornets trapped in a flask. Part of him wondered if this was how Nagash had seen the world. It was as if everything was moving in slow motion. He could see motes of dust drifting past him, and the sparks that made up the flames that spread from his hands. He could see what was to come and how to make it so with searing clarity, and he laughed as he cut his way through the bowels of the mountain.

Then, one final wall exploded outward and, wreathed in the smoke of his passage, W'soran stepped through, into a massive cavern. A hundred pairs of glittering eyes stared at him in shock. There were skaven everywhere and they all froze. He smelled their fear and smiled.

The cavern was larger than any yet encountered, and full to bursting with the stuff of construction. It reminded W'soran of the ancient ruins of the dwarfen workshops he'd discovered high in the mountains. It was lit, as with the rest of the mountain, by great braziers and censers exuded foul-smelling smoke. Rats scurried underfoot. Baskets full of abn-i-khat were everywhere. Great chains hung from the roof and half-built war-engines occupied most of the cavern floor. The skaven appeared to have been caught in the process of dismantling the engines for transport.

Suddenly, the determined holding action made sense. The skaven were trying to get their creations out of the reach of their enemies. W'soran could almost admire their persistence in defending the objects of their artifice. He held up a hand wreathed in black flame. The skaven tensed, watching him like vermin caught in sudden torchlight. He savoured the fear-stink rising from them.

'Run,' he hissed, 'or die, it makes no difference to me.' His voice carried to every corner of the cavern.

The skaven ran. W'soran laughed and killed those too slow to get out of his reach as quickly as their fellows. His magic speared out, killing them in droves. Skaven ran burning and screaming. The cavern was filled with the stink of cooking rat as W'soran stalked towards the contraptions, intent on claiming them for his own. As he strode, his thoughts uncoiled and slithered ahead and around him, latching onto the guttering life-sparks of dying skaven. With a mental jerk, he pulled the dead to their paws and set them scrabbling after their fellows. In an orgy of mindless hunger, the dead fell upon the living and the cavern echoed with the sounds of slaughter.

Abruptly, the euphoria he'd felt was replaced by a gnawing pain. For a moment, the world skidded around him, out of sync and blurry as his stomach lurched and the bile in his veins became turgid and weighty, dragging his limbs down, causing him to stumble. With a moan, W'soran staggered against one of the war-engines as a cold shudder ran through him. He felt like a punctured waterskin, leaking and deflating all at once. The temporary burst of energy the abn-i-khat had given him was leaving him. Bubbling pus leaked from his wounds and pores as his body expelled the last traces of the stone he'd eaten. He felt weak and wrung out. He shook his head and shoved himself to his feet.

A moment later, the blade of a spear cut through the spot where his head had been. The blade gashed his shoulder and threw him backwards. The wound burned and he saw that the blade of the weapon that had cut him was crafted from pure wyrdstone. Hissing, he pulled himself up into a crouch, one hand pressed to his injury.

A skaven crouched on the war machine, clutching the spear in its heavy gauntlets. Serrated black armour covered dirty robes, and its fur was a pure white where it peeked out through both armour and cloth. A heavy helm hid its head, and its eyes glowed green through the eye-slits. He wondered, as he examined it, if this were one of the so-called 'warlocks' the few captives he'd taken over the past months had spoken of.

The skaven pulled back the spear and spat his earlier bravado back in his face, 'Run-run or die-die, man-thing. It makes no difference to Iskar of Skryre.'

W'soran rose. He'd taught himself the rudiments of the

rat-things' language, with the unwilling help of the captives they'd taken in the campaign so far. He'd always had
a facility for tongues, even ones as animalistic as that of the
skaven. 'There's always a third option, vermin. I kill you and
wring the blood from your furry carcass.' He snapped his
fangs together. His keen ears caught a new sound above the
cacophony of the battle going on in the cavern. Weapons
clashed somewhere, followed by a roar that might have been
Vorag. W'soran chuckled. 'You're out of time.'

'There is always time,' the skaven snarled. It sprang from its
perch, wielding its weapon with skill. Only W'soran's speed
saved him from being gutted and he backed away from
the stabbing blade. The skaven pressed forward, seeking to
impale him.

He loosed a sorcerous bolt, hoping to catch the creature
unawares, but it simply raised its weapon and caught the
spell on the blade. The bolt evaporated, and the glow in the
skaven's eyes seemed to grow brighter. 'Weak man-thing,' it
chattered. 'I see-see your weakness.' It tapped the side of its
helm with a talon.

'Silence, beast,' W'soran said. More magics flew from his
gesticulating hands. The skaven's blade swiped out, cutting
through his spells as if they were nothing more than an
evening fog. The creature loped forward, its tail lashing.

W'soran staggered back and tripped over a corpse, toppling
backwards. The white-furred skaven darted forward with
a high-pitched cry of triumph. W'soran's palms slammed
together on either side of the blade, trapping it. The skaven

planted its paws on his chest and put all of its weight on the spear, trying to force the blade into his skull. W'soran grimaced and resisted. Slowly he sat up, and the skaven was shoved back. For the first time, he saw fear in its eyes.

With a growl, W'soran pressed his palms together. The wyrdstone blade shattered in his grip. The skaven stumbled back. It opened its mouth, as if to scream.

W'soran gave it no chance to do so. He let loose a final spell, and a corona of heat engulfed the creature. Without its blade, it had no way of dispersing his magics and it stiffened as its fur shrivelled, its robes caught fire and its armour melted to its quivering frame. It fell backwards with a loud clank, smoke and steam rising from its body.

He rose and squatted beside it. It still lived, albeit not for long, unless something was done. Almost gently, he pried the helmet from its head, causing it to thrash in agony. Ignoring its squeals of pain, he examined the helm. 'Ingenious,' he muttered, tapping the green lenses.

The cavern was silent now. The survivors of his attack had either fled or joined the ranks of the dead things that stood still and stiff, waiting for his next command. The sounds of fighting were growing louder. After the explosion, the Strigoi must have continued to press forward. Vorag wouldn't let the loss of his army stop him. W'soran laughed, imagining the expression on Stregga's face when she saw him waiting for them.

He looked at the skaven. Its eyes had been cooked in their sockets, and they rolled madly as it writhed. W'soran patted its blistered snout fondly as he looked from the helm to the half-constructed war machines. 'You were right – ah – Iskar was it? There will indeed be time aplenty. Time enough for me to flay your cunning little secrets from you, and make them mine.' He looked down at the trembling creature and licked its blood from his claw-tips. It moaned.

'Won't that be fun?' he said, smiling.

—< CHAPTER FOUR >—

Nagashizzar
(Year -1168 Imperial Calendar)

Ushoran screamed. He snarled and gibbered like a wild beast as the wights held tight to the chains which bound him. A dozen of the dead men were required for the task, and W'soran had serious doubts as to whether it would be enough. Ushoran's strength had been great even before he'd accepted Neferata's gift of immortality.

The chains rattled as the vampire thrashed. His arms were pinned to his sides and the bonds had been looped about him multiple times. Even so, Ushoran managed to yank one of his captors from his feet. The wight slid across the forecourt, armour rattling. Ushoran pounced like a desert-fox, jumping straight up and bringing both feet down on the wight's chest like the talons of a raptor. Armour crumpled and burst and the wight flailed as Ushoran crouched and fastened his jaws on the front of the dead man's skull. Bone crunched and Ushoran jerked back, spitting fragments.

'Impressive,' Arkhan murmured. They stood on a balcony overlooking the forecourt, watching Ushoran's struggles as they debated his fate. Arkhan wanted to leave him out for the sun. W'soran, however, thought Ushoran might prove useful, after a fashion.

Arkhan flexed his hand. After they'd cornered Ushoran in the ghoul-warrens beneath Nagashizzar, the vampire had attempted to bite off Arkhan's hand. He would've succeeded, had W'soran not intervened. 'He is far stronger than I was led to believe your kind could be.'

'He is nothing. A cur, to Neferata's lioness,' W'soran said. He had been surprised to see the other vampire in the depths. He'd thought Ushoran dead and good riddance. Somehow, however, the Lord of Masks had managed to survive and find his way to Nagashizzar. He had changed much in his time in the wilderness. W'soran had always suspected that something unpleasant lurked beneath Ushoran's bland exterior. He was a monster now, slab-muscled and animal-faced, with eyes like lanterns and fangs like daggers. He was mad as well, driven insane by the wounds he sustained so many years before at the final battle of Lahmia. In time, with the proper nourishment, he might come out of it – or perhaps not.

Ushoran had led them a merry chase for many months in the depths. The ghouls had swarmed at his command, attacking their forces with a surprising ferocity. There were thousands of the corpse-eaters in the warrens below the fortress, and somehow Ushoran had roused them all to war. What he had been planning for his army, he had yet to share. They had captured him in the mines, ambushing him in a battle that had taken hours. In the end, the ghouls had been put to flight, and Ushoran captured.

'Neferata,' Arkhan said, and looked at him. W'soran wondered whether it was only his imagination that made it seem as if the liche's eye-sockets blazed more brightly at the thought of the queen of Lahmia. 'Yes, she is a lioness. And you, W'soran, what are you?'

'I am true to myself,' W'soran said, with a shrug.

'AND WHAT IS THAT, W'SORAN?' The voice was as cold as the grave and as deep as an ocean trench. Both Arkhan and W'soran froze at the sound of it. A heavy hand, more metal than bone, settled on W'soran's shoulder, its talons not quite piercing the flesh beneath his robes. 'WHAT IS W'SORAN OF LAHMIA?'

'Your servant, my master,' W'soran whispered.

'AHHHH,' Nagash breathed. Metal squealed as he moved past them to the edge of the balcony. Flames crackled silently around his grinning skull. The Undying King loomed over his servants. In death, he had become a giant. He grasped the balcony and the stone cracked beneath his weight. 'AND WHAT IS THIS?' he asked.

'A beast,' Arkhan said.

'A tool,' W'soran interjected. He glared at the liche.

'WHAT NEED HAVE I OF ANOTHER TOOL?' Nagash rasped. The sound of it scraped across W'soran's nerves. Nagash turned. 'I HAVE ALL THE TOOLS I REQUIRE.'

'Ushoran is… he is another of my kind, master. And cunning,' W'soran said quickly. 'He could be useful in your coming campaign to take that which is yours. They all could, master…'

'ALL?'

'*Neferata, Abhorash, Ankhat, the others; imagine what sort of champions they would make, master,*' W'soran said. '*Imagine the horror they could wreak in the Great Land, at your behest. They – we – are walking plagues, master. Our numbers can swell and grow with ease, and we can hunt the treacherous men of Nehekhara like dogs.*'

'A PLAGUE,' Nagash said slowly. *The fires around his skull seemed to curl higher and brighter as he turned back to gaze down at Ushoran once more.* 'YES…'

Crookback Mountain
(Year -323 Imperial Calendar)

The orc howled in brute agony as W'soran carefully peeled back the flesh of its barrel torso and pinned it to the wooden table. Even with its vitals exposed, the creature refused to either give in to shock or, as was more common, die. W'soran stepped back and gestured sharply. The ghouls squatting to either side of the table lunged up, grabbing the chains that dangled above the table and hauled on them. With a grinding squeal, the table was cranked up from a horizontal position to a vertical one.

W'soran had taken the skaven workshop for his own after the final battle and where it had once been full of squirming brown-furred bodies and strange machines, now only the latter remained, carefully disassembled and placed so that he might examine each cog and pulley. Great cages crafted from bone and wood now occupied a large portion of the space, crammed full of bellicose orcs and screaming goblins, taken captive in raids. Piecemeal zombies, crafted from the limbs of skaven, men and orcs, crawled, lumbered and scuttled about the cavern on various tasks.

Great alembics bubbled and hissed atop the heavy workbench W'soran had installed, as strange fluids sluiced through them. It had taken him months to craft the alembics, teasing the glass out of black sands brought from the shores of the Sour Sea. Bellows constructed from the vertebral plates of the monstrous beasts that roamed the deep caverns and the tanned and stretched hide of a rat ogre wheezed and whispered as zombies unceasingly pressed on them, circulating the fluid in the alembics. Other pathetic patchwork corpses saw to the grinding and sifting of W'soran's ever-dwindling supply of abn-i-khat, or the cleansing and arrangement of gathered bones for future purposes. Generations of skaven, and before them goblins, had lived and died in and on the mountain and W'soran's mindless servants scoured every crevasse and crag, hunting for remains. Vorag required an army, and W'soran knew of no better way to provide him one than to use what was at hand.

In the months following the capture of the mountain from its previous owners, W'soran had again begun his interrupted experiments in bone-craft and flesh-weaving. Even as he had created the crypt horrors, he had devised more warrior creations, based on ancient theories passed down to the priests of the Great Land. Giant scorpion-engines crafted from bone or slithering serpent-things made from stitched flesh and stretched muscle patrolled the lower depths ceaselessly for any new incursion from the skaven. It only took a bit of magic to give a semblance of life to the conglomerate horrors.

The table settled at a steep angle and the orc bellowed in pain as his centre of gravity descended, and his weight pulled on the heavy iron spikes that had been driven through his meaty wrists and ankles to hold him in place. Another chain had been looped beneath the orc's neck and as the beast slumped, the chain caught tight around its neck. It gagged and its piggy eyes bulged in mingled pain and hatred as it glared at its tormentor. Fresh, brackish blood oozed from around the spikes and the creature shuddered.

W'soran watched it twitch and writhe. Then, with the air of a *gourmand*, he reached below the orc's ribcage and pulled something out. 'Redundancies of redundancies,' he murmured. He glanced over at the crouched shape of one of his apprentices. The vampire was robed and cowled, and only its clawed digits were visible as it scratched out notes on a roll of parchment with a pen made from a fingerbone. 'Its heart and lungs show variation from human or skaven organs. Rudimentary, but still significant,' W'soran said, more loudly. Dutifully, the apprentice scratched out his master's observations.

Idly, W'soran took a bite of the lump of meat he held. He chewed slowly, sucking the blood from it. For all that it tasted foul, he'd found the blood of the greenskins to be a potent stimulant. He tossed the nearly-drained hunk of meat to the closest of the ghouls, which snapped it out of the air like a starving dog. Each of the ghouls was covered in jagged branding marks as well the pale weals of old incisions.

The orc groaned and its prognathous jaw gaped, showing off its splintered tusks. Crude blue tattoos covered its flesh and its musculature was overdeveloped to the point of ridiculousness. W'soran watched its powerful heart thud inside its cage of bone. Its heartrate wasn't slowing, despite the partial vivisection.

W'soran sniffed and leaned close to one of its brawny arms. With a flick of his talons, he sliced open its flesh and slid the quivering green hide back from muscle fibre and bone. 'Increased muscle strength,' he said. He hooked a section of its bicep muscle and gave it an experimental tug, eliciting a shriek from the orc. 'The muscle roots are anchored far more firmly than in men or skaven. And the limbs continue to function well after separation from the rest of the body.' He jerked the muscles free of the arm and the orc arched its back. Its skull drummed on the table and froth gushed from its mouth.

W'soran paid no heed to its writhing. He peeled back the layers of the muscle as if it were a fruit, his good eye narrowing. 'Hnf, it's attempting to repair itself. Intriguing,' he muttered. His eyes flickered to the side, where a heavy cage hung from the ceiling. 'What do you think, Iskar?'

The huddled shape inside didn't move. W'soran frowned. He gestured sharply and the sigils that crowded the heavy brass collar on the skaven's neck flared with an eerie light. Iskar shrieked and uncoiled like a spring.

The skaven looked the worse for wear from its years of captivity; its once white fur, what remained of it, was dingy, yellow and matted with filth. Burn scars covered its hairless skull and most of its body. It was completely blind, its eyes the colour of fish-bellies. W'soran had kept it alive out of curiosity. He had been intrigued to learn of the sturdy malleability of the species. Skin grafts from dead skaven and goblins had repaired most of the damage that W'soran's flames had done to the creature in their battle, and he felt, given the proper raw materials, he could repair the creature's eyes. Of course, it was more amusing to leave the beast blind and helpless.

Iskar hissed in his general direction, exposing blackened gums and brown teeth. 'Kill you,' it tittered. 'Kill you.'

'Yes, yes,' W'soran said, prodding the cage. Iskar huddled back, whimpering. 'After two years of those same two words I'm beginning to wonder if I actually managed to repair your voice box or not. Remind me why I keep you alive, rat.'

Iskar's nostrils flared and its lips writhed back from its fangs. The blistered tail lashed and it made a sound like a giggle. W'soran shook his head, disgusted. He wondered if perhaps he had gotten everything out of the beast that there was to get. With a sniff, he turned back to his current study.

With a roar, the orc wrenched its good arm free of the spike that had pinned it and flung out a hand, clawing for W'soran's throat. A blade flashed, cutting through the heavy clouds of incense before chopping into the orc's forearm. The brute yowled as the blade was wrenched free and then sent slicing into its skull with a sound like a melon being dropped.

Melkhior jerked his blade free and examined it critically. 'Damnable brutes are too tough by half,' he growled. He looked at W'soran. 'You should pay more attention to what's going on around you, master.'

'Why would I bother? That's what you're for, Melkhior,' W'soran said. He tossed the chunk of muscle to the still furiously scribbling apprentice. 'Collect muscle tissue from the remaining specimens and let it soak. We'll begin crafting our newest warriors tomorrow,' he said. He turned to Melkhior. 'Come to help, or to ask for it yourself, my son?'

'What are you planning?' Melkhior asked, avoiding the question.

'Orc muscle combined with goblin frame and skaven flesh and hide – small, sturdy and less prone to rot. Perfect scouts for the depths and high reaches,' W'soran said, rubbing his hands together gleefully. 'They'll hold together for months before they begin to degrade; longer if they're properly preserved.'

'Why not simply resurrect more skaven?'

'Where's the fun in that?' W'soran said. He patted Melkhior's cheek. The other vampire flinched and W'soran chuckled. 'Death is not the end, my son. And we must learn to husband our meagre resources in these harsh climes. To improve upon base creation and make something glorious here, in our citadel.'

'It might not be our citadel for much longer,' Melkhior said. 'What are you talking about?'

'Neferata… has sent word. From the north,' Melkhior said. 'She has succeeded. The Silver Pinnacle is hers, and the army Ushoran sent with her – what's left of it – is hers as well. Two Lahmians arrived not an hour ago.' His gaze turned accusing. 'They bypassed your defences.'

W'soran grunted. 'That is… unfortunate. What about Vorag?'

'They are with him now. He is holding a council.'

W'soran frowned. 'Why was I not informed?'

'Why do you think?' Melkhior snapped. W'soran caught him by the throat even as the words left his mouth and hefted him. The ancient vampire stepped towards the cages, propelling Melkhior back against them. Orcs howled with glee as they grabbed at Melkhior, tearing his robes and gouging his flesh. He spat and snarled, but couldn't free himself from W'soran's grip.

'Watch your tone, my apprentice. You are not irreplaceable,' W'soran said, with deadly mildness. He stepped back and let Melkhior drop. The younger vampire rubbed his throat and stooped to scoop up his sword. W'soran said, 'Why wasn't I called to the council?'

'Stregga,' Melkhior spat. 'She has Vorag wrapped around her finger. It's all Zoar or I can do to counter her machinations, while you've been holed up down here.'

W'soran glared at him. 'What good are you if you cannot outthink a blood-addled fishwife?'

Melkhior hissed, but looked away. W'soran shook his head. He ran a hand over his leathery pate. His words to the contrary, he wasn't surprised. Melkhior had all the subtlety of a starving wolf and Zoar, while cunning, had never been the most independent thinker. Lupa Stregga seemed like little more than a feral blood doxy at first glance, but he'd grown familiar with how her mind worked. She possessed a peasant's cunning and a ruthlessness that he could almost admire.

'Take me to them. Now,' W'soran grated.

With Melkhior leading the way, they left the cavern and moved upwards through the mountain. Even with slaves, it would have taken decades to make the mountain habitable. With the dead, however, the rudiments of civilisation had been constructed within a few years. Thousands of zombies and skeletons had worked day and night, bracing caverns and widening tunnels. The corridor from his workshop was braced by the uncomplaining shapes of massive skeletal conglomerations – things composed from the skeletons of many beasts and ghouls, their overlarge limbs bound in sturdy chains and leather straps and the surface of their mouldering bones inscribed with runes of abn-i-khat. They were a parody of the great *ushabti* of Nehekhara, and like those monstrous statues, there was a faint flicker of aware-ness in the eye-sockets of their wide, blended skulls.

More such creations – part guard dog and part decora-tion – lined the corridors and tunnels. A chattering skull, wreathed in sorcerous flames, cast light across a small bend in a tunnel, and the bones of a multitude of skaven had been used to craft a bridge across a gap. Everywhere there were guards, clad in the remnants of the armour and furs they had worn while alive.

'Who came?' W'soran asked as they walked. 'Who was it, the courtesan or that spindly nomad? Who did she send?'

'No, neither of them,' Melkhior hissed as he idly traced an old scar on his chest. While they had been in Mourkain, W'soran's followers and those of Neferata had clashed more than once in the shadows of the blighted city. Melkhior had nearly had his head taken by one of Neferata's witches – a nomad woman named Rasha. She had transformed into some form of desert cat and torn his apprentice open and hurled him from a rooftop. Melkhior, far from burning with a desire for vengeance, seemed to consider her murderous assault as a form of flirting. There was no accounting for taste with barbarians. W'soran himself had never been inclined to the company of women.

Melkhior shook himself. 'One is a Strigoi named Layla, the other an Arabyan named Khemalla.'

The names sparked no memories in W'soran's mind. He grunted irritably. 'Do you know them?'

'One was a scullery maid, the other a slave, or so I heard,' Melkhior said. 'Neferata prefers her pets already broken.'

W'soran didn't reply. Melkhior's biases were showing, and he felt no urgent need to correct his apprentice. If anything, the opposite was true – Neferata chose her followers for reasons other than devotion. Sometimes, he thought she had the right of it. W'soran had always chosen scholars, men like himself. Like minds made for easier work.

But when he'd arrived in Mourkain, Ushoran – damn his eyes – had thrust a bevy of unlettered savages upon him, and demanded he teach them his arts. It was the price of sanctuary and after everything that had occurred in the east, he was happy to pay it. Still, it had meant long years of training brutes like Melkhior in the subtler thought-processes required of a scholar – of them all, only Morath had shown a natural inclination in that regard. Zoar had been helpful in those early days, and the few others who'd accompanied him from Nagashizzar.

Of that group, only Zoar remained. As to whether he or Melkhior, or even Neferata was responsible for that, W'soran had no interest. He cared nothing for any particular acolyte. They were simply tools.

'What will you do, master? Vorag might be angry if you simply intrude uninvited...' Melkhior went on.

W'soran smirked. 'Only if he's cavorting with them,' he said. The smirk faded. 'No, Vorag needs me and he knows it. That slattern of his is the one behind this insult. Where is Zoar?'

'I left him to watch over our guests,' Melkhior said. 'Vorag is giving them a tour, and crowing of his conquests.' He hesitated. 'Do you think – could this be a trap? He abandoned her, after all. She is not forgiving of betrayal...'

W'soran chuckled bitterly. 'She is if there is an advantage for her in it. No, knowing her, she's already scheming to pull Ushoran's empire out from under him.'

They reached the main cavern – the courtyard to Vorag's citadel – a moment later W'soran realised that something was different. There was a smell on the stale air, a whiff of familiar magics. 'Morath,' Melkhior growled. 'I can smell his stink on the air.'

'No,' W'soran said. 'Not quite.' He looked around the cavern. It had changed much in the years after the skaven had been driven out. The mountain had been all but hollowed out by the burrowing ratkin, and thus easy to make over into something more fitting for the kind of warrior-king Vorag imagined himself to be. The unstable walls of the cavern had been stabilised by the addition of smooth stone slabs and beams of petrified wood which criss-crossed the vast belly of the cavern like the bracers of a mine shaft. Stone stairways and balconies had been constructed, overlooking the interior from on high. Vorag had wanted it to look as much like Ushoran's palace as possible, though he hadn't admitted as much openly. It amused W'soran to think of Vorag aping his former king even as he sought to filch his kingdom.

There were cosmetic differences, of course. The nooks and crannies of the cavern had been filled with skulls, and the pelts of skaven, trolls and other beasts of the mountains lined the walls, flayed and stretched as trophies to Vorag's might. In the years they'd fought and occupied the mountain, Timagal Vorag had made himself quite at home.

Vorag stood in the centre of the cavern, hands behind his back, and a wolf-skin cloak across his brawny shoulders. Stregga stood beside him, as well as Sanzak and a few other

Strigoi besides. With them stood Neferata's envoys, apparently listening to Vorag's blustering braggadocio with keen interest.

Both were dark-headed, though one was quite obviously of Strigos and the other an Arabyan – not a nomad, but one of the city dwellers. They were dressed in travel-stained leathers and furs, and both had heavy swords belted to their waists. The Arabyan wore a gold band around her head and the other had her hair bound in ratty coils. Zoar lagged behind the group, nervously rubbing his hands.

W'soran and Melkhior strode swiftly towards them, and it wasn't until they got closer that W'soran realised that there were dead men in the cavern, and not ones who had been raised by his magics. These were different. They were old things, steeped in death, and heavily armoured. Great bat-winged helms covered their skulls and coats of rusty mail hung from their mummified frames. Ancient cuirasses, embossed with new symbols, covered their torsos. Each carried a heavy shield and had a blade belted at their waist. The dead men examined the newcomers with glowing eyes and W'soran bristled. 'That witch,' he spat.

The dead men were wights. Though they resembled skeletons, the wights were as far beyond those pale remnants as vampires were beyond men. There were minds within those brown, root-encrusted skulls, albeit minds warped and shredded by dark magic. It took more skill than he had thought Neferata possessed to bring such creatures back from the grave.

'Morath's doing,' Melkhior snarled as his hand flew to the hilt of his sword. The wights reacted instantly. Bronze swords gone green with age sprang from rotted sheaths and the long-dead warriors stepped forward with deadly intent. W'soran raised his hands, ready to unleash a fatal spell.

'Stop,' Vorag bellowed, throwing up his hands, his face mottled with fury. 'If a spell leaves your withered lips, W'soran, I will rip out your scrawny throat.'

Reluctantly, W'soran lowered his hands. Melkhior had already released his sword and stepped back. Zoar hurried over to them, gnawing his lip. 'I wanted to warn you master, but–'

'Never mind,' W'soran snapped. Stregga grinned insouciantly at him, and the two new vampires giggled.

'Frightened, were you, old monster?' Stregga said.

'Simply surprised; Neferata was never what you'd call bright. I thought even the rudiments of the art of death were beyond her,' W'soran said, pulling his cloak and his dignity about him. It was a childish response, but it had the desired effect. The newcomers hissed like angry cats. Stregga, more used to W'soran's insults, merely frowned. W'soran looked at Vorag. 'I was not invited.'

'No, you weren't,' Vorag said. The Strigoi smiled slightly – a dangerous expression. Vorag only smiled when he was killing something, or preparing to kill something. 'I am capable of speaking without you at my elbow, sorcerer.' The gathered Strigoi sniggered and laughed. All except Sanzak, who remained silent, W'soran noted. 'Or have you at last come to tell me that my war-engines are ready to take the field?'

W'soran paused. Vorag had been growing increasingly impatient in regards to the war machines. He wanted to take to the field, now that he had a citadel and a growing army. Exactly what lands he intended to claim in these barren mountains, he'd never said. Their army was, as yet, too small to confront Ushoran's forces. Unless...

'What word, Lord Vorag?' W'soran asked, smoothly changing the subject. 'What news do our guests bring?'

'Neferata lives, old monster. And she has conquered,' one of the newcomers said. 'Khemalla and I have come to bring word – Lahmia lives again.'

'And what would you know of Lahmia, little creature?' W'soran asked. 'What would you know of its grandeur, of its glory? What would you know of anything pertaining to the Great Land?' He snorted. 'Or has Neferata been filling your heads with stories?'

'Watch your tone,' the Arabyan, Khemalla, said as her dark eyes flashed. 'Layla speaks the truth – Lahmia lives. And it stands against Mourkain, and the usurper, Ushoran.'

'Funny how he wasn't a usurper until he made Neferata bow,' Melkhior murmured.

Khemalla snarled, and her sword was in her hand in an eye-blink. Melkhior drew his blade in the nick of time. Steel rang on steel and Khemalla spun about Melkhior. Her blade lashed out, nearly drawing blood. But W'soran intervened, grabbing her wrist with a speed that shocked all of those present, and slung her to the ground.

'Insulted and attacked as well,' W'soran snarled. He glared at Vorag. 'Has my time here come to an end, Bloodytooth? Should I and my followers leave you to your dreams of empire and wandering doxies?'

Vorag swept back the edge of his cloak. 'And you think I would simply let you leave? No, I require your aid, necromancer. I need your magics. But perhaps you don't require all of your limbs, eh?' The Strigoi hunched forward, spreading talon-tipped fingers.

W'soran knew he wasn't bluffing. He also knew that he could likely dispatch the Strigoi with little difficulty. But dispatching the others at the same time might have been a tad too tricky. So, instead of responding, he merely met Vorag's gaze and held it just long enough. Then he looked away and stepped back, hands lowered.

Vorag glared at him for a moment longer, and then grunted, satisfied. 'Neferata sends word that Ushoran's attentions are on her now. Abhorash has been recalled to Mourkain,' he said.

W'soran shrugged and said, 'And?'

'And, it is an opportunity,' Stregga said. 'One we have been waiting for, the opportunity to put the true heir on Kadon's throne.' She gestured to Vorag, whose grin widened. 'In his veins runs the blood of Kadon and Strigu, the first *hetman* of Strigos, and in his hands, the empire will prosper, even as it rots on the vine with Ushoran.'

'And what of Gashnag or the other nobles who stand at Ushoran's side?' W'soran asked. 'They might have something to say about that, especially given that Strigu's blood runs in their veins as well.' He raised a hand to forestall a rebuttal. 'No, no, I'm in favour of overthrowing Ushoran, of course. I simply dislike these games of semantics your mistress insists on playing.'

'And here I thought scholars liked words,' Stregga said.

'We prefer truth,' W'soran said. 'Better the truth of the blade than the lie of the sheath. Ahtep of Mahrak said that, in his scroll, *Higher Truths*. I have a copy, if you wish to read it? No?' He looked at Vorag. 'What does she want, Vorag?'

'Lord Vorag,' Vorag rumbled.

'What does she want, *Lord* Vorag,' W'soran said.

'For us to invade Strigos's eastern territories,' Sanzak said, speaking up for the first time. The scar-faced Strigoi fiddled with his scalp lock, his ugly face grave. 'A task which we have neither the resources nor the time to accomplish properly, not if Ushoran intends to pitch Abhorash and the northern *Tekes* – the warrior lodges – against the Silver Pinnacle. Which he will do unless he's gone addle-brained,' he said. He looked at W'soran. 'Has he?'

'No, more's the pity,' W'soran said, sucking on a fang. 'Mad, yes, but stupid… no.'

'What about the engines you promised me?' Vorag asked. 'With those, we could devastate the eastern marches and even the vaunted Red Dragon himself will not be able to stand against us!'

W'soran fought a smirk as he caught the bitterness and scorn in Vorag's words. The enmity between Abhorash and

Vorag had begun even before he'd arrived in Mourkain, and it lasted to this very day. Vorag had been the pre-eminent champion of the nascent empire and Ushoran's sword arm, until the Champion of Lahmia had arrived, with his small band of savage killers. Ushoran was no fool. He'd put Abhorash in charge of as much of the army as he could get away with, and more since, and Abhorash had created a martial engine more deadly than anything that had marched across Nehekhara in Settra's time. The champion had a gift for war and for making men into warriors. He'd built Ushoran a juggernaut of an army and then used that juggernaut to pave an empire.

When it came to military matters, Abhorash was the next-best thing to a god. It was in every other endeavour that he failed miserably, and always had. W'soran still remembered the grim champion, dogging Lamashizzar in times long past, as hungry for the secrets of immortality as the rest of them, himself included. And when Neferata had usurped those secrets and made them into something infinitely more terrible, Abhorash had bared his throat as quickly as the rest of them.

Just why he'd done it, what he'd wanted out of it, W'soran still didn't know. For the fools like Ankhat or Ushoran, immortality was an end in and of itself. For Neferata it was simply her due. For himself, the power that came with immortality had been his goal. But for Abhorash, what?

Even as he thought of the champion, he said, 'The engines are not ready. Not yet.'

'You have had almost two years, sorcerer,' Vorag growled.

'I need more abn-i-khat,' W'soran said. 'Those war machines require inordinate amounts of the wyrdstone to function, and that means I need more than I have.'

'And where do you suggest we get that stone? Perhaps we should crawl down into the skaven burrows and borrow a bushel or two?' Stregga said.

'No.' W'soran smiled. 'We take Nagashizzar.'

━◄ CHAPTER FIVE ►━

The Sea of Claws
(Year -1166 Imperial Calendar)

The great bat shrieked in hunger as it swooped high over the choppy, frigid northern waters. That it was dead, and had, indeed, been dead for a number of years, and thus could not be hungry, made no difference to it. W'soran, astride its back in a saddle crafted from furs and tanned human skin, felt a distant kinship with the massive beast.

'Death is not the end,' he murmured. His words were lost in the rushing wind. Below him, a galley made furiously for the mouth of a river. W'soran smiled. 'Well, not for all of us,' he added. He bent low in his saddle and hauled sharply on the reins. The giant bat folded its wings and plummeted towards the galley with another shriek.

The craft was Nehekharan in origin, though it had been much patched and repaired since it had first set sail from the City of the Dawn. Saurian hide patches marked its hull and Cathayan sails billowed from an Ind-style mast. Its crew were men, despite the nature of its master. Then again, he had never been entirely comfortable with the dead.

In the months following Ushoran's capture, W'soran had sent out spies and searchers, hunting for word of the rest of the Lahmian Court. Word of Abhorash had been sparse, and Neferata seemed to have disappeared entirely. W'soran held out hope that she had died in the fall of Lahmia, but knew better than to do more than hope. Neferata had a habit of surviving the best laid plans of others.

Of all the former members of the inner circle, only Ankhat had been easy to locate. In the years since Alcadizzar's destruction of the City of Dawn, Ankhat had not remained hidden. Indeed, he had discarded subtlety entirely. In Cathay, he had claimed to be an immortal sorcerer-prince, and he had led the Dragon-Emperor's armies in hurling back an invasion from the north that had attempted to breach the Great Bastion.

Soon after, his nocturnal feedings had apparently been uncovered by a secretive society of courtesans and Ankhat had been exposed. A fighting retreat had left the Port of Dogs in flames and Ankhat's forces reduced to a few vessels and some hundred men. He had prowled the oceans, raiding and hiring out his services to various coastal lords and masters, including the petty chieftains of the icy north. Freed of the responsibilities of royalty, Ankhat had apparently taken to the life of a freebooter. Being a sea-borne thief suited him, W'soran thought.

The crew reacted to the appearance of the bat much as W'soran had expected. Arrows cut through the air, striking the dead beast. W'soran laughed. The bat landed on the prow with a heavy, wood-splintering thump, its wings folding up and its claws crushing the rail. W'soran stood in his saddle and gestured, sweeping the life from the closest men with a single spell. 'Come out, come out wherever you are, Ankhat,' he called out. 'I have a proposition for you, oh mighty lord of Lahmia.'

The door to the cabin's quarters was flung open and a lean shape clad in light armour and a dark cloak stepped out. Ankhat had not changed much since the fall of Lahmia, W'soran noted. He still had the same arrogant bearing and supercilious expression on his face that W'soran remembered. His hair had gone white, but he was still darkly handsome and of noble position.

'W'soran,' he said, his hand fondling the pommel of the heavy eastern blade that hung at his side. 'If there was one face I had hoped to go without seeing for the rest of eternity, yours would be it.'

'I'm flattered,' W'soran said, leaning over the pommel of his saddle. He motioned to the galley. 'You have been on quite a trip, it seems. I have tracked you from the Port of Dogs to the Bay of Pirates. It's almost as if you're running from something, Ankhat. Whatever could that be, hmmm?'

'You know damn well what I'm fleeing,' Ankhat snapped. He pointed at W'soran. 'After all, you clutch at its skirts and bony ankles like a trained ape.'

Stung, W'soran exposed his fangs. 'Watch your tongue, Ankhat, or I'll tear it from your head.'

'Come and try it,' Ankhat spat. Then, without warning, he

shouted an incantation and night-black fire roared from his out-
thrust hand. It crashed across the mast and caught the giant bat
full in the face and chest. The creature hopped back with a squeal
as flames crisped its dry, dead hair. W'soran cursed and slashed
out a hand, summoning an icy wind to put out the flames.

Ankhat grinned at him and spread his arms. 'I always wondered
where you'd gotten to, in the end. You left behind a library of
scrolls and tomes, you know. Then, maybe you thought Alcadizzar
had burnt them, eh?' Ankhat folded his arms. 'So many interesting scrolls... so much knowledge, for a man smart enough to see
it.'

'You never struck me as smart,' W'soran said. 'So, you've pil-
laged my old library and think yourself now a match for me? Is
that it, Ankhat?'

'Enough of a match to give you a fight,' Ankhat sneered. 'But
I'd rather not, if I don't have to. I can only think of one reason
for you to hunt me down, W'soran, and the answer is no. I assure
you that the others will answer in similar fashion, if you ever find
them.'

Something about his tone caught W'soran's attention. His eyes
narrowed. 'You know where they are, don't you?'

'Perhaps, but why should I tell you?' Ankhat asked. He smiled
smugly.

'If you don't, I'll burn this galley to the waterline and take you
back to Nagashizzar in chains, even as I did Ushoran,' W'soran
said.

The smile slipped from Ankhat's face. 'I'll fight you,' he said.

'Why would you, when you could fight for the Undying King?

Why whore your powers out for the petty tribal kings of these bar-baric shores when you could serve a true power?'

'If you have to ask why, you'll never understand, W'soran,' Ankhat said, exposing his fangs. *'A trade, then. I'll tell you what I know and you leave me be.'*

W'soran frowned and sat back in his saddle. The bat stirred restively and he stroked its skull. In truth, Ankhat was hardly a catch – W'soran had always considered him a subpar general and subpar sorcerer. But, if he knew where the others were…

He sniffed. 'Fine, then. If you wish to remain in these inhospi-table climes, who am I to gainsay you? Where are they – Neferata and Abhorash? Tell me where the queen and her champion might be found…'

Crookback Mountain
(Year -322 Imperial Calendar)

When W'soran stepped out of the tunnel and onto the ledge of the crag, Sanzak was waiting for him, even as he'd prom-ised. The Green Witch, the smaller of the two moons, hung full and ugly in the sky alongside its larger sister, and pale streaks cut across the darkness in the distance.

'Wyrdstone,' W'soran said, causing Sanzak to turn from his study of the heavens. 'Those streaks are the tears of the Green Witch, which take the form of the abn-i-khat when they strike the earth.'

'Interesting, but not why you asked to see me, I trust,' the

Strigoi said. W'soran examined his scarred features in the eerie light of the moons. Sanzak looked like a lump of raw meat with fangs, but his eyes sparked with a keen intelligence. Of all the Strigoi W'soran had met, he was the closest to Ushoran in terms of guile, though that cunning was tempered by an unfortunate propensity to unquestioning loyalty.

'Knowledge is its own reward,' W'soran said.

Sanzak snorted. 'Then why are you so determined to garner other glories?'

'Vorag's plan is madness,' W'soran said bluntly, ignoring the question. 'It is madness and you know it.'

Sanzak crossed his heavily muscled arms and tilted his head. 'And if it is? And I do? I will not be a party to betrayal, W'soran. Vorag is my friend and he is my lord. I will give my life for his before I let him come to harm.'

'Fine sentiments, but would you risk losing everything we have built here, on a whim of Neferata's?' W'soran asked, pulling his robes more tightly about himself. Overhead, vast shapes slid through the skies, and faint shrieks drifted down. The great bats of the deep caverns were out and on the hunt.

In the months since the arrival of Neferata's envoys, Vorag's army had begun to mobilise for war. Raiding parties scoured the mountains for supplies and new recruits both. Great herds of orc prisoners were being driven into the newly constructed pens in the belly of the mountain, and those who resisted and did not survive that resistance were added to the ranks of zombies that Vorag intended to lead into the eastern marches of Strigos.

Vorag himself, accompanied by Stregga, had begun leading raids on those far-flung holdings of the Strigoi Empire that abutted the territories he himself had claimed. Ushoran's vassals were put to the stake and torch, unless they swore fealty to Vorag, or somehow managed to escape north. Word was also beginning to filter to the frontier agals and ajals, and as little love as they had for Ushoran, many were flocking to Vorag's banner with their retainers. Sanzak knew all of this as well, and he had his own doubts, W'soran knew. Sanzak's loyalty was a weapon that he could hone to a killing point, if he were careful.

Now, Sanzak peered at W'soran and rubbed his chin. 'What do you mean?'

'She's using him, using all of us, and you know it. Neferata won't put Vorag on the throne any more than she'd put me or you. No, that one wants to rule herself, and Vorag is playing right into her hands. She's done it before, Sanzak. She builds heroes and then casts them into the dust when they've served their purpose.'

'She doesn't strike me as a woman interested in ruling. Now, telling others how to rule, perhaps...' Sanzak smiled. The expression made his features even more hideous. 'I fought at her side, W'soran, against the greenskins. I know full well what she's capable of. She'll put the Bloodytooth on the throne and feed him speeches, true enough, but he'll be king nonetheless.'

'You have no idea, Strigoi,' W'soran said. 'You fought beside her? You think that tells you anything about the way her crooked mind works? Neferata pulls you into an embrace only so that there's less distance across which to drive a dagger. Vorag is nothing to her. We are nothing to her, save pawns to be expended in some obtuse game of power.'

'Then tell Vorag,' Sanzak said.

'I have,' W'soran said. He chuckled. 'As have you, if what Zoar says is true.'

Sanzak grimaced and said, 'Zoar?'

'Oh, spare me – did you think he would betray my secrets so readily unless I had given him permission to?' It was W'soran's turn to snort. 'How many of you grubbing barbarians tried to co-opt my followers in Mourkain, to learn their secrets without having to bother with joining my circle, eh? Ten maybe, or twenty, or a hundred… my only question is, was it you who decided you needed to learn the art of the winds of death, or Vorag?'

Sanzak turned away, and that gave W'soran his answer. 'Ah, and isn't that interesting?' he said silkily. 'You're using your own initiative, Sanzak. That's a bad habit, in times like these and in a place like this.'

'Vorag doesn't trust sorcery,' Sanzak said.

'Yet he is happy to use it, at least at a remove,' W'soran said. He looked out over the mountains. 'He trusts you?'

'He did,' Sanzak said.

'Before Stregga, eh?' W'soran said, clasping his hands together. 'You served beside him for how long? A century or so, before Neferata and her creatures arrived, as I recall. A century of brotherhood, tossed aside for a blonde strumpet.

So much for loyalty,' he said and made a dismissive gesture. 'Pah. Vorag is a warrior, but nothing more. He only sees what is in front of him and not what lurks off the path.' He looked at Sanzak. 'She will destroy him. She will use him as a weapon against Ushoran and break him on Mourkain's battlements. And you will be broken with him.'

Sanzak said nothing. The Strigoi stood silently, waiting. W'soran held up a finger and continued, 'Unless, we do something about it now.'

'Like what?'

'We cut the cord of influence,' W'soran said. He made a chopping gesture. 'Mourkain will be a battleground for centuries yet. Neferata is hoping to ensure that Vorag and Ushoran are the two armies in the field. Instead, we force her to fight her own battles for once.'

'Vorag hungers for war,' Sanzak said doubtfully.

'And war he will have, but not with Mourkain. At least not directly,' W'soran said. He swept out a hand, indicating the mountains. 'A great empire sits silent and waiting to the south, over these mountains. And its doorway, the citadel of Nagashizzar, sits open and empty. If Vorag were to sweep south and take it, all of Araby would be ripe for the plucking and the dead cities of the Great Land as well.'

'Dead cities are right. Neferata spoke of what crouches in those distant ruins, sorcerer,' Sanzak said. 'The way is hardly open and you know it. We will have to fight for every scrap of rock and sand.'

'Yes, yes, yes, but it will be a war that Vorag can easily win, with my help. With *your* help, Sanzak,' W'soran said testily. 'The dead of Nehekhara are old and brittle and few. We will have all of the dead of Nagashizzar and these mountains at our back. More, we have ourselves. The Strigoi are preeminent warriors. Your people are born conquerors, so, why not go forth and conquer?' He laughed. 'Vorag will have battle aplenty, for years to come and his – your – rewards will be greater than any mouldering mountain city or stagnant hardscrabble empire.'

'Stregga will not hear of it,' Sanzak said, after a considering silence. 'She will try and convince him to move towards Mourkain himself, with all of his forces. And you are forgetting that that is what he wants to do as well. Empires be damned, Vorag wants Ushoran's head on a pike, aye, and Abhorash's as well – more than he wants a crown or a throne.'

'And he will have them,' W'soran said. 'But those things will be easier to take with the resources of an empire of our own at our back than the pitiful dregs we possess now.'

'That still leaves Neferata's women...' Sanzak began.

'Not for long,' W'soran said.

Sanzak lifted a hand. 'Say no more. I do not wish to know.'

'Squeamish, are you, Sanzak? How unexpected,' W'soran cackled. 'Never mind then. My plan does not require your assistance or even your acknowledgement. I only ask that you lend your voice to mine, in the moment to come.'

Sanzak hesitated. 'And Vorag will not be harmed?'

'I swear by the hackles of Usirian that Vorag will not be

harmed,' W'soran said. 'In fact, he will gain everything he wishes, in the end.'

Sanzak nodded sharply, after a moment. Then, without another word, he left the crag, stalking back into the tunnel. W'soran didn't watch him go. Instead, he sniffed the air and said, 'You heard all of that, I trust?'

'How long have you actually known Zoar was teaching that fool?' Melkhior hissed, detaching himself from the upper reaches of the crag. He scrambled down to join W'soran, moving like a spider. In their time in Mourkain, Melkhior had learned how to hide his scent and sound from their kind – all save W'soran, who knew how to look for what was not there as well as what was.

'Long enough,' W'soran said.

'And yet you didn't discipline him?' Melkhior demanded.

'Why would I do that? I did not forbid you from taking your own apprentices, Melkhior,' W'soran said, relishing the look of fury that passed across Melkhior's face. 'Besides, it has proven useful, has it not? Did you do as I commanded?'

'Yes master,' Melkhior said. 'I have pulled the sentries from the deep warrens. The way is unguarded. Do you truly think the skaven will attack?'

'They've been skittering through those tunnels for months now, sniffing for the stores of abn-i-khat they left. Even a single shard would be enough to impel them to attack. With the guards gone, they'll jump at the opportunity for mischief. And Vorag won't be able to resist such a direct assault on his "kingdom",' W'soran said. 'And when he moves to counter them, we will have an opportunity of our own to seize.'

'The deep warrens, you mean,' Melkhior said. He smiled nastily. 'I know you, master. And I know that this isn't just about getting rid of those interfering creatures of Neferata's, is it?'

W'soran eyed Melkhior for a long moment before he chuckled. 'You've always been something of a disappointment to me, Melkhior. Up until this moment, at any rate... yes, there are obvious goals and subtle ones. I've learned quite a bit from Iskar. The mad little rat has finally begun talking, and what stories he weaves. I thought the skaven were a localised phenomenon, but according to him, they lurk everywhere, under every mountain and molehill. Most importantly, there is more to this mountain than what we have found. A whole secondary fortress beneath the fortress we took. With armouries, breeding pens and workshops of filthy creation, all for the taking, if we are quick enough and cunning enough to do it.' He rubbed his hands together in glee. 'There is more to this citadel than those dullards the Strigoi know, and it will all be mine.'

'And how do you intend to escape Neferata's vengeance, in the interim?' Melkhior asked.

W'soran glanced at him. 'With a citadel and an army, I will have little need of "escape", Melkhior,' he said. He leaned over the crag, his hands clasped behind his back. 'In truth, the story I have spun for Sanzak is just that – a story. A deception, Melkhior, for Neferata is, at best, merely an obstacle. She is not a threat to us, not in the same way that Ushoran is. Oh yes, she is scheming even now to forge us – forge Vorag, I should say – into a blade to drive into Ushoran's heart. This is because, despite all that I taught her in lost Lahmia, she lacks the ability to grasp what is truly at stake here, and what sort of war is being waged.'

He tapped his head. 'She thinks like a queen still, and thinks that this is a war of kings and queens and thrones. Like Vorag, her strategies revolve around passes and supply lines, territory… material things. Oh, but Ushoran knows now, even as I know, that this is not a war of men, but of magicians. Men, and their valour and their greed, are incidental. The throne is incidental. Empires are but the dust beneath our feet. Neferata does not see that. She is not our enemy, Melkhior. She is but a tool, like Vorag and Abhorash and all of the others – pieces in the game Ushoran and I are playing.'

'I'd wager she thinks the same of you,' Melkhior said.

W'soran smiled. 'I'm certain she does. She's wrong; but then, given her history, that's not surprising.' He chuckled. 'It serves my purposes to build her as an enemy in Sanzak's eyes. And, should he survive, in Vorag's. It keeps them from seeing the true game, and gives them an enemy equal to their understanding. And, well, if I did not strike at her, she would become suspicious. And we can't have that. So, I will take her pieces, and counter her puling attempt to bully her way into mine and Ushoran's game, and keep her busy striking at shadows, even as I did in Mourkain. And, when she finds Vorag's forces nowhere to be seen, she'll realise that she's overextended her hand and she'll retreat.

'And Ushoran... Ushoran will pursue and pull her pathetic little mountain down around her ears. If we're lucky, she'll come running to us for sanctuary, grovelling on her belly as she always should have done, seeking the favour of her betters.' He snapped his fangs for emphasis. 'Stupid preening cow, always so assured of her own righteousness, of her own intelligence. It was she who ruined it, you know... all of it. She mooned after that lout Alcadizzar instead of ringing the cities of the Great Land in fire and steel and squeezing them until they wept blood. It was she who ruined Lamashizzar's plans to tease the secrets of immortality out of that fool, Arkhan.

'And if she had allowed me to make an offer of alliance to Nagash early on, Lahmia might yet stand – the City of the Dawn, reborn as the City of Eternal Night, where an ageless aristocracy ruled the dead sands forevermore!'

'And where were you while she was doing all of this, master?' Melkhior asked, after a moment of silence.

W'soran didn't reply. Where indeed? He had been in a jar, with a splinter in his heart and only the spiders for company. He stared out over the mountains. To the north and east, he could see the flickering blacker-than-black aura that crossed the dark sky like a ribbon. He felt a distinct tug on his mind, like hooks settling gently into the meat of it, and hissed in irritation. 'Fool,' he said softly, then, almost sadly, 'you foolish, foolish man.'

He had never had friends, either as a child or as a man grown, for such petty social concerns had always been beneath him. But if he had indulged, Ushoran would have been one. W'soran looked at his withered hands. It had been Ushoran who had, all those many long years ago, helped him escape Mahrak. It had been Ushoran who had brought him into the conspiracy and then, after Neferata's murderous attack, back out of the darkness.

Ushoran had feared him, and had hated him, had kept him around only because he was useful, but nonetheless... there it was. For no matter how W'soran twisted and schemed, only Ushoran had never lost patience, or decided to do away with him. Only Ushoran had seen his potential, had seen him for the power he truly was. Even Nagash had denigrated and underestimated him.

Only Ushoran had ever cared enough to truly fear W'soran for his capabilities, rather than his looks or his proclivities. That was why he was the only one worth playing against. Fear bred respect, after all. Neferata was nothing, and Abhorash even less than that. They were primitives, besotted by blood and unheeding of the true currents of power. But when Ushoran's fear had been driven from him by the power of the twisted iron crown that now ensnared him, W'soran had run. He'd done as he'd always done, scuttled for the shadows, his tail between his legs. He'd left Mourkain and Ushoran.

But then flight had ever been his first choice, even as a boy in Mahrak. In flight, there was no risk, only gain. To fight was to risk pain, or death. But to flee was to live, to borrow a bit more time from inevitability. That was why he had sought immortality. He knew well enough now how fragile it was, but at the time it had seemed the ultimate escape. But in fleeing Mourkain, he had sacrificed much.

He closed his fingers, letting the tips of his talons pierce his flesh. When he'd sent Neferata to Nagashizzar, he'd half-hoped she would fail. That she would fail and die; that if the skaven failed to kill her the dead of Nehekhara would have succeeded. But she had won through, and brought back those resources he'd requested. Another shadow-chase he'd sent her on that she'd preened at seeing through, as if she had actually accomplished something.

He hadn't truly needed the book. He could have drawn Alcadizzar's spirit from the stones of Mourkain at any time, and bound it once more to its tattered flesh for Ushoran to maul to his heart's content. But he'd hoped to distract Ushoran from his growing obsession. Even now, he couldn't say whether that attempt had been for his own ends, or out of some misguided attempt to protect the only creature he had even the smallest shred of affinity for.

But Ushoran's demands had grown ever more strident. He had sat atop that damnable crown longer than any, had felt it caress his mind every night, been tormented and seduced by it, until finally it had snapped him up and pulled him under. It could have been any one of them, in the end. Ushoran had simply gotten there first. He had always been quick to seize an opportunity.

Even now, even here, the thought of that moment, of that horrified realisation that had risen from within Ushoran's eyes, sweeping aside madness, pricked him. Anger bubbled in him, for himself, and perhaps for all of them. The struggles of ants, eclipsed by the whims of gods; but ants could bite and kill.

As if in response to his thoughts, the distant black aura seemed to brighten and pulse. W'soran looked at it and snarled. He could feel it creeping up on him, drawing close about him, beckoning him on. Was Ushoran fighting for control even now, or had he already surrendered? Was his seeming opening to attack true weakness or a feint, designed to draw them all in once more? Was it all a ploy to draw in W'soran, for who better to be the bearer of the Crown of Nagash than his former disciple? Not Ushoran, or Abhorash or Neferata, but W'soran. Whose game was being played? Though there was no sentience in that crooked diadem, there was a malign *drive*. A compulsion, woven into the metal in its forging, that fools like Neferata confused for intelligence.

He closed his eyes and shuddered as the black aura seemed to blaze beneath the moons. He could sense the daemonic challenge that rode the charnel winds from Mourkain. Ushoran, unlike Neferata, would be a worthy opponent. Who else but Ushoran suspected the full power that lurked in Nagash's crown? Who but Ushoran was left to vie with for such a secret? Arkhan cowered somewhere to the south, and the rest of Nagash's disciples had either gone to their final deaths or fled the lands of men entirely. Only the two of them were left. Would he, W'soran, be able to rise to the occasion?

OR WILL YOU RUN AS YOU HAVE ALWAYS RUN, W'SORAN OF MAHRAK?

The voice – Ushoran's voice – rumbled in his head like ice sliding from a crag to crash against slopes far below. His hands flew to his skull and he gasped. In his mind's eye, he could see the throne room of distant Mourkain as if through a pool of water. He saw the great and the mighty of that realm, clad in barbarous splendour, as they roared out Ushoran's name.

Ushoran strode through their ranks, a demigod clad in gilded armour and bearing a handsome face. On his head, he wore the iron crown, and shadows seemed to sweep in his wake like the wings of some mighty bird of prey. But there was another face beneath his, another figure occupying his space, just out of sync with him, but yet connected – a massive shape, twisted and dark and mighty in that darkness, but unseen by any save he, W'soran knew. Ghostly brass claws held tight to Ushoran's broad shoulders, guiding him towards his throne as musicians played a triumphal march and his people cheered.

W'soran could see the tightness of Ushoran's muscles, the resistance in every movement. The ghostly claws tightened, slicing into him, and Ushoran's lips peeled back from his fangs in a grimace that his court likely took for a smile. The crown pulsed and burned to W'soran's eyes, like a gangrenous wound wrought in iron. Strands of hateful magic stretched from it and spread down into Ushoran, digging into his vitals like a torturer's hooks.

Ushoran took his throne, and Abhorash moved out from the crowd to stand at the foot of the dais that supported his throne. From Abhorash's face, W'soran knew that he knew and that he saw what W'soran saw. And yet he stayed. What madness compelled him, W'soran wondered? Was he too under the power of the crown, even as Neferata had been, or was it something else?

Before he had more than a moment to contemplate those questions, he saw Ushoran, slumped on his throne, turn slightly, as if looking in his direction. Then, with sickening certainty, W'soran knew that he was. Pain rippled through him, a dull, pounding ricochet of agony, searing him. Again, he felt Khalida's arrow at the Gates of the Dawn, and the wet tearing of Neferata's improvised stake as it punched through his sternum. His claws dug into his skull as he quivered in agony.

Looming above Ushoran, skull wreathed in balefire, something looked at him and then Ushoran asked, *WHAT ARE YOU? WHAT IS W'SORAN OF LAHMIA?* Ushoran's eyes blazed as the words thundered in W'soran's head, spiralling into agonising incandescence. And Ushoran twitched upon his throne, as if trying to pry himself free of what held him. His eyes met W'soran's and there was a terrible plea in them. The Lord of Masks was caught in a trap that not even his cunning could set him free of.

Then, all at once, the vision was done, and there was nothing in his head save the sound of the night wind howling through the crags and the dull warble of Melkhior's voice as he reached out a claw. 'Master, are you unwell?'

W'soran spun about, and he slapped Melkhior off his feet, nearly knocking him from the ledge. One hand clutching his aching head, W'soran snarled, 'Never touch me!'

Then, without a backwards glance, he left the winds and his cringing apprentice behind as he strode back into the mountain, shaking and shivering with rage and fear.

There was murder to be planned and a war to be won. And perhaps, just perhaps, an old – what? – friend, that was as good a word as any, to be saved – saved from himself, from the ghosts of the past, from his unearned throne.

But most importantly of all, there was an empire to be had. 'What is W'soran of Lahmia, old friend?' W'soran asked himself as he swept his cloak about himself. 'Why, he is your master. He is the Master of Death, and he will break you on the altar of your own hubris!'

—◄ CHAPTER SIX ►—

The City of Bel Aliad
(Year -1152 Imperial Calendar)

'Nightfall crept into our souls and changed us all,' Abhorash said softly, sitting slumped in his chair, clad in armour that was unadorned but well-kept. He was dressed as a kontoi, one of Bel Aliad's noble horsemen. The night-wind coiled softly through the open windows of his chambers. He had been awarded a small palace, near the centre of the City of Spices, for his efforts in helping the Arabyans make it their own.

He raised his hawk-like features and his lip twitched, revealing a length of fang. 'Some more than others,' he added. His hand found the pommel of the long blade that leaned against his chair, still sheathed, but no less intimidating for all that. He smiled coldly and said, 'and some of us not at all, eh, W'soran? Except for that eye, I mean.'

W'soran stiffened and made to retort, even as his hand flashed *to his unseeing eye. The arrow that had pierced it at the Battle of the Gates of the Dawn was long gone but the damage was done. His eye had yet to properly heal, instead remaining a milky, sightless orb. Ushoran held up a hand. 'Be quiet, old monster. If you insult him, we will achieve nothing,' he hissed.*

'You will achieve nothing regardless, Ushoran.' Abhorash pushed himself to his feet, his armour creaking. 'I have left mercy long behind me, and am in no mood to take part in your damned fate, whatever it might be. Go back to your fell master and leave me be.'

'But surely it won't hurt to hear us out, eh? Otherwise you'd have set those ravening devils of yours on us,' Ushoran said, indicating the silent, unmoving shapes of Abhorash's Hand – the four men who'd stood by him since Lahmia's fall. W'soran knew them by name, if not by appearance. Walak of the palace guard and his cousin Lutr, of the harbour guard, were both Harkoni hillmen rather than true Lahmians, and had been given position in the military by Abhorash in better times. Mangari of the Southlands, a savage-turned-soldier, and Varis of Rasetra, a cunning duellist and former mercenary. Each was almost as formidable as their master and their eyes glowed red through the chainmail masks they wore beneath their ornate, high-peaked Arabyan helms.

W'soran seethed at the touch of those gazes. He longed to burn the impertinence from them. But Ushoran had convinced him to approach Abhorash peacefully, in contrast to his aggressive pursuit of Ankhat and, later, Neferata. In the months since his capture, the Lord of Masks had swiftly – indeed, more swiftly than W'soran had anticipated – regained his faculties. Even as W'soran had hunted for Ankhat, Ushoran had begun his hunt for the others, infiltrating the cities of the coasts of Araby and Nehekhara, his guise switching and changing month to month as he moved once more among mankind.

Nagash had already enacted the initial stages of his great plan. Soon, there would be no time to search for the wayward members of the Lahmian Court and bring them to heel at Nagash's behest, and once again W'soran would be the fool. He imagined Arkhan's look of arrogant triumph – no mean feat, given the liche's lack of a face – and ground his fangs in annoyance.

He had already lost Neferata to a moment of foolish indiscretion. He had thought to overawe her with his power, and had attacked her where she laired in the desert, surrounded by an army of ragged tribesmen. He traced the barely-healed scars that covered his throat. Neferata had resisted more strongly than he'd anticipated, and her handmaidens were as deadly as he remembered. They'd almost killed him. Only Ushoran's intervention had allowed them to escape.

Now, she was in the wind, and Ushoran had convinced him to cease hunting her and to instead set a trap. W'soran grunted and the moment of reverie passed. Ushoran and Abhorash were still speaking. 'And you are sure she is coming here?' Abhorash said. He crossed his arms over his chest and glared at them.

'There is nowhere else,' Ushoran said. 'She is not a creature of the deserts and the discomforts of the wilds. She wants a city to rule, with civilised folk, not barbarians. Bel Aliad is the closest, and the tribes will be inclined to attack anyway given their history. The question is, what are you going to do about it?'

'Why should I do anything?' Abhorash said.

'*Because otherwise she will take this city, and when she has done that, Nagash will take it from her, as he intends to take Nehekhara,*' Ushoran said bluntly. He made a fist for emphasis. '*This city – these people – they will die for her ambition, even as Lahmia did.*'

'*Again, what is that to me?*' Abhorash said, but more softly this time. W'soran felt a flash of disdain. Ushoran knew Abhorash's weaknesses well enough, it seemed. Abhorash had always been too concerned over seeming to care as to the fate of his inferiors. Even as he had supped on them, he had taken no more than was necessary, and had treated it as one might a distasteful duty. He curried favour from insects and played hero to apes, greedily supping on their adulation even as the rest of them did so with blood.

'*Perhaps nothing or perhaps everything… you've served the masters of this city for months, Abhorash, training their household cavalry in the ways of war. You have seen off desert raiders and brigands aplenty. The people hail you as a hero. Will their hero vanish, as the long, final night descends? Will you leave them as you left us?*' Ushoran asked.

'*Quiet,*' Abhorash growled.

'*It's true and you know it, champion,*' W'soran interjected, spitting the word. '*You abandoned the city to Neferata and she bled it dry and served its husk up to Alcadizzar. Will you do the same again?*'

Abhorash's snarl was terrible to hear. There was a depthless fury there, and W'soran stumbled back. He raised his hands, ready to defend himself, when Ushoran stepped between them. He faced Abhorash unflinching.

'Nagash is coming, Abhorash, and he will be unstoppable. The things we have seen…' Ushoran shook his head. 'But you can spare this city his wrath, just as you can spare it Neferata's.'

Abhorash narrowed his eyes. After a long moment, he said, 'What would I need to do?'

Ushoran glanced at W'soran, and then turned back. 'What you should have done the moment you first learned what Neferata had become, champion,' he said.

'I will not kill her,' Abhorash growled.

Ushoran raised a placatory hand. 'No. She is a queen, after all. And one does not simply kill a queen.' He smiled grimly. 'No, you will capture her, champion. You will capture Neferata for us…'

Crookback Mountain
(Year -321 Imperial Calendar)

'Why did you run here, W'soran?' Stregga asked, sliding a hank of skaven fur across the wet surface of her sword to clean it. She sat on a dead rat ogre, her limbs clad in battered leather and bronze armour, her hair hidden beneath a conical Strigoi helm. She peered down the length of the blade, one fang exposed as if in consternation. 'Surely there were safer places?'

'Safer than at your lord's side, you mean,' W'soran said, wrenching his scimitar from the body of a skaven. 'And yes, quite likely,' he added. Dozens of dead skaven littered the corridor. 'I could have returned to Cathay, perhaps, or gone into the west. Perhaps I have become a patriot, in my dotage, eh?' He looked at her slyly. 'Why has your mistress remained? Why does she not flee far from these climes? Why tempt fate?'

'Neferata does not flee,' Stregga said stiffly.

'Neferata always flees. She has always run from that which she does not wish to confront,' W'soran said. 'I have no doubt that when Ushoran trounces her rabble in the field, she will flee yet again.' He looked at her. 'Will you go with her then, I wonder? Or will you remain here, with your new master?'

'Vorag is not my master,' Stregga said, rising smoothly to her feet. 'He is my lover and my king, but I have but one mistress, and he is not it.'

'You didn't answer my question.'

'It wasn't a question worth answering,' Stregga said, turning away from him. 'Besides, you didn't answer mine, either.'

W'soran grinned and gazed about the corridor. Several ranks of skeletal spearmen waited patiently for orders, the points of their spears dark with skaven blood. There were a number of Strigoi with them, including several newcomers – frontier ajals unhappy with Ushoran's reign, mostly, though there were a few who were genuine idealists, looking to create a vampiric utopia free of so-called 'outsiders'. Vorag had sent them all down into the tunnels as a test of loyalty when the skaven had come to call. Most were returning relatively unscathed, though there were a few missing faces. The skaven had refined their methods for dispatching lone vampires – lassos, hooks and flames, if the remains were anything to judge by.

As he'd predicted, the skaven had attacked within a month of the sentries being pulled from the depths. The ratkin had boiled out of the darkness like the waters of a flood, sweeping through the lower reaches of the mountain with a speed that belied their habitual cowardice. They'd made for his laboratories straight away, and he'd defended them with a ready savagery that had set the skaven to flight amidst a cloud of fear-musk. But other sections of the mountain had not been so well defended. The lower corridors had fallen quickly, and were soon filled with squirming hairy bodies.

Even now, the great central cavern, which stretched up into the uppermost reaches of the mountain, was the scene of massed combat. Rank upon rank of skaven hurled themselves against the dead with a frenzy that bespoke chemical or perhaps sorcerous inducement. The echoes of that struggle carried dully through the rock around them. Battle had been joined in full several days earlier, and the pace of it had neither slowed nor ceased since. The skaven were determined to recapture their citadel at any cost, and were apparently willing to sacrifice as many of their kind as it took to do so.

'We should return to the main cavern, Stregga,' Khemalla said, loudly. Like her sister-in-darkness, she was clad in armour, and carried one of the heavy, cleaver-like blades that the Strigoi favoured. 'We've stymied this flanking effort, but Vorag could still be overwhelmed.'

'I doubt we've stymied anything,' W'soran said, speaking

over the assenting grunts of the Strigoi. 'There'll be more of the ratkin coming. These were only meant to establish a strongpoint.'

It hadn't taken much in the way of cunning to ensure that the Lahmians – as they insisted on referring to themselves, much to W'soran's annoyance – had stuck to him. He had no doubt that they were planning to play witness to his end, even as he plotted to do the same. The cramped, dark tunnels were the perfect murder-ground. In the confusion of battle, a ready blade could slide into an unaware back with little difficulty.

He'd left Melkhior and Zoar with Vorag, to help him hold the skaven in the central chamber. His remaining apprentices guarded his laboratories and the repurposed skaven workshop, slaughtering any skaven foolish enough to attack and then animating them and sending them back into the tunnels to kill their living companions. He himself had volunteered to lead the flanking effort, knowing that the Lahmians would insist on accompanying him.

'What do you know of war, leech?' one of the Strigoi growled. He was a burly creature named Faethor and he belonged to the Lahmian called Layla. Even amidst the current conflict, Faethor had been accosting any Strigoi who stood against declaring open war on Ushoran and marching into the eastern reaches and challenging them to duels. Many fangs hung from a rawhide thong about his neck, attesting to his success in that regard.

'Oh, is it my turn then, Faethor?' W'soran said. 'Is it time for you to deprive Vorag of yet another strong arm for your pale lady?'

'Careful with those barbed words, old monster,' Layla said, as she stepped from behind Faethor. 'The Strigoi are a warrior-people, and they may take your insults and accusations more seriously than you intend.'

'My accusations were serious enough,' W'soran said. 'Though I doubt even Faethor is foolish enough to challenge a withered old thing like myself amidst a battle...' He grinned at the Strigoi. Faethor purpled, the skaven blood he'd glutted on flushing through his pale skin.

Before he could respond, however, the sound of pattering feet and squealing filled the air. Part of the corridor wall crumbled suddenly, unleashing a flood of rag-wrapped skaven tunnellers, wielding short, heavy blades and long knives. The skaven crashed into the skeletons, shattering them before they could react. Faethor and Layla spun about, striking out at the ratkin. One, clad in a strange mask complete with heavy goggles and bulbous tubes, bounced beneath a sword-blow from a Strigoi and flung a heavy globe of some viscous liquid towards W'soran.

W'soran reacted swiftly. He lashed out with his sword, striking the globe in mid-air. A foul-smelling gas billowed from its shattered remnants and W'soran hissed, tasting abn-i-khat. The masked skaven hurled two more globes before Khemalla reached him and brought her sword down on his skull, splitting it from crown to neck. More gas exploded out, rapidly filling the corridor. The surviving skaven had retreated as quickly as they had come, slithering back through the hole they had made.

'What is this foulness?' Stregga snarled, swiping her sword through the gas.

'Poisonous gas,' W'soran said. 'If we breathed, we'd be dead. I don't think they've quite figured out what we are just yet.'

'Small favours,' Khemalla grunted. Then, she screamed as a spear-point burst through her shoulder and sent her stumbling forward. W'soran and the others turned as more skaven burst through the gas clogging the corridor. The tunnel-attack had been a diversion, meant to allow the newcomers to get close. All of the ratkin had masks similar to that worn by the slain globadier welded to their flat, skull-fitted helms. These were not the brown-furred common vermin who normally led such attacks, but the heavier, black-furred variety. Clad in thick armour, the skaven charged relentlessly forward, spears thrusting out.

Stregga stooped to haul Khemalla out of the path of the advancing vermin, and W'soran was tempted to strike her then and there. But there were too many witnesses, and even if he'd succeeded, he'd have still had to fight his way free of the tunnel. 'Fall back,' he shrieked, 'fall back! Let the dead earn their keep!'

'Coward,' Layla spat, even as she and Faethor followed him back into the ranks of skeletons.

'But in one piece, which is the important bit,' W'soran said. The Strigoi were following his example, melting back through the lines of the dead, even as the front rank of skeletons raised their shields and lowered their spears. 'A shame you left your wights with Vorag,' he said. 'We could have used them.'

'They'll serve us better keeping the Bloodytooth alive,' Stregga said, holding Khemalla upright. 'At least until we can get back to him. Can your bone-bags hold them, sorcerer?' She looked at W'soran, who shrugged.

'It depends on whether they're planning any other tricks,' he said, even as he knew full well such would be the case. The skaven had begun launching attacks similar to the one that had nearly seen him permanently entombed several years previously. They caught the undead forces by surprise and dropped the weight of a tunnel on them. There was more than one Strigoi still trapped in those collapsed corridors, screaming into the silent dark.

The plan was childishly easy to discern, if you knew, as W'soran did, how the ratkin thought. Collapsing the tunnels choked off the avenues and approaches to the central cavern, forcing the Strigoi to retreat and reform their lines. The skaven, however, were burrowers without peer, and used tools and simple brute force to dig twenty new tunnels for every one they destroyed. The Strigoi, on the defensive, had no time to do the same, even if such labour had been their inclination. There was only one tunnel remaining now, the one they occupied. Once it fell, and reinforcements were cut off from the main cavern, the skaven would make their final assault.

While the thought of being caught in such a collapse again caused him no end of discomfort, there was no other way to achieve his ends without making an enemy of Vorag. The Lahmians had to die, and it was best if it seemed as if the skaven were responsible. He touched the top of his cuirass, where the fraying cords of the abn-i-khat amulets he wore were bunched, for reassurance. When their flanking effort failed, the skaven would likely launch their attack. And, if his luck held, he would be in the perfect position to play the hero.

The first line of the skaven crashed against the skeletons and W'soran gestured, pulling tight on the skeins of death-magic that animated the ancient bones. The skeletons wavered and the skaven took advantage, smashing them aside with victorious squeals. W'soran looked up, and saw the tell-tale cracks forming in the ceiling and walls. The corridor shuddered slightly. None of the Strigoi seemed to have noticed yet. It was a pity that so many would have to be sacrificed, but W'soran took the long view, and besides, what need had he of preening bully boys?

Despite having the advantage, the skaven began to retreat, backing away up the tunnel. Faethor gave a bellow of triumph. 'They run! At them, wolves of Strigos,' he roared, lunging through the ragged ranks of the dead, even as W'soran had hoped. With the others occupied, he could ensure that Neferata's pets met their well-deserved fate. The Strigoi gave tongue to the war-howls of their people and loped free of the thicket of bones.

It took W'soran a moment to realise that Faethor wasn't with them. The big Strigoi had leapt for the wall even as his brethren streamed past, and now scrambled across the cracked ceiling of the tunnel like an oversized spider.

Danger had always lent clarity to thought for W'soran. Obviously, the Lahmians had decided that his time had come, and Faethor was to be their weapon. With a snarl, Faethor dropped towards W'soran, chopping out with his notched blade. W'soran barely interposed his scimitar in time and was forced back against a shifting, groaning wall. He looked about wildly, trying to spy the Lahmians. They would not leave his death to a fool like Faethor.

'Now you die, leech,' Faethor said, hacking at him with determined savagery. 'Rudek was my kin, and I know full well how you served him. And just now, I felt your magics as our dead men quailed. The Lahmians are right – you cannot be trusted!'

W'soran didn't bother to reply. He blocked another blow and lashed out, trying to drive Faethor back, to clear enough room to work magic. At the other end of the tunnel, the Strigoi tore into the skaven ranks. The dead hesitated, turned and retreated from the battle, closing in on Faethor. Spears dug for the Strigoi, forcing him to leap aside, away from W'soran. 'Treachery,' he roared.

'Indeed,' W'soran said, almost amused. He directed the dead forward. 'Kill him.'

The corridor was shaking now. There was no sudden explosion this time, but instead a gradual shifting of weight, as if the skaven were coaxing the mountain to move. Dust and bits of rock fell from the ceiling, pattering across his head. Faethor stepped back, cursing and snarling as the skeletons closed in.

A whisper of sound tugged at W'soran's attention. He whirled and saw a thread of movement, almost too quick to catch. Black blood burst from his throat. The pain struck him a moment later. He clapped a hand to his torn jugular as he choked on his own fluids. For a moment, just a moment, he was back in Lahmia, in the temple, and Neferata was loping towards him, inexorable and deadly. Again he felt the hot flash of the old familiar terror – the fear that took the form of the dark and cramped confines of a jar.

Layla darted forward, her eyes alight with murder-lust. Her blade bit into his as he wove a desperate defence. 'She warned us about you, old beast. She warned us that you would try and turn Vorag against us, that you would strike at us through cunning and deception. And she has decreed that you must die!'

W'soran could respond with only a gurgling snarl. He saw Stregga moving in on him from the side, and Khemalla as well, circling him as Layla drove him back. Behind them, Faethor gave a despairing howl as the relentlessness of the true dead won out against the ferocity of the near-dead. Spears pinned the Strigoi to the wall, puncturing his heart and skull. W'soran flung out the hand that had been clutched to his throat, spattering blood across Layla's face. She reeled with a cry of disgust. W'soran sank beneath Stregga's blow, and the Lahmian's sword drew sparks from the tunnel wall.

She grunted as W'soran crashed against her, knocking her from her feet.

W'soran whirled, barely countering a blow from Khemalla. The three Lahmians were all on their feet again, and closing in. He swung his scimitar in a wide circle. He was stronger than they, but they were better warriors, and faster. They were hemming him in, keeping him from concentrating for even a moment. Neferata had schooled them well in how to combat sorcerers. The Strigoi were falling back. They had realised that they were alone, and unsupported. The tunnel was shaking now, and the rocks were grinding loudly.

Khemalla shrieked like a banshee and lunged. Her blade skidded along the side of his cuirass as she sought to spit him. Layla darted to the side, climbed the wall, and leapt down, her blade smashing against his pauldron, and he was sent spinning about by the force of the blow. Stregga's blade chopped down into his forearm. W'soran screamed.

Then, at last, the roof caved in. The returning Strigoi were blotted from sight by the falling rocks. Stregga pulled back for another blow and gaped upwards as the world fell in on them.

W'soran seized his moment. He slithered through the falling rocks like a striking snake. His talons pierced the flesh of Stregga's throat and he coiled around her with every iota of speed he possessed. Then, with a hiss, he bit down on the other side of her neck, savaging flesh and cartilage, and finally bone, as her black blood – Neferata's blood – pumped down his throat.

He swallowed Stregga's final scream as the tunnel fell in on them. Amidst the thunder of rocks and the growl of the mountain, he slapped his palm down flat on the ground and the shadows swirled about him like a swarm of insects. Ghostly scarabs the colour of oil and the grave fluttered around him with a sibilant clatter, their phantom shapes somehow protecting his thin one from the falling rocks. The scarab-jars he had used to escape his enemies in Nehekhara were long gone, but the fluttering spectres of the insects that had been contained in those jars were still his to command, bound to him by unhallowed rites and the force of his own will. They protected him now, their constantly moving forms deflecting the rubble that pounded down on him, creating a cone of safety.

The last rock fell with a crash. It had been his intention to simply allow the skaven to bury his problems for him. The Lahmians had forced him to get his hands dirty. Dust stung his eyes and nose as he slid his fangs from Stregga's throat. She flopped limply from his grip, her eyes opaque and white and her once lush form withered and thin. He had drained her dry. Her vitality coursed through him, adding to his own and filling him with a feeling of invigoration that left him feeling slightly light-headed. It warred with the old familiar fear of being buried, numbing it.

W'soran paused for a moment, looking down at the corpse, searching for any hint of life. There was none. If a vampire could be said to have met the true death, Stregga had. Perhaps he would tell Vorag that the skaven had taken her captive. A slow grin pulled at his thin lips. Yes, that would be amusing.

The forms of the scarabs faded like an evening mist and he drew his cloak to him. He pulled his amulets from beneath his cuirass and rubbed one with his thumb. It had been years since he had eaten one, but he already felt the craving, almost as strong as his thirst for blood, rising in him. It was like an itch he could not scratch. A soft whisper, just out of earshot, tempting him, reminding him of the power that could be his, if he had but the courage to take it. Stregga's blank eyes glared at him contemptuously, as if she saw his hesitation and mocked him for it. 'Your mistress has tried to kill me more than once, witch. And she has failed this time, as she has failed in every other attempt,' he said to the body.

'She... only... needs... to... succeed... once,' a voice coughed, startling him. He turned, and snorted in amusement. Layla had been attempting to reach him, perhaps to save her sister-in-blood, or perhaps simply to take advantage of the distraction Stregga's death provided. She had been caught in the collapse, half-buried in the rubble. Her head and one arm protruded from the tightly packed rocks and dark blood stained the stone in a cruel halo about her pale flesh. More blood coated her chin and streamed from her nose and eyes. Even with the weight of the mountain on her, the Lahmian still somehow lived. 'Just once, old monster,' she whispered hoarsely.

'Yes, but perhaps she will think better of it henceforth, eh?' W'soran said, sinking to his haunches in front of her.

Still clutching his amulets in one hand, he reached out with his other and grabbed her crimson-stained hair, twisting her head up and to the side so that he could examine her face. 'Especially when her hunting beasts do not return to their kennel, bearing my scalp,' he said. 'If your mistress bothers to rip your screaming spirit from the audient void to question you, you will say this – no more running. W'soran of Mahrak makes his stand here. In this place, I will build my own Lahmia, my own Nagashizzar. A city of the new dawn and corpse winds, wherein I shall build the chains that will drag down this fallen world and make of it something perfect. I will show both Neferata and Nagash for the frauds they are and were, mewling things demanding titles that are not their right. I spit on queens and grind kings beneath my heel, witch.' He yanked on Layla's hair, eliciting a grunt of agony. 'You will tell her this, when you next see her,' he snarled. 'Your noisome shade shall pass my words on to your queen, squatting in her tomb.'

He released her and stood. There were half a dozen amulets dangling from his long fingers and they seemed to pulse in time to the beat of sour blood in his head. He stared at them, half in longing and half in fear. The first time, there had been no choice. It had been the wyrdstone or entombment, perhaps forever. But now he had a choice. He could escape without them. He was not injured this time.

He looked about him, and felt the closeness clawing at the edges of his mind. He fought it down, wrestling the gibbering terror that clung to him like an unwanted passenger into a box in the back of his mind. 'I'm not afraid,' he hissed. 'I'm *not*.' His words sounded petulant, even to him.

This wasn't about fear this time. It was about expediency. That was all. He needed power. The amulets provided power. And what they took in return, he was willing to sacrifice. He had ever done so, so why hesitate now? He held the amulets up and examined them. The darkling glow of them was comforting at first glance, but it grew less so, the longer he looked.

He needed power, if he was to do what needed doing. He hissed and opened his jaws to skin-splitting width, and dropped the amulets in, one after the other. Fire burst along his mummified nerves, greater than before. His shrivelled muscles swelled and his eyes bulged as a daemon-heat was kindled within him. It happened more quickly than before, and he was almost overwhelmed. Oily smoke issued from his pores, wreathing him in a cloak of foulness. His hands twitched jerkily as he sank to his knees, wheezing and hissing. The mountain seemed to press down on him from all directions – he could feel its weight in every nerve and on the tip of every hair.

He coughed, trying to dredge up a scream, but all that escaped his mouth was an explosion of boiling gas. He felt like a fire-pit overstuffed with kindling, and the very air wavered about him as a vile heat radiated from his scrawny form. He clutched his sides, fearing that the surging energies that roiled in his gut would tear him apart.

The world pressed in on him, and for a moment, he could

see everything, every part of the mountain, every battle taking place from its roots to its tip, including those that had
yet to take place and those that never would. He saw the
heaving veins of raw magic that threaded through the air
around him and the frothing abominations that they ema-
nated from, and he knew that they saw him as well. He saw
faces as wide across as oceans and full to bursting with such
hideous malignancy that even his sour, stunted soul qua-
vered at the atrocities promised in the thinnest of smiles or
the briefest flicker of an eye. For a moment, his sanity trembled on the edge of that vast, crumbling precipice.

Then, the rocks echoed with the sounds of insects scrabbling. For a moment, he thought that he had somehow
inadvertently summoned his scarabs once more, before he
realised that they were not his, for these, rather than being
pale phantoms, were as black as Usirian's pit. Their shells
swallowed light and even his inhuman gaze could not fully
discern them. They were equal parts smoke, filth and insect
and they spun about him in a wild dance.

The voice, when it came, seemed to thrum through him,
riding the fires of the abn-i-khat into the very recesses of his
soul. *I SEE YOU*, it seemed to say. *I SEE YOU, MY SERVANT,
MY MOST FAITHFUL SON.*

He watched in horror as the skittering insects flowed over
one another, forming the crude approximation of a great
face at his feet. It was Ushoran's face, and yet not. Another
face looked through Ushoran's – a hateful, terrible face that
seemed at once pleased and angered.

'No,' W'soran said, covering his face. 'No, not yet! Not yet!' His former bravado was gone, stripped away in a moment of uncomprehending terror. He was trapped, sealed in rock with the King of Nightmares and beyond him, the Court of Chaos, his mind and soul open for the flaying. He howled and gibbered, flailing at the faces that leered at him, promising torments of exquisite intricacy.

The voice did not respond to his maddened screams. When he finally lowered his hands, the scarabs were gone, as if they had never been. The only sound, in the cramped confines of the space, was Layla's hoarse, croaking laughter. 'You – you're… mad,' she wheezed. 'K-killing you would be a mercy…'

W'soran shrieked and threw out a hand. Black energy burst from his crooked fingers and struck the trapped and cackling Lahmian, washing over her face and boiling the flesh from her head. Her screams ended abruptly. Only a blackened skull remained. Panting, W'soran turned and raised his hands. The tumbled rocks turned to slag as he gestured.

Even as he stepped into the newly-made tunnel, he knew that Nagash was watching. He knew, as he strode quickly into the darkness, erasing the stone from his path, that Nagash would always be watching. The shadow of the Undying King would cover his path until he forcibly removed it.

Chewing the shards of abn-i-khat, W'soran lurched onwards, to claim his citadel in fire and blood.

—◄ CHAPTER SEVEN ►—

The City of Bel Aliad
(Year -1152 Imperial Calendar)

'Where is she, Abhorash?' W'soran growled. He glared at the former champion of Lahmia, his good eye blazing with fury. Ushoran gripped his arm in a calming gesture, but W'soran shook him off irritably. 'Where is our beloved queen, eh? I would gaze upon her beauty once more,' he said bitterly.

'She is… contained,' Abhorash said, looking out the chamber's window, down at the war-torn streets of the City of Spices. Neferata's desert raiders had been driven back, but only at great cost and the city had suffered in the doing of it. Many had died, and many more had been taken as captives by the retreating raiders. Neferata's handmaidens too – those who had survived – were still at large, prowling the shadows of the city, pining for their imprisoned mistress.

That was the reason Abhorash's Hand was absent. The four

killers were leading the hunt for Neferata's followers, though, given their proclivities, likely not very seriously. Ushoran had offered to aid them, but Abhorash had turned him down flatly. W'soran suspected that the champion was less than pleased to see them. Then, when had the champion ever been happy to see them? Even in better times, now long dust, Abhorash had been an aloof one.

'Then the weapon we procured for you was satisfactory?' Ushoran said, stepping forward. He wore his bland-faced human seeming. It had taken Ushoran some months to gain possession of the sword that Abhorash's factotum had used to disable Neferata. It had belonged to an eastern war-chief of singularly vicious disposition. The tribe had come west, raiding and burning as they crossed the Badlands. Nagash, unwilling to ignore such an affront to his burgeoning empire, had sent W'soran and Ushoran to deal with the flea-bitten marauders.

In a single night of blood-soaked murder, the two vampires had wiped out Karadok the Conqueror and his pathetic tribe of daemon worshippers. The howling blade had been wrenched from Karadok's grip by Ushoran, even as the vampire throttled its former wielder. W'soran had driven the remnants of the tribe into the darkness of the Badlands with a barrage of sorcery, and set stalking hounds crafted from the skeletons of desert jackals wrapped in the stitched skins of orcs and men on their trail. It had been an amusing diversion from his duties.

W'soran had, at first, thought that the blade was intended as a trophy for Nagash – Ushoran was forever currying favour with the Undying King. Instead, the other vampire had kept and concealed the weapon, eventually delivering it to Abhorash, who had in turn gifted it to the young nobleman, Khaled al Muntasir. True to form, Abhorash had refused to strike directly at Neferata, until forced to by circumstance.

'For the most part,' Abhorash said. 'I was forced to intervene, in the end. Khaled is a strong warrior, but too easily distracted by a pretty face or an unexpected situation. He thought the blade made him invincible, and he was unprepared for Neferata's strength.'

'Something we've all experienced from time to time,' Ushoran said, somewhat ruefully. W'soran reached beneath his robes and rubbed the ancient scar on his breast unconsciously.

Abhorash's smile was tepid. 'Some of us more deservedly than others,' he said.

'Enough of this... where is she?' W'soran demanded, stung. Abhorash's supercilious, self-righteous pose grated on his nerves. Soon, Nehekhara would fall, and Alcadizzar would bend knee to his betters once more. Then, the Great Work would begin in earnest. 'I would have her with us, for our reunion with the puppet-prince of Rasetra. I think she would... appreciate it.'

'No,' Abhorash said, not turning from the window.

'Excuse me?' W'soran said.

'I said no, priest,' Abhorash said. He turned towards them, his palm resting on the pommel of his blade. It bore neither enchantment nor curse, but all the same, in that moment, it was the most terrifying weapon in the world. W'soran silently cursed himself for that flush of fear. It was Abhorash who should fear. It was Abhorash whose existence could be ended with the flick of a finger, or the whisper of an incantation.

But Abhorash was not afraid. Abhorash was too stupid, and too proud, to be afraid. He looked down his nose at them, like a lord examining peasants, and W'soran bristled. Ushoran remained as calm as ever, though W'soran felt him tense, ever so slightly, which made him feel better. Ushoran was too placid, too calm. It was no wonder that Nagash barely acknowledged his existence.

'Why?' Ushoran asked, speaking up before W'soran could.

'She is contained. It is enough. I will not surrender her to slavery or death,' Abhorash said.

'Those are her only options, Abhorash,' Ushoran said, stepping forward. 'Why are you protecting her? She will not appreciate it.'

'And she should not. She is a queen. It is my duty to protect her, while she lives. I could not protect her from herself, but I can protect her from you,' he growled. 'You will not turn her over to the Usurper.'

'And if we insist?' W'soran asked. Power crackled between his hooked fingers. He was almost happy that it had come to this. He had waited for years to match himself against the brute.

'Don't,' Abhorash said softly.

W'soran hissed and flung out his hands. He spat an incantation, and Abhorash reeled as he groped for his blade. W'soran knew, on some level, that this was a mistake. Attacking a killer like Abhorash was tantamount to suicide, a small part of him screamed. But another, larger part of him was determined to rip the look of mockery from Abhorash's face. The champion had never feared him, never respected him. Well, he would respect him now.

Obsidian-hued lightning curled from W'soran's fingers, stretching towards Abhorash. The champion jerked like a marionette, but refused to fall. A snarl rippled across his features as he staggered forward, his blade springing from his sheath. W'soran backed away, goggling as Abhorash pressed towards him. Steam rose from his rapidly blistering skin, but Abhorash refused to retreat. The tip of his sword closed the gap.

W'soran gave a gasp of relief as Ushoran crashed into Abhorash's back. Ushoran moved like lightning, coiling about the warrior. His human face had bled away, revealing the beast beneath. Talons that could puncture armour and bone with ease sank into the champion's shoulders, and his muzzle dipped towards Abhorash's throat.

W'soran's relief was short-lived, however. Abhorash roared, grabbed Ushoran's muzzle with his free hand, tore the Lord of Masks from his back and hurled him into W'soran, knocking them both sprawling. Abhorash leapt towards them, blade raised. Only Ushoran's quick recovery saved them, and he dragged W'soran aside as the blade came down, cracking the floor.

The three vampires faced one another silently, as the dust settled. Abhorash smiled tightly at them. 'If you run, I will not kill you,' he said.

'The day you kill me, warrior, is the day I deserve to die,' W'soran spat as he scrambled to his feet, Ushoran at his side. 'I'll flay the flesh from your treacherous bones!'

'No,' Ushoran said, forcing W'soran's hand down. 'No. We are finished here.'

'What?' W'soran barked, looking askance at his ally.

'We are done,' Ushoran said, looking at him. 'She is contained. That is enough.'

'But–'

'I only attacked him to save your miserable hide, W'soran, so shut up and kindly allow me to do so,' Ushoran hissed, jerking him away. He turned to Abhorash. 'We will go, champion. But you have made enemies this day, when you could easily have had allies.'

'I think I'll live,' Abhorash said. The sneer in his words rattled in W'soran's head as they made their way from his palace...

Crookback Mountain
(Year -320 Imperial Calendar)

The skaven squealed as Vorag bit down on its head. His powerful jaws cracked the creature's skull and the helmet that supposedly protected it. The Bloodytooth tossed the twitching body aside, his jaws and chest covered in dark blood. He roared, and the line of skaven flinched back as one. He wore neither armour nor furs, and his flesh was corpse-grey and pulled taut over inhuman muscle.

It had been a year since Vorag had lost his woman, and in that year, he had scoured the skaven from the mountain, from crag to canyon, from peak to root, butchering them in his rage. Now, the skaven defended their deepest warren – the last warren of Crookback Mountain – as Vorag and his snarling Strigoi made to fall upon them.

W'soran watched from within his bodyguard of hulking, scar-covered crypt horrors as Vorag slung another skaven into the air with a backhanded swipe. The line of black-furred beasts was crumbling beneath the relentless assault of the Strigoi and the slavering ghouls that bounded at their side. W'soran watched and chuckled. He rubbed his hands together, thinking of what secrets might be housed in the warren. He felt certain that it would contain breeding pens, at the very least.

Still chuckling, he extended a hand and unleashed a sorcerous blast at the shrieking wolf-rat that lunged at him. Hundreds of the berserk quadrupeds had been released as the Strigoi pressed their assault on the remaining tunnels – a last-ditch defence. They attacked both sides in their fierce hunger, however, and as many skaven as corpses had fallen to their bestial appetite.

More bounded towards the knot of mammoth ghouls, who growled warningly and clutched their great hammers and clubs more tightly in anticipation. As always, their pointed, ape-like heads had been sealed inside bronze cage-helms, to lessen their chances of biting their masters, and their bulbous, malformed torsos were protected by crude studded cuirasses of banded bone and leather. One gave a shrill roar and slapped a leaping wolf-rat from the air with its maul. W'soran left them to it, and turned his attentions back to Vorag's efforts.

The skaven had their own warlords and war-chiefs and it was one such, clad in heavy armour and wielding a sword and a hooked war-pick, that bounded forward to meet Vorag in the centre of the blood-slick cavern, accompanied by its bodyguard. The creature was larger than most of its kind. W'soran wondered whether that was due to blood or simply having access to more food than its followers. It wore a crested helm and back-banners reminiscent of the horsemen of the eastern steppes, and a spiked ball was mounted on the end of its tail. Foam gathered at the corners of its mouth, indicating that it had consumed a number of the strange potions and brews that the ratkin employed to circumvent their instinctive cowardice.

Vorag met it with a howl. He ducked beneath the slash of its cleaver-like blade and gouged canyons in its cuirass with his claws. The creature bounced off him. The war-pick sank into Vorag's thigh and he roared in pain. Nonetheless, he jerked aside as the tail-ball swung towards his head. He slapped aside the sword and grabbed for the beast. He only managed to snag a handful of its helmet crest and his howl of outrage was audible over the sound of battle.

Finally, he caught the tail-mace in his palm and held tight, ripping the creature from its feet. He swung it up and brought it down, spine-first, against the cavern floor with a shuddering *crump*. The creature lay, breathing heavily, obviously broken, as Vorag tore the pick from his thigh and sent it slicing down into the skaven warlord's chest. Crouching over the squealing creature, Vorag shucked it of its armour and flesh, digging open its chest in a bid to extricate its heart.

When he'd reached the morsel, he plucked it free and stood, holding it aloft. Then, with the air of a starving man, he shoved it into his mouth and tore it to shreds.

'He's lost all sanity,' Melkhior hissed as the grisly scene played out. His features were hidden within the folds of a heavy hood, to hide the still-healing burns that further marred his unpleasant countenance. He and Zoar had defended Vorag in the skaven's final assault on the citadel's central cavern, and had suffered for it. The skaven had unleashed new weapons that vomited wyrdstone-created flames and had, with unerring accuracy, apparently caught both Melkhior and Zoar with them. When W'soran had arrived, at last, to that final battle, he had been greeted by the sight of his ghoul-borne palanquin burning like a merry torch, and his oldest remaining apprentice screaming in his death-throes as he clawed at his burning flesh.

Melkhior had sworn that Zoar had shoved him aside, in a split-second gesture of brotherhood, and been caught full by the blast meant for Melkhior himself. He had sworn it, even though W'soran had not asked, and did not truly care. Zoar had been useful, in his way, but W'soran wouldn't miss him.

He glanced at his apprentice and said, 'Perhaps he did love that she-wolf after all.'

'Vorag has never loved anything,' Melkhior said.

'There speaks the voice of experience,' W'soran said. 'At any rate, what does it matter? For the price of a witch, we gain a fortress, unthreatened by vermin.'

'Yes… Vorag's fortress,' Melkhior said sourly.

'In name, perhaps, but in truth, it will be mine,' W'soran said. 'Everything falls into place, my son. At last, we are unencumbered by obstacles.'

'There are still over a hundred skaven between us and that moment, my master,' Melkhior said hesitantly. 'What if–'

'What if *nothing*,' W'soran snapped. A wolf-rat lunged between his hulking bodyguards, vile jaws snapping. W'soran plucked the creature out of the air and slowly crushed its throat, enjoying its death-agonies. 'Everything is going the way it should. Soon, I will be master here and these stones will stink of death, rather than rats.' He tossed the body aside, nearly hitting Melkhior, who staggered back.

'And what then, master?' Melkhior asked, drawing his robes about him as he stepped over the dead beast. 'Mourkain still stands, and the Silver Pinnacle as well. The immediate obstacles might be dealt with, but we still have enemies…'

'Yes,' W'soran said. He reached up to trace the rim of his cuirass. He could feel the heat of his remaining amulets. They called to him, and bitter saliva built at the base of his tongue. He longed to taste the strange fire of the abn-i-khat again, and to feel it burning in his veins, but he resisted the urge. There was no need now, and he refused to fall prey to the addiction that had claimed Nagash. The wyrdstone was a tool, nothing more. It was not his master. He had no master, unloving or otherwise.

Irritated by the sudden flush of need, he shoved past his bodyguards and thrust his gangly arms forward as if stabbing the air. It responded, thickening and curling around his gesturing fingers. He motioned towards the line of skaven and suddenly, the cavern echoed with the moan of spectral winds.

Cold and cacophonous, the air rushed across the dips and gullies of the cavern and washed across the skaven. Even as it did so, strange shapes seemed to gain shape and form within the roll and weft of the wind and they struck, grasping the skaven and tearing at them like phantasmal beasts. Everywhere the wind touched, skaven died, collapsing like grisly puppets that had just had their strings cut. And as they fell, wisps of something rose from their bodies to join the howling wind, adding to the spectral ranks that were now, like some deep-sea tick, freshly infused with blood, fully visible to the horrified eyes of the survivors.

The spectral host spread like the water from an emptied bucket, splashing over more and more of the skaven, ripping whatever vile essence passed for their souls from their bodies and adding them to its own ghostly ranks. Skaven died in droves, toppling in heaps and piles, the ghastly vapour rising from their twitching corpses. W'soran stepped forward, grinning happily. 'That's more like it,' he said. The spirits of the dead swirled about him like leaves caught on the wind, and their moans caressed his ears like the sweetest music.

It was in these moments that he felt as close to peace as he thought he could get. Surrounded by agonised spirits and standing on the corpses of his enemies, he felt whole.

He opened his mouth like a viper, inhaling the effluvium of battle and death, drinking it in. It made him feel almost as good as the abn-i-khat, almost as strong. He battened on death the way a leech did on blood.

Then again, he needed blood as well. It was a sour note, ruining his enjoyment of the moment. The need his kind had for blood was a weakness, nothing less. It was a link to detestable life and a hook which bound them to the living. Nagash had understood that. Perhaps that was why he had never fully trusted them, never taken them into his confidences. Vampires were bound to the living, as all predators were bound to their prey. In Nagash's world, vampires were little better than living men.

The thought irked W'soran. Even now, after all this time, he still felt as if he was being found wanting by his old master. 'Then, at least I'm still walking around, eh, old skull?' he muttered. He gestured and more ghosts rose and swirled about him, forming up on him as if he were a general and they, his honour guard. He caught sight of Vorag loping towards him. The other vampire looked angry.

'How dare you?' he growled. 'They were my prey, sorcerer! Their lives were mine!'

'Is your sorrow not yet glutted, Vorag?' W'soran asked, meeting the Bloodytooth's glare through the haze of writhing spirits. 'Would you toss the corpse of every skaven in this mountain on her savage pyre yourself?'

'Her pyre will make the sky boil, sorcerer, even if I must feed the mountain itself to the flames,' Vorag hissed, talons flexing, 'And I will wash these rocks with the blood of her killers. I will swim in their blood and crush the life from every one, in her name. And you will call me *Lord Vorag*.' He snapped his fangs like a maddened dog and took a step forward.

W'soran hesitated, noting that Sanzak and the other Strigoi were watching. Sanzak's expression was contemplative. The Strigoi had kept himself at a distance since the moment that W'soran had burned his way into the central cavern and carved the heart out of the skaven horde. Sanzak knew what W'soran had done, even if he didn't know the particulars. But he had kept quiet, which was all that mattered.

W'soran had gone back into the darkness of that collapsed tunnel after the battle was over to ensure that Stregga was truly dead. Ostensibly, he had been leading a rescue party. Vorag had clutched Stregga's withered form to him and keened for hours, shrieking his sorrow to the unheeding rocks.

Of the other two Lahmians, Khemalla was missing, and likely buried somewhere. Layla, however, provided a moment of unpleasant surprise. Despite the state of her head, despite the damage to her body, the Lahmian yet lived, though only just. Unable to provide her the ending she so thoroughly deserved, W'soran had had her body removed along with that of Stregga. The latter's corpse lay stiff and still on a bier in Vorag's chambers; the former was ensconced in a stone box in W'soran's laboratories, awaiting his further examination. He had never imagined that Neferata's creatures could prove so durable. A bit of luck, perhaps – he yearned to continue his study of vampiric flesh, and Neferata had unwittingly provided him with the raw materials he needed.

'Surely one torment is as good as another,' W'soran said to Vorag carefully, gesturing to the hovering spirits. 'This way, they can be of some use, at least. And you had no complaints when I did the same, a year ago, and saved your hide from decorating a skaven banner pole.'

Vorag thrust his head through the spirits, sending them fluttering like bats. His eyes bulged wildly and his scalp-lock was undone, leaving his lion-like mane, now turned ice-white, to curl about his head. 'She was mine, W'soran,' he hissed. 'Mine and mine alone, just like these...' He swept out a talon, indicating the dead skaven. 'Everything is mine, sorcerer. I am king here, I am master and lord. Or do you doubt that?'

'If I have given offence, I am sorry, my lord,' W'soran said, forcing out each word. He wanted nothing more than to burn Vorag's leering face off, but he needed the Strigoi, as yet. He needed the raw strength that they provided, to wrest an empire from the sour soil of the mountains. And, annoying as he was, he needed Vorag. 'I merely sought to aid you in your task.'

'Not for any love of me, I suspect,' Vorag hissed. He leaned close. W'soran could smell the thick odour of blood and offal wafting from the Strigoi. In the months since Stregga's death, Vorag had sunk further and further into barbarity. It was as if, in killing his helpmeet, W'soran had inadvertently stripped him of all remaining humanity. The proud frontier lord who had set out from Mourkain, determined to wrest control of Strigos from the man he saw as a usurper, was gone, replaced by something that was all hunger and savagery. 'I do not claim what loyalty squirms in your rotten heart, old monster. I know traitors. I *am* a traitor, and I can smell your treachery. Are you growing impatient with my grief, W'soran, or with my presence?'

W'soran did not flinch as the skeletal gargoyle face drew close to his. He had faced worse monsters than this jumped-up brute. Vorag's claw flickered up, tapping the scar on W'soran's face, where Nagash's brand of obedience had once burned. 'Sanzak says we should go south. He says that there is war there, for me to lose myself in. That we should ignore Neferata's entreaties for now,' Vorag murmured. 'That is easy to do, now that her envoys are gone, eh?'

W'soran met Vorag's hateful gaze. 'Have you sent messengers, Lord Vorag, to tell the Queen of Silver Pinnacle about the deaths of her servants?' he asked, knowing that the other had not. That had not been his doing, and it had surprised him, somewhat. The idea that Vorag might be somewhat more cunning than he had anticipated, and that the Bloody-tooth might welcome a moment of respite from Neferata's web of schemes, had not truly crossed his mind.

Vorag looked away. His shoulders slumped and he gestured lazily. 'I am weary of slaughter. Send your phantoms into the darkness, sorcerer. Cleanse these vaults of infestation.'

W'soran nodded and turned. The entrance to the warren gaped welcomingly. He could smell the fear of the remaining rats as they huddled within, waiting for the end. He flicked his fingers and the spectral host swept forward, flowing through the entrance and into the tunnels beyond. Every skaven they killed would add to their number until those last tunnels were peopled only by ghosts. Faint screams echoed from within and he smiled.

'I sometimes wonder which of us is the worse beast,' Vorag said, from behind him. W'soran glanced at him, frowning. Vorag was examining his talons, watching the play of muscle beneath flesh and the drying blood on the cruel curves of his claws. 'Which of us enjoys this more, W'soran? I am a warrior, and slaughter is the hymn of war. But you – you bask in it, like a snake sunning itself on a rock.'

'One simply grows used to such things,' W'soran said.

'Ushoran awakened something in me. I know this,' Vorag said, making a fist. 'I don't think you were much changed by Neferata's bite. I think you have always been what you are.'

W'soran didn't reply. Vorag laughed. 'What sort of empire will we build, W'soran?' He sank into a crouch and hefted a dead skaven. With a grunt, he fastened his mouth to its throat and tore it open, gulping the thickening blood.

'A better one than I helped Ushoran build,' W'soran said harshly. 'A better one than Neferata desires.' He turned to Vorag. 'You allowed me to join your rebellious band because

I am your best bet for gaining that which you desire.'

And what he desired, what they all desired in some way, though they knew not why, was the crown of Mourkain. Nagash's crown wrought in iron and fire and made strong with his power. It tugged at them all, every vampire, pulling at something in their blood. Granted, only a handful of them had come to Mourkain, following the black call of the crown. The others had been either too far away or... he growled and shook his head. The idea that a fop like Ankhat could be more strong-willed than he, or even Neferata, was laughable.

He frowned again, feeling the ghosts within the warren twist and writhe on his sorcerous hooks. He was strong enough now to manipulate hundreds, if not thousands of spirits in a similar manner. He felt the tormented spark of each spectre as it sought to numb its pain by swallowing the life of its former companions. The screams from within the last warren rose to a crescendo and he stretched, tasting the ashes of souls on his tongue.

Vorag desired the crown, deep in his brute brain, just as they all did. Only W'soran had recognised it instantly for the poisoned meat that it was. He knew Nagash's stink and had smelled its foetid odour in every crack and crevice of Mourkain. It was in the soil and water of the place and it tainted the blood of the Strigoi, making them beasts, even as Nagash had corrupted the Yaghur. The crown sought to make them all into beasts of burden.

'Perhaps I do not want it any more,' Vorag said, dropping

the pitiful remains of the skaven. 'I saw what the crown did to Ushoran, sorcerer. Can you promise me that it will not do the same to me?'

W'soran paused. Then, 'Yes. I can rip the secrets from that detestable circlet, given time.' That was not quite a lie. In time, he could indeed discover the secrets that Nagash had woven into the forging of that crown. He would learn the secrets that had broken Kadon and Ushoran in turn, and make them his. 'I can make you the master of Mourkain and high hetman of all Strigos, Vorag – emperor of a vastly expanded empire, even. All I need is time.'

'So you keep saying,' Vorag growled as he stood. His eyes glittered eerily. 'Neferata will not be happy.'

'Neferata will have her own war to keep her occupied. And while she and Ushoran fight over Mourkain, we can take Nagashizzar. Within its bowels lie the tools I need to make you chief of chiefs, Vorag. It sits waiting to be garrisoned by a powerful host – provide that host! Take Nagashizzar! Take the Great Land and Araby beyond it, and create a kingdom to rival Strigos – a fruitful kingdom, and one that will provide you with the strength you need to beard the beast in its lair.'

The warren had fallen silent. Even the echoes had faded. Vorag seemed to deflate. His features became more human, though his eyes remained as black as polished onyx. He tilted his head backwards and inhaled the smell of death emanating from the entrance to the warren. Then, with a faint smile, he looked at W'soran.

'I am not a fool, sorcerer. I am not a beast. And I would make right what Ushoran – what you all – made wrong. He made me in his image, but I would have more. I would have an empire of men, not monsters.' He dropped a heavy hand on W'soran's shoulder. 'And you will build it for me.'

W'soran smiled. 'It would be my pleasure.'

—◄ CHAPTER EIGHT ►—

Nagashizzar
(Year -1151 Imperial Calendar)

Alcadizzar screamed. Nagash held the last king of Khemri aloft in one hand and used the other to carve symbols of fell power into his bruised and tattered flesh. Arkhan and his fellow liches watched silently. Ushoran and W'soran stood off to the side, watching as well, but not quietly.

'What is he doing?' Ushoran hissed. 'Is it just torture, or something else?'

'His agony fuels the magic,' W'soran said, watching enthralled. 'He is using Alcadizzar's life to craft a spell of death.' Nagash's skill for necromantic improvisation was unparalleled. Where W'soran had to study and experiment until his mind staggered beneath the weight of it all, Nagash seemed to simply wrestle the winds of magic into whatever shape he desired. He was all raw power, with neither nuance nor ritual to hinder him from

simply forcing reality to bend to his terrible will.

'Why?'

'What do you mean "why",' W'soran whispered. *'You know as well as I do what Nagash intends. And it will be beautiful.'* Even as he said it, the doubts, new and old, crowded at the forefront of his mind. Some he had come by himself, in his years in Nagashizzar. While he had once thought of Nagash as a god, in truth, the Undying King was something else. Just what he was, W'soran couldn't say, but he was no god. He was no invisible master, speaking through oracles and dusty tomes, but a hard, cruel presence. What went on within that blackened skull no one could say, but Nagash at least thought as a man, and an exceedingly petty and spiteful one at that.

Why else would he have brought Alcadizzar before him, to gloat over him as he had done only moments earlier, before beginning his current ministrations? W'soran shook his head. *'Beautiful,'* he said again. *'The sands will give birth to generations of the dead… entire dynasties will bow before the Undying King and we will lead them to war against the men of Araby and Ind. We will bring order and peace to this world, Ushoran. And all for the glory of–'*

'Nagash,' Ushoran said, softly. *'Just Nagash.'*

W'soran looked at him. Alcadizzar screamed again and writhed in Nagash's unyielding grip as blood poured down his body to drip and collect in the stone runnels set in the floor. Ushoran watched and his eyes were like stones. Whether he was enjoying the king's agonies or not was impossible to tell. His face might as well have been a mask. *'Why do you call him the Undying King, when he is no kind of king at all?'* he asked, as

*if to himself. 'Just because he wears a crown, that does not make
him a king...'*

W'soran grunted and glared at him. 'What are you talking
about?' he asked.

'Nothing; it is a shame Neferata is missing this. I'm sure she'd
have enjoyed seeing her old pet flayed by inches,' Ushoran said.

'Whose fault is that, then?' W'soran asked quietly. 'We should
have beaten Abhorash and brought them both here in chains.
Nagash would have thanked us. Instead, see – he honours Arkhan
and those bags of bones. It is we who are his true servants – they
are but tools.'

As if he'd heard them from across the throne room, Arkhan
turned to look at them. The green glow in his gaze was gloating,
and W'soran bristled. Ushoran didn't react. He ignored Arkhan,
and the liche returned the favour. Indeed, save W'soran, few took
notice of Ushoran at all, least of all Nagash, though Ushoran had
sought to curry favour at every opportunity.

'Do you truly think she would have been content to serve,
W'soran?' Ushoran asked. He looked at the other vampire. 'Are
you?'

'I – what about you, Ushoran, are you content?' W'soran asked,
after a moment's hesitation. 'Neferata would have served. She
would have had no choice.'

'There are always choices,' Ushoran said, turning back to watch
Alcadizzar's agonies. W'soran frowned and turned as well, and
just in time – Alcadizzar gave a bull-bellow of pain and anger and
flailed his way free of Nagash's grip.

Emaciated as he was, broken and weak as he was, Alcadizzar

was no coward. He sprang towards Arkhan and the other liches, and tore the black blade from the sheath on Arkhan's hip even as he gave a desperate shove, knocking the liche back into his fellows. Blade in hand, Alcadizzar spun about and lunged for Nagash.

W'soran intercepted him, catching the downward stroke of the blade on the bracers of his crossed wrists. 'You,' Alcadizzar groaned, pallid face twisted in fear and loathing.

'Me, little prince,' W'soran said. 'And this time, your women aren't here to save your hide.' He shoved Alcadizzar back, knocking him to the ground. W'soran made to pounce, when he felt the chill clutch of Nagash's gauntlet on the back of his head. Fingers like iron hooks dug into the thin flesh and he was ripped into the air and flung casually aside, his howl of pain trailing after him.

'NO! YOU WILL NOT KILL HIM, LITTLE LEECH,' Nagash said. W'soran landed hard enough to crack the stones of the floor and he felt things break and burst within him. He had felt Nagash's strength before, but never in such a way. He lay panting as Nagash hefted Alcadizzar once more, after divesting him of his weapon. 'HE IS WORTH MORE TO ME THAN YOU. HIS BLOOD IS WORTH MORE TO ME THAN THAT OF A THOUSAND OF YOUR KIND.'

'I simply sought to aid you…' W'soran wheezed.

'I HAVE NO NEED OF YOUR AID.'

Nagash turned back to his work. Arkhan scooped up his sword and looked down at W'soran. 'On your feet, old monster… we'll soon have an army to lead.' The liche turned without waiting for a reply. W'soran staggered upright, clutching his healing ribs tightly. He looked around and saw Ushoran, still standing in the

lee of one of the great columns that lined the throne room. Before
he could say anything, the Lord of Masks turned and faded into
the shadows...

The Badlands
(Year -300 Imperial Calendar)

W'soran gave vent to a howl of fury as he caught the arrow
mere inches from his head. He snapped it in two and hurled
the pieces aside. More arrows sailed through the deeply
overcast sky, slicing through the falling snow to pierce the
tattered mail of the marching dead that trudged towards the
crude, but massive, palisade that blocked the mountain trail.
'Tear it down,' he snarled, batting aside another arrow with
his scimitar. 'Leave not one piece standing!'

The pace of the dead quickened as he let his anger fuel the
incantation that sprang to his lips, invigorating them. They
were almost running now, bones sheathed in frost and bronze
moving with inhuman fluidity. The warriors on the palisade
– living men, these, and soldiers of Strigos – cried out and
redoubled their efforts. The compact horse-bows the Strigoi
favoured thrummed as the rate of fire increased, and broad-
headed arrows crashed home, knocking skeletons sprawling.
The ones that reached the wall set up the heavy scaling ladders they carried. There was no telling how many would make
it to the top. The Strigoi were already hurling rocks down on
the climbing skeletons, battering them from the ladders.

The palisade, and the small border fort beyond it, had been built in the years following his departure. Ushoran had not been idle. With determined efficiency he had begun fortifying the mountain passes that provided the most direct routes into his empire. Border palisades occupied the most distant points, and further in, larger fortifications watched over the frontiers. This one was one of the smaller ones – the pass it sat astride was a minor gouge in the spine of the mountains, barely fit for a raiding party, much less an invading army. That was why he had chosen it.

W'soran had always favoured the swift, unseen blow over the give and take of regular combat. He knew from Vorag's newer recruits that Strigos was at war with a number of the larger tribes occupying the north and west, including the Draka and the Fennones. In centuries past, the Strigoi had driven the ancestors of those tribes west and out of the mountains, and there were old grudges aplenty waiting to be settled. The savages cascaded into the mountains, burning and raiding before retreating back to the lowlands. The Strigoi, long used to martial superiority, were finding it curiously difficult to handle tribes they'd long since thought effectively cowed.

W'soran thought he detected Neferata's pale fingers in that particular pie. She had wormed her way into the good graces of the larger tribes, supporting this chieftain over that one and providing this bit of that to those, and welded them into a web of nonaggression pacts. Too, she had spread the stories of Mourkain's wealth and decadence, convincing the

barbarians that Strigos, far from being a vibrant and dangerous foe, was nothing more than a sick old wolf, ripe for the
killing.

He'd hoped that Ushoran's eyes were full on the lands
of the tribes, and Neferata's new fastness, and that he'd
decided to ignore Vorag's ever-growing band of rebels. No
such luck, however, as this fastness attested to. Ushoran was
many things, but a fool wasn't among them. The mountain
fortresses were only temporary stumbling blocks, set up to
slow any advance from the east, to enable Ushoran to divert
forces to repelling a substantial invasion, whether it be renegade Strigoi or orcs.

W'soran jerked the reins of the skeletal horse he rode in
frustration, and turned it about. 'We need to find another
way over that palisade,' he said. He and his coterie sat some
distance from the battle, protected from what weak light
managed to pierce the clouds by a large, heavy pavilion
made from tanned skins and held aloft by uncomplaining
armoured wights.

Melkhior, sitting on his own bone nag not far away, nodded. 'As I said earlier, my master,' he said, carefully not
meeting W'soran's gaze. 'The pass is too narrow, and they've
done too good a job bolstering that palisade. It'll take us
days to knock it down.' He peered up and around the edge
of the pavilion and continued, 'by which time, the snow will
be coming down too heavily and we'll be trapped.'

'Careful, my son,' W'soran grated. 'One would think you
were chastising me.'

Melkhior flinched. 'Never, master. I was merely pointing out the facts of our situation.'

'Facts are good, Melkhior. Let's stick to those, shall we, and leave any commentary aside,' W'soran said pointedly, looking at his commanders. 'Well, my lords, any suggestions?'

The Strigoi were a varied lot. There was the wolf-grinned Arpad, who wore the serrated-edged armour of a *timajal* and a peaked, crested helm that covered all of his face but for his lower jaw. Then there was Tarhos the Hook, a burly, barrel-chested Strigoi who wore his namesake in place of his left hand. The hand had been bitten off by one of the great bull-headed beastmen that haunted the mountains and Tarhos, with the customary practicality of his people, had taken one of the beast's horns after he'd killed it, and made it into a replacement for the missing limb.

Last of the trio was Ullo of Carak, a minor frontier agal from one of the far northern provinces. Ullo was a raw-boned monster, all slope-skulled and pebble-skinned, like a shark wrapped in furs. He had served with Abhorash in the north and wore a profusion of amulets torn from the necks of northern champions and chieftains, and played with them constantly. He and the others rode sturdy, stubborn Strigoi mountain horses, and scalps aplenty dangled like tassels from their saddles. All three had been given the blood-kiss by Ushoran. All three had turned on him in the years following Vorag's exile, seeking better opportunities with their fellow agal.

Ushoran had inadvertently created a stagnant aristocracy

for his empire. Undying lords rarely made way for their heirs in a timely fashion. The Strigoi, already given to duelling, had begun to kill each other with startling regularity not long into Ushoran's first century of rule. Then, perhaps that had been Ushoran's plan to control a rowdy and often overly-ambitious people. It had his characteristic, light touch – Ushoran had always enjoyed letting others do his work for him.

'Get above them,' Tarhos grunted, scratching his chin with his hook. 'We could scale the cliffs, descend on them.'

'And then what?' Arpad asked, leaning over his saddle horn. 'A few men against a small army? I know you fancy yourself a hero from the sagas but I'm quite particular about how I spend my blood.'

'Abhorash would have taken the wall himself,' Ullo said, his dead eyes meeting W'soran's.

'Well, Abhorash isn't here, for which we should all be thankful,' W'soran snapped. 'Otherwise all of our heads might be decorating the walls of Ushoran's palace.' He glared at the trio of Strigoi. Vorag had long since gone east with the bulk of his forces, leading them towards Nagashizzar and the lands beyond. He had left a garrison at Crookback Mountain, nominally under W'soran's control. But Ullo and his fellows were there to keep W'soran in check, and to see that he didn't get any ideas above his station.

It would be easy enough to see them dead. But he needed them. He needed their experience, and their men. Each had brought with him a complement of living men; or, as W'soran liked to think of them, raw materials. With them, W'soran had an army capable of holding off both Ushoran and, should she choose to make an issue of it, Neferata. That was Vorag's intention, at least.

But W'soran had other plans.

Plans that would be stalled for a season or more, if he allowed this pathetic palisade to hold him back for even one day longer. He opened his mouth to snarl an order when something almost familiar brushed across the surface of his mind, like the touch of a bat's wing. His mouth snapped shut and he turned his horse about, peering at the palisade. As he watched, a Strigoi on the wall was gutted by a skeletal warrior. The dead man slumped. Then, with a familiar jerk, he shoved himself up, his blank gaze fixing on the corpse that had done for him, and he lurched into it. The two corpses, one fresh, one long dead, tumbled from the palisade to crash into the hard ground.

'Necromancer,' Melkhior hissed. W'soran nodded.

'Well, that changes things a bit,' he murmured. 'I wondered whether Morath managed to find a place for himself in Ushoran's kingdom. It seems he has.' Melkhior growled and W'soran chuckled. 'All the more reason to break this obstacle, it seems. And for lack of better ideas, I suppose I'll be doing the breaking.'

With a snap of his reins, he urged his undead mount forward, into the swirling snow. The Strigoi and Melkhior followed, at a distance, uncertain as to his intentions.

As W'soran rode through the ranks of the dead, a curious ripple spread through them. Skeletons dropped their weapons and grabbed hold of one another. Bones shifted and locked with a loud, squealing clatter. W'soran ignored the arrows that rattled around him. The bones rose over him in a wave, and then became something else. Fifty skeletons, then twice that, drew close and joined, and the pile heaved forward and grew steadily as it did so. Skulls rolled upwards as if tugged by invisible strings and arm bones descended, pressing together tightly as hundreds of fingers curled and clicked.

The conglomeration rose and stepped forward, and the cliff face shuddered. W'soran's mount reared and then its bones joined the mass as well, and fleshless hands reached out, passing him upwards towards the chattering crown of a hundred-hundred skulls. The thing stooped low over the palisade as it bent forward, its conglomerate hands tearing at the barrier. Logs cracked and burst asunder in a spray of splinters and men went screaming into the air from the force of the attack. Even as W'soran stepped onto a platform crafted from ribs and skulls, part of the palisade burst inwards, crushing its defenders like scuttling insects.

He had learned the art of crafting such creatures in Nagashizzar. Dead flesh and bone was much more malleable than living, and it could be welded into a million different shapes, if one had but the imagination and will to do so. It required a certain exhalation of energy to do it on this sort of scale, but W'soran had fed earlier in the day on a prisoner, and had the strength to burn. Such magics were beyond living men, however. Only the undead had the dark strength required to bend the dead into such monstrous shapes.

But the living had their strengths. Dead men rose bloody and broken, and threw themselves upon the giant, scaling it like fleshy spiders. W'soran had hoped his little demonstration would attract the enemy's attention, and his hopes had been borne out. The zombies were fast, thanks in part to their animator's desperation as well as their relative freshness. W'soran swept his scimitar from its sheath and lopped off a reaching arm as the first of the dead men flung itself up onto the platform. It stumbled forward and he grabbed its sagging, pulped skull with his free hand. He could see the dark threads of magic which bound it to its master. Invisible to any but one trained in the art of seeing, they blazed like cold fires to his eyes.

Beyond the palisade was a second, smaller wall. And built into that wall was a stone bunkhouse. Less a fortress than a wind-break, it was nonetheless a strongpoint, built to withstand punishing weather and the inevitable greenskin attack. It was also where the enemy necromancer was located, to judge by the flickering darkling skeins that stretched like ghostly leashes from the dozens of dead men who scaled his creation.

Below him, Ullo and the others had joined the assault. They rode pell-mell through the ranks of the dead, eager to be in at the kill. Melkhior followed them, cloak flapping, and the wights running in his train, their barrow-blades drawn and their eyes glowing like hell-lamps.

'The bunkhouse,' W'soran bellowed, gesturing with his blade. 'Take him, Melkhior!'

The human defenders of the palisade broke and retreated as Ullo and his companions crashed into them. There were more than a hundred men left, enough to put up a hearty defence. Their courage, however, broke in the face of the snarling trio of vampires riding down on them. Their courage had been linked to the solidity of their defences, and with those defences only a memory, so too was their fighting spirit.

The zombie squirmed in his grip, bringing W'soran's attentions back to the matter at hand. More of them had gained the platform and they stumbled towards him, even as his conglomerate giant ripped another section of the palisade apart. It was a simple enough matter to reach out and snag the magics that bound the zombies to their animator, and the work of but a moment to break them, and usurp them. The dead stiffened and slumped, his will now theirs.

Down below, he saw Melkhior's undead steed spring into the air and clear the heads of the panicking soldiers. Even as its hooves touched the hard ground, horse and rider were galloping towards the bunkhouse where men, braver than the rest, had made their stand. Arrows pierced his apprentice's cloak as Melkhior rode them down, laying about him with his blade, his gruesome features twisted in an expression of fierce glee.

W'soran looked down at the zombie. 'Morath, Morath...
you would not forget what I have taught you in the heat of
battle. You wielded spells as an archer does arrows,' he said.
'Still, that one's unbridled savagery has its place...'

As if he'd heard him, Melkhior gave a pantherish growl
and vaulted from his mount, striking the head from one
of his remaining foes even as he landed, the few men still
standing scattering in terror. Melkhior gestured and the
iron-banded doors to the bunkhouse exploded into fiery
fragments.

The air suddenly blistered with the stink of ozone and
Melkhior staggered as talons of lightning clawed at him
from within the bunkhouse. Another crackle of lightning
and he reeled back, smoke rising from him. The enemy necromancer stepped through the shattered doors, surrounded
by a cluster of armoured corpses. The latter were clad head
to toe in the sharp-edged, banded mail of Ushoran's personal guard, their rotting faces hidden behind the visors of
hair-crested, bat-winged helms. The wights lunged towards
Melkhior, blades hissing as they cut the air.

W'soran's own wights met them there, as Melkhior fell
back through their ranks. The two groups of dead men
duelled in silence, trading heavy blows with an empty
remorselessness. Melkhior circled the group and bounded
towards the necromancer, his jaws wide and his cloak flaring
about him like wings.

W'soran examined the man as he wove defensive gestures. He was a Strigoi, and had the characteristic broad

build, but was pasty from lack of sunlight. He wore thick robes, a pitted iron cuirass and ornately engraved pauldrons. A wooden case, containing a number of scrolls, was attached to his belt, and a small tome, with a locked clasp, was chained to his belly like a piece of extra armour. On his pale skin curled the black tattoos of Mourkain's Mortuary Cult.

W'soran grunted, as if struck by a blow to the gut. He didn't recognise the man, and as once-head of the cult, it was he who had inscribed the tattoos of obedience and subservience on all the members. He fancied it had been one of his better ideas. Neferata wasn't the only one with experience in twisting faith, and the cult – a backwater version of the Great Land's own far-reaching priesthood – had given W'soran access to hundreds of fresh corpses on a daily basis. It hadn't been difficult to introduce the cult to the Strigoi, and Ushoran had seen the wisdom of a state religion – especially one that he controlled – at once.

The cult had spread rapidly. The Strigoi, given their history, were quite comfortable with death, and it had been a matter of mere decades to introduce them to the worship of Usirian and the other charnel gods, albeit suitably altered for W'soran's purposes.

In the night of fire, the night he'd left, he'd burned the temple to cover his escape, slaughtering those priests and students that he couldn't bother to have with him in exile. He'd ripped the guts out of the cult and left it for dead, wanting Ushoran to have nothing of his to exploit. He hadn't expected that it would continue in his absence. Was Morath responsible for that as well? If anyone could have rebuilt what W'soran had destroyed, it would have been Morath. 'Ah, Morath, you cunning boy,' he said, stroking a zombie's head as the corpses clustered about him. 'I should have expected that Ushoran would find some use for you. Still, for it to come to this...' He clucked his tongue.

The enemy necromancer spat spells with rapid-fire enunciation, ripping apart the air with the force of his magics, and words of withering and burning spun about Melkhior as he cut through the air. As he pounced on the necromancer, he screamed in pain. But the necromancer's screams were louder. Melkhior had lost his blade in that first surge of magics, and he tore into the spell-caster with fangs and claws. The fight was over in moments, and the sweet scent of hot blood filled the air.

W'soran gestured and the bone-giant began to disassemble itself, bit by bit, returning to its component parts, even as it passed him from hand to hand to the ground. He stepped lightly across the snowy ground and trotted towards Melkhior, who crouched over the dead man, his jaws hooked into the man's throat. 'That's enough,' W'soran said.

Melkhior ignored him. His eyes were red with blood-greed and he snarled like a cur with a bone. W'soran frowned and reached out, swiftly grabbing Melkhior's unruly mane and jerking him from the body. With a twist, he hurled his apprentice aside. Then he sank to his haunches and ripped the tome from the dead man's body. It was a heavy thing, its covers made from some hairy animal hide stretched over a bone frame, with a brass spine and iron nails holding it together. He snapped the lock with a flick of his finger, and scoured the pages.

They were made from tanned skins, and were blotchy and flabby. As he'd thought, the incantations and spells within were his own, albeit changed slightly. He stood, still flipping through the pages. Morath had adapted what he'd been taught, changing it to compensate for the lack of raw magical strength that afflicted men. 'Bold, my student,' he muttered. 'To twist the gifts of the gods, rather than accepting what should be.'

It had never occurred to him that such could be done. Oh, the old tomb-priests of the Great Land had done it, but they had had the gods to intercede for them, to hear them tell it. But if Morath's scribbling was correct, then skill might provide a balance to strength. Morath had never accepted that the blood-kiss was the logical next step in his tutelage. He had stubbornly held tight to his humanity. Perhaps there had been something to his stubbornness after all.

W'soran clapped the tome shut as Melkhior picked himself up. He looked at his apprentice and shook his head. 'You are an eternal disappointment in a sea of inevitable frustration, Melkhior. You brawl like a beast, when you should duel like a king. Have I not taught you my magics? Have I not equipped you with the arts of death and divinity? And still,

still, you resort to the basest carnage. Perhaps I made a mistake, eh? Perhaps I am an old fool, hmm? Perhaps I should have chosen others to accompany me, to become my good right hand, eh?'

He hefted the tome and gesticulated with it. 'Maybe Morath, who, at least, seems to have learned something from my poor efforts.' He shook his head again. 'Ah, if only Zoar had not been so selfless, I might have the help of a bright student. Poor W'soran! To be so alone, abandoned by his pupils, and left only with dullards to aid him in his task.'

'Are you finished... master?' Melkhior growled.

'Only until you disappoint me once again,' W'soran said and tossed him the tome. 'Collect his other scribbling. If Morath has assumed my duties as head of Mourkain's Mortuary Cult, it would behove us to learn exactly what he is teaching them.' Hands clasped behind his back, he looked about the inside of the palisade. While he and Melkhior had dealt with the necromancer, the butchery had continued. The dead that the necromancer had controlled – including the wights – had fallen like string-cut puppets with his passing. The living had continued to fight for some few minutes more, but save for a few, strangled cries the defenders of the palisade were now silent.

Ullo and the others strode towards him, kicking aside snow and bodies. 'This place is ours,' Arpad said, removing his helmet and tucking it beneath his arm. 'Now what are we planning on doing with it?'

'Oh, we'll find a use for it, I'd wager. Beyond that other

wall there are the far frontiers of Strigos, my lords,' W'soran said, throwing out an arm. He did not look in the direction he had indicated, for he knew what he would see. The black, flickering blotch that spread oily coils across the horizon, day or night, a brooding malevolence that beckoned him even as it caused his mind and spirit to quail in terror. The shadow of Nagash was spreading daily, lending the sting of urgency to W'soran's natural impatience. He did not know whether the spreading shadow implied that Ushoran was growing more powerful, or simply being more swiftly hollowed out by the nightmare mind that resided in the iron crown he wore. 'Lands that should have been yours and mine, and now belong to puppets of cursed Ushoran. Let's go take them back, shall we?'

'Vorag's command was to assume control of the high passes and then wait for him to return,' Ullo grunted, his tiny eyes glittering.

'Why wait to do later what can be done now?' W'soran asked, shrugging. 'I have never been a patient man. How many years will it take Vorag to wrest control of the gateway to the east from the skaven and the unbridled dead, eh? Even with the aid of those of my students that I sent to accompany him, it will take time.'

'We have nothing but time, sorcerer,' Tarhos said. The big Strigoi's hook hand was scarred and cracked and he ran a whetstone over it, clearing the bone of imperfections. 'We are immortal, after all. What do a few centuries, more or less, mean to us?'

'Ah, so, that is the reason,' W'soran said, with a nod. He wrapped his cloak tight about him and turned away. 'I had wondered why you three were chosen to be my watchdogs. And now I see.' He chuckled. 'You are *cowards*. Of course he left you behind!'

Arpad gnashed his teeth and Tarhos growled. Only Ullo remained silent. 'Watch your tongue, sorcerer!' Arpad snarled, gesticulating with his helm. 'We have bathed in oceans of enemy blood and taken the tusks of thousands of *urks*! The greenskins fear us even more than the ratkin!'

'Orcs and vermin are one thing – but the might of Strigos? It is no shame to be afraid of Abhorash, or the warriors he has chosen to replace you in defence of Mourkain. Even Vorag is afraid…' W'soran purred, glancing at them.

Tarhos roared and leapt for him, hook swinging up as if to perforate W'soran's skull. Melkhior lunged to meet him, his sword locking against the hook. The two vampires strained against one another in the swirling snow. Arpad, as if shocked by his companion's attack, had his blade half-drawn, but Ullo grabbed his arm, forcing the sword back into its sheath. The grey-skinned Strigoi looked at W'soran, and then reached out an arm, hooking Tarhos by his scalp-lock and yanking him backwards off his feet.

'Sanzak warned me about you, sorcerer,' Ullo said, idly kicking Tarhos in the side of the head to calm him. He shoved Arpad back and grinned, displaying a mouth full of triangular razors. 'He said you couldn't be trusted, that you would lie to us to serve your own ends.'

'And what if our ends happen to coincide, Ullo?' W'soran asked.

Ullo's grin became a smile. It was an unsettling expression. 'Then we would follow your lead. Wherever it may take us,' he said.

—◄ CHAPTER NINE ►—

Nagashizzar
(Year -1151 Imperial Calendar)

Nagash was dead.

W'soran stared at the remains of the throne, and the deep, black score marks that covered it. The throne had been crafted from large blocks of stone and sections of petrified wood and lined with the bones of beasts and men. Still-glimmering strands of abn-i-khat shot through the stone, casting a sickly illumination over the floor all around it. Nagash's corpse was missing, perhaps taken by the skaven his minions had reported were mobilising in the antechambers and lower levels of the citadel. With the Undying King dead, the ratkin were readying themselves for war once again. Too, the dead of Nehekhara, raised from their slumber by Nagash's Great Working, would soon be banging on the gates, looking to separate his flesh from his bones. Without Nagash's will to bind them, they were as much the enemies of the remaining inhabitants of Nagashizzar as the vermin that seethed in the depths, or the orcs howling in the slave pens.

W'soran hissed and thumped his head with balled-up fists. He glared about him at the throne room, at the flagstones of black marble and the wide columns, covered in elaborate and grotesque carvings, which loomed upwards to meet the arched ceiling. It had seemed so magnificent, the first time he'd seen it. Now, it seemed facile and empty, as if Nagash's death had drained away the malevolence that had once been imbued in the stones and columns.

'How,' he muttered. 'How could this have happened?' How could Nagash have been felled? How could a god… die?

No answer came to him, in the vastness of the now-abandoned throne room, but he knew, regardless. Nagash hadn't been a god. His claims to the contrary, and all hubris aside, it had become increasingly clear to W'soran that Nagash was many things, but a god was not one of them.

Would a god have had to bargain with the ratkin? Would a god have taken such pleasures in the torture of a mere mortal, as Nagash had Alcadizzar? That Nagash had not allowed him to extract the price of his stolen eye from Alcadizzar had been a disappointment; he had gorged on the fallen king's pain like a flea, keeping it all for himself. W'soran closed his eyes. And would a god have denied his truest servant, in a fit of pique?

He went to the throne and traced the gouges. A tingle of magic – ugly and acidic in nature – coursed through his fingertips. He pulled his hand back quickly, flexing his fingers. He could see it in his mind's eye. Nagash's final moments had likely been swift ones.

That was the only way he could have been overcome, with speed and ferocity. W'soran had considered it himself, in those private moments in recent months, when he was far from Nagashizzar.

The attacker had probably taken him as he sat slumped, exhausted after his Great Ritual. That would have been the perfect moment, and Nagash had known that. Why else would he have sent them all – W'soran, Arkhan and the others – from Nagashizzar while he did it?

He saw his master now for the paranoid creature he truly was. Nagash had been afraid of them all. He had been afraid of their power, afraid that they might usurp his much-vaunted dominion of the dead. He feared that once more the usurper would be usurped and tossed down by his followers.

W'soran had returned first. He had felt Nagash's death reverberate through the winds of magic and the pain had nearly driven him mad. The tattoos of obedience that Nagash had scratched into his flesh had burned like acid and he had nearly toppled from his palanquin into the Mortis River. Carried on a cloud of scarabs, he had returned to Nagashizzar to find the dead there toppled at their posts, and ratkin swarming the corridors, armed for war.

He glanced around, at the pathetic, smoking heaps that marked the final moments of a number of the latter. They had attacked the moment he arrived, and he had been sore pressed for several confusing moments. The pain of Nagash's death had disorientated him, and Nagashizzar, once a place of safety and strength, now seemed menacing, like a beast that had slipped its leash. Without Nagash, Nagashizzar crouched ready to serve a new master.

'Master,' Zoar said, stepping into the throne room. 'The ratkin

have retreated for the moment. We have revivified a number of the citadel's guards, but we require your might to bring them all back from the dark vale.' The Yaghur looked tired. W'soran had left his acolytes behind when he'd made his sudden journey, and they'd pushed themselves hard to catch up. Undead as they were, the magics they'd used still drew on their strength and will, something none of them had in abundance. W'soran chose for certain qualities, and initiative and endurance were not among them.

'I am coming,' W'soran said, examining his hands. Slowly, his fingers curled into fists. 'We have much to do, and the night slips by.'

'What are we going to do, master? What will we do now, with the Undying King… taken from us?' Zoar asked. Nagash had been a certainty for the Yaghur for centuries. Zoar and his brethren had been shaken to their core, no less than W'soran, by the destruction of Nagash. If they could know fear, they did so at this moment.

W'soran looked at Zoar. 'What will we do?' he asked. 'Anything we want, Zoar, for Nagashizzar is ours, as of this moment, and Nagash's empire with it!'

The Worlds Edge Mountains
(Year -290 Imperial Calendar)

'We welcome you, oh speaker of the dead,' Shull, High King of the Draesca, wheezed, his white-haired head bowed beneath the weight of the tall, bat-winged helm he wore.

He sat slumped in a throne constructed from wood and the bones of a great cave beast, killed by some ancient tribal champion in the mists of history. Bronze braziers stood to either side of the throne, their flames both warmed and lit the lodge-house that served as Shull's palace. It was mostly empty. A great fur rug covered the floor before the dais that held the throne, and rough benches lined the path to it.

In normal times, the sub-chieftains of the Draesca would sit on those benches, as their high king welcomed official guests. But these were not normal times, and W'soran was not a normal guest. He stood before the throne, cloaked and hooded, with his face hidden by the bronze mask he'd worn as high priest of Mourkain's Mortuary Cult, and inclined his head.

'And I give thanks for that welcome.' W'soran examined the old man carefully and could see the weight of unnatural years that clung to him. There was a cruel power in the helm the old man wore; W'soran knew this, because he'd put it there. The metal helm was as much a vampire as the man who'd created it, and no high king had yet lasted longer than seven years wearing it. 'Many have forgotten me, in my exile,' he continued. 'Many have turned from the ways of the charnel fields, and the teachings of the Mortuary Cult, in these dark times.'

'Not the Draesca! Never the Draesca, my lord,' the high king coughed, bending forward to hack up a spatter of blood onto the rough-hewn planks that made up the floor of the lodge-house. 'The Draesca hold tight to the old ways,' he continued thinly, gesturing to the great berths that marked the walls of the structure. In the berths sat the dusty, shroud-wrapped bodies of the previous chieftains. W'soran could practically taste the flicker of dark magic nesting in each of those corpses, like maggots in a wound. 'We hold tight to our ways and our mountains both,' Shull croaked, and a darkling power flared deep in his sunken eyes. He was on the sixth year of his reign, and his body was weighed down by decay and nearing death. 'Thanks to you, my lord,' he continued, essaying a gap-toothed smile.

The Draesca inhabited the mountains of the northern fringes of Strigos, and the south of the Draka and the Fennones. They were a large tribe, made of dozens of feuding clans, and ruled by the high king, who was chosen by tribal coronation. Neferata had gotten her hooks into the other tribes early, but the Draesca had been W'soran's the moment he had forged their helm of kingship for them.

There was a part of him in the helm, even as there was a part of Nagash in the crown that now occupied Ushoran's head. It had taken him centuries of research and failed experiments to create the process that had gone into the forging of the helm. It had not been an idle whim.

He had known from the first what black presence squatted brooding beneath the crude pyramid that Kadon had built and Ushoran usurped. Ushoran had as well, though he had not truly understood. But W'soran had. What he had not known was how it had gotten where it was, many hundreds of miles from where it should have been. Those last few days in Nagashizzar, in the wake of Nagash's destruction, he had scoured the citadel for any sign of the crown. It had been the symbol of Nagash's authority, and somehow, Nagash had sealed a portion of himself – of his essence – into the black iron. It was that shard of the Undying King that had drawn first Ushoran and then the others, one by one, to Mourkain.

It was a strange sort of immortality, but one that occupied W'soran's thoughts more and more. Somehow, some way, Nagash had defied the utter destruction of his physical shell. Some small, but steadily growing shard of him was anchored to the world by the crown. And like a burrowing insect, it had found both shelter and sustenance in the masters of Mourkain; first Kadon and now Ushoran.

Yes, it was a peculiar sort of immortality. It was a bodiless eternity, existing as pure intellect, until settling within another shape, usurping bodies as he had the throne of Khemri at the beginning of the whole sad history of things. And W'soran desired to know just how he'd done it. Thus, he'd created the helm of the high kings for the Draesca.

'I merely sought to lend aid to the faithful,' W'soran said smoothly. Shull's frame quivered, racked by shuddering coughs. *And I wanted to see if I could improve upon Nagash's artless craftsmanship*, he thought. He did not see his own eyes staring back at him from within Shull's, though that didn't bother him overmuch. After all, had Nagash's crown possessed its raw, mad sentience before his doom had fallen upon him in the form of a crazed Alcadizzar? 'Your people have prospered since I last journeyed to these lands, oh mighty chief-of-chiefs. It pleases me to see it.'

He had taken a small contingent and gone north from the Badlands, after breaching the ring of protective fortifications that blocked the high pass, to take the lay of the land himself. His were the only eyes he could trust. He'd left Ullo in charge. Melkhior had not been happy, but W'soran had seen little reason to abet his acolyte's delusions of military prowess.

In fact, he was beginning to wonder if it might not be best to remove Melkhior from the field entirely. Like all Strigoi, he fancied himself a warlord in the offing; in the first tentative raids they'd made into the fringes of Strigos, he'd relied less and less on his magics, and more and more on his sword-arm. A muscle unused soon withered, W'soran knew.

Not that one more or one less apprentice mattered; W'soran had begun collecting a new coterie of acolytes as he travelled around the edges of Ushoran's crumbling empire. Itinerant shamans and exiled hedge-witches had found new homes and new purpose beneath his wing. That was ostensibly his reason for visiting the Draesca who, above all the other tribes, birthed men with a great capacity for controlling magic. Among them, he'd find a number of willing apprentices. Part of him wondered if it were due to the helm... whether it corrupted them, even as the crown had the Strigoi.

Besides his scholarly interest, the Draesca were one of the few fonts of information about what was going on in Ushoran's lands available to him. His old spy network had been systematically dismantled or re-purposed by Ushoran in the months following his flight. And before the next stage of his plan could be enacted, he needed to know how things stood.

From the Draesca he'd learned about orcs proliferating once more in the eastern reaches of Strigos, and of the internal revolts within the Strigoi settlements along the Skull River. He'd learned that the tribes in the Vaults and the Black Mountains were attacking all along the Strigoi frontier. The empire was fluid at the best of times but it had become positively porous since the last time W'soran had been within its boundaries. The Draesca were among the largest of the tribes of the western heights, and they had taken to warring regularly with their fellows. It was a very encouraging picture, all things considered – Mourkain's belly was exposed and the empire of Strigos was ripe for the plucking.

'We have had nothing but good fortune since you made us this gift,' Shull said, reaching up with trembling, liver-spotted fingers to stroke the grotesque gargoyle skull carved on the front of the helm. 'We are unassailable, and invincible. The ancestors themselves ride to war with us, bringing death and terror to our enemies.' He gestured to the berths and the bodies therein. 'The tribes of the lowlands shudder in their lodges when we descend upon them with fire and sword.'

W'soran nodded and said, 'And what of your relations with Mourkain, High King?' The Draesca had been included in those early negotiations centuries before, when Strigos had begun trading dwarf-crafted weapons to the mountain tribes in return for unmolested trading routes and aid against the orcs that filled the mountains like toadstools. Since the fall of the Silver Pinnacle, the *dawi* had slammed their doors against the men they shared the mountains with, even as they waged incessant war with the greenskins, who seemed drawn to the burrows of the under-men with a passion that W'soran found alarming. The battles between the stunted ones and their enemies stretched across the mountains, sweeping up any unlucky enough to be caught in the middle. More than one tribe of hillmen had been extinguished, caught between the immovable object and the irresistible force.

Shull spat a glob of blood to the floor. 'That for Morgheim,' he croaked. That was the name the mountain folk knew Mourkain by. It meant 'place of death', which, W'soran supposed, was as accurate a title as any. Shull went on, 'It is a sick beast, staggering on two legs to its dying place. The wild men of the far hills carve portions from its hide daily, and the Great Red Dragon cannot be everywhere at once.'

W'soran's eyes narrowed at the mention of Abhorash. The champion had been given the nickname not long after his arrival in Mourkain, and it suited him. He was certainly just as arrogant, not to mention just as dangerous, as one of those semi-mythical beasts. 'So it is true, then…' he murmured. Part of him had suspected that Neferata's agents had been exaggerating.

'They say you have gone east, lord,' Shull said. 'That you serve under the banners of the Bloodytooth and that he is the true hetman of Mourkain.'

'Oh? And who says this?' W'soran asked.

'The Handmaidens of the Moon, oh speaker of the dead,' a sibilant voice purred. 'And we would know.'

Thin, elegant shadows detached themselves from the darkness behind Shull's throne, and W'soran cursed himself for not having noticed them earlier. The Lahmians were slender creatures, with eyes like lamps in the darkness of their cowls. There were three of them and they wore the thin robes of the followers of the hill-goddess Shaya. That was another of Neferata's innovations.

One threw back her hood, revealing crimson tresses and a feral beauty. 'I am Iona,' she said.

'I know who you are,' W'soran said.

'Oh? I was not aware that we were acquainted.'

'Not you personally, but one of you is as much the same as another,' W'soran said stiffly. The others were slowly circling him, like a pack of lionesses on the hunt. He tensed, wondering if they intended to attack him here. Had they been waiting for him? Had Neferata come to the obvious conclusion, when her handmaidens failed to return, and when Vorag had not launched an invasion of Strigos? The scar on his chest tingled painfully, and he remembered the thrust of the wood and the darkness of the jar. Ruthlessly, he pushed down the twinge of hesitation.

'The handmaidens carry word from one tribe to another,'

Shull said. 'Even as they have since the time of the first high king, Volker Urk-Bane.' He coughed into a clenched fist, and Iona stepped to his side, as if concerned. 'They bring us joyful tidings, my lord. They give hope that the tyrant who rules Morgheim will soon be staked out for the birds, and that a true king, and friend to the tribes, will rule.'

W'soran stepped back, trying to keep the Lahmians in sight. His escort were outside, waiting for him. He'd brought only living men with him, reasoning that it would make travel easier and less noticeable, and, if worse came to worse, he could butcher the lot and raise them. Now he was regretting it. The Strigoi warriors, tough as they were, would not provide much obstacle for the Lahmians. And his new apprentices were untested, and far too ignorant for his liking. For a moment, he wished he'd brought Melkhior with him, rather than leaving him behind.

'Do they? How curious. I'd heard nothing of that, though I do indeed serve the Bloodytooth,' he said. He glanced to the side, at the berths, and reached out with his mind to fan the embers of dark awareness in the mummified Draesca kings to life. 'Perhaps the handmaidens are not as all-knowing as they claim.'

'Or perhaps you are not as much in the confidence of the Bloodytooth as you think,' Iona said softly. 'Perhaps your services are no longer necessary. Perhaps the Bloodytooth requires better advisors than withered old priests.'

'Will you allow your guest to be insulted, High King?' W'soran demanded. *Neferata knew.* He could feel it in his bones, in the barbs that edged the words of the Lahmians. She knew and she was angry. It had been foolish to think that he could infiltrate these mountains without alerting her. She had eyes and ears in every lodge-house and yurt from the lands of the daemon-worshippers to the Vaults. Once again, he'd allowed his impatience to get the better of him. Now he was once again forced to deal with her petty distractions.

Shull blinked owlishly on his throne. 'What?'

'You are tired, High King. The burden you bear is heavy,' Iona murmured, and W'soran could hear the hypnotic thrum in her words. She reached out to stroke the old man's cheek and he trembled. How long had they been soothing him with soft whispers and gentle words? 'Sleep now, and let us speak with your guest.' She shot a venomous look at W'soran and walked over to him as Shull sagged in his chair, his eyes closed. 'He is dying, you know. Your magics are eating him up from the inside out,' she continued, in a low voice.

'There is a saying… something about eggs and breaking them,' W'soran said. 'It is of no matter. He is mine, hag. The Draesca are mine. I can do as I wish with them. You are not welcome here.'

'We do not require your welcome or your blessing, old monster,' one of the other Lahmians hissed, exposing her fangs. 'We require only your scalp, preferably wet.'

'Assassins, then,' W'soran said mildly. 'How boring – I had thought better of Neferata. I had thought she might have more pressing affairs, what with Vorag's absence from the field.' He grinned beneath his mask. 'How is that working out for her, by the way? As I recall, she was always something of a poor general.'

The Lahmian who'd just spoken hissed and struck, bounding towards him with impressive speed. Iona threw out a hand and shouted, 'Varna – no!'

Varna's claws tore through W'soran's robes as he spun away from her. The third Lahmian leapt for him then, and her blow tore the mask from his face. He slapped her aside with a snarl. Varna's claws tore across his back and he staggered.

From outside the lodge-house came the screams of men and horses. W'soran whirled towards the doors, his good eye blazing with anger. He could smell spilled blood and death. It had been a trap after all. He glanced at Shull. The old king still slumbered; whatever the hags had done to him still held.

Varna came for him again and his rage lent him strength. He caught her wrists and slammed her into the benches. He turned, robes flaring, and saw Iona speeding towards him, her feet barely seeming to touch the floor.

'We did not come here to kill you, old monster, despite Varna's impetuousness,' she said, easily dodging his wild blow. Her fists crashed against his belly and shoulder, staggering him. She bounced out of reach and fell into a strange serpentine stance, arms raised and legs bent.

'Cathay,' he grunted, rubbing his shoulder. The blow hadn't – quite – hurt. 'I see Neferata has learned the fighting arts of the war-monks of the Bastion.'

'Priestesses – women – should not be seen carrying blades,' Iona said. 'We did not come for your life.'

'Then why did you?' W'soran asked.

'She wants to see you. She requires your counsel.'

'Then let her come see me. I'm sure she knows by now where I reside.'

Iona made a face. 'She has doubts as to your hospitality.'

'As well she should,' W'soran growled. 'Did she ever tell you the jar story?' Iona frowned in puzzlement. W'soran went on, 'She once stabbed me and stuffed me in a jar. It was an experience one does not easily forget... or forgive. But I did try. I offered her palaces and power undreamt of and she turned on me again. She has tried to kill me numerous times since. And now... now she wants to see me? Now she asks for my counsel?'

He gave a bark of laughter. 'No. She just wants to stuff me in another jar. But here is my counsel, regardless... huddle in your tomb. Close the doors. And leave the world to your betters, oh queen of dust and bones. This war does not concern Neferata. It never has. The sooner she realises that, the better.'

Iona did not react with anger. She inclined her head and said, 'It was not a request. Our people have taken yours, by now. You are alone, and we will take you to the Silver Pinnacle in chains, if we must.'

'Try, by all means.' W'soran spread his arms with a smile. As the three Lahmians closed in on him, the dead kings of the Draesca sat up as one. There had been almost forty kings in the years since he had first gifted Volker with the helm, and their bodies had been wrapped tight and packed head to foot in the berths in the walls. They had been interred in full ceremonial panoply, with bronze breastplates and winged war-helms, and the best weapons of their tribe, whether sword, axe or spear, had been strapped to their hands. Now, they moved and shifted, ancient armour creaking and squealing as they dropped to the floor, mummified faces contorted by rictus snarls and their ancient majesty and brutal authority bound to W'soran's will. Almost forty wight-kings, made stronger in death than they ever had been in life, turned their faces towards him, eyes blazing like will-o'-the-wisps.

The three Lahmians had frozen in shock as they suddenly found themselves surrounded. 'What–? ' Iona asked, eyes wide.

W'soran took a moment, savouring their sudden confusion. 'Chains, was it?' he asked. 'Did you think me a jackal in a trap? That this place, amongst the entirety of these pathetic mountains, would be the place to attempt to take me? I told you… these people *are mine*. Dead or alive, they belong to me. I wonder – am I hurting Neferata by killing creatures as foolish as you, or helping her?' He looked at the wights and raised a hand. 'They grow tiresome. Kill them, mighty kings of the Draesca. Kill them for your master.'

Weapons, ranging from crude rust-splotched iron affairs to ornate dwarf-wrought blades and axes decorated with ceremonial inscriptions, were drawn with a collective hiss as the wights turned towards the trio of vampires and began to advance. W'soran stepped back, off to the side. Eager to see the carnage as he was, he thought he might be needed outside. It was becoming something of a habit, this disposal of Neferata's pets. Perhaps it was time to see to her once and for all.

He reached the doors even as the first wight struck. One of the Lahmians screamed. He thrust the massive oaken double doors open with a single shove and examined the pigsty beyond. He clucked his tongue as he looked around the courtyard. Shull's palace was located at the top of the uppermost barrow, and heavy paving stones marked the descent down from the upper courtyard, where the most important warrior lodges were located, to the bowl-shaped depression amongst the barrow fields below, where the bulk of the population of the settlement resided.

To call the main settlement of the Draesca a city, was to befoul the term. It was barely a town – squatting lodges and huts, occupying a series of descending and expanding plateaus, huddling behind a series of rough palisades, and the smell of cooking fires and unwashed bodies thick on the evening air. The Draesca had built their city on the barrows of their ancestors, carving themselves a place in a hill of burial. Even the lowest palisade rose above the hummocks of earth and stone that held untold generations of Draesca dead. The air, water and soil were saturated with the stuff of death. The people lived with it. They marched to war with their ancestors and their homes were built on bones and barrows.

Nonetheless, they were not noticeably quick to join the great majority. The Lahmians had struck with commendable swiftness, while the Draesca watched. His men, whom he'd left on the lower plateau, were dead or dying, all save a tiny knot of warriors who had sought refuge in one of the warrior lodges that spread out in disorganised fashion in a semi-circle around Shull's laughable palace. One or two of his prospective apprentices lay dead as well. The others were with the Strigoi, watching the approach of the Lahmians with horrified awe through shattered wooden walls and tatty fur windbreaks. There were only six of the Lahmians, and in as many minutes, they had butchered three times their number.

'And to think, Neferata once accused Ushoran of being profligate with our gift,' he said, loudly. 'Six little scullery maids, all in a row.'

His voice echoed down through the courtyard. The Lahmians below were not clad in robes, but in travelling leathers and piecemeal armour. In helms and cloaks, at a distance, human eyes might mistake them for men. Up close, there were too many curves and too few scars. They turned like hunting hounds at his call, their gear spattered with blood, their jaws agape and their weapons dark and dripping.

W'soran clapped his hands together, once. 'Well then, little maids. Here I am. Come and get me,' he said. They did so, and in a rush, moving like quicksilver blurs up the stairs. They came at him from all sides, closing in too swiftly for his eye to follow.

Even as they drew within a sword's length, the ground beneath them ruptured and split, disgorging the dead. Bony talons clawed the air and gaping skulls bit blindly. The moment he had set sandalled foot on the ground, his magics had seeped down into the loose soil, caressing the closest dead into semi-awareness. Besides the honoured interred of the tribe, there were also mass graves at the entrance to every lodge-house, where enemies of the Draesca were buried alive in order to bring good fortune to those who resided in the lodge. These skeletal horrors, wrapped in roots, rags and chains, burst from their pits to grapple with the surprised vampires and drag them down into the churning dirt. One alone managed to avoid the clutching hands, and she hurtled towards W'soran, blade scything out towards his neck.

His palm brushed aside the blade as the talons of his free hand buried themselves in his attacker's throat. He met her doomed gaze with one of amusement and gave a chortle as he twisted and yanked, tearing out her throat in a spray of black ichors. The body toppled past him as he stepped daintily aside and started down the stairs. The other vampires were tearing themselves away from the dead, albeit slowly. They would be free soon enough, however. W'soran paid them no heed. He clasped his hands behind his back as he walked.

'It should come as little surprise to you, or your mistress, that I am not a worldly man,' he called out, over his shoulder. 'I know little of spying or politics. But I do know quite a bit about faith. I was a priest once. I was a speaker for the dead, a preparer of corpses and a master of the mortuary rites. I prepared the dead for their final journey to the gods, and saw to the proper sealing of tombs. I buried poor men and rich men, powerful men and weak. All were equal in death, I thought. Foolishly, as it turned out. Even the dead have their own hierarchy.'

He stopped before the crumpled bodies of the men who would have been his apprentices. Even in death, their bodies so much cooling meat, there lurked a kernel of dark magic within them. One had been the shaman of a hill tribe, and still wore furs that stank of dark caves and bat droppings. The other had been a hedge-witch, surreptitiously plying his trade on the fringes of settlements. Both had had the potential to be something greater. W'soran had smelled it in them, and he found it almost insulting that they had been so casually slaughtered before achieving that potential.

At the top of the steps, the doors to Shull's palace were torn from their hinges by the flying body of a Lahmian. Iona had struck them with crossed forearms and she spun about, landing in a crouch, her snarling features pointed towards the wights that pursued her. She was bloody, but seemingly unbowed. Yet another failing of Neferata's teachings – her creatures did not have the good sense to know when to give up.

He turned back to the bodies. With an almost gentle gesture, he raised a hand over them. The essences of the two dead men rose at his motion, seeping through the rents and gouges in their mutilated bodies like smoke through the slats of a burning hutch, to coalesce beneath his palm in two swirling spheres of absolute darkness. Yes, there had been great power in them, waiting to be unlocked and honed. And that power was frustrated and angry. He let slip a bit of his own magic to join theirs, and the spheres bulged and bristled, forming twin shapes, quite unlike anything he'd seen before. Then, he had never before tried to draw forth the spirits of slain magic users.

There was a hideous beauty in the slow flowering of the nightmare shapes. He could feel them drawing strength and substance from the stuff of death which inundated the town, in a way that was at once familiar and strange. Smoky shapes that might have been bones or serpents or something in-between roiled within the masses.

'Fascinating,' he murmured, watching as the shapes writhed in the air before him, changing and stretching. A surge of curiosity snapped through him, as strong in its way as his thirst for blood. He had been too long away from his laboratory and library, too long away from his alembics and tomes. He thought of the entombed Lahmian, Layla, and blind, mad Iskar. He'd ordered the skaven to be fed regularly on gruel made from its own kind, laced with abn-i-khat, and the result was an impressive longevity. Layla, on the other hand, was rotting on the vine, kept alive only by his good graces and the vat of skaven blood he'd ordered her submerged in.

As he thought of one Lahmian, a second almost killed him. Only the hiss of parting air alerted him to the passage of the blade. He whirled and struck her wrist with bone-splintering force, knocking her sprawling. Even as she fell, however, Iona lunged to take her place, red hair wild and knotted with gore. 'Murderer,' she snarled. He stumbled back as she struck at him with her palms and feet, bending and snapping and spinning so fast that it was all he could do to avoid the blows. 'Monster,' she growled, dropping low and kicking his legs out from under him.

He fell atop the bodies of his late followers. Behind Iona, two more Lahmians approached. Their sisters, including the creature called Varna, looking decidedly the worse for wear, were busy holding off the wights. W'soran squirmed back, chuckling. 'If I am a monster, I am not alone, little maid,' he said.

He looked up, at the ethereal shapes coiling and twitching above him. They looked like nothing so much as rag-clad bones wreathed in smoke. He flung out a hand. 'Kill them!' he bellowed. He had no idea what sort of spirits he had conjured. Now was as good a time as any to see what they were capable of.

The two rag-clad phantoms shot forward, spiralling through the air towards the Lahmians. Iona, quicker on the uptake this time, leapt to one side. The two following her were not. One was jerked into the air by bony hands like a toy. She screamed as her alabaster flesh puckered and blistered at the touch of the thing. A gout of frigid air burst from her open mouth and a hellish frost formed on her limbs and face, even as her struggles weakened. The other suffered a similar fate, her flesh blackening with an impossible cold, and her hair cracking and falling from her scalp in brittle lumps as she was dragged into the air and wrapped in fluttering rags and rattling bones.

'Oh my,' W'soran said. Lost for a moment in the beauty of his new discovery, he sat on the ground and clapped his hands like a gleeful child. His excitement was interrupted by a savage thrust from the Lahmian whose wrist he'd shattered. Her sword carved a red trail across his scrawny chest and he fell back and bent beneath the blade as it hooked around, biting for his neck. He scrambled backwards like a spider, his crouched body crooked unnaturally as the Lahmian tore the ground in pursuit, skittering after him like a mongoose on the trail of a serpent.

With a creak and a pop of old bones he bobbed to his feet just in time to avoid another palm-strike from Iona, who spun about him, catching him in the shoulder, elbow and knee with a further flurry of swift blows. She moved like one of the cruel apes of Ind or one of the Dragon-Emperor's pet water-snakes, always gone by the time his eyes reached the last space she'd occupied. The natural speed of a vampire, coupled with the deadly skill of a war-monk, made for a lethal combination. A hand held flat like a blade skidded across his cheek, opening the dry flesh to the bone, and he staggered. The sword of the other Lahmian kissed his spine and he gave a cough of pain. He had to get clear of them, to give his newest creations a chance to come to his aid.

Moving swiftly, he trapped the thrusting sword beneath his

arm and threw himself forward, tearing it from its owner's grip. The Lahmian staggered and W'soran seized the opening, whipping the blade about in a wild but powerful blow, almost severing the other vampire's head from her shoulders. Iona gave a cry as her sister fell and dived towards him. A crackle of sorcerous lightning flung her back before she could reach him. He watched her tumble to the ground, hissing in pain, and then turned back.

Shull stood in the doorway of his palace, a hand raised, and his eyes alight with a weird glow. He looked even closer to death than before, and his ceremonial armour hung from his shrivelled frame. Nonetheless, his crooked, arthritic form radiated a terrible power. Shadows snapped and surged around him like pennants caught in a strong wind and the wights had formed about him like an honour guard.

'I beg your forgiveness, my lord. The whispers of my beloved brother-kings awoke me from the cursed slumber these witches placed upon me.' Shull's glowing eyes fell upon Iona. She had clambered to her feet, and Varna and the other surviving Lahmians had joined her. 'The Handmaidens of the Moon are no longer welcome in the lands of the Draesca. You have proven false, and dead or living you will find no friends here.'

His words echoed strangely across the settlement, slithering through the oily air and alighting in the ears of every watching tribesperson like bats seeking a roost. Weapons were drawn, and looks of grim determination replaced the previous expressions of fear and worry.

W'soran stepped away from the Lahmians, and grinned as Shull continued. 'Wherever you go in our lands, the hand of every man will be turned against you, for this betrayal. You are accursed and I bid you go and trouble my sight no longer.'

The Lahmians hissed, and one – Varna – made as if to launch herself at Shull. But Iona grabbed her shoulder, halting her. She looked at Shull and inclined her head. 'Let it not be said that the servants of the goddess of mercy and moon do not heed the commands of kings. We do not go where we are not invited.' Her gaze switched to W'soran. 'This could have been avoided, old monster. Now… it is war between us.'

'Were you under the impression it was ever anything but?' W'soran said. He exposed his fangs. He laughed. 'Neferata and Ushoran both think they are entitled to rule this fallen world, one by blood and the other by delusion. But they are wrong,' he called out to the Lahmians as they took their leave. 'Only one among our accursed crew is fit to rule. Tell her that, little maid. Tell her what her old counsellor has said. Tell her that W'soran has decided to take what he is owed, and that the debt to him will soon be repaid *in full and in blood!*'

—◀ CHAPTER TEN ▶—

Marshes of Madness
(Year -1149 Imperial Calendar)

The dead had pursued them for days.

Relentless and untiring, the soldiers of the Great Land marched through the marshes, ever on their trail. For two years, the servants of the newly awakened Tomb Kings had hunted the remaining followers of Nagash from one end of the Great Land to the other. Some, like Arkhan, had fled west, across the burning sands to Khemri, in an attempt to carve out a kingdom for themselves. Others, like Mahtep, had gone south, hunting safety in the distant jungles.

W'soran himself, after losing control of Nagashizzar to that wretched liche Arkhan, had thought to seek sanctuary in Araby, but he had been driven back by the overwhelming armies of the newly-awakened dead. The crypt legions of Numas had shattered his small army and scattered his ghoulish retainers, leaving he and his few remaining acolytes stranded in enemy territory. Now, they made their way to the shores of the Great Ocean, where he hoped to procure a vessel of some kind and kick the dust of Nehekhara from his heels.

He cursed for the fifth time in as many minutes as his keen hearing caught the clatter of brown bones moving through the sharp-bladed marsh grass. He pulled his damp robes tight and kept moving. Zoar and his remaining apprentices hurried to keep up. 'Hurry, fools,' he spat. 'We need to find high ground.'

The apprentices were moving more slowly than he would have liked, burdened as they were by grimoires, scrolls and baskets of abn-i-khat. He'd taken everything he could from Nagashizzar – he'd picked the bones of the fortress, snatching anything that looked like it might be useful. There was no sense leaving any of it to the Undying King's other servants, worthless lot of bone-bags that they were, especially Arkhan.

Unfortunately, Arkhan had interrupted him before he could complete the rituals that would have given him complete control of Nagashizzar. It had been all he could do to get away. He'd built a small army from the dead that littered the black shores of the Sour Sea and set off to carve a path through the Great Land to Araby. If he could have made it to Bel Aliad, he had no doubt that he could have made himself king, whether Abhorash opposed him or not...

Bones rattled and then a skeletal steed, adorned in golden barding, galloped through the murky waters of the marsh, a mummified king on its back. More skeletal riders joined the first. W'soran's apprentices scattered in panic, dropping their burdens in the process. W'soran himself, shaken from his reverie, nearly lost his head to the king's khopesh. He sank into the murky waters of the marsh as the horsemen charged past, seeking a moment's shelter.

Zoar and the others shrieked incantations as their pursuers sought to separate them and ride them down. Ancient spears dipped, and the vampire closest to Zoar screamed piteously as he was hoisted into the air to dangle helplessly, a spear in his guts. Another was pierced from three different directions, and torn apart by the momentum of the skeletal horseman.

Zoar fared better, spitting destructive magics. A horseman exploded into dust and fragments and another was consumed in black fire. Another acolyte had forgone magic in favour of the bronze-headed barrow-axe he carried, and he swung, shattering a horse skull with vampiric strength. He fell a moment later, as a spear-point punctured the back of his head and exploded out from between his gaping jaws. The rider lifted the spear, dragging the vampire into the air, where more spears soon sought his vitals.

In the two years since their first clash, the dead of the Great Land had learned the ways of dispatching their blood-drinking foes. Invariably, they sought to pierce the heart or remove the head, even if it cost them a hundred dead men to bring down one vampire.

W'soran recognised the leader of the horsemen easily enough – King Ptar of Numas had been hunting them since that fateful day W'soran had run afoul of his legions. To say that the newly-awakened kings of the Great Land were not happy about their resurrection would be an understatement. 'Eater of filth,' Ptar roared. His voice was a crackling rasp that nonetheless carried easily. 'Sneak-thief of eternity,' he continued, urging his mount around. 'Your head is mine!'

W'soran rose from the water, fangs exposed. 'Only if you can take it,' he snarled, thrusting out a hand. A sorcerous bolt shattered the rider closest to Ptar, disintegrating both horseman and horse. Ptar rode on regardless, khopesh whistling through the air on a curved arc towards W'soran's neck. He twisted to the side and avoided the blade but not the horse. It struck him, and he was dragged beneath its hooves. Pain exploded through him as he was stomped into the muck. Foul water flooded his mouth and stung his good eye as he flailed.

His fingers touched long-buried bone. A ghost of a memory spiked through him – of the marsh-tribes that Nagash had butchered upon arrival. Thousands of corpses littered these marshes, it was said. Black sorcery boiled from him in speeding tendrils, seeking the closest of those corpses. Even that small effort exhausted him – it had been months since he had tasted blood, and he was already fatigued.

As Ptar galloped past him, W'soran was hauled up by the momentum of the king's charge. He rose again from the water, spitting blood, but not alone. Waterlogged corpses, crudely preserved by the murk of the marshes, rose and reached for his fleshless attackers. As the horsemen reeled, surprised by the sudden onslaught from below, W'soran scrambled away, clutching his chest. The horse's hooves had shattered his ribs and one of his legs wasn't working. He would heal, but not in time. Nonetheless, he scrambled for the sanctuary of the marshes, hoping to escape Ptar while the latter was distracted.

That hope dwindled as a spear slid through his shoulder, knocking him to one knee. Another spear dug for his side, and grated across his ribs. With a howl, W'soran grabbed the first and broke it, freeing himself. He grabbed the second in both hands as he was shoved sideways by its wielder.

'Pin him, my warriors! Pierce his heart and chain him! We shall deliver him to Settra so that the King of Kings and Lord of Lords might punish him for his effrontery!' Ptar roared, jerking on the gilded reins of his mount.

Panic flared in W'soran's withered heart, and he thrashed like an animal. More spears dipped towards him, more than he could avoid. He screamed in rage.

Then, without warning, something massive and leather-winged fell upon the closest horseman and crushed him in his saddle. The great bat shrieked and darted towards another of the skeletal riders. And not alone – more bats, dozens, perhaps hundreds, pierced the murky sky of the marshes and descended like living arrows, battering riders from their saddles and biting at those who refused to fall. Ptar cursed and flailed at the trio of bats that clung to him like hairy barnacles, their needle teeth tearing at his mummified flesh.

'What are you waiting for, old monster?' a voice called out from somewhere in the depths of the marsh. Ushoran's voice, W'soran realised, belatedly. 'Get up and run!' the Lord of Masks roared...

The Worlds Edge Mountains
(Year -285 Imperial Calendar)

Men and women screamed as they were herded into the wheeled cages by skeletal overseers. Behind them, a walled village burned and its former defenders, mutilated and blank-eyed, helped their new comrades herd the survivors into the cages. W'soran watched it all with a satisfied air. 'Excellent,' he hissed. 'How many of these detestable little border villages does that make?'

'Fifteen,' Ullo growled, his black eyes reflecting the light of the fire. 'We use more corpse-men to guard the cages than we do to fight.' For several weeks, W'soran's forces had ravaged the border. First one legion would strike, and then another and finally a third, smashing a village or border fort to oblivion and then vanishing before the Strigoi could respond in force.

'Good,' W'soran purred, fondling his amulets. 'Just a few more and then we'll return to the mount for the season.' He looked up, considering. In a few weeks, the full force of a mountain winter would descend, making travel more difficult than he liked, especially through the high passes. They would retreat back to Crookback Mountain, and wait for the spring thaw. The slaves wouldn't last long, but they would provide ample raw materials. And while Ushoran was distracted with the tribes that Neferata had stirred up, W'soran could do as he liked. He needed slaves for his mines, food for his acolytes, and materials for his experiments – all of which these pathetic frontier villages provided.

In the five years since he'd visited the Draesca, and in the nearly three decades since Vorag had left for the east, W'soran had begun to build his empire. With Crookback Mountain as the aleph, he had begun to scour the lands to the west and north, gathering human and greenskin slaves by the hundreds and building his armies. The sound of hammers rang in the depths of the mountain, as the forges of the skaven were repurposed by dead hands. He had five tomb-legions at his disposal now, armoured and armed at his command and ready to march beneath his banners. His vampiric commanders, though nominally loyal to Vorag, eagerly followed his orders.

And he had acolytes aplenty these days – outcasts and dark scholars from as far as the republics that clung to the southern reach of the Vaults and the feudal morass of the western peninsula. Arabyans as well, and men from the north, wearing cloaks made from wolf-hide and crow feathers. Dozens of them flocked eastward, as if drawn by a black beacon.

True, some had gone to Mourkain, but others, the wisest of the lot, or at least the most discerning, had continued east until they reached his burgeoning empire. Like called to like – there were men aplenty in the world who desired to learn Usirian's mathematics – and their blood sang in his veins, binding each of them to his will. A bit of him in each of them, lending them something of his focus and will, making each of them, whether savage Norscan or subtle Arabyan, more than a match for the puling whelps that Morath had inducted into his false cult.

More than just the forges were lit in his mountain fastness; his new students, under Melkhior's watchful eye, had partitioned off laboratories and libraries for themselves, and brought the watered-down, yet still useful knowledge of their own backwater principalities with them. They had brought scrolls and treatises written by men who had been but motes of possibility when Nagash had dragged the dead of Mahrak to their feet.

And some – a rare, precious few – were older than Khemri. Dark tomes, bound in dawi hair and written on the marble flesh of the *asur* – the elder race – that had been found in northern temples or places hidden in the empty vastness of the Great Desert. All of which spoke to W'soran's growing understanding that Nagash was not the first man to wrest control of the stuff of death from the gods. He had simply, with characteristic arrogance, assumed he was.

Of the greater war, between Mourkain and the Silver Pinnacle, he knew only a little – only what news his new followers brought. The Draesca waged haphazard war, attacking and retreating, and they knew little of the ebb and flow of greater events. W'soran himself refused to give open battle to Strigos's armies, and retreated from them when he could not easily overwhelm them. Occasionally Arpad or Tarhos would grumble, but Ullo restrained them. Ullo understood the strategy. Or he thought he did, at least.

The Strigoi was presumptuous, but W'soran allowed him his presumption. The strongest chains were those a man forged himself. Ullo thought that W'soran intended to snaffle off chunks of Strigos for himself, as his enemies warred on each other; a war of scavengers, picking bones while the great predators roared and fought over the carcass. But that was not his true goal.

What need did he have of an empire? Empires were ephemeral things. No, power was his goal. That and the payment of debts owed him. But to gain power, he needed the resources an empire provided. To beat and break his enemies, he needed a weapon equal to theirs. Granted, his weapon was of simpler construction – the only living beings in his empire were slaves. He had no need of diplomacy or of politesse as Ushoran did. Let him waste his energies and resources on manipulation and military stratagems, while W'soran sat and waited.

He was good at waiting. He had waited twenty years for someone to pull him from his jar. He had waited centuries to discover Nagash's secrets. He would wait millennia to see his foes kneel at his feet. The thought warmed him, and he turned his attentions back to the hapless Strigoi peasants being herded into the cages. He felt neither pity nor interest in them – then, he never had. For W'soran, his fellow men could be divided into two, often equally despised camps... obstacles and tools. The latter were only such until they invariably, inevitably became the former. They served him, until they had to be disposed of. They could not be trusted, for trust was power and W'soran would suffer no one to have power over him, if he could avoid it. When he couldn't, his very nature made him squirm and strike like an asp when that power weakened even a fraction. And like an asp, W'soran only knew two solutions to a given problem, despite his wealth of knowledge – either kill the problem or flee from it.

It had always been thus, even in his youth in Mahrak. When he had ascended to the priesthood, he had become acquainted with plenty of tools and obstacles both in his early, puerile attempts to gain the power he so craved through generous application of manipulation and poison. Then Nagash, after usurping the throne of Khemri, had reached out his hand and snuffed the life from Mahrak, and he thought, at last, he had found the path to true power.

Nagash, the Undying King, had reduced every man to the status of a tool. To W'soran, in that moment when the first of the corpses clogging Mahrak's streets had risen unsteadily to its feet, it had seemed as if the way to true power had, at last, been made clear.

He clutched his amulets and felt the tingle of power in his fingertips. The abn-i-khat whispered to him, and his eyes drifted to the horizon, where the ever-present black blotch of Mourkain's shadow caressed the stars. 'Soon,' he whispered. 'Soon the only shadow cast over these mountains – over this world – will be mine.' That was the point of power. To be the strongest was to be the safest. With all of his enemies broken, with all men made over into tools for his will, he could cease striving. He closed his eyes. He could rest. There would be nothing left to fear.

Would Ushoran thank him, he wondered? He liked to think so. He cherished the image. They would all thank him and fear him, as they always should have done. They feared Nagash, but W'soran would prove a greater horror than the Undying King. 'King,' he whispered. 'Pah, I will be emperor– an emperor of blood and a lord of the dead.'

He felt a stirring in the winds of death, and wondered if Ushoran had heard him. He hoped so. He was not afraid, and he wanted the king of Mourkain, and the darkling spirit that whispered to him, to know it. *I am not afraid. It is you who should fear me,* he thought.

His eyes popped open as Arpad rode up to join them, lashing his mount in his haste. 'The scouts have sighted a column!' he shouted as he yanked on his mount's reins, causing it to rear. 'They think it's Abhorash!'

W'soran hissed. Courage faded, replaced by consternation. 'Impossible. He's off fighting the Draesca,' he snapped. He wasn't ready to face Abhorash yet.

Arpad made a face. 'From the description, if it's not the Red Dragon it's one of his damnable claws, which is almost as bad. Those bastards are tougher than I like,' he said.

Ullo shook his wedge-shaped head. 'How far out are they?'

'A day, maybe two,' Arpad said. He looked at W'soran. 'If we leave the prisoners, we can outpace them.'

'And why would we want to do that, eh?' W'soran asked, not looking at either Strigoi. He thought quickly, weighing, gauging. 'This is perfect. Perfect!' He pounded his saddle with a fist. He looked at Ullo. 'Tarhos is only four days north of here, seeing to the greenskins that threaten our endeavours. Send riders to him. Have him fall back to rejoin us.'

'The orcs will follow him,' Arpad protested. 'He'll lead them right down on us!'

'Exactly,' W'soran said. He leaned back and stroked his

chin. 'We have been presented with an unparalleled opportunity, my friends, and one we would be foolish to ignore.'

'What do you mean?' Ullo asked, looking at him.

'Whether it's Abhorash or merely one of his lickspittles,
their presence implies that the approaching force is no
rag-tag frontier force, but a hardened legion. And it is one
that he would not lightly spare.' He clutched his amulets
tightly. 'And we have the opportunity to destroy it and deal
Mourkain a definite blow.'

'And weaken them in the process,' Ullo said. He nodded
brusquely. 'Yes,' he said. 'We will draw them in, and distract
them, until it's too late – the *urka* will crash into them.' He
displayed his mouthful of fangs in a too-wide grin. 'Even if
they win, they'll be shattered. Excellent, and here I almost
believed Melkhior when he asserted that you lacked a warrior's instinct, W'soran.' He eyed W'soran, obviously gauging
his reaction.

W'soran restrained his first impulse, and then his second.
He settled for a grimace. Melkhior was growing ever more
vocal in his dissatisfaction with his current lot as castellan
of W'soran's citadel, for all that it was a position of high
honour to W'soran's way of thinking. In truth, he did not
enjoy the vagaries of war, though he was self-aware enough
to admit that the customary acts of violence required of all
warriors scratched a certain itch. But war itself was a tedious
affair. One of several reasons he had kept his involvement to
a few reputed raids.

Yet, he was looking forward to this. If it was Abhorash

who was coming, it would be the sweetest of nectars to draw him into a trap and watch it snap shut about his priggish, unbending neck. To watch the champion of Lahmia die, pulled beneath a filthy green sea, would be a joy second to none. He rubbed his hands together in glee, savouring the anticipation. He wasn't ready to meet Abhorash in open battle, but he'd happily watch him die, oh yes.

'Arpad, load up the slaves and take them ahead with your legion. Take my acolytes with you. Dead or alive, I want every slave to reach Crookback Mountain. Ullo and I shall draw Abhorash – or whoever it is – off with the rest and join up with Tarhos. We shall find ground and hold them in battle until the orcs arrive and then, we shall vanish like a morning mist.'

'And what of our warriors? We may not have time to disengage,' Ullo said.

W'soran made a dismissive gesture. 'Our warriors are dead. Once we have drawn the enemy in, there is little need to keep them moving. We can always make more, later. Especially if we return after the battle… I'm sure we will find more replacements than we can effectively use.'

'And what if they are using the dead as well?' Ullo asked.

In answer, W'soran looked at Arpad. 'Well?'

'Living men, veterans of the northern frontier, by the description,' he said. 'They've got some sort of red beast's skin on their standard…'

'It's a manticore,' Ullo said. 'The Red Lions, they're Horda's men. That means it's likely that honour-obsessed bastard

Walak is with them.' His teeth scraped against one another. His eyes, normally as dead as stones, flashed with something that might have been rage.

'Bad blood?' W'soran purred.

Ullo glared at him. 'That's none of your concern, sorcerer.'

'It was just a simple question,' W'soran said, looking away. Ullo had served on the northern frontier, before he'd left Ushoran's service. From what little W'soran knew, that leaving had been helped along by an attempted coup of some kind, with Ullo attempting to lead a revolt against the iron authority of Abhorash and his hand, for reasons as yet unknown to any save Ullo himself. W'soran could respect that sort of ambition, and he could not fault Ullo's courage. If the Strigoi, as a whole, had one saving grace it was their courage. 'What sort of commander is this Horda?'

'He is a fool and a plodding one.'

'And what of Walak?' W'soran asked. He had never concerned himself with either of the brutal Harkoni who followed Abhorash. That Walak and his brother Lutr had been in Lahmia's army, he knew, but that was as far as it went. 'Is he a plod as well?'

Ullo's expression turned dark. 'No,' he hissed. Hatred warred with respect in the Strigoi's eyes. 'He's a devil, just like his master. Worse, maybe... the Dragon holds tight to his honour, even at cost to himself. Walak fights dirty.' He snapped his teeth, biting off the end of the word. There was a story there, W'soran knew. But not one he cared to inquire after.

'Handy to know,' W'soran murmured. He watched the fires that consumed the village for a moment, considering. Then, 'We shall simply have to make sure that we fight dirtier.' He looked at the Strigoi. 'You know what to do, my lords. Time is not on our side. Let us begin.'

Time might not have been on their side, but it was a simple enough matter to make sure the weather was. One of the first incantations that W'soran had learned was a spell to darken the sky and cause the clouds to grow black and angry. Though he was not as sensitive to light as his followers, he saw no reason to endure even that limited discomfort. It didn't require much effort in any event – winter was stalking down from the mountains on bone-white paws. By the time Tarhos had joined them, the sky was the color of a frost-bitten limb and the clouds were heavy with incipient snows.

It had taken six days for Tarhos to reach them. In that time, Arpad had led the slave wagons south-east, towards the safety of Draesca territory, while W'soran and the others went in the opposite direction. If Abhorash had been with the enemy, W'soran would have worried that he might have bullied the other commander into following Arpad, but Walak, true to Ullo's assertions, seemed disinclined towards the mock-heroism that Abhorash was unable to avoid indulging in.

What followed were days of running battle. With deft application of his forces, W'soran caught and held the attentions of the enemy's scouts and outriders. Dead wolves, dragged from icy graves by his craft, lunged through the curtain of falling snow to drag down lone horsemen or to hurl themselves, slavering, their fleshless jaws spread wide, into the packed ranks of marching men. Skeletons squatted beneath snow drifts and rose to the attack amidst their enemy, striking out in all directions. He sacrificed hundreds of the dead to buy mere hours, knowing even as he did it that it would inflame and provoke his pursuers. As Ullo had said, Horda was a beast with a gnaw-bone.

The enemy left a trail of corpses in their wake. W'soran wondered, briefly, at the lack of necromantic magics, and the waste of such wonderful material, but then pushed the thought aside. What business of his was it if his enemies deprived themselves of a useful tool? Abhorash had never approved of sorcery, and it was likely his brood felt the same way.

On the tenth day, they made their stand. The ground was thick with snow, and uneven, broken by rocks, hills and scrub trees. At their back was a vast frozen lake, and the air was redolent with the sounds of grinding, cracking ice and the dull slap of freezing water. W'soran ordered the dead into neat ranks, their backs to the water, ready to meet the enemy's charge. Then, with Ullo and Tarhos, he retreated to a safe distance to wait.

'Tell me about the orcs,' W'soran said, as they waited. He glanced at his acolyte, a Draesca named Merck, who'd been assigned to aid Tarhos. 'Their numbers, their disposition, anything pertinent to this affair, Merck...'

'The Red Eyes are a large tribe, master. They came down

through the Peak Pass and swept most of the smaller tribes west. They're heading south, though not in any great hurry,' Merck said, stroking his ratty beard. His flesh was thick with wrinkles and his eyes were like black pits. Rodent-like fangs left shallow cuts in his thin lips.

W'soran nodded. He'd sent Tarhos to divert the orcs from rampaging into the path of his legions, while he conducted his own raids. He'd assumed they were a local tribe, however, like the Iron Claws.

'They've come farther than I would have thought,' he said. 'I'm surprised Abhorash hasn't… ha.' He blinked. 'Oh, oh you old fool, W'soran. Poor old W'soran, your mind has turned to stone!' He laughed. 'South, you say? From the Peak Pass, you say, yes?' He looked at the Strigoi. Tarhos had a blank look on his face, but Ullo–

'The witch,' he rasped.

'Yes! There might be hope for you yet, Ullo. Neferata! She always was good at handling savages. Somehow, she's diverting them, sending this large tribe directly for us, while funnelling the run-off, the dregs, west into Strigos.' He pounded a fist into his palm. 'Two birds with one stone was always Neferata's preference, greedy girl that she is.' He could see her plan now, as if she'd laid it out for him herself… an orc Waaagh wasn't like a normal army. It was more like run-off from a mountain stream, gathering force and strength as it crashed down. The Red Eyes wouldn't be weakened, if they fought their way across the mountains, into the east. To the contrary, they'd only grow stronger and fiercer.

'Another splinter in my heart, eh?' he muttered. 'Well, let's hope that the Strigoi can put a dent in them for us, eh?'

They caught sight of the first horsemen a few moments later, galloping through the distant trees. Ullo gave a grunt, attracting W'soran's attention. 'They're here.'

'Of course they are. They smell blood. We are cornered prey, and our kind finds it hard to resist that,' W'soran said. He glanced over his shoulder. 'The hill-tribes call this place the Black Water. They swear there are beasts in the water.' He turned back, and looked at Tarhos. 'Where are the orcs?'

'A few hours out, maybe less, if they get a scent of man-flesh,' the big Strigoi said, scratching his cheek with his hook. 'Your sorcery and the weather have kept them hidden, and they've been taking advantage of it, the green-skinned animals.'

'Good,' W'soran said. 'When the time comes, you know what to do?'

The two Strigoi looked sullen. Tarhos nodded, but said, 'I dislike running from a fight.'

'Then by all means stay and battle on,' W'soran said, 'but I intend to run, when the time comes, and this army, once it has done its job, will collapse, so you'll be fighting alone.' He grinned. 'Of course, I'd have thought that that would appeal to brutes like you.'

'Careful, sorcerer,' Ullo said, waving down Tarhos's snarl of anger. 'You still need us just as much as we need you, if only to keep Vorag happy. You recall Vorag, I trust? Your master and ours, for whom we wage these battles,' he continued.

W'soran frowned. 'Was that a threat?'

'Merely a reminder,' Ullo said. He looked towards the trees. 'Tarhos has a point – why should we retreat? Why not crush the orcs as well? With your sorcery, we could have quite the army after a few hours. And end two threats at once.'

'You have fought orcs, Ullo. Do you think we could crush them? Or do you think we would become bogged down, fighting an ever-growing number of greenskin savages?' W'soran flung out a hand, indicating the dark peaks that rose around them like monstrous fangs digging for the throat of the sky. 'There's a reason the dawi simply close their doors and let the savages wash across their moun- tains… they are not an army, but a storm. You do not fight a storm – you wait for it to pass. Neferata might have shattered the great Waaagh centuries ago, but the orcs still cling to these crags like limpets. They are growing in strength, and I want that strength directed away from us and towards Mourkain. Let Ushoran shed the blood of his slaves on orc blades. And even if the Red Eyes continue their pursuit, I would rather face them from a position of strength, than in enemy territory.'

'And what if his necromancers raise an army from them?' Ullo asked shrewdly. 'For Ushoran will defeat them. Of that I have no doubt.'

'And so,' W'soran shrugged. 'We have enslaved tribes of the beasts ourselves, and Vorag sends more westward as he tears a bleeding hole in those mountains. And it will take Ushoran years to do so. Even with our help, it took him cen- turies to do the job the first time. Without us – indeed, with

Neferata actively working at cross-purposes – it will take him much, much longer.'

He leaned towards Ullo. The sound of Strigoi horns was carried towards them on the wind, but he ignored them. 'We are merely buying time, my lords. Every battle we fight, every raid we conduct is to buy us – to buy *Vorag* – a few more days of grace. We will bleed Strigos white and set it stumbling towards doom, and then, at the last, *we will take it!*' His hand snapped out, snatching a tumbling snowflake from the air for emphasis. Tarhos flinched back, as if W'soran's hand were a striking spider. Ullo merely grunted. He looked back towards the trees.

'And what of Neferata?' he asked. Horsemen threaded through the trees, clad in the loose armour and furs of Strigoi horse-archers. There were lancers as well – *vojnuk*, the Strigoi called them. They were heavily armoured, and their armour was all swooping curves and serrated edges, engraved with scenes of battle and slaughter. Their helms, rather than being the simple conical affairs the Strigoi normally wore, were grotesque things, all bat-winged flanges and gargoyle visors. Their lances were not the thin spears of the Arabyan kontoi, but heavy things, more like iron-banded staves. The vojnuk did not pierce the enemy, they crushed them.

The infantry followed; archers mostly, but a few units of spearmen, carrying large, square shields that could be anchored to the ground to create a makeshift barricade. The Strigoi had long since learned the arts of fighting their more disorganised enemies, whether those enemies were orcs or men. W'soran wondered whether this legion had come east looking for orcs, and merely stumbled upon him. It didn't matter; he would destroy them regardless. Even better, the Strigoi would think that the orcs had done it.

'Time and patience,' he murmured, watching the enemy draw up their lines. 'Those are weapons you never learned how to use, Ushoran.' Idly, he played with his amulets. He was tempted to eat one, but there was no need. Not for this. There was no need for a sword when a knife would do.

He looked at Ullo and said, 'As to Neferata, what of her? She is no threat to us. Merely an annoyance – she is a child, attempting to join the games of her elders. No, Ushoran is the true threat, and it is he that we face here, or his proxies, at any rate.' He smiled. 'I'd wager he knew all about the orcs. He was probably hoping to send us fleeing right into them. Instead, we shall slip aside and let our enemies have at each other.' He sat up in his saddle. 'Ah, there they are.'

The enemy commanders were easy enough to spot. Horda rode with the horse-archers, his manticore-pelt banner rattling in the snowy breeze. Like most Strigoi nobles, he wore the bare minimum of armour, and no helm. Instead, he wore the tatty hide of a beastman over his head and shoulders, and golden clasps on his muscular arms and wrists.

Walak was more impressive looking. He was as big as W'soran recalled, and plated in the armour of a vojnuk, save that it had been enamelled crimson. His helm was topped by two flaring wings and his visor was crafted in the shape of a snarling face. A crest of black wolf pelt hung from the top of his helm, and a cloak of the same was wrapped about his armoured bulk. He carried no lance, and instead wielded a heavy blade which was sheathed across his saddle, his hand resting on the hilt. There was a stillness to him that put W'soran in mind of Abhorash, though Walak was smaller and thinner than the champion. He was still bigger than any Strigoi.

Ullo snarled at the sight of him, and his grey flesh seemed to ripple with anger. W'soran peered over at him and smirked. 'Calm yourself, Ullo. I'd hate to lose your counsel to foolishness.'

Ullo snapped his teeth and shook his head, like an animal stung by an insect. 'I am quite calm, sorcerer. I am merely eager for the fight. It has been too long since our last proper one.'

'Aye,' Tarhos rumbled, swiping the air with his hook. Even as he said it, the horns of the enemy split the air. W'soran hunched forward in his saddle. The beginnings of a plan crouched in his mind.

'It'll be Walak,' Ullo said, noting his expression. 'The vojnuk will charge first, to break our lines. It's been long enough since Vorag's exile that they've fought your kind many times since, sorcerer. He'll be looking to take your head.'

The words startled W'soran more than he cared to admit. What if Ullo was correct – what if Walak was looking for *him*? What if Ushoran were searching for him, even as Neferata had been? What if this wasn't just a battle, but a hunting expedition? The thought wasn't a pleasant one. W'soran didn't like to consider what Ushoran might have planned for him, should he fall into his clutches.

He grunted and pushed the thought aside. 'Let him come. There is a reason I chose this ground, Ullo, as you will soon see.'

'I hope so, for your sake, sorcerer, for you will hold the centre, while Tarhos and I take the flanks. If we're simply keeping them occupied, there's no reason to hold our horsemen in reserve, eh?' Ullo grinned and snapped his reins, urging his red-eyed mount forward. The black beast whinnied in annoyance, and pawed the snow with obsidian-hued hooves. The horses the vampires rode had been fed on blood and abn-i-khat, and turned into something else. W'soran wasn't sure there was a ghoulish equivalent for an animal, though he'd heard tell of herds of man-eating horses on the steppes. His own mount was thankfully quite dead, and as such, not prone to making noise.

Ullo was correct, of course. There was little need for reserves in this battle, though the enemy would suspect desperation in the tactic rather than design. W'soran knew little of military stratagems, but he knew enough to understand that a battle unfolded not all at once, however it might appear, but in stages. Move and counter-move, thrust and counter-thrust, back and forth in a dull little dance; it was less a game here, in these grim mountains, than it had been in the Great Land, but the pattern was the same. There were only so many pieces and only so many moves.

Walak drew his great blade and chopped the air with it. All

at once, the ground began to tremble as the armoured lancers began to trot forward, gaining speed. They intended to
crash through his lines, crushing and destroying the forma-
tions. W'soran smiled thinly. They wanted to make a path...
so be it. He was nothing if not accommodating.

Soon the vojnuk were galloping towards his lines, lances
lowered, back-banners streaming. Snow fell around them,
and at any other time, if he were any other man, W'soran
might have felt a stirring at the sight. Instead, contempt
filled him. He had felt the same, watching the chariots of the
Great Land. Thugs and bullies, thinking power came from
their hooves and weapons. But power came from the mind,
from within.

'I will show you power,' he spat.

The vojnuk drew closer. He could feel their approach in his
belly and in his bones. Beside him, Merck cringed, exposing
his teeth in a worried snarl. 'Master...' he began.

'Calm yourself, acolyte,' W'soran said. He could see the
faces of individual vojnuk now. He could see Walak's eyes
widen slightly, behind his visor. He had been recognised.
Good. W'soran grinned. He and Merck were well out of the
line of the charge.

'Master,' Merck yowled. The ice behind them cracked and
burst, vibrated free by the thunderous charge. W'soran gestured and the dead collapsed, like puppets with their strings
cut.

It was a simple enough ploy. He controlled their every
action, and the very stuff that held them together. To drop

them all at once required no more thought than pulling them to their feet.

The vojnuk charge was unimpeded, the expected impact never came, and men and horses rode on, straight into the Black Water. A hundred men and horses rode onto the cracking ice, their momentum carrying them far past the shallows. They realised their plight quickly, and men began yanking on reins, trying to turn their horses about. Animals squealed as hooves slipped and slid on the ice, and men bellowed and screamed. The riders in front were the first to feel the bite of the Black Water, as the weight of the front ranks caused the ice to snap and snarl and gape. Men and horses plunged into the water into shrieking knots, and W'soran chortled.

W'soran gestured again. The dead stood, even those that had been trampled and broken, and they turned as one, shields locked and spears levelled. The charge was broken; it was no longer a thundering engine of destruction, but simply a scrum of desperate men, trying to reach shore as the ice began to give way beneath them. The dead began to march onto the ice, pushing against the horsemen, forcing them back through sheer weight of numbers.

W'soran laughed and clapped, gleeful. 'Oh, see, Merck! See how the mighty become the meek at the merest whisper of my power, eh?' He turned. The battle had begun in earnest. Tarhos and Ullo had engaged Horda's horse-archers and the bulwark of infantry. Tarhos's skeletal riders crashed through the infantry line, heedless of casualties and blind to even the most rudimentary tactics. There was a certain blunt beauty to such an attack, but if their goal had been victory rather than simple distraction, it would have failed.

Ullo had engaged his enemy head-on as well, if with more surgical precision. Like the shark he resembled, the Strigoi had gone for the weak spot, closing swiftly and removing the horse-archers' advantage. Now, amidst the swirling melee, Ullo and Horda traded heavy blows with superhuman energy. The two vampires were evenly matched.

'Raise the dead as they fall, Merck,' W'soran said, as he turned back to his apprentice. 'We must keep our guests occupied, until–'

His words were lost in Merck's scream. The vampire was lifted from his saddle by the sword jutting from his chest, and sent hurtling towards the Black Water like a shrieking comet. Walak, covered in water and frost, his armour battered, growled and urged his mount forward towards W'soran. 'Sorcerer,' Walak roared. 'I shall take your head back to the Captain, and lay it at his feet!'

The vampire had hacked his way through the dead. His horse was on its last legs, bleeding from a hundred wounds, its eyes rolling. Walak himself didn't look much better, but he seemed determined. He swept his blade out, aiming to cleave W'soran's head from his shoulders. W'soran leapt lightly from his saddle, avoiding the blow. He drew his scimitar as he landed and cut the legs out from under his opponent's mount. The animal tumbled with a squeal and Walak with it. But he rolled quickly to his feet and renewed his attack.

They traded blows for a moment. W'soran was impressed by the other vampire's strength. His was still the greater, but Walak was a trained warrior, and deadly. W'soran had learned much of swordplay in his centuries, but Walak had been trained by the greatest warrior to ever tread the world's sands. They spun about, their blades weaving a wall of steel between them.

They broke apart a moment later. On the Black Water, the surviving vojnuk had reached the shore. They battered through the dead with all the fury of men determined to survive. There weren't many left, but enough to cause trouble.

Then, from the north, came the unlovely sound of orc drums and the raucous wailing of their horns. W'soran hissed in pleasure and looked at Walak, who circled him warily. 'Do you hear that?' he asked.

'I hear,' Walak growled. 'It makes no difference, old man. I will take you back to Mourkain, even if I must wade through the blood of every greenskin in these mountains.'

'Just a moment ago, you intended to take my head,' W'soran spat. It seemed his earlier suspicions had been correct. They had come for him. That boded ill. 'What purpose does your Captain – does Abhorash have for an old man, eh? What need has the Great Dragon for a humble priest such as myself?'

'He doesn't,' Walak said. He sprang forward. W'soran caught his blow and heaved him back. Walak slid to a stop several feet away, snow billowing around his legs. Beneath their feet, the snow shifted and W'soran could feel the approach of the orcs. Walak's sword came around, forcing W'soran back a step. 'But Ushoran does...' Walak said.

A moment of fear flared through him. Was it truly Ushoran who required him... or Nagash? And if the one, and not the other, what did it mean? He opened his mouth, ready to attempt to draw the answers from Walak.

'Walak,' a voice roared. Incensed by the interruption, W'soran saw Ullo galloping towards them.

Walak whirled and was knocked sprawling by the base of the standard that smashed into his helm. Ullo rode past, hefting the enemy banner like a spear. The Strigoi howled and shook it. 'Take my legion from me, will you?' he snarled, launching himself from his saddle to bring the standard crashing down on his dazed opponent. 'They were mine! The glory was mine!'

He roared, slapping Walak from his feet hard enough to splinter his makeshift club. With a growl, he hurled aside the shattered standard and leapt upon Walak, his talons sinking into the other vampire's much-abused helm. In his frenzy, he tore the helm from Walak's head and smashed the vampire to the ground. For a moment, W'soran thought Ullo would kill the Harkoni. Then Walak's hand flashed and Ullo reeled, pawing at the heavy Rasetran-style dagger jutting from his chest.

Walak staggered to his feet and retrieved his sword. He was grinning through the mask of blood that obscured his features. 'You're a good fighter, Ullo, but you're a piss-poor general. You always have been. A good fighter, though. I'm almost sorry to take your fangs...' He raised his blade. W'soran hesitated. No one could blame him, if Ullo fell here. It wasn't as if he hadn't contemplated the same...

Tarhos galloped past, hunched over his mount's neck. 'They're here,' he shouted. 'The orcs are here!'

W'soran looked past him and saw that the Strigoi wasn't wrong. The orcs had arrived, in their numberless ranks. Snorting boars, their bristles lank with rime and filth, burst from the scraggly tree-line and made a beeline for the closest of the enemy. Behind them came the rest of the horde, panting with exertion and roaring out a multitude of nonsensical challenges. The trees burst and shattered as the ponderous shape of a giant forced its way through them. The mammoth creature uprooted a heavy rock and hurled it at the distant Strigoi. Men and horses were crushed beneath the rock and the giant gave a thunderous bellow of satisfaction.

Walak cursed and his blade dipped. W'soran made his decision. He lunged. His scimitar crashed down on Walak's pauldron, rocking the warrior. He staggered and W'soran darted past him, hauling Ullo to his feet as he went. Then, half-dragging Ullo, he made for the latter's mount. Flinging the Strigoi across the saddle, he climbed up and dug his heels into the horse's flanks, setting it in pursuit of Tarhos. Walak made no effort to pursue. The first of the boar riders had reached the remaining vojnuk, and battle commenced. W'soran grinned as, behind him, men and orcs died.

Regardless of who triumphed here, the ultimate victory would be his.

It was simply a matter of time.

—◄ CHAPTER ELEVEN ►—

The Black Gulf
(Year -1149 Imperial Calendar)

It was less a fishing village than a pirate enclave. One of a hundred nestled along the coast. Corsairs, smugglers and slavers from Araby, Sartosa and Cathay walked the crude boardwalks that connected the pontoon-balanced lodges. It squatted on the edge of the marshes, where the salt waters of the Black Gulf met the sour, but fresh waters of the marshes. Ushoran had claimed one of the outer lodges, just outside the sea-wall palisade. W'soran did not ask what happened to the previous occupants, and the other inhabitants of the enclave kept their distance. Ushoran had no get and W'soran's surviving followers had made themselves at home.

'I should have expected that you would find sanctuary amongst pirates and thieves,' W'soran said, sipping from the crude goblet. It was the first taste of human blood he'd had in weeks, and he gave a small sigh as a burst of long-absent strength filled him. He

had learned early on that their kind could, if necessary, subsist on the stuff of sorcery, but it was in blood that they found pleasure. Ushoran, sitting nearby, grunted.

'Not for long. The dead move fast, and the kings of the Great Land have woken in their hundreds, to reclaim their ancient demesnes. Numas once claimed these marshes. Ptar and the other kings will soon put this place to the torch. A matter of weeks, I estimate, until the pecking order is sorted out amongst the awakened kings, and the sortie is launched.' He set his own goblet down and ran a finger across his lips, wiping away the blood that clung there. It had belonged to a young woman that Ushoran had purchased from a disreputable Arabyan slaver of his acquaintance that evening and subsequently gutted. 'I, for one, do not intend to be here when they arrive.'

'Sensible,' W'soran muttered, clutching his goblet in both hands. He hesitated, then asked the question that had been bothering him since they'd arrived. 'Why did you save me?'

The bats had done their job well. The dead of Nehekhara had been distracted while W'soran made his escape. With Ushoran as their guide, they had come to the settlement within a few days. The pursuit had broken off after Ushoran's ambush, though W'soran doubted that Ptar was once more safely in his grave. Nehekhara was in upheaval, despite the unloving state of its people. King fought king in the streets of every city and silent legions clashed in the wastes between. Ptar likely couldn't waste the time hunting W'soran any longer, not with eighteen generations of his fellow kings jostling for control of his territories.

Ushoran was silent for a moment. Then, he looked through the flattened strips of marsh-reed that made up the curtain over the entrance to the lodge. It was night outside, and a silvery moon graced the sea with its kiss. He picked up his goblet and took a sip. 'I never let a useful tool go to waste,' Ushoran said.

W'soran grimaced. 'I am no tool of yours, Lord of Masks.'

'Not at the moment, no,' Ushoran said. 'But who can say what the future holds?'

W'soran gave a snort of laughter. He sobered quickly. 'I could have used your aid in Nagashizzar.'

'It wouldn't have made any difference,' Ushoran said dismissively, watching the moon.

'It might have,' W'soran said. He cocked an eye at the other vampire. 'Where were you? The rest of us were sent out, but you…'

'Nagash forgot about me.' Ushoran tapped the side of his head. 'He forgot a lot, towards the end.'

W'soran was suddenly alert. 'You saw how he died?'

'I saw much, in those final days,' Ushoran said, softly. 'He wasn't a god, you know.'

'I'm well aware of Nagash's failings,' W'soran said. Then, suspiciously, 'What did you have to do with it, Ushoran?'

'Nothing, W'soran,' He said and smiled. 'Then, perhaps something.' He sighed and looked away. 'It was Alcadizzar. The ratkin freed him and gave him a blade. They almost didn't find him.' He took another sip of blood and made a face. 'They were quite surprised, at the time. But they are a race used to treachery, and they didn't question.'

W'soran stared. 'You treacherous animal…' he hissed. 'You helped them. You helped them!' He stood and gestured accusingly.

'It was your fault – all of it was your fault!' A flush of rage filled him – not for Nagash's sake, or even for what had been lost, but for himself. He'd seen no hint of treachery in the other vampire, and it annoyed him to be made a fool of.

Ushoran leaned back in his seat. 'Yes. It was.'

'Why?' W'soran demanded, looming over the seemingly unconcerned Ushoran.

'Why?' Ushoran asked. He set his goblet aside and stood slowly. 'He killed us, W'soran. He killed our people – every man, woman and child. He killed every animal and every oasis. He killed our history and our future. He killed the Great Land for spite, and for spite's sake, I helped his killers in turn.'

W'soran stepped back, frowning. 'Don't tell me you felt something for them. You were happy enough to bleed the living when we ruled…'

'It was ours, W'soran,' Ushoran said, and there was heat to his words, now. 'The Great Land was ours. It belonged to us. We lifted it from the muck and made it a land to be feared once again!'

'And then you let it slip through your fingers,' W'soran said. 'Was this about revenge, then? Dead is dead. What matters the how of it, or who made the killing stroke?'

Ushoran smiled and shook his head. 'You don't understand, do you?' The smile faded. 'We could have made an empire to rival Settra's, and instead we allowed it all to fall to dust. And Nagash… Nagash was a monster. He would have seen the end of everything. Does that prospect truly appeal to you, W'soran? Is a slow march to oblivion what you truly want? Or do you desire something else?' His eyes narrowed. 'Why did you serve Nagash,

W'soran? Men only serve when they are too afraid to rule.'

W'soran hesitated. 'You served Neferata,' he said. 'And Nagash!'

'Yes. I was afraid. But I have seen the grinning skull beneath the skin of the world now, and fear is no longer in me. But you – you stink of it, W'soran. You always have, you know. Fear and need. Just like me.' Ushoran laid a hand on his scrawny shoulder. 'What do you fear, W'soran?'

W'soran brushed his hand aside. 'I fear nothing.' It was a lie, and he could tell Ushoran knew that it was a lie. The other vampire smiled slightly.

'Then why do you keep running?' Ushoran asked. He emptied his goblet. 'I am going north. You are free to accompany me, or seek your own fortune.'

'What do you intend to do in the north?' W'soran asked, looking down into his goblet, and the dregs that remained there. 'There's nothing out there but mountains and savages.'

'I told you – fear has been burned out of me. There are kingdoms over the mountains, crude brawling child-kingdoms, where a strong man… a smart man, might rule. Where dust might be stirred, and glory once again awakened.' Ushoran exposed his fangs.

'I will go north and build an empire.'

Crookback Mountain
(Year -280 Imperial Calendar)

'Has there been any word from Vorag?' W'soran asked, climbing down from his saddle. Brackish blood coated his limbs and robes and he could still taste the throat of the last orc he'd killed, though it had been several days ago. Mindless corpse-servants waited nearby, clutching heavy buckets full of cistern water. As he walked towards them, W'soran stripped off his armour and tossed it to his acolytes, who followed him like a bevy of baby chicks.

The stable was a recent innovation, built to house the substantial force of skeletal cavalry that the citadel now contained. None of the scents and sounds a living man would associate with stables were evident, for all the beasts in it were dead, and were, if not quietly rotting, then simply quiet. Their riders, clad in verdigris-coated mail, slumped against the stalls, waiting for the moment they would be commanded to mount and once more ride to war.

'Not for some months,' Melkhior said, passing a gore-encrusted pauldron to another acolyte with a grimace of distaste. He had been waiting in the stables for W'soran to arrive, fresh from the destruction of the final remnants of the Red Eye Waaagh. It had taken five years, but the deed was done, and, to W'soran's way of thinking, done well indeed. 'Then, is that any surprise?'

'No. In point of fact, it means everything is going according to plan,' W'soran said. He snapped his fingers, and the zombies with the buckets upended them over him, sluicing off the majority of the blood and offal that covered him. While hygiene was not one of his main concerns, there was a point where even his fossilised sensibilities were offended.

Across the stable, several Strigoi were receiving the same

treatment. In the years since the Battle of Black Water, more dissatisfied vampiric noblemen had crossed the high peaks, looking to join the Bloodytooth in forming a new and better empire. Not many, true, but enough to provide W'soran with a coterie of experienced commanders whose thirst for battle was only rivalled by their annoying tendency to vocally, not to mention loudly, wonder when Vorag was coming back to lead them in glorious final battle with the forces of the usurper, Ushoran.

Thus far, W'soran had only had to kill two of the newcomers. At a remove, of course, but he had overseen their destruction as surely as if he had pierced their hearts himself. If he had learned one thing from his time in Mourkain, it was that troublemakers should be removed immediately before they could upset the spice cart. Ushoran was paying for his leniency in that regard even now.

'And what plan would that be, my master?' Melkhior asked, watching as W'soran wrung out his sopping robes. 'The plan where you conquer the east, using Vorag as your weapon, or the plan where you conquer Mourkain, while Vorag is busy elsewhere?' He made a face. 'Or, perhaps is it some plan which you have yet to deign to share with me, your most loyal acolyte?'

'Speaking of troublemakers,' W'soran muttered.

Melkhior blinked and asked, 'Master?'

W'soran gestured airily. 'Nothing, my son. The plan is as it has always been. We proceed apace and on schedule. Our citadel stands, despite greenskins and treachery, our armies grow steadily, and our enemies grow weaker.' He glanced at Melkhior. 'Speaking of our enemies – how is our guest?'

'Which one do you mean,' Melkhior snorted, 'the rat or the witch?'

'Both, either,' W'soran said with a shrug.

'The same,' Melkhior said. 'The rat almost died a few months ago. It tried to swallow its tongue. I stopped it. It's been... restrained, for the moment.'

'And the woman?' W'soran asked.

'Little change there,' Melkhior said. 'She is still unconscious, though her wounds have healed. She is no longer as lovely as she once was, however.' He seemed pleased by that. Given his own degraded appearance, W'soran could understand, though he was slightly disappointed in Melkhior's vanity.

They left the stables, W'soran leading the way. They ascended the curving steps that coiled about the innards of the mountain like the interior of a conch shell. Undead sentries tromped past, their glowing eye sockets scanning the rock walls for any signs of infiltration. As they ascended, the acolytes were joined by W'soran's scribes – dwarfish, crooked, broken things, made from the remains of goblins, skaven and men, wrapped in sackcloth and cowled, carrying heavy rolls of papyri on which they scratched out W'soran's words for posterity.

He had conceived the idea early in his bid for empire. A true history of Mourkain, its master and the events surrounding its rise, fall and return beneath his iron rule, from his unbiased perspective, with the musings and philosophical quandaries which had brought him to his path. It would be a true *liber necris* – a book of the dead, for the dead. He would not countenance the lies of Neferata or Abhorash to taint his new world. He would not let their deranged philosophies infect future generations.

Not that there would be future generations, as such, but nonetheless, only W'soran's words would be remembered. His heroism in Mahrak and Lahmia, at the Battle of the Hot Gates and in the struggle for Nagashizzar would be remembered, as would his great discoveries in the arts of sorcery and the natural sciences. He would write a new, glorious history, even as he trampled the old into the dust. Poor W'soran – never respected, never feared; but no longer. He would no longer be poor W'soran, a tattered carrion crow flapping in the wake of others. He would be the new Undying King, for a silent, perfect world. And he would cast the old king down soon enough.

'What of Ullo? Has he reported in from the Black Water?' W'soran asked as he clasped his hands behind his back. 'And Arpad as well – he should have completed his pacification of the settlements along the Blind River.'

'Both have sent riders. And Tarhos has joined up with the Draesca. He claims that the entirety of the Vaults will fly our banner within a few more months,' Melkhior said sourly.

W'soran heard the sour note and smiled thinly. 'You doubt our brave captain?'

'Tarhos is barely better than the savages he's leading,'

Melkhior said. 'Even when he was alive, he was reckoned one of the stupidest ajals in the empire. Being undead has not noticeably improved his cunning.'

'Harsh words,' W'soran murmured. 'Still, as long as he keeps those tribes that still bear allegiance to Mourkain and Ushoran on the back foot, he serves a useful purpose. Too, the slaves he'll send us will fill our mines nicely.'

'We are still playing for time, then?' Melkhior asked.

W'soran ascended a few more steps before replying. He gazed up at the eternally-burning, yet never-consumed skeletons that cast a weird light across the vast stairs. They were held in great cages chained to the dips and nooks of the stone walls and wreathed in a sorcerous fire that never went out. He and his kind did not truly require the light, but it was somehow... comforting. A visible, simple reminder to himself of the power he wielded. He admired his handiwork a moment before replying. 'Yes,' he said. 'Strigos totters, but it is not yet ready to fall.'

'And in the interim, Ushoran grows stronger,' Melkhior said harshly. 'That daemon-crown he wears grows stronger.'

'Ah, I see you have finally resumed your studies,' W'soran said, looking down at his acolyte. 'And what have you learned, hmmm? What gleanings have you gathered from my knowledge, eh?'

Melkhior glanced at the other acolytes, and then at the crouching scribes before replying. 'I know that while Strigos may falter, our true enemy only grows more powerful. Do you fear him... master?'

W'soran blinked. Then he smiled. 'What are you implying, my son?'

'Why are we playing a waiting game?' Melkhior flung out a hand. 'We have the strongest army in these mountains. We are the greatest sorcerers and the Strigoi will flock to us, even with Vorag's absence! Even the Lahmians would join us, if we made tacit reparations. We could close the trap and finish this charade!'

'Could we? Or would we merely hasten our own defeat, eh? The Lahmians – and the Strigoi too, don't doubt it – would turn on us the moment Ushoran was toppled from his damnable throne,' W'soran said, descending towards Melkhior. 'Yes, Ushoran grows stronger and more sure of his new power, but so too do we.' He spread his arms. 'Let him rise, unbridled and roaring like Nagash reborn, then, and only then we will meet him in a clash of death, in dead lands, from which only one will emerge the victor. They will all see then, Melkhior. They will see our might, *and know fear.*' He made a fist and exposed his fangs in triumphal sneer. 'Only then, will our foes know our power, and bow to us.'

'You... you *want* him to tap into the full power of that damnable crown?' Melkhior asked.

'Of course,' W'soran said. 'If this is war – if I am to be emperor – I must prove myself to be the strongest, the fittest to rule. By my brain, my strength and my sorcery, I will be declared the master of death, and none will gainsay me. I will defeat Ushoran, and impose my will on the others in the doing of it. I am owed that much, for my services and struggles, wouldn't you say?'

'You're mad,' Melkhior hissed, forgetting himself in his shock.

W'soran let the comment pass. 'No. I am *efficient*. In Mahrak, we had a saying... take the tail, you only anger the serpent. But take its head... ah.' He held up a finger and twitched it with pedantic precision. 'The thing that drives Ushoran crouches just past the skin of the world, pressing its talons against it – it is nothing but will without mind, intent without intelligence. It is not Nagash, but simply the last shreds of the power that grew in him. I intend to let that power in, then finish it for good. Otherwise... what is the purpose of immortality, eh? What is the purpose of an eternity of fearing such a thing? No! Let Ushoran drape himself in Nagash's might. I will kill him. I will break his black soul on the charnel rack of the Corpse Geometries and smash down the sour light of that foul crown for all time. I will take every secret, every forgotten thought from Nagash's creation and make it mine – *as they always should have been*! I was his student! I was his heir – not that fool, Arkhan, and certainly not Ushoran! And I will not have that which is mine to claim taken from me by an inferior mind,' W'soran rasped and chopped the air with a stiffened hand. Abruptly, he calmed and straightened, lowering his hands, and said, more quietly, 'I am owed this.'

He looked down at them. His other acolytes cowered behind Melkhior, who looked fairly uncertain himself. The scribes continued to write, unheeding. 'Do you know what it is like to see the face of divinity and have it ripped aside to expose the flawed, weak thing within? They say – or said, rather – that that is what happened to Nagash. That he saw that the gods of the Great Land were not truly gods, but simply... powers. And that he could rival them in their power, and in knowing that, he thought them weak and pathetic.' He shuddered slightly. 'Nagash was no more a god than those ancient powers. He was not infallible, or omnipotent. He was a stupid, crippled thing, addicted to these stones,' he continued, gesturing to his amulets of abn-i-khat, 'and addicted to his spite. And he is dead and that of him which remains is nothing but a nightmare that I will disperse to claim my due.'

They were strong words, words for posterity and words of power. They were lies. He knew that they were lies, even as he spoke them. An errant memory bubbled to the surface, even as he spoke: a memory of Ushoran, sitting across from him, asking him what he feared.

He had not answered then. He did not truly know the answer, nor, in truth, did he truly understand the question. There was much to fear in the world. As his power grew, so too did the fear. The fears of the mighty were far greater than the fears of the weak. He felt contempt for Nagash, but he also feared him still, though he was long gone from the world. He feared the one being that he could not fight – could not even confront, as he had confronted others.

That fear gave Nagash power over him still, even now.

Perhaps that was the real reason he stalled and dithered and waited. The thought struck him like a bolt from the blue, a moment of realisation that made him more tired than any battle or contest he had yet faced.

'Enough. A good student should ask questions, Melkhior, *and* answer them. How go the mining operations in the depths?' he asked, changing the subject.

Melkhior coughed and straightened his robes. 'Satisfactory, we have thousands of slaves – both dead and alive – down in the pits, mining the ores we require. If – when – Vorag returns, he'll have a treasury greater than any yet seen by the kings of these mountains. Iron ore as well, and quarried stone for the fortifications we will build.'

'Excellent. I think your services as an overseer far outweigh your abilities as a sorcerer, Melkhior,' W'soran said mildly. He began ascending the stairs once more. 'With what's left of the Red Eye tribe added to the slave pens, our production capabilities will increase dramatically. Not to mention our raw materials…' He smiled gleefully. 'Oh, the things I will make.'

'And what of the weapons you promised Vorag so long ago, master? When will you create them?' Melkhior asked, shushing another acolyte.

W'soran didn't pause. 'Oh, I never intended to do that,' he said, gesturing airily. 'No, we'll strip those engines of their secrets, but we have no need of such crude ballistae. We can craft more reliable war engines from the materials at hand. I simply wanted to study them, and distract Vorag from his obsessions.'

'As opposed to yours, you mean,' Melkhior snapped.

W'soran laughed. 'Oh, you are in a rare mood aren't you, my son. Accusing me of cowardice, and then of being obsessed...' He glanced over his shoulder. 'One would think you're feeling left out of the war-mongering.'

'I should be at your side!' Melkhior said. 'Not here, in this stone kennel. Let Urdek or one of these others keep your books and catalogue the mine proceeds. Let me loose, master, and I will lead your legions into the heart of Mourkain.' Several of the other acolytes murmured assent. They were as eager to be rid of Melkhior as he was to be rid of them.

'Would that I could trust you to do so, my son,' W'soran said, mock-gently. 'But your way of waging war is too savage for my plans. You would attempt to gut the beast, before properly bleeding it. You have no patience.'

Melkhior opened his mouth, as if to protest. Then, with a grunt, he fell silent. W'soran nodded in satisfaction. 'Maybe there is hope for you yet,' he said. 'Now, tell me – our envoys to the ogre tribes and the dawi of the eastern wastes... have they returned yet?'

'The dawi have agreed to provide us with arms and armour, in return for slaves,' Melkhior said. The dawi – or *dawi zharr*, as they called themselves – were an odd lot, quite unlike the stern rulers of the mountain deeps. It had been a lucky accident when his legions had stumbled across them. They were vile creatures, with a penchant for casual cruelty that W'soran could almost admire. But they made wonderful arms and armour; things far better than the crude armour crafted by his dead smiths. The armouries of Mourkain were full of wargear manufactured in the workshops of the Silver Pinnacle previous to Neferata's usurpation of the mountain hold from its previous owners. W'soran intended to match that with dwarf-forged weaponry of his own.

'Excellent,' he said. 'We'll send out the first caravan this month. And the ogres?' he added.

'I believe they ate our envoy,' Melkhior said.

'How many does that make?'

'Sixteen,' Melkhior said.

W'soran grunted. The ogres rarely travelled far west enough to trouble the tribes of the mountains, but when they did, nothing but death and destruction followed in their wake. They were fearsome beasts, and all the more so if they were under his banner. 'Send another,' he said.

Melkhior nodded. 'Should we send riders in pursuit of Vorag?'

W'soran hesitated. Then, 'No.' He did not elaborate. Let Melkhior draw his own conclusions. They continued their ascent until they reached the uppermost levels of the mountain. W'soran forced Melkhior to run through everything that had occurred in his absence; even the smallest of matters did not escape his notice.

By the time they reached his laboratories, W'soran's keen mind was scheming anew. Plans always sprouted more plans. Neferata wasn't the only one who could spin webs within webs. When he entered his chambers, the smell of Arabyan incense and spoiled meat coiled about him. He closed his eyes and inhaled, tasting the sour scent of the dark magics that stained the stones after almost a century of experimentation.

When he opened his eyes, his gaze was drawn immediately to the cage hanging from the ceiling, where Iskar crouched, watching him with his new, glittering eyes. W'soran had plucked the skaven's ruined orbs from their sockets and replaced them with new ones, cultivated and grown in a febrile tumour of flesh kept alive by a serum crafted from powdered abn-i-khat and vampire blood. Iskar's eyes looked like faceted emeralds, and they cast a sickly glow on anything the ratkin looked at. It hissed silently, baring its rotted fangs around the strange leather and iron muzzle that simultaneously pinioned its jaws and trapped its tongue. Drool dripped from its maw and dried foam coated the corners of its mouth.

Despite this, the skaven looked stronger than it had in a decade. No longer was it a withered thing, but instead muscled and sleek. W'soran leaned close to the cage and made satisfied noises. He looked at Melkhior. 'I see the improvement in its diet has had gratifying results,' he said.

'I still don't understand why it's still alive. What use is it now – especially if you're not intending to use those weapons?' Melkhior asked. He stepped aside quickly as a severed hand, a coiled, sharpened spinal column grafted to its wrist stump, skittered past like a fleshy scorpion.

'Knowledge is sometimes its own reward, and I am loath to dispense with a potentially useful tool,' W'soran said. 'At the moment, I'm merely curious as to how long this beast will live. I'd wager it's already survived well past its allotted span.' He sniffed and turned.

Half-dead, half-living things hung from the great chains that draped the open spaces of the cavern like a massive web of iron. He had begun experiments in grafting living flesh to dead, to see what effect the one had on the other. A thing that had the heads of an orc and a skaven on its mal-formed shoulders squealed and thrashed as he drew close to it and traced the suture marks that marked where green flesh had joined hairy. 'Wonderful,' he chuckled, 'so persis-tent.' He looked at Melkhior. 'I do so miss this place, when on campaign.'

'Then perhaps it is time for you to leave the dirty business of war to me, my lord,' Melkhior said. 'I am ready to serve you, in any capacity you desire, and I would be happy to lead our legions to war.'

'Are you deaf, or simply forgetful?' W'soran asked. 'My decision is final, no matter how much you whine.' He stretched out a hand and whistled. Slack-jawed human heads bobbed obscenely through the air of the laboratory at his call, fluttering on bat wings that had been grafted to their skulls. A cephalopod-like mass of spinal columns and squirming intestines, protected by sheaths of crusty blood and bile, flopped towards W'soran like a dog welcoming its master home. He clucked welcomingly and bent to stroke the quivering, bulbous face that briefly surfaced from the writhing morass, its tongue lashing across his fingers. He moved on, and it squirmed into the shadows after giving Melkhior a wet growl.

Rank upon rank of heavy sarcophagi, plundered from Nagashizzar by Vorag in earlier years, lined the walls of the cavern, and W'soran's servants inspected, measured and tested the dead things within. Ancient experiments he'd long thought lost, now returned to him again – old kings of the long-extinct Yaghur now mummified and wrapped in sorcer- ous linens. W'soran paused to examine them and nodded as one of his cowled scribes croaked a reply to a brief question. He patted the squatting creature affectionately and turned to a heavy half-sphere, constructed from thick shards of amber set into a bronze frame that occupied a space nearby.

Over it hung the limp, bloodless corpses of a dozen orcs, the bodies hung head-down, so that their foul fluids might plop into the sphere. More of the crooked scribe-things scuttled about the place, stirring its steaming contents and striking the bodies above with long poles in order to free the last drips of blood.

'And is this a matter of curiosity as well?' Melkhior grunted.

W'soran sank to his haunches and peered through the thick amber. A dull form floated within, barely discernible in the opaque stew of blood. Layla of Lahmia yet lived, albeit after a vastly diminished fashion. 'In part... more, I wish to know at what point our kind finally give out. Removing the head or the heart will drop even a being of my age and potency, but if they could be reattached or healed somehow... would these old bones still live?'

He gestured to himself. 'We are not true immortals, Melkhior. We are merely more persistent than the run of the mill beast. Even the resurrected dead are not immortal. They suffer cessation, if not true death. I believe we do the same. Both Neferata and I were pinned through the heart, and left for dead, and we both walk now among the living. Abhorash, I'm told, was devoured by a great beast in the Southlands during his exile, and yet even now bestrides the earth like an infuriating colossus. And Ushoran was set on fire and eaten by jackals. I wish to know why our flesh resists the corruption of death. Rather, say, I wish to know why it does it in some cases and not others…'

He placed a hand against the glass. 'I wish to know the secrets of life and death. I wish to know where the dividing line is, and how it might be erased entirely. There is a saying, in Araby… *what is not dead can eternal lie and over strange eons, even death may die*. It is as true as it is trite.' W'soran stood. 'Nagash is both dead and yet not. Something of him, of his black will, persists, like a flea in the fold of a jackal's skin. True immortality…'

'Is it?' Melkhior asked. 'It seems like no kind of immortality to me.'

'You place too much importance on the body, my son. That has ever been your main failing,' W'soran chided. He strode towards the cages where a number of orcs crouched snarling, fresh from the mountains. They were survivors from the Red Eye tribe, given the pernicious pink tint that afflicted their piggy orbs. W'soran strode close to the cages and the orcs howled and lunged at the bars, grasping at him wildly. 'These husks are like anchors, holding our minds in bondage. Nagash was a fool – clutching at the physical, when he should have concentrated on the spiritual. The raw stuff of magic flows in us, pumping our blood and allowing us to wield it as a weapon, or to embrace it to transform, moulding our shapes as we see fit. Not without good reason do the Cathayans call our kind *Yiangshi*, or "corpse-ghost".' He held up his hand, as if to examine it in the light of the braziers that lined the cavern. 'We are ghosts possessing our own bodies. In time, I will know the secret that Nagash stumbled upon, like a cave-dweller learning of fire.'

'That's why you want Ushoran to unlock the secrets of the crown,' Melkhior said, quietly. 'That is the debt you wish to collect.'

W'soran looked at his apprentice. 'Among others, yes.'

Melkhior shook his head. 'Plans within plans,' he muttered.

W'soran snorted. 'Where you see complexity, I see subtlety. Birds and stones, boy – the only lesson Neferata ever took from me was that of the subtle plan. Plans are like layers of armour, insulating you from failure. You would do well to remember that,' he said pointedly.

Melkhior frowned. 'I have taken your every lesson to heart, my master.'

'A beautifully parsed sentence, my boy,' W'soran said. 'I have long feared that the art of rhetoric and grammar died with the Great Land.'

'You are a good teacher,' Melkhior said.

W'soran smiled. 'Another beautiful sentence. Now, I dislike having these Strigoi hanging about, getting up to mischief. We'll need to organise a new campaign for them. Something that takes them far enough away to not trouble me with their incessant complaining, but close enough that – eh?' He stiffened. 'I smell something.'

Melkhior tensed, and his hand flew to the hilt of the sword on his hip. The other acolytes reacted more slowly, but reacted all the same, clutching at their knives or scrolls. It had been years since the last skaven incursion, but there were more tunnels than even W'soran's diligent vermin-hunters had been able to ferret out.

W'soran turned in place, head cocked. The only sounds he heard were the bubbling of the alembics and the screeching of his captives. But he smelled something out of place. As he looked about, the great web of chains suddenly rattled. W'soran spun around, raising a hand.

A dark shape launched itself from the chains. A blade flashed. W'soran staggered back as the flesh of his palm parted and he howled. He slammed back against the cage of orcs and they grabbed at him, pinioning him. Tusks sank into his flesh and bellicose roars deafened him. The dark shape seemed to skate towards him, blade angling for his heart.

Then Melkhior was there, deflecting the blow. He shoved the would-be assassin back. The dark shape crashed among the acolytes, who scattered. It bounded to its feet, revealing itself to be a man – no, a vampire – clad in dark leathers. A scalp-lock whipped about his head as he slashed the air with his sword and drew a heavy dagger from his belt.

'Assassin,' Melkhior snarled.

'Really, how observant of you,' W'soran shrieked, ripping his arms free of the orcs. 'How impressive that you were able to deduce that,' he continued with a hiss. Another hiss, 'It's almost as if you have eyes and can use them. Imagine that!' He whirled about and barked a sibilant incantation. The orcs writhed as if lashed by invisible whips and shied back from the bars, cowed.

He jerked back just in time. A second assassin dropped from the top of the cage, his sword burying itself in the stone. It snapped off, and the vampire tossed it aside with a curse as he leapt for W'soran, his fingertips extruding claws.

W'soran backhanded the assassin, shattering his neck and spine with a single blow and sending the body hurtling across the laboratory. 'You dare,' he roared. 'You dare attack me *here?*'

'Master, look out,' Melkhior bellowed, flinging himself against W'soran even as a third killer materialised from the shadows, wielding a short, stabbing spear. The blade, edged with silver, hissed as it pierced Melkhior's side and he screamed in agony. He chopped down on the spear, shattering it as he fell. W'soran shoved him aside and spat another incantation.

A knot of blackness formed on the assassin's chest. The vampire stepped back, confused. The knot billowed and blossomed into something else; tendrils of purest darkness exploded from it, ensnaring the hapless assassin. He had time for one, single scream, before he was drawn into the small obsidian knothole in a cacophony of snapping bones and tearing flesh.

W'soran rose to his feet with impossible grace and turned to search for the last assassin. The vampire was gone. W'soran's lips writhed back from his fangs and he turned, stooped, and plucked Melkhior from the floor like a man snatching up a hare. 'How did they get in here?' he roared, clutching Melkhior by the throat. 'Where were my guards? This is *my* citadel, Melkhior! *Mine!* How did they get in here? Fool. Fool!' Melkhior could only respond with a weak gurgle. 'You worthless ape, you spawn of flea-bitten jackal,' W'soran howled.

With a frustrated shriek W'soran tossed his acolyte aside. He turned, fixing his acolytes with a burning, one-eyed glare. 'Find him. Find any others who might be with him. Scour this mountain peak to root and *find him!* I want to know who has dared to invade my sanctum! Find him, find him, *find him,*' he howled as the mountain echoed with his fury.

—◄ CHAPTER TWELVE ►—

The City of Lashiek
(Year -1147 Imperial Calendar)

*The soldiers of the Dowager Concubine burst through the door
of the villa, even as they had burst through the gates outside
only minutes before. The battering ram they used fell heavily to
the floor as they reached for their weapons. The zombies lurched
towards them, groaning. W'soran scooped up the tomes he'd been
scribbling in and pressed them to his chest as he whirled about
and slapped the life from an extraordinarily quick – and extraordinarily unlucky – soldier in the same motion.*

'Kill them,' he snapped. 'Kill them all!'

*More zombies lurched past him, their jaws champing mindlessly
as they fell upon the invaders. W'soran looked down at the thing
on the table – a patchwork cadaver, built from the most perfect of
parts, excised from the freshest corpses – and hissed in frustration.
Another experiment, ruined.*

He was alone in his dwelling, having sent Zoar and his other remaining acolytes out to prepare his new lair for his arrival. Araby was no place for him, not any longer. Not with Arkhan the Black storming the walls of every city within reach. The last thing he wanted was to become bogged down in a conflict with his old foe, especially when there were more important matters to be attended to. There was a ship in the harbour waiting for him, and he had intended to crew it with the dead he now hurled into battle with the invaders.

The servants of the Dowager Concubine had been hunting for him for weeks. The crippled old witch had sought his aid in resurrecting her dying son, in order to maintain her stranglehold on the city. He had done so, and taught her the limited arts she needed to keep the zombie of her firstborn relatively inoffensive-looking. With a puppet corpse-caliph on the throne, she could rule safely. He had thought that would have earned him a few weeks grace at the least, but the wily old crone had turned on him the moment she no longer needed him. He had planned for betrayal, but he was astounded that she had discovered his lair in an abandoned villa in the heart of the port city so quickly.

'Stand and face justice, butcher,' the warrior leading the soldiers bellowed. Something in his voice tugged at W'soran's attentions and he peered at him. He saw a flash of red through the slits in the chainmail mask that covered his face. He did not wear the armour of a common soldier, or even one of the esteemed Royal Harem Guards of Lashiek, but was clad instead in the war panoply of one of the kontoi of Bel Aliad. Ragged silk strips flared from the spiral point that topped his helm as he spun about, cleaving the heads from a trio of zombies with one fluid blow.

Then he was upon W'soran, who jerked to the side as the war-rior's blade hammered down onto the edge of the table, splintering it. His attacker wrenched the blade free and it spun in his hands as he lunged for W'soran again. With a snarl, W'soran grabbed the swordsman's wrists and they stood for a moment, muscle locked against muscle. That close, W'soran could smell the stink of sour blood and death that marked the kontoi as one of his kind, if an unfamiliar one.

'What are you?' W'soran growled. 'Who are you?'

The kontoi hissed, 'Neferata sends her regards, butcher.' As W'soran's good eye widened, the kontoi kicked him in the belly, flinging him back. He crashed through a bevy of zombies, but regained his feet quickly, avoiding a blow from the kontoi's blade. W'soran sank his talons into the wood of the floor and ripped a number of boards free. Gripping one, he caught his opponent's next blow. The heavy blade sank into the wood and W'soran twisted the sword from his enemy's grip. The kontoi did not hesi-tate; with a roar, he flung himself at W'soran, smashing him in the face with an armoured forearm.

'Get off me,' W'soran spat, catching the next blow on his palm and closing his fingers about the warrior's fist. With a heave of his shoulder he jerked the vampire into the air and swung him about, smashing him into the wall of his domicile and through it, ruptur-ing the mud-brick easily. The kontoi crashed against the wall of the building opposite and tumbled into the alleyway.

W'soran turned. More soldiers thrust forward, jabbing at him with spears. He hissed and took the obvious path. In a single *bound, robes flaring, he leapt the hole and struck the opposite building, clinging to the brick like one of the colourful tree-dwelling frogs of the Southlands. He turned about and craned his neck, giving the horrified soldiers a parting hiss.*

Then, quickly, he scuttled for the edge of the roof. He could recreate his experiments elsewhere, under more convivial circumstances. However, even as he cleared the edge of the roof, he heard the scrape of armour on brick. He turned to see the kontoi hauling himself up, eyes flashing with rage.

'Do you really think you stand a chance against me, dog?' W'soran cackled, raising his hand. 'And weaponless and alone at that?'

'What made you think he was alone, old monster?'

W'soran whirled. Neferata crouched on the roof behind him, surrounded by her handmaidens. She extended the blade she held and smiled cruelly. 'The Dowager Concubine has asked – monarch to monarch – that I remove you from her demesnes, W'soran. Being as you are still my subject, I could not, in good conscience, refuse her.'

'I am no subject of yours,' W'soran hissed. 'Why do you persecute me?'

*'Why,' Neferata said, her smile sliding from her marble features. 'Why? Is the span of your memory so fragile a thing that it cannot bear the weight of what you have done, old monster?' She slashed the air with her blade. 'You **killed** our land! You destroyed everything, alongside Nagash! It is your fault Lahmia fell, it is your fault the Great Land is now nothing more than a sandy tomb, and I shall extract that blood-debt from your wrinkled hide.'*

W'soran stood. Rage washed over him. How dare she blame him? How dare she put her failures at his feet? With a snarl, he said, 'Then by all means… come and try your hand, oh queen of nothing!'

Crookback Mountain
(Year -279 Imperial Calendar)

The assassin managed to avoid W'soran's search parties for six months. For half a year, the vampire hid in the depths or scaled the peak, avoiding hunters of every shape and description – from Strigoi to wights to the giant bats that lived in the vast caverns far below the mountain. In the end, it was the smallest thing that caused him to meet his end – a common slave.

Unlike W'soran's brood, the assassin required regular nourishment. And in the mountain, the only nourishment to be had for one of their kind was the slave pens. Mostly, the slaves couldn't tell one predator from another. Indeed, it wasn't his identity that proved the assassin's undoing, but simply that he was a vampire, in the wrong place at the wrong time.

The Red Eye orcs had been growing restive for months. As more and more guards were diverted to the hunt, the orcs, ever-surly and unfailingly aggressive, took advantage. Revolt in the pens was not unheard of. But it was usually squashed quickly and effectively. But on that day, at that moment, there simply weren't enough dead men to contain the living. The orcs seized their moment well – as another troop of skeletal guards marched out of the cavern, bound for a search of the southern crags, leaving less than a hundred in place to guard three times that of greenskins.

Crude tools, intended for mining, smashed down on bone, battering the unfeeling sentries from their feet. The overseer, an acolyte named Hruga, sounded the alarm before launching himself into the fray. And the assassin, in the pens to assuage his thirst, was caught up in the green tide as the orcs, seeing only another vampire, attacked him as readily as they attacked everything else.

Such were W'soran's conclusions after the fact. When he arrived, the pens were in complete disarray. Orcs battled the dead throughout the large cavern. He saw a half-dozen orcs bring down an armoured skeleton, dragging the dead warrior from his feet. The revolt was disorganised, chaotic. It had no centre – it was merely a tantrum of beasts, flinging themselves at their tormentors en masse. The orcs required no lightning rod to incite them to violence, only to organise them. In time, if they won free, a new warlord might arise to lead the Red Eyes to battle.

'Kill as many of them as it takes to herd the rest back into their pens,' W'soran growled, flinging the edge of his cloak back. 'We stop this here, *now*. Go!' Melkhior and the other acolytes moved quickly. They knew the danger that faced them as well as W'soran did. There were close to ten thousand orc slaves in the bowels of the mountain. Even a third of that number could threaten their control of the hard-won citadel.

A howling orc burst past the acolytes, swinging a mattock. It was a big brute, covered in scars and blue tattoos. W'soran drew his scimitar and bisected the beast in one smooth motion. His acolytes hesitated. W'soran gestured with the bloody blade. 'What are you waiting for? Kill them!'

The battle that followed was no sort of battle at all. A dozen sorcerers unleashed the most devastating spells and incantations that they knew within a confined space. Orcs were incinerated, torn apart, shrunken to screaming mummies, or otherwise massacred in minutes. And through it all, W'soran stalked, killing the rebels with gestures and the edge of his blade.

In a way, it was a relief. For six months, frustration had piled upon frustration for him. The body of the assassin he had slain in the initial attack had revealed nothing. The killers were Strigoi, but again, that meant nothing. There were Strigoi scattered to the four cardinal directions, serving four different masters, including himself. Ushoran's empire had splintered and fragmented like a stool bearing too much weight, just as W'soran had planned. There were no clues to those who had sent them, no subtle signs or indications of their loyalties. They could have even been freebooters – lone vampires looking to take territory for themselves.

But until he knew for certain, he could not plan his next action. *Give me facts, I must have facts,* he thought, beheading an orc with a casual blow. What if they had been sent by

Vorag? What if the Bloodytooth had at last discovered that W'soran was responsible for the death of his woman? Then again, it might have been Neferata – an easy assumption to make, given her recent treacheries. But what had she hoped to gain? Even Neferata was not so arrogant to assume that a bevy of hired blades would be put to him.

But Ushoran might be. Yes, the Lord of Masks had ever assumed that his cunning was greater than that of his enemies. But to send assassins – unless, had they been assassins, or kidnappers? More possibilities crashed through his brain, even as he disembowelled a bellowing orc. Could his own allies have decided to dispense with him? Ullo might consider it, perhaps, or Arpad, certainly… perhaps even one of his own. Suspicion burned in his mind as he caught sight of Melkhior striding through the cavern, flinging death from his hands. Had he finally decided to serve his poor master as he had so many of his fellow acolytes?

As focused on these questions as he was, W'soran almost missed the assassin. The vampire, like all of the others, was engaged in fighting the orcs, but upon sighting W'soran, he moved to complete his mission. W'soran saw it out of the corner of his good eye – saw the assassin, recognised him easily as close as he was thanks to the smell of spoiled blood and bear-fat that seemed to cling to him, and recognised the blade in his hand as it drove for his brainpan. Even W'soran was not quick enough to block or dodge that blade.

Then, with a roar, an orc crashed into the assassin. The blade skidded off W'soran's shoulder and cheek, drawing blood, and he screamed and spun about. The assassin was on the ground, the orc's hands on his throat. W'soran, never one to bother with gratitude, beheaded the latter with a contemptuous slash and grabbed the assassin by his bottom jaw, hoisting him into the air.

'Well, well, well,' he hissed. The assassin grabbed for him, and W'soran drove his scimitar into the other vampire's gut, slowly, a bit at a time. 'Six months I've wasted on you, my friend,' he said, as the cross-guard of the hilt struck the assassin's belly. 'Six months of effort and questions.'

Then, with a flick, he withdrew the blade and sent the wounded vampire to the ground. The Strigoi tried to push himself to his feet, but W'soran planted a foot between his shoulder blades and shoved him back down. 'No, don't get up. I insist.' He looked around. The revolt had been put down, and sufficiently bloodily. Once his acolytes had entered the fray, it had only taken a matter of minutes to put things in order. Heaps of smouldering green carcasses covered the floor of the cavern. Only one of his acolytes had faltered, and been dispatched by the maddened orcs, or so Melkhior said. Hruga, as it turned out, which was just as well, as W'soran had intended to punish him severely.

'He wasn't paying attention,' Melkhior said, meeting W'soran's calculating gaze. Idly, he touched the ruptured flesh that marked the spot where Hruga's head had once rested. 'The orc tore it off.'

'I see that,' W'soran said, leaving the assassin to his servants. 'Orcs are strong, but it is odd to find one quite that strong.'

'They are a varied species. I incinerated it, better safe than sorry,' Melkhior said, rising to his feet. W'soran smiled.

'Yes,' he said, 'Better safe than sorry. He was the closest to you in ability amongst the current crop, was he not, poor Hruga? Ah well, no matter.' He glanced at the wounded assassin, who was now held aloft on the points of several spears kept by his servants. The vampire's blood ran down the spears to patter across the floor in thick, ropy streams and W'soran reached out a palm to catch some of it. It tasted of grave-mould and rot, and he grimaced.

'He is a Strigoi,' Melkhior said, looking at the assassin. 'Ushoran sent him, obviously. As I have said,' he said.

'As you never cease saying,' W'soran corrected. 'For six long months, you have said it, and I have said – what was it – ah, better safe than sorry,' he continued, flinging Melkhior's words back at him. 'Yes, that was it. I want to be sure who my enemies are before I begin flailing at shadows, my son. Is there perhaps some other reason you are so eager to convince me of Ushoran's guilt, eh? Is it a desire to press Strigos, perhaps?' He glared at his acolyte for a moment before turning about and gesturing for his servants to carry the weakly struggling assassin away.

W'soran favoured the fuming Melkhior with a final glance. He motioned to the cavern and the bodies that littered it. 'Clean up this sty, my son. That is your duty, after all.'

In the days that followed, W'soran questioned his would-be killer with the same single-minded intensity he had used in the hunt. To make an assumption, he knew, could prove fatal. He was surrounded by enemies both real and potential, and to divert his attention from one to the other wrongly was to court disaster.

For years, he had realised that he was fast approaching the knife-edge of things. The sharp end drew close, bringing with it the culmination of plans and schemes decades in the weaving. Since the fall of the first border-fort, he had spread his shadow further and farther across the mountains. His agents moved through the settlements and fortified villages of Strigos, spending gold freely, buying loyalty or indifference as the situation warranted. Fools like Melkhior thought war was a thing of armies and engagements, when W'soran knew, from experience, that it was more about the ground and time you chose, than the forces you brought. Battles could be won or lost for a matter of space or moments.

'I will not fight until I am ready,' he murmured. The assassin had been nailed to an examination table. Heavy iron spikes had been driven through his wrists and ankles and silver chains draped his neck and chest. The touch of that metal on his bare flesh filled the air with a scent reminiscent of burning pork and W'soran sniffed in satisfaction. The assassin was awake, though in tremendous pain. W'soran gestured to the chains, careful not to touch them.

'Silver,' he said. 'I have been aware for many years of its more unfortunate properties in regards to our kind. Oh, we do not require it to kill or maim one another, but it does give one a certain edge, I'm sure you'll agree.' He waited for a response. When none appeared to be forthcoming, he sniffed again and snapped his fingers. Several of his crooked scribes lurched forward, bearing his tools and instruments. Carefully, W'soran selected a delicate blade, covered in curving sigils. 'This belonged to a creature of my limited acquaintance who was as foul a torturer as has ever trod the jewelled sands of this world, despite her ageless beauty.' He smiled, lost for a moment in a pleasant memory. 'I have her head somewhere.'

He chuckled and deftly sliced open the assassin's leg, ignoring the vampire's scream of agony. 'But I learned quite a few things from her before our sudden, but inevitable, falling out. From her, I learned of certain men in the South-lands, who can draw the secrets from an enemy simply by devouring them.' He sliced the assassin's tendon and stripped it free of its cage of meat. 'It's a similar belief to that of the sadly now-extinct Yaghur of the Eastern Marshes, who ritualised the… consumption of human flesh in order to gain the strength of enemies and placate the souls of the slain. Barbarity at its worst, I'm sure you'd agree, but not without its… points of interest, shall we say?'

W'soran held up the tendon and examined it in the torch-light. 'It was an interesting theory – the consumption of a thing to reveal its secrets. Blood is a potent sorcerous tool, of course, but flesh… in flesh there is a strange sort of magic, I have found. I have never tried it at length of course, being no savage. But, needs must when the devils drive, eh?' Then, he dropped the quivering shred of muscle into his gaping jaws. Chewing, he watched as the assassin thrashed and snarled.

Swallowing, he said, 'Nothing yet. Well, we have plenty of time.' He raised the blade, and bent to extract another piece.

Days flowed into weeks. Every day W'soran ate a bit more of his would-be killer, working his way up from soles to crown. As his teeth tore the tough flesh, as his tools flayed the thrashing body, he sucked out every secret contained in the Strigoi's mind, all save one. One secret, and one alone, the Strigoi took into oblivion with him – the name of whoever had sent him and his fellows to murder W'soran. W'soran was forced to admit that his prisoner might not have known it.

The Strigoi had screamed many names, true, in his torment, but none bore the ring of authenticity. The names of Strigoi nobles and Lahmian courtesans, of village headmen and kings; hundreds of enemies, rather than simply one, and for a brief moment W'soran contemplated conspiracy. It had been a conspiracy that had driven him from Mahrak, and a conspiracy that had ruined him in Mourkain, so why not another?

But things were different now. A conspiracy required order and necessity to function – only one of those things was evident in the incident. All that remained were furtive facts. Someone required his death, and they had acted on it. They would try again, that much he was certain of. But who had made the move? Whose game was this?

Webs were spun within webs, overlapping and interconnected. A complex arrangement of action and reaction, a murderous geometry that caused an ache in his skull – even as it raised more questions. How had the assassins bypassed his defences? How long had they been in his citadel? The last had seemed far too familiar with the hidden places of the mountain to be a new visitant.

W'soran sprawled on his chair – *his throne*, part of him whispered, for where else would he make his throne room but his laboratory? – and stared unseeing at the ruins of the assassin. He stroked his bloody chin, trying to puzzle out the problem. But for every strand he teased out, two more became knotted. It was Neferata's way to attack openly if only to drive in the subtle blade, thus, the orcs to distract him and the assassins to kill him. But why use Strigoi, when her handmaidens were more effective killers, unless she intended to throw suspicion elsewhere?

But, she would know. She would know that W'soran would suspect such, and thus would not bother. So, the assassins were sent by someone else. Ushoran, then, but Ushoran was not fool enough to attack so haphazardly. No, Ushoran wouldn't have sent two assassins, or even twelve. He'd have sent hundreds. Unless he knew that W'soran would suspect Neferata, and was trying to pit his enemies into open battle against one another.

W'soran hissed and dug his claws into his scalp, as if to extract all of his suspicions and toss them aside. He had to know. If he did not know – if he made a move, and it was wrong, the game was lost. When Ullo arrived a week later, W'soran realised that, intentional or not, he had been distracted and that the game had continued without him.

The blunt-headed Strigoi burst into his laboratory, trailed by acolytes and crooked servants, stalking forward in the face of Melkhior's shouted protests. W'soran had ordered that he not be disturbed, and for once, Melkhior had obeyed him unquestioningly. Ullo brushed him aside in a casual display of strength and tossed something onto the ground at W'soran's feet.

W'soran's good eye narrowed as he peered at the thing. He recognised it easily enough – it was Tarhos's hook, badly cracked, scorched and stained. Given its condition, he doubted that there was much left of its owner. '*That* does not bode well,' he murmured. His gaze flickered up to Ullo. 'What happened?'

'Abhorash happened,' Ullo snarled. 'While you've been busy chasing shadows, Ushoran has launched a full scale assault on our borders. Every pass and every valley we hold is under siege, sorcerer!'

'I knew it,' Melkhior crowed. 'I knew it. It was a distraction – no, a prelude!' He pounded the air with his fists. 'It was Ushoran, master. He has declared open war on us – on Vorag!'

'Has he? I wonder…' W'soran stroked his chin and looked down at the hook. Gingerly, he bent and retrieved it, letting it dangle from one long finger. 'It stinks of magic. One of his false Mortuary Cult members did for the brute, I assume?'

'Not just any member. Arpad said it was Morath himself,' Ullo growled.

W'soran stiffened. 'Well… well, well, *well*. And where is Arpad now?'

'Attempting to save our little empire, sorcerer,' Ullo snapped, crossing his arms. 'Just as I was – I only returned to bring word and to see if I could dislodge your rump from this musty hole. We must act and soon, or everything we've won these past few years will be gone.'

'And we can't have that, can we,' W'soran grunted as he pushed himself to his feet. 'Fine then, to war once more, I suppose.'

'Not just war. It is time, master,' Melkhior said. He turned and began barking orders at the other acolytes. 'It is time to teach our enemies what fear truly is. Urdek, Gavok, ready our forces! Today, the sons of W'soran march to Mourkain and throw the pretender from his throne. Spiro, send word to the east, and recall Vorag – let him know what is happening and that he must return! Malang, send riders to our envoys to bring their forces home–'

'Stop,' W'soran said, raising his hand. The acolytes froze, like mice sighted by a hawk. All save Melkhior, who turned, a look of confusion on his grotesque features.

'Master, what is it?'

'I need only two. Urdek, Malang, you will come with me. The rest of you will stay here and oversee the citadel. Melkhior, as ever, is castellan.' He stepped away from his throne and caressed Melkhior's cheek. 'You are more useful here, my son. Guard well my tomes and house, and I will reward you upon my return.'

'I can serve you better in the field. Urdek and Malang lack my power,' Melkhior protested. 'They are nothing – weaklings!'

'You are more powerful. But you lack their skill,' W'soran said. 'You are as much a brute as Tarhos was. You smash when you should slice, and roar when you should retreat. Thus, you will stay here, where your power will more than make up for their absence.' It was a bald lie. Melkhior had skill aplenty, but what he lacked was subtlety.

His apprentice had been pushing for war for months; longer even, when W'soran stopped to consider it. Once again, he ruminated ruefully on his choice of his servants. Melkhior lacked the temperament for sorcery. He was powerful, true, and a sponge for the stuff of magic. When he honestly reflected on the matter, W'soran suspected that the former nobleman was almost his equal in that regard. But he could not be trusted. Not on the battlefield.

Melkhior opened his mouth to respond and W'soran grabbed his jaw in a painful grip. 'I'd advise you to make your next words ones of gratitude, my son,' he murmured.

'What of Vorag?' Ullo asked.

'What about him?' W'soran asked, not breaking eye contact with Melkhior. 'This is why he left us here, if you'll recall. I'd hate for him to think that he could not trust us.' He released Melkhior and his apprentice stumbled back into his fellows. 'Where are your fellows, Ullo? Those who are not heroically engaged in the defence of our mighty empire? Have they flown the coop, looking for safer pastures, or are they with us still?'

'Unless you've stuck a knife in their guts, they're still here,' Ullo said.

'Wonderful. Let us go give them a rousing speech, yes? Get
them ready for the war they claim to desire, eh?' He bustled
past his acolytes, leading Ullo out of the laboratory. 'Come,
Ullo, come!'

W'soran had lost track of those Strigoi still in the mountain. He left such details up to Melkhior these days. Most,
easily bored by what amounted to garrison duty, made up
missions for themselves, and led savage raids on what could
loosely be termed 'enemy territory'. The rest, not really interested in conquest or glory so much as in not being under
Ushoran's thumb, lounged about the mountain, getting on
his nerves or making idiotic demands of his acolytes when
they weren't engaging in barbaric duels or slipshod intrigue.

Those ones in particular would make excellent shock
troops, he thought. When he broached the suggestion as
they left the laboratory and descended to the section of the
mountain that the Strigoi had made their own, Ullo agreed.
They found the bulk of them easily enough. One of the
larger caverns had been converted into a crude facsimile
of the great arena of Mourkain, where captured beasts and
prisoners of war fought for the amusement of the populace.
It had been easy enough – the Strigoi weren't alone in their
love of blood sports, for the skaven had had their own fighting pits, and this cavern had once rung with the squeals of
excited skaven as they watched rat ogres tear apart slaves or
captured trolls.

It rang now with the bellows of bloodthirsty Strigoi,
who crouched on the wide, brazier-lined walkway ringing

the open pit, watching and wagering on the vicious battle below. One of their own bounded through small hills of offal and decomposing corpses to meet a charging monster. It resembled a wolf, albeit a wolf that had been inflated and stretched over too-long bones and the wrong kind, at that. Matted hair, stiff with blood, sprouted from it, and hunks of raw, pink flesh hung from its frame like some form of grotesque decoration. There was something of the ape in it, and something almost daemonic as well, and the cavern seemed to quake with its howls as it charged to meet the Strigoi. The vampire ducked beneath a wild swipe and slithered around the brute, finding purchase on its back. Fangs flashed, and the wolf-thing screamed chillingly as it reared and clawed for its attacker.

'Another northern freak,' Ullo muttered as he led W'soran up onto the viewing platform. 'More of them drift south every season. I wonder where they found that one.'

W'soran could tell that the wolf-thing stank of dark magic, even from such a distance. A foulness akin to that which clung to the abn-i-khat amulets still dangling from his neck seemed to seep from the beast's pores. With a roar, it ripped the Strigoi from its back and sent the vampire tumbling across the pit. After shaking itself, it loped forward with an awkward gait, like something not quite sure whether it should be running on two legs or four.

'There're whole packs of these things north of the mountains. Every time the witch-moon rises, they boil out of the wastes like locusts. Damn things refuse to die, even if you rip them apart,' one of the nearby Strigoi said. He was a handsome creature, as such things were judged, with a well-tended scalp lock and cunning features. 'Took three of us just to knock that one out and drag it back here for a bit of entertainment. We've been throwing it slaves, but that got dull.'

W'soran grunted, still watching the battle below. 'Which one are you?'

'Tarka of Tzimtzi, at your service, great one,' the Strigoi said as he made a courtly bow. 'Newly arrived from the demesnes of Mourkain.'

'Courtier,' Ullo spat. 'Thin-blooded fop.'

'Ah, Ullo, the others mentioned you were here as well – it's like no time has passed at all since I last saw you. How did your little military coup go? Not well, I'm guessing.' Tarka grinned mockingly, and Ullo hunched towards him. W'soran interposed an arm.

'No better than your attempt to poison Ushoran,' Ullo said, stepping back and dropping his hand to his sword pommel. 'I heard he drained the doxy and returned her to you after the fact, with his compliments.'

W'soran watched the byplay, amused. The Court of Mourkain was a snake-pit in more ways than one. Ushoran had used the blood-kiss as a reward for service and had turned hundreds of nobles in his reign, and they in turn had done the same. Assassination had quickly become the pre-ferred method of social and political advancement among the undying aristocracy. Immortality made inheritance a tricky prospect, even among a people for whom duelling was a common solution to a variety of problems.

'Well, aren't we a pretty party of traitors, then,' Tarka said. 'Unless Vorag sets his primitive fundament on the throne, then, of course we're heroes.' His dark eyes found W'soran. 'And where is Vorag, by the by? I've been here three years without seeing either hide or hair of the Bloodytooth.'

'I'd consider that three years well spent,' W'soran said. 'But the time has come to earn your keep – aye, you and the rest of these fools.' He gestured to the other Strigoi, who were now watching them, as opposed to the fight below.

'Oh?' Tarka asked. 'And just how will we be doing that? And, who are you to suggest it? You are no more master here than I am,' he continued, smiling slightly. The other Strigoi drew closer. Down below, the vampire fighting the wolf-thing had regained his perch on the creature's back and his hands fastened on its jaws, prying them open. With a heave of mighty shoulders, the Strigoi snapped the brute's neck.

W'soran cocked his head. 'I? I am the ruler of the citadel. I am your host, and I'd say you owe me a debt of hospitality, if not loyalty.'

'A debt of hospitality, you say?' Tarka asked, turning slightly to include the other Strigoi. 'Ruler of this citadel, you say? I came here to serve the Bloodytooth, not some withered old bat! I know you, W'soran. They say you fled from Mourkain with your tail between your legs, looking for sanctuary in Vorag's coterie.'

W'soran laughed softly. Ullo had stepped back, his gaze

calculating. The Strigoi had become complacent in their sanctuary. That was partly his fault, he knew. He was used to the unquestioning obedience of the dead, and had not considered that the Strigoi might, in their own, unsubtle way, have plans of their own. Those who desired battle were out defending his empire already; all that was left here were those who desired to be on the winning side, but did not necessarily desire to contribute to that victory.

Thin-blooded fops, cowards and conspirators, these were to be his generals. W'soran exposed his fangs, wondering if, in some odd way, this had been Ushoran's plan all along. Ushoran had, in one of his thousand disguises, fomented rebellions and conspiracies aplenty in Lahmia, and then crushed them. Perhaps this was something similar – a centuries-long purging of untrustworthy elements, now that their use had ended. That alone proved Ushoran as the most deadly of those who pitted themselves against him. Neferata would butcher hundreds in a moment of spite, but she was incapable of the pragmatic bleeding that Mourkain had required. But Ushoran thought like W'soran. He saw his followers for what they were – tools. Tools to be discarded or re-forged as circumstances dictated.

He dismissed the thought a moment later. Even if it were true, there was no help for it now. One worked with what one had. He met Tarka's gaze and inclined his head. 'As you say, but Vorag left this citadel in my command. And I have built it into the centre of a growing empire, an empire of which you are subjects, an empire I am calling upon you to defend.'

'Under your command,' another Strigoi barked.

'Who better?' W'soran asked.

'Anyone,' Tarka said bluntly. 'You are no warrior – you are barely a castellan. We see more of your bat-faced servant than we do of you, W'soran. You hide in your stinking lair, or scuttle about on the fringes, clinging to Ullo's skirts. You are no Strigoi.' Tarka spat, and a gobbet of bloody spittle struck the hem of W'soran's robes. 'You are barely a man. Even that witch, Neferata, is more of a warrior than you.'

'Then why did you not go to Silver Pinnacle to serve her?' W'soran asked. He smiled thinly. 'I'll tell you why – she wouldn't have you. Neferata has no use for creatures like you. But I do.'

'Maybe we have none for you,' Tarka said. His smile was wolfish. The other Strigoi were watching intently. The one from the arena had joined them, covered in the wolf-thing's foul-smelling blood. Belatedly, W'soran noticed the necklace of fangs dangling from Tarka's neck, and a flutter of amusement passed through him.

He had been expecting this, or something like it, for some time. Vorag's authority had grown distant and thin, and not every Strigoi possessed Ullo's remarkable strain of competent self-interest. Vampires had short memories when it came to authority. Unless it was obvious and undeniable, they inevitably attempted to wriggle out from under it.

'Oh, I'm sure you could find some use for my poor self.

Old W'soran knows a few tricks,' he said. He glanced at the crowd of Strigoi. There were more than a dozen of them. He didn't need all of them, certainly not Tarka. 'For instance...'

Tarka lunged, as quickly as a shadow. W'soran completed his surreptitious gesture regardless, and caught the Strigoi's throat with his free hand. The Strigoi's eyes widened as he realised just how strong the withered vampire was. In the arena pit, the mounds and heaps of dead flesh began to quiver. W'soran turned and Tarka's feet scraped the palisade helplessly as he found himself dangling over the edge of the pit, W'soran's claws hooked into the meat of his throat.

Below him, the dead had risen. They circled beneath the helpless Tarka like jackals on the hunt. He thrashed in W'soran's grip, but couldn't break it. W'soran ignored his flailing and focused on the other Strigoi. 'Yes, I know a few tricks. And those tricks are all that keep you safe in these lands. Our enemies circle us, like the dead below circle this fool, waiting to rip him lip to loin. You think to challenge me for leadership? I welcome your challenges. If one of you would prefer to take the burden of leadership from my poor, tired shoulders, let him step forward. If one of you has tricks comparable to mine, if one of you can wring loyalty from the great majority of the charnel field, by all means, *step forward.*' He shook Tarka for emphasis. With his good eye, W'soran glared at the muttering Strigoi. 'Well? Who's it going to be, my fine, brave lords of Mourkain, hmm? Who steps forward, eh? Just Tarka, then – perhaps he speaks for you all, eh?' His gaze slowly slid to the red features of Tarka, who hammered at W'soran's forearm with no more effect than a feather beating against an iron bar.

'Did you think me weak, Tarka? Did you think to add poor, old W'soran's fangs to your collection? *Is that what you thought?*' he snarled, shaking the Strigoi. 'In my youth, I was something of a teacher – a humble tutor to aristocrats and the puling whelps of kings. You are certainly older, but definitely no wiser than those scheming brats, so I will teach you as I taught them. Lesson the first… I am to you as you are to those rotting carcasses below. I am the first and in me is the strength of ages. I have killed nations and drained the lifeblood of empires, while you are nothing more than fleas in the hide of history. Lesson the second… never forget lesson the first, or I shall dispense with you as easily… as… *this*.' So saying, W'soran crushed Tarka's throat, rendering it a gory, gaping ruin. Gagging and choking, the Strigoi slid from his grip and crashed to the arena floor.

The dead, as one, peered up at their master. W'soran gestured, as a man might to his faithful hounds, and they fell upon the wounded Strigoi. Tarka fought as best he could with broken bones and gaping throat, but when the wolf-thing fell upon him, its horrid corpse sparking with unnatural vitality, the fight ended abruptly as Tarka was scattered across the arena.

W'soran retracted his bloody arm and examined it. 'Today's lesson is ended. We march at dusk, my lords. See that you are ready, or we shall have another lesson.'

─< CHAPTER THIRTEEN >─

The City of Magritta
(Year -1017 Imperial Calendar)

W'soran lashed out with his blade, decapitating the guard and sending his body spinning aside. 'Onward,' he shrieked, gesturing for his acolytes and the dead legions that followed them to advance after him as he stormed up the great marble steps of the Temple of Myrmidia.

The very stones of the city of Magritta howled in agony as his undead legions stormed through the streets and washed the sun-baked bricks with blood. On his right, Zoar tore the head from another temple-guard and lashed the ranks of panicking city militia with sorcerous fire. The Yaghur howled with laughter as he killed men by the dozens.

W'soran raced up the stairs, brushing aside the guards in their archaic bronze armour and robes. He had spent the past three decades killing many such men – in Araby, Tilea and now Estalia,

where he was known as Nourgul the Wamphyro. The gods of
Nehekhara might be dead and dust, but there were newer gods
with newer wisdoms, and W'soran wanted them. He had spent the
years since his expulsion from Lashiek hunting secrets. Nagash,
he knew, had learned some of his wisdom from the druchii. They
had bargained dark secrets for sanctuary, for all the good it had
done them, in the end.

He had run across several members of that race in his hunt.
None had been particularly forthcoming, but he had gotten what
he needed regardless. As he would claim what he desired this time,
even if every follower of this paltry hill-goddess thought to stand
in his path. He had defeated the silent stranglers of the Black
Oasis in Araby, and slaughtered the corsair-witches of the Sarto-
sian reefs to claim the secrets they guarded, and he would do the
same to these so-called Myrmidons. It was said that the Temple
of Myrmidia housed one of the greatest libraries in the known
world. It was a storehouse of knowledge, and W'soran intended
to plunder it.

A warrior met him as he ascended the last stair, leaping heroically to the attack, his wide-bladed spear sliding across the surface
of his shield in a screech of metal-on-metal. W'soran caught the
head of the spear and flung it to the side, even as his blade crashed
into the guard's shield. The man staggered back, off balance, and
W'soran lashed out with a kick. Metal buckled and the warrior
was flung backwards. He slumped against the doors and let his
dented and crumpled shield roll free of his grip. With a groan, he
drew the short, leaf-shaped blade sheathed at his hip and staggered to his feet, sword in one hand and spear in the other.

W'soran gave him no time to recover. He lunged beneath the spear thrust and batted aside the short sword, and sank his fangs into the man's thick neck. With a twist of his head, he ripped out the guard's throat and sprang over the body as it fell. The doors had been blown off their hinges by an earlier sorcerous blast, and he easily stepped inside.

The central forecourt of the temple was massive. Vast marble columns rose upwards, holding up the great domed roof. A giant statue of the goddess herself stood sentinel in the centre of the fore-court, leaning on a shield and clutching a heavy spear, an eagle on her shoulder, its wings fully spread. Her eyes seemed to glare down at W'soran and he grinned.

A phalanx of at least fifty Myrmidons awaited him, shields raised and spears lowered. They were clad in bronze cuirasses and greaves, and wore full-face rounded helms topped by flaring horse-hair crests. As one, they stepped forward in tight formation, as if to drive him back through the doors.

'Oh no, I'm not leaving without what I came for,' W'soran hissed, acknowledging their intent. 'I didn't raise every pox-ridden corpse between here and the northern coast just to get chased off by a bunch of bully-boys.' He gestured, pulling tight the strands of dark magic that swirled about him like an infernal halo. The spirits of the dead, some from the marshy barrows he'd discovered near Magritta and some newly wrenched from their cooling bod-ies, billowed through the open doors and washed over him, roiling and splashing silently towards the Myrmidons.

The Myrmidons met the rushing wall of ghosts with silent stoi-cism, even as many of their number fell and died and joined the *spectral throng. They pressed forward, ignoring the dead, and men from the rear rows moved to fill the gaps in the front ranks. By the time they reached him, barely a third remained, but impossibly, they did not stop.*

W'soran gaped, nonplussed, but then swept his sword out and spat a flurry of incantations. Black lightning jolted from his eyes, punching holes in the phalanx, and sorcerous fire engulfed men. The ghosts tore at the rest, but still, they came on. The first spears reached him a moment later, driving at him with cruel inexorability. Desperate now, he slashed out, chopping through them. Shields struck him, pushing him back. He was stronger than any man, any dozen men, but nonetheless, they forced him back towards the doors, even as he cursed and railed.

Zoar came to his aid, followed by those of his acolytes who were at the forefront of the battle. The vampires hit the phalanx like a thunderbolt, tearing through it and giving W'soran the room he needed to use his full strength. Soon enough, it dissolved into red ruin, as men died where they stood, trying to prevent the vampires from entering their temple.

W'soran stepped over the bodies, gore dripping from his armour and skin. 'Shut those doors. I want no interruptions,' he barked, gesturing behind him without turning. He met the goddess's marble gaze and laughed softly. 'It's mine,' he said.

'Perhaps – then again, perhaps not,' a deep voice murmured.

W'soran hissed and turned. Abhorash, clad in bronze mail and a cuirass emblazoned with the face of the goddess, stepped from around the statue, holding a heavy spear. Behind him came his Hand, the four vampires spreading out around their leader. Each was arrayed in a similar fashion, though they carried swords rather than spears.

'What are you doing here?' W'soran sputtered.

Abhorash didn't reply immediately. Instead, he looked up at the statue of the goddess. An expression, wistful and sad, crossed his hawk-like features. Then, he smiled slightly and looked back at W'soran. 'Repaying a debt,' he said, simply. Then, he tossed the spear up, caught it easily and sent it hurtling, point-first, towards W'soran's heart.

The Worlds Edge Mountains
(Year -265 Imperial Calendar)

Strigoi arrows bit into W'soran's lines as they marched towards the enemy where they crouched in among the thick scrub trees. The broad heads of the arrows crunched through bone, dropping his dead soldiers where they marched across the frost-covered open ground. Spines and skulls burst at the point of impact, or were simply obliterated by the heavy catapults that lined the ridge above the trees. A large rock crashed down nearby, burying a group of skeletons, and he flinched slightly in his saddle. His will pulsed and a troop of mounted corpses, clad in heavy, dwarf-forged mail, thundered towards the war-engines. Normal riders and normal horses would not have been able to make it up the slope, but for dead men it was no more difficult than open ground.

His forces had crossed the mountain passes that divided

the edges of the Strigoi Empire from the territory nominally controlled by Vorag a fortnight before, and this was the first time he'd been able to bring the barbarians to battle. They'd set their scouts and flankers to draw his forces into the bowl-shaped valley amongst the smaller peaks of the mountains on the eastern border of Strigos and he'd obliged them, despite gleaning their intent. They'd set a trap for a jackal and caught a mountain cat. He did not know where they were exactly – he left such pedestrian matters to Ullo and the others – but he knew they were close to Mourkain. He could practically follow the buzzards.

His grand strategy was playing out to perfection. Patience and cunning had won out over bloodlust. He had bided his time, stalling and reining in his more over-eager followers, waiting until his enemy's attentions were overwhelmed by the myriad threats besetting him. Ushoran was surrounded by snapping jackals – Neferata, renegades in his own court, the wildling tribes and the orcs – and he was unable to prevent the approach of the mountain cat that would tear out his heart. Strigos was a dying beast, stumbling towards its final stand, and W'soran would deliver the killing blow. Smiling, he looked out over his army, the tool by which he would extract Ushoran's heart.

As ever, there were no living men in his forces – only easily biddable bones and dead meat filled his ranks. Skeletons clad in armour or scraps, mounted on equally bony steeds or on foot, marched or galloped at his direction. War machines crafted from fossilised timber and the bones of great beasts flung heavy stones; swarms of scuttling half-things, part spider, part skaven, part scorpion and goblin, crafted in his laboratory and animated by his malice, swarmed towards the enemy. The bones of great giants, clad in patchwork mail and bearing armoured howdahs across their shoulders holding ranks of skeletal archers. Massive mockeries of Nehekharan ushabti, created from boiled and congealed flesh and the bones of ogres and orcs, loped forward, wielding crudely forged khopeshes and monstrous bows. Overhead, the corpses of ancient carrion birds of immense size cut through the darkly overcast sky alongside fluttering clouds of bats, and the gigantic cousins of the latter swooped low over the Strigoi lines, plucking men into the air to drain them of blood or simply tear them to pieces. All these things and more trudged, marched, stomped and slithered through the melting snows and dust of the field, at his command, and the commands of his acolytes.

'Their left flank is crumbling,' Arpad howled gleefully, suddenly riding past him, a train of mounted skeletal horse archers following in his wake as he made his way to where the fighting was the thickest. 'Ullo has that preening fop Gashnag on the run, sorcerer! The day is ours!'

W'soran waved a hand to indicate that he'd heard. He had expected as much, but his attentions were on the right, where several of his acolytes duelled with those of Morath. There, the battle was going worse. His students were masters of the death-winds, each worth a handful of Morath's disciples, but they were outnumbered here. If W'soran seemed to never have enough students to hand to accomplish what he desired, Morath seemed to suffer from a surplus. For every one of W'soran's, Morath had three. Then, the Strigoi needed many necromancers to do what a single one of W'soran's minions could accomplish with a wave of a claw.

The two groups of necromancers were at a standstill, and the dead caught between them, frozen in the midst of the fray. The Strigoi had dragged their own dead to their feet to meet W'soran's corpse brigades, and both groups of dead men trembled where they stood, pinned by the opposing magics. Controlling the dead was all a matter of will, and bending them to yours. It required discipline, focus and patience as well as raw force. W'soran's followers had the latter in excess, but the former were alien concepts to many of them. They had been barbarians when he'd given them the gift of immortality, and they were savages still.

But strength alone could make the difference in struggles like the one playing out before his eye. Discipline frayed, patience fractured, and focus crumbled before overwhelming strength. As he watched, one of his students, a former shaman of one of the Vault tribes called Niscos, extended a hand, as if pushing against a great weight. A zombie jerked and staggered, taking a step towards one of the Strigoi, who made a complicated gesture. The zombie twitched and bent around, reaching towards Niscos.

Niscos bared his fangs and clenched his hand into a fist. The zombie whipped back around, body rupturing with the force of the motion. Bones cracked and shattered and its skin bubbled and tore as it lurched towards the Strigoi. The Strigoi stumbled back, waving his hands. The zombie staggered on, unheeding, shoved forward by Niscos so forcefully that it began to shed pieces of itself. It seemed to explode as it crashed into the Strigoi, its jaws clamping shut around the man's throat. Niscos gave a whoop, and his concentration wavered.

W'soran winced as the Strigoi's companions made Niscos pay for his inattention – a dozen corpses fell on the vampire, bearing him down. Shattered bones stabbed into his flesh, seeking his heart. Niscos howled and backhanded a corpse, sending it spinning head over heels into the air. W'soran let his gaze drift towards the other combatants. If Niscos survived, he would have learned a valuable lesson. If not – well, he could be replaced, eventually.

Similar scenes played out all around the duelling necromancers. A group of skeletal spearman shivered to dust as two opposing wills sought to control them, and a number of fresher corpses simply burst, as if they'd been left out in the sun too long. Broken bones shaped and re-shaped themselves in complex, chaotic geometric patterns as the two groups of necromancers sought to employ them. Missiles crafted from chattering skulls hurtled across the battlefield and cages and traps made from stripped flesh and cracked bone fastened themselves about the unwary. Black fire washed across a number of corpse-constructs, unravelling them as they lumbered forward. For a moment, W'soran wondered whether he would need to become involved.

When he caught sight of the wolf-tail standard of the king of the Draesca bobbing over the fray, however, his concern faded. Chown, the latest to bear the weight of W'soran's gift, was a more vigorous battle-sorcerer than Shull had been. W'soran's keen gaze found the necromancer-king easily enough. Chown was burly, even with the weight of years clinging to him, and he was wreathed in the stuff of death as he rode at the head of his ancestors. A mace made from the skull of an ogre whirled in one hand as he crashed into the Strigoi lines, and he beat an enemy vojnuk down from his horse with a smash from his heavy shield.

The dead kings of the Draesca charged with him, wielding the weapons they had used in life. Shull was there, his mummified skull split in a silent howl as he swept his sword out to lop off the head of a rider before he rode down a frantically gesturing enemy necromancer. Morath's students would find their petty magics availed them nothing against the wight-kings. They were too much at one with the stuff of death to be controlled by any but a master of the Corpse Geometries.

He grunted, satisfied that the Draesca could bolster the flagging flank. His attentions switched to the centre, where the ranks of Strigoi spearmen waited, unmoving. Living men these, and seemingly disinclined to attack his silent ranks of skeletal soldiers. He wondered whether they had grown used to the dead in the intervening years, or whether their fear had only grown worse from the proximity.

'Why aren't you moving?' he hissed, trying to gauge

whether it was cowardice, or strategy. Then he caught sight of movement in the enemy's rear – men, falling back and fleeing into the tree-line. Cowardice then – not unexpected, given how hard his forces had been pressing those of Strigos.

In the years following their attack on his watchtowers and border forts, W'soran had moved rapidly, striking multiple points at once and driving the invaders from his territory. His legions marched unimpeded across the frontier, burning and pillaging as they hammered the Strigoi lines, driving them back again and again. The Strigoi had gone from being on the offensive to being on the defensive, and quite rapidly. One by one, their forces crumpled and fell back, streaming through the crags and bowers of Ushoran's domain.

It had been surprisingly easy. Ushoran's forces outnumbered his, but Strigos's defences were stretched thin. Wild tribes of men and orcs continued to attack the frontiers, and undoubtedly, Neferata was taking advantage of the situation in some fashion. Nonetheless, it was easier than he'd expected. And that worried him. But not enough to make him stay his invasion – the time had come.

Eventually, he knew, Ushoran – the thing that Ushoran had become – would have to face him. Nagash could never abide a direct challenge. Ushoran, possibly, but not Nagash. It was just a matter of applying the right amount of pressure. He leaned forward over the horn of his saddle, watching the Strigoi centre disintegrate. With a whisper, he set the ranks of skeletons standing before him to advancing. It was just a matter of pressure. What a torturer did to the body, a general did to the enemy army. It was a simple thing, taken in that regard, and he wondered that he had never before seen the simplicity of it.

The assassination attempt had been the signal, he now knew. It had been obvious – *obvious!* Ushoran was a wolf in a trap. W'soran wondered whether he could feel himself slipping away, to be buried beneath the black soil of the crown's thoughts. He thought perhaps that Ushoran did, and that the attempt on his life had been a desperate ploy to end his threat obliquely. Perhaps Ushoran thought it a way to circumvent the crown's prodding and pushing, and to stave off the inevitable.

The lines of the living gave way before the relentless march of the dead, and W'soran urged his horse forward with a slight smile. 'Pressure,' he murmured and gently clasped his amulets. Soon, he would need them. They would give him the power he needed to confront his old friend and rip him from his perch. A moment which was approaching swiftly – the Strigoi were retreating all across the frontier, falling back before his followers, the ragged remnants of their armies returning to Mourkain, ceding territory to the invaders. Horns blew, catching his attention.

He twisted in his saddle, and made a sharp motion. His bodyguard formed up in a protective phalanx. The wights wore heavy armour and had, in life, been chieftains of those tribes that W'soran had beaten into submission in the Vaults and the other nearby ranges. Now, in death, they served him as an imperial guard more than a hundred strong, ready to carry him through the fires of war to inevitable victory.

The horns belonged to the Strigoi, of course. In the tangle of battle, a group of riders had become separated from the rest, and they were galloping hard for their receding lines as his skeletal horsemen harried them. They crashed into the rear of his lines and he hissed in annoyance. The lead rider wore the black armour of Ushoran's personal guard, and his snarling-visaged helm was decorated by trailing streamers of coloured cloth.

W'soran reacted quickly. At his silent command, the dead began to shift position, to encompass the riders. There was little sense in letting them reach safety, especially if the one in the lead was, as W'soran suspected, the enemy commander, Gashnag.

'And won't it be nice to see him again, eh?' he muttered to himself as his steed charged. He leaned forward in the saddle, and his bodyguard spread out around him, smashing aside their own forces at his command. He could always resurrect them later, after all.

He straightened in his saddle as they closed and gave a ringing shriek. It was answered by several nearby packs of ghouls, all clad in primitive armour and adorned with coarse tattoos and brands. They wielded rough weapons – femurs with blades hammered through them, maces crafted from skulls, and crude digging implements repurposed for battle. Among them were several of the large war-ghouls of his own creation, and it was these beasts who answered his call and chivvied forward their smaller pack-mates. They loped towards the riders at W'soran's cry, seeking to cut them off.

W'soran caught up with them a moment later. He jerked his mount to a trot as his wights thundered ahead, crashing into the enemy. When a hole had been punched through their ranks, he let his mount lunge forward through it. His sword licked out, lopping off the top of a rider's head, and then he was face to face with Gashnag.

He'd been infamous among the court for his vanity and a maddening obsession with Cathayan silks and foreign trinkets. A slim creature, golden-haired and prone to fits of poetry, he'd nonetheless earned a reputation as a fierce duellist and ruthless killer. That was one of the reasons that W'soran had seen fit to employ both Gashnag and his cousin, Zandor, as his agents against Neferata's machinations in better times. Zandor had perished at the Silver Pinnacle, but Gashnag seemed to have come into his own. His heavy helm had been struck from his head, and his hair was unbound, whipping about his thin face. His armour was black, but edged in gold and of fine craftsmanship. Intricate scenes from Mourkain's history had been engraved on his cuirass and his pauldrons bore grimacing devil faces. His eyes widened as he caught sight of W'soran.

'You,' he snarled. His sword snapped out, hissing as it sliced the air. W'soran easily avoided the blow, jerking back in his saddle. Their mounts circled each other as they traded blows, their blades crashing together. 'Traitor,' Gashnag shouted.

'Opportunist,' W'soran corrected, scoring his opponent's cuirass with a swift blow. Gashnag grimaced and aimed a slash at W'soran's head. W'soran interposed his blade and pressed the blow aside. 'If Ushoran put you in command, I must say I made the right decision. Not quite like those epic poems of the glorious wars waged by ancient Strigu, eh, Gashnag?'

They spun apart. The wights continued to fight with Gashnag's men. Gashnag jerked his mount around and the horse smashed into W'soran's bony steed. W'soran squawked as the other vampire slashed the straps of his saddle. He toppled from the top of his steed with a distinct lack of grace and crashed to the ground. Trapped by the thicket of stomping hooves that surrounded him, he instinctively curled into a ball, trying to make himself as small a target as possible. Nevertheless, sharp-edged hooves struck him and he crawled through the mud, trying to get clear.

A pair of hooves thudded down on his back and pain rippled the length of his spine. The hooves lifted, and W'soran flung himself onto his back, hands out-thrust. He spat a guttural stream of words and the rearing horse squealed as javelins of purest darkness pierced its belly and chest. It toppled like a cut tree, carrying Gashnag to the ground with it.

W'soran rose. He winced as his spine popped, realigning itself. Gashnag kicked his way free of his dying mount and rose to his feet, hands twitching as he sought the sword he'd dropped. Then he thrust out a hand and barked strange syllables. The air seemed to ignite and W'soran stepped back as his robes caught fire. Hissing in anger, he swept his arms out sharply, snuffing the fire. 'That's a new trick,' he said.

'I've got more than that,' Gashnag said. 'Some of us are not fools, old man. And sorcery isn't so difficult when you've got centuries to learn it in.' Then, as if to twist the knife, he added, 'And Morath is a much better tutor than you ever were.'

W'soran snorted. 'You always were an arrogant fool, Gashnag.' Gashnag gestured and more fire splashed across the air mere inches from W'soran's face. Behind him, the corpse of his steed flopped over and twitched. 'Sorcery is not a bludgeon, it is a scalpel.' The horse's hide split, peeling away, and its carcass opened like a flower as bones and organs uncurled and spread. Gashnag shouted crooked words, trying to hook the winds of magic to his will, to pierce W'soran's mystical defences. 'It is a subtle art, requiring skill and will in equal measure – neither of which you possess in any great quantity.'

The flopping horse-flower fell upon Gashnag with a convulsive heave, hunks of flesh and chains of bone wrapping about the vampire's limbs. He yelped in surprise, and turned. He tore at the thing as it bore him down. Spears of splintered bone punched through his shoulder and belly, piercing his mail with sorcerous strength as slithering organs sought to tighten about his head. W'soran watched intently, his hands clasped before him.

'To manipulate the winds of death requires the temperament of an artist, and the patience of a philosopher. Any fool can learn to bark a few incantations, if his blood is sour with the stuff of dark magic. Ushoran's bite might have given you the ability, but you will never know the true power of it all,' he said, raising his arm. The effluvium of the battlefield rose at his gesture – blood and offal swirled about him in a foul cyclone. The bodies of Gashnag's men twitched and jerked, rising. 'Not even Morath will know, for he is too frightened to see. He fears the power, when he should embrace it.'

Howling ghosts rose from the blood-soaked soil, both ancient spirits from battles centuries old and the recent dead, and sped towards W'soran. He glanced at them, seeing the black strands of magic which bound them to a trio of approaching riders. They bore the tattoos of the Mortuary Cult, and they wore flapping furs and bronze skull masks. They galloped towards him on their stubby Strigoi steeds, gesticulating and shouting, racing to Gashnag's aid. Gashnag tore at the thing holding him captive, struggling to get free, as the spectral host surrounded W'soran and slid over him like shadows, unable to reach him thanks to the swirling cloud of battlefield detritus. W'soran looked around without concern, ignoring the moaning phantoms.

The battle had collapsed into a disorganised melee. The living fled from the dead, and the Strigoi lines had collapsed. His followers were pursuing their defeated foes with gleeful howls or grave silence. He smiled as the spirits of the departed approached him, followed by their summoners. They needed to salvage Gashnag. Ushoran likely didn't have many generals left, given the defections and deaths. Not that Gashnag was much of a general. W'soran chuckled. In a way, letting the vampire escape would hurt Ushoran more than help him. 'Fine,' he said, decision made. 'A trade, then.'

He cocked a hand and then snapped it forward, as if hurling a spear. The typhoon of blood and offal swirling about him shot forward at the gesture, hurtling towards the approaching necromancers like a rain of gruesome arrows. Bits of bone and boiling blood pierced their bodies, plucking them from their saddles and dropping them to the ground. 'Three talented students for a brute, a good trade, eh, Gashnag?' he said, glancing at the vampire as he tore his way free of the horse carcass. They locked eyes through the swirling cloud of ghosts and W'soran said, 'Run away, Gashnag. Tell Ushoran that I'll be along shortly.'

Gashnag ran. Not quite with his tail tucked between his legs, but close enough. He sprinted for the trees, avoiding battle, joining his men in harried flight. W'soran raised a hand and caught the loose threads that bound the ghosts that continued to swirl about him like a semi-sentient fog bank, and he stalked towards the trio of necromancers. All three were quite dead, and he examined the fading glimmer of the magic that had inundated them. 'Yes, three for one is quite fair, I think,' he said.

He stretched out his hand, stirring the embers of their magic the way a man might stir a campfire. He had not seen fit to craft any more such creatures as those he had summoned that day when the Lahmians had come for him. Their presence had annoyed him on a spiritual level, their proximity grating on his senses like a file on iron. He had freed those wraiths, but had remembered and refined the method behind their creation, like a blacksmith hammering out imperfections.

Words slipped from his mouth. The words were meaningless, a vocal focus as all incantations were, stabbing his will into the corpses at his feet, stirring the ashes of their souls into white-hot fury and drawing them forth in a cataclysmic display of power. As before, so many years ago, that power burst from the bodies like coruscating clouds of inky darkness. The ghosts that fluttered about him seemed to shrink back from these new spirits. If the dead could be frightened, the bound souls of dead necromancers would be the thing that did so. He watched the things gain shape and form and sniffed in satisfaction.

'Mighty magics indeed, my lord,' a voice growled behind him. W'soran turned to see Chown riding towards him. The Draesca king's body and armour were covered in blood, and his great mace dripped a trail as it dangled from his grip. The bat-winged helm seemed to pulse with a satisfied hum upon his white-haired head, and, as ever, W'soran examined it closely, peering up at it, wondering if the piece of him that lurked within it had yet flowered into malign sentience. 'I would know those secrets,' Chown continued, his eyes glowing with an eerie light. Then, a moment later he added, 'If it would please you, my lord.'

Yes, there's definitely something of me in you, man, W'soran thought in amusement. 'In time, oh mighty king, you shall know this and many things besides.' He gestured to the blood that coated Chown's mace. 'Victory, then, I take it?'

'Victory and death,' Chown said, grinning fiercely. 'The dogs of Morgheim have fled the field, and my riders harry them. We shall hunt them to the very walls of their lair and bring them to battle, my lord.' Around him, the dead kings of the Draesca seemed to groan softly in agreement, and their glowing eyes sought out W'soran. He met their gazes and raised his hand in benediction, and the dead seemed to sigh.

'Aye, that we will, King of the Draesca, and soon to be Lord of the Vaults,' W'soran said. Chown's face betrayed his surprise and pleasure. W'soran smiled thinly. 'Emperor Vorag has sworn it, and as his castellan, I shall ensure it. You will be lord of those mountains, though we must scour them of life.' Chown gave a grunt of satisfaction. The barbarians were easy enough to placate, W'soran reflected, and their wants were minimal at best. He could easily take back his gift at a later date, should he so desire, after all.

Ullo and Arpad rode towards him, the former holding a knot of heads by their scalp-locks. The slack jaws of the heads sagged, revealing their fangs. By the condition of them, it appeared that Ullo had simply ripped them loose from their owners' necks. He held up the gory trophies and his black eyes glittered. 'Ushoran must be desperate if he's reduced to employing such thin-blooded weaklings. These pups barely had five decades apiece. They were no sport at all.'

'You say that as if it's a bad thing,' Arpad said, grinning. 'I prefer an easy fight, me.' He twisted in his saddle, looking around. 'That's what this has been from the first.'

'Too easy, maybe,' Ullo said, examining the heads, as if trying to glean an answer from their vacant stares. The black gaze flickered to W'soran. 'What do your magics tell you, sorcerer? Is the empire dying?'

'Can't you smell it?' W'soran asked, spreading his arms and tilting his head. Overhead, lightning flashed in the bellies of the clouds. 'We are in at the death, Ullo. Strigos lies panting in the mud, our arrows and spears jutting from its hide.' He inhaled the stink of the battlefield, inflating his narrow chest. 'Why else would I have stripped my – Vorag's – territories of troops? Why else would my agents spread the gospel of fire and sword through these black hills as openly as they do? Mourkain will be ours before the first snows of the season fall.'

'If your acolytes at Crookback Mountain send us reinforcements, aye,' Ullo rumbled. He scratched a flat cheek with a bloody talon. 'Have you had word from Melkhior these past weeks?'

W'soran looked at him. 'What are you implying?'

'We are far from our territories, sorcerer. We might not have supply lines, as such, but neither do we have an easy route ahead of us. We might be able to raise the dead with every battle, but even they don't last forever. Our enemies know how to fight them, and how to fight us. We lost Orcuk and Scabeg of Illios in this battle, both of them pinned like flies to the ground by men – mortal soldiers. And half of my spearmen, dead though they were, are no more – burnt by sorcery and blasted to ashes. And Ushoran has been sending smaller and smaller forces against us. There's not enough dead to replace our losses. We're fighting for every stretch of ground and our armies are being ground down, slowly but surely.' Ullo said it all flatly, and without accusation. Nonetheless, W'soran was stung by his words.

'What would you have us do then, Ullo? Retreat, perhaps?' he snapped.

'I speak of caution, not retreat,' Ullo growled back. 'Perhaps we should wait until Lukas and Vaal the Thirst have rejoined us,' he added, naming two of the other renegade Strigoi, both of whom who had taken smaller forces to the west and the north-east, respectively, in an attempt to lead off any reinforcements for Gashnag's now-destroyed force. 'With their forces added to ours, we could punch through the ring of fortifications that line the Plain of Dust and reach Mourkain within a fortnight. But if Melkhior doesn't supply us with reinforcements soon, it's going to be a slog. We'll be lucky if we've got enough cold bodies to throw at Abhorash when the Great Dragon inevitably unfurls his wings and moves to stop us.'

'Not to mention that they've got their own sorcerers,' Arpad interjected, gesturing hesitantly to the floating, black spectres that W'soran had wrought from the remains of Morath's acolytes. Even creatures as brutal as the Strigoi feared the wraiths on an instinctive level, like wolves faced with a maddened bear. 'Three less now, I admit, but who knows how many he's got...'

'One or a hundred, it matters not,' Chown said. 'For we have our Lord W'soran, whose might is unparalleled.' The

Draesca flashed his blackened teeth in a grin. W'soran glanced at the savage necromancer and felt a twinge of something that might have been affection, as a parent for an extremely stupid, yet loving, child. The Draesca had always held him in some reverence, a fact that often slipped his mind. The brutal tribesmen viewed him with less fear than the Yaghur had felt for Nagash, for his touch had ever been light. Strangely, they were more than willing to fight and die for him, despite that.

'Be that as it may, you might be right,' W'soran demurred. Ullo wasn't; he was a fool, and over-cautious, frightened as he was of Abhorash. Nonetheless, Ullo was too valuable to ignore or supersede. W'soran knew that the shark-faced Strigoi's loyalty was held only by that thinnest of threads – a debt of honour. He had saved Ullo at the Battle of the Black Water, and the Strigoi seemed to feel that he owed W'soran his grudging service in return. And Ullo was the only reason that the other renegade Strigoi remained loyal.

W'soran was not deaf to the mutinous whispers of his bloodthirsty servants. Some Strigoi thought he had done away with Vorag, since his disappearance into the eastern mountains. That W'soran was only using the name of the Bloodytooth as a mask for his own desires. That was true as far as it went, though he'd done nothing to Vorag. Indeed, the Bloodytooth's fate was as much a mystery to him as it was to the others. He'd been too busy, and disinclined besides, to find out what had happened to the would-be emperor of Strigos.

Perhaps Vorag had run afoul of the unbound dead of Nehekhara, or some other enemy, and been destroyed. Perhaps Neferata had gotten her vengeance for Vorag's abandonment at last, and his brute head decorated a spear in the Silver Pinnacle.

Perhaps he had simply decided not to return.

That last thought was the most disturbing. He had expected Vorag's army, whatever was left of it at any rate, to slink back to Crookback Mountain sooner or later. Though he had convinced Vorag of the victories that awaited him in the southern reaches, he knew that there was little way that such a brute could take Nagashizzar, let alone conquer the risen kings of the Great Land. He had simply wanted his figurehead safely out of the way while he drew Ushoran – Nagash – out of hiding and into the open. If Vorag returned triumphant, fine, and if he returned beaten, even better, so long as he returned. With W'soran as his vizier, Vorag could rule, and rule well and long. And W'soran would have the order he needed to make a true and uninterrupted study of Nagash's crown and the secrets therein.

And then, once he had those secrets...

But none of that mattered now. *Carts before horses*, he thought. For now, it was Ullo who was the key to his victory. It was Ullo who held the loyalties, or at least the respect, of his Strigoi generals. Not poor W'soran, who was regarded, at best, as a necessary evil by his followers, despite everything he had done for them. And while Ullo did not require as much placation as Vorag, it was best not to press him too far.

The vampire had a ruthless sort of practicality, and would, if push came to shove, easily forget his debt to serve his own ends.

W'soran sniffed and looked around, meeting the gazes of his commanders. Then, his gaze travelled to the horizon, where blackness seemed to spread across the sky like spilled ink on paper. Nagash was waiting, he knew, crouching like a beast in a cave. He grasped his amulets, succumbing to a sudden nervous impulse. He felt as if he were standing in a storm wrapped in iron and waiting for the lightning to fall. 'We will make camp and await our allies. I will send messages to Melkhior, inquiring as to his tardiness. And then we will march to Mourkain, and lay claim to an empire!'

—◄ CHAPTER FOURTEEN ►—

The Worlds Edge Mountains
(Year -950 Imperial Calendar)

The beastmen died swiftly, their crooked bodies blasted to bloody chunks by W'soran's destructive magics, and the mountains echoed with their screams. He swept aside his tattered cloak and thrust out his talons, gesturing. Dark magic coursed from his hands, washing over a charging bull-headed giant. The beast screamed in agony as its flesh was flayed from its thick bones. Its remains toppled into the snow at his feet, still smoking. The survivors of the first attack turned to flee back into the snow-capped trees, squalling and bleating like the herd animals they resembled.

'Do not pursue them,' he snarled to his acolytes. Zoar made as if to protest, but a glare from his master caused his mouth to snap shut. 'Let them run, boy. I want to study that stone of theirs uninterrupted,' W'soran continued, lowering his arms.

The stone in question occupied the centre of the clearing. It was a massive fang of rock, covered in sigils daubed in blood and filth, and hung with thick chains that were heavy with skulls, skin-sacks and other, even more grisly trophies. It radiated a strange magic, one that W'soran was only familiar with in passing. He stepped over the corpses of its defenders and approached it. He was careful not to touch it.

It reeked of old blood and bodily fluids and it was crudely carved in places. He glanced aside, at the heavy stakes set into the ground around it at intervals, and the bodies that had been tied to them. They were men, though of a tribe he was unfamiliar with: brawny and pale, with sharp features and their scalps shorn clean save for greased scalp-locks. There were a number of them, and all were dead. The beastmen had been eating them, a bit at a time. Most had died before the creatures got past their waists, though at least one had lived long enough to see his intestines chewed like sausage. Bits of the dead men had been smeared on the stone, like a primitive offering.

W'soran had encountered the beasts before, though their numbers seemed to be increasing the farther north he went. He had seen their herdstones as well, though none quite this... decorated. The warping magics contained in the fang of stone reminded him of a starving cur, equally likely to bite off his hand as lick his palm. It was untrustworthy, and while he had several tomes containing incantations relating to similar sorceries, he had yet to experiment with them.

'Master,' Zoar began, 'is this...?'

'No,' W'soran said harshly. It wasn't the dark beacon he had sensed all those weeks ago, the beacon that had drawn him ever *further into the wilds, pulsing in the sky like a black sun. It was not a real sun but instead more akin to an afterimage, a darker-than-dark blotch on the retina of his mind's eye, burning cold and hungry beneath the moon. He felt it calling to him in his quiet moments, purring seductively in his mind, infiltrating his thoughts. There was a malign familiarity to the voice, and something in it made him very afraid. It was a ringing depth that he could not plumb, no matter how hard he listened. It pulled him on, like a bell in the night, summoning him.*

Instinctively, his eyes slid away from the stone and his gaze rose, finding the blotch. The voice was whispering again, just a brief hiss of dim noise, just on the edge of his hearing. Irritated, he shook his head. 'Stop it, stop hissing at me,' he growled to no one in particular.

'Master,' Zoar said.

'What?' W'soran snapped, turning.

Men watched them, men with bows, who had seemingly crept out of the trees as silently as ghosts. They closely resembled the bodies slumped against the stakes, albeit more vital. W'soran watched them approach calmly. They stank, not just of bear grease and sweat, but of something else... something familiar.

Then, something heavy landed on the herdstone and W'soran spun, fangs exposed. Ushoran, his features human and handsome, crouched on the spur of stone. He was clad in heavy furs and leather armour, and his hair was bound in a thick lock. A simple gold band encircled his head.

'When my scouts reported that there was thunder among the trees, I half-expected it to be you, old man,' Ushoran said,

dropping down from his perch. He carried no weapon, but he'd never truly needed one. He gently touched one of the dead men and he sighed. 'Poor Garek,' he murmured, closing the dead man's staring eyes. 'I wish you had accepted my gift, my friend.'

W'soran said nothing. His mind whirled, calculating. So this was where the Lord of Masks had decided to make his empire. Coincidence, or… no; W'soran didn't believe in coincidences. Ushoran was here for the same reason he was. Something had called him, had perhaps, been calling him since the last time W'soran had seen him. Ushoran ignored him as he cut each of the bodies free and laid them gently on the ground. When he had finished, he looked at his men and said, 'Gather wood. We will commit them to the fire, and lay the bodies of their killers at their feet, as befitting the sons of Strigu.' He turned to W'soran. 'So, old monster… you have no idea how glad we are to see you.'

'We?' W'soran inquired, his good eye narrowing. A length of cold metal dropped onto his shoulder, its edge pressed lightly to the side of his neck.

'We,' Abhorash said.

Crookback Mountain
(Year -263 Imperial Calendar)

W'soran cursed as the hooves of his steed slipped and slid on the ice encrusting the rocky path leading to the entrance to his citadel. The wind howled through the crags, and sheets of snow and frozen rain pelted him as he hunched forward in his saddle, his tattered cloak providing little protection. He did not feel the cold, but the snow and ice made it hard to move and even harder to see. Winter in the mountains was never pleasant, even for a being such as him.

The difficulty in reaching his citadel had only added to the pile of steadily building frustrations that threatened, at times, to crush him under. It had all been going so well, and, to an extent, it still was. His army maintained its position, and had thrown back a number of Strigoi assaults. Palisades had been erected and trees cleared. The temporary camp had become a fortified bulwark, a wedge of influence in enemy territory. He was forced to trust that Ullo and the others could hold it, especially given the lack of reinforcements.

Vaal the Thirst had not rejoined them. His forces had been ambushed by unknown enemies in the hills to the west. Lukas, the other Strigoi outrider, had found Vaal's head on a spear, standing amidst the detritus of his forces. Lukas's own force had been harried all the way back to the main body of the army, attacked by small parties of the dead. W'soran recognised Neferata's handiwork, though not a single quicksilver killer had been seen. There was something going on in the west, something she didn't want him to see. Perhaps she was simply shielding the flanks of the tribes of the lowlands, whose barbarous warbands were streaming into Strigoi territory with a relentless savagery. Or perhaps she was finally mobilising her own forces for the final battle. She could smell the scent of Ushoran's weakness as well as he could, though she had no hope of defeating Nagash in a direct confrontation.

You had your chance, witch. It's my turn, he thought sourly. Or, it would have been, had he not been dragged from the forefront of battle by the negligence of his supposedly capable castellan. Melkhior had much to answer for. He had sent no reinforcements, and the citadel was woefully undefended, as evidenced by the lack of any sentries accosting him upon his arrival. For a moment, he ruefully contemplated the lack of exterior fortifications. He had never considered them necessary, despite Melkhior's protestations to the contrary. There were defences within, and strong ones at that, but he had never thought it necessary to add any to the slopes of the mountain. Why advertise the citadel's presence, after all?

It wasn't only a matter of men and materials; the proceeds from the mines had dried to a trickle and the mineral wealth that had bought him the loyalty of certain tribes and served to bribe others into inactivity was threatened. It was all his agents could do to keep the hillmen of the Vaults from attacking the Draesca while their king was away. If the gold stopped coming, they would attack and a third of his army would melt away as Chown took his men home to defend his kingdom.

Everything hinged on the mines and the reinforcements. He had thrown everything into this attack, had planned and prepared for years for this moment, and now it was all teetering on the edge of a knife held by a dithering, twitching fool. He angrily scrubbed snow from his shoulders. He'd known Melkhior was too unreliable to serve him in battle, but had hoped that he'd prove an adequate major domo. Instead, he was beginning to regret ever having bothered to turn the idiot Strigoi in the first place. What a waste of blood and power that was turning out to be…

The only forces W'soran had brought with him were his bodyguard of wights. The dead chieftains looked about slowly as they rode into the crooked cavern that marked the entrance to the mountain and acted as the forecourt of the citadel. Scorch marks marred the cavern walls and debris covered the rough floor – bits of bone and armour, and patches of melted rock.

Something had happened.

Perhaps reinforcements hadn't come because there were none to send. W'soran growled deep in his throat. What foolishness had his acolyte perpetrated?

Eyes were on him, and he brought his dead steed to a halt in the centre of the forecourt. He looked around. There were no torches lit, no burning skulls to greet him. Leather brushed against rock. W'soran's gaze rotated. Thousands of bats clustered on the ceiling of the cavern, their tiny bright eyes staring down at him. Hairy bodies squirmed against one another in a living carpet of teeth and wings, and he wondered at their number. There had always been bats in the deeper reaches of the mountain, but never so many, he thought.

He grunted and swung out of his saddle. His wights followed suit, drawing their weapons even as their feet touched the floor. W'soran didn't bother to draw his scimitar. He looked to the wide flat steps that curved up into the mountain. The slap of leather soles on stone sounded dully out of the darkness. A moment later a cloaked shape stood at the summit of the steps, glaring down at them. W'soran frowned.

'What is this? No happy greeting from student to master? No cry of welcome, no reception befitting my status?' he called out harshly. There was no reply. Irritated, W'soran raised his hand and a soft corona of sickly light formed above his upturned palm. Light washed over the cavern and the shape at the summit threw up a hand to cover its eyes.

'I expect an answer when I ask a question, Melkhior,' W'soran said. 'Or have you forgotten all of your duties, rather than just a few?'

'Master, is that you?' Melkhior rasped, peering down at them.

'Who else would it be, you idiot?'

Melkhior visibly hesitated. W'soran's good eye widened slightly as he caught sight of the creatures behind Melkhior. He thought they were ghouls at first, but then saw that they weren't alive, in the traditional sense. Stained wrappings were wound round their blistered and scarred flesh, and their faces were a gruesome blend of man, beast and corpse. They seemed to be caught between life and death, and they reeked of *wrongness*. Their mottled flesh blended easily with the darkness and they crept forward around Melkhior in a protective manner. W'soran felt a sting of pleasure at the thought that Melkhior had created them. Perhaps he wasn't as much of an idiot as he seemed.

'I see you have been keeping up with your studies, at least,' he said.

Melkhior's hand fell to the flat skull of the closest of the beasts, and he stroked it idly. He seemed to relax slightly. 'There have been… incidents, in your absence, master.'

'So I see,' W'soran said, gesturing about him. 'What has happened?'

'The ratkin have returned,' Melkhior said bluntly.

W'soran hissed. He looked about him. Now that he knew what to look for, he could see the signs of collapsed tunnels in the walls and floor of the cavern. He had half-expected it, but not so soon. Not now, when he couldn't deal with them as they deserved. 'When?' he asked, starting up the stairs.

'Months ago,' Melkhior said. He watched his master approach, a strange expression on his face. 'But their scouts infiltrated the mountain a year ago or more. We didn't detect them until too late.' He hesitated. 'They freed your… pet.'

'Iskar is still alive?' W'soran asked, bemused. 'Fascinating, I'd have thought he'd have died in my absence.' Then Melkhior's words fully sank in and he snarled. 'Freed him? How, when?'

There was another hesitation. Then, Melkhior said, 'Two years ago.'

'Two…' W'soran repeated and shook his head.

'They snuck in and destroyed the laboratories. They freed him then. At first, I thought he'd died, but we never found a carcass...' He stopped and shrank back as W'soran glared at him.

'My laboratory,' W'soran said, his hands clenching. Fury built in him. 'What of the vaults?' In the aftermath of the first attempt on his life, W'soran had realised that his most valuable treasures – the carefully hoarded books and scrolls of dark design upon which his power was based – were vulnerable to theft or destruction, as they were. They had been copied again and again by his acolytes, and it was true that if they were lost, the knowledge in them could be recovered, but there was a malevolent power in those original manuscripts that could not be replaced. Not wishing to risk it, he had overseen the construction of a specially prepared vault, guarded around the clock by unsleeping guardians.

'Safe, master, I swear,' Melkhior said quickly. 'They are under guard day and night. I created the perfect guardian to replace those destroyed by the skaven. Come, come! I will show you!' He spun about and started up the steps, his creations scuttling after him. W'soran watched him flee, and then, more slowly, followed.

The citadel bore mute testimony to Melkhior's assertions. W'soran had no real cause to doubt his acolyte's word, but he knew better than to trust him. He knew better than to trust any man, servant or no. Nevertheless, the citadel showed signs of conflict that put him in mind of those early months just after their arrival, when they had battled the skaven for control of the mountain. He saw patrols of battered skeletons, much repaired and moving slowly. Rotting zombies crafted from orcs and men guarded the entrances to the side caverns, and he saw more of Melkhior's creations prowling the side-tunnels and darkened ledges. But not many – when he had marched for Strigos, Crookback Mountain had echoed with the sounds of industry and marching dead men. Now, an eerie, empty silence hung about the place and his every step seemed to echo and re-echo.

'Where are the legions I left for you, Melkhior? Where are your fellow acolytes?' he asked.

'Dead – the final death,' Melkhior said, not looking at his master. 'The skaven returned with deadly weapons, master... weapons that spat sorcerous fire and monstrous creatures that tore vampires apart as if they were nothing more than men. You cannot resurrect ash and char. I have... had to make do.'

'All of them, Melkhior?' W'soran pressed.

'Those who did not die in the destruction of the laboratory fell in battle,' Melkhior said. He paused and glanced over his shoulder at W'soran. 'I am your only remaining apprentice, master.'

'All save those who accompanied me to war, yes. How unfortunate,' W'soran murmured. Melkhior was lying. He knew it as surely as he knew that the other vampire had gone mad. He could smell that madness seeping from Melkhior's pores. W'soran recognised it, for he had smelled the same stink on Ushoran and on Neferata – the madness of certainty, of a single overwhelming design. If W'soran had felt even the slightest amount of affection for his acolytes, he might have been angrier. As it was, he only required one to see to the citadel – if Melkhior had elected himself to be that one, fine.

Melkhior appeared not to have heard W'soran's insult. 'But the citadel remains in our hands, master. I have thrown back the skaven every time they have attacked, no matter the losses. I have scoured their old warrens with armies made from their own dead and I have filled the deep tunnels with my eyes and ears...' Here, he gestured upwards. W'soran looked up and saw more bats, all watching him. 'I have done all that you asked of me, master.'

'Except supply me with reinforcements,' W'soran said. He stopped and turned. 'I would see my laboratory,' he said, stepping through an archway.

Melkhior hurried after him. 'It is dangerous, master. The abn-i-khat has tainted everything, and your experiments–' he began, reaching for W'soran, who caused him to freeze in place with a glare. As Melkhior shrank back, W'soran turned back to the great doors that marked where his laboratory had once been.

'My experiments are of no concern. I can recreate them, in time. What of our other guest?'

'Other...?'

'The Lahmian witch, Melkhior,' W'soran said, pressing one hand to the doors. The amulets around his neck grew warm and they caused his flesh to tingle where they touched it. He could smell the essence of abn-i-khat beyond the doors. The scent was almost overpowering, and the old need rippled through him, making it hard to think. 'Or was she destroyed as well?' he continued.

His curiosity was almost impossible to ignore – what sort of weapon had the skaven used to destroy his labs? More – how had they gotten in? His labs had been warded both inside and out, the very stones wrapped in layers of sorcery. The doors bulged slightly, though they had been chained shut. The thick wood was scorched and the metal warped by a great heat, a heat which was still present. W'soran drew his hand back and examined the raised blisters on his palm with some interest. Through the cracks in the door, he could see a strange flickering light, and there was an eerie tang to the air. Everything seemed greasy, as if it were covered in a thin film of... something.

'I... don't know,' Melkhior said. 'There were fires – fires that still burn! Not even we could stand it for long. The wyrd-stone fires burn without consuming, master, and I can find no way to extinguish those flames. I have had to seal it off.'

W'soran stepped back from the doors. He turned to Melkhior. 'You disappoint me. The vaults,' he snapped. Melkhior scuttled away, and W'soran followed. 'What of the mines?' he asked.

'The orcs grow rebellious,' Melkhior grunted. 'There is a band of them loose in the bowels of the mine, led by a creature called Dork.' Melkhior shuddered. 'It broke free of the work gangs in the last revolt. It was whelped here, I think. Grown in the dark like a mushroom, and raised in the mines. It – it is not like the others.'

'What do you mean?' W'soran asked. 'And how much trouble can one band of orcs be?'

'More than I expected,' Melkhior said hesitantly. He twitched. 'The creature employs sorcery.'

'Impossible,' W'soran said. The orcs had shamans, but their magics were primitive, and more likely to kill the caster than an enemy.

'He is smart. It is as if he has learned,' Melkhior continued, as if W'soran hadn't spoken. He shook his head. 'I thought it was impossible for the greenskins to learn, but this beast has. It employs cunning, avoiding my patrols. Every day, more orcs vanish in the mines, freed or killed by this creature, and I do not have the resources to both find him and guard against the skaven.' He looked at W'soran, and his expression was sour as he added, 'Or to send you reinforcements, master.'

W'soran didn't reply. He fingered his amulets thoughtfully, studying his acolyte. 'Show me the vaults,' he said.

The vault was set into a hollowed-out crag, with only one entrance, and only one purpose. The entrance was normally guarded by a coterie of wights raised specifically for that task, but they were not in evidence now. The door was crafted from stone, with a great iron pull-ring set in its centre. Melkhior moved to open it, but W'soran shoved him aside and grabbed the ring himself. He grunted as he shifted it, eliciting a grinding groan from the stones of the portal. He could feel the spells he had worked into the vault washing over him, determining his identity. Only he and his most senior acolytes were allowed within. At this point, of course, Melkhior was the only one of the latter remaining.

But with a word, he could render the vault impenetrable save by himself, or transport its contents to a pre-arranged location, set up years before and in secret. One of Zoar's final services before he'd met his sad fate. Not even Melkhior knew of that place, nor did he know of the simple spell that would remove W'soran's most prized possessions from the vault. W'soran stepped past the door. He ignored Melkhior's cry of warning.

His library was as he'd left it. Dozens of tomes sat on an equal number of stone podiums, and more books and rolls of papyri and scrolls sat piled around the bases of the latter. The vault was featureless save for the podiums, which were themselves little more than fangs of melted and re-shaped rock, drawn upwards to serve as book rests. The pages of the grimoires rustled as he stepped into the vault, as if in greeting. The scent of age and dark magic washed over him. He stroked the cover of a hairy book and flipped through the thick, slightly damp pages of another.

There was no light in the vault, save for that which he'd brought in with him. In the darkness, something rustled and W'soran froze. He looked up and saw fangs. Each was the length of a sword and equally sharp, and that thicket of death descended at speed.

W'soran raised a hand and the fangs halted, their curves kissing his palm. Two eyes like balls of balefire bobbed beyond the grisly maw and he was suddenly overwhelmed by a miasmic cloud. The odour of rot and age filled his nostrils, and he could just make out the shadowy shapes of two great wings and the vaguely serpentine bulk they were attached to, filling the vault from ceiling to floor. He felt a monstrous pressure from the gaze of thing, and was, for a moment, reminded of Nagash at his most terrible.

But even Nagash's fury paled before the sheer unadulterated rage in those glowing orbs. It was the rage of something at once divine and bestial that was now trapped in a cage of sagging muscle and rotting meat. He knew that the dead were, on some level, aware of their fate, but never to this extent, and never before had he felt such hatred from a corpse.

'My minions found it on the Plain of Bones, to the southeast of here while scouring for raw materials,' Melkhior said from outside the vault. 'It was too big to use in battle, save in the deepest bowels of the mountain, and I thought it better utilised here, as a watchdog. I took it apart carefully and reassembled it in here, bit by bit, piece by piece. '

The fangs, and the maw they occupied, rose away into the darkness, as if the thing were assured that W'soran was no threat. He cautiously sent his ball of witch fire bobbing upwards to reveal the monstrous enormity that now called his vault home.

He had seen dragons before, though only once or twice, and at a distance. The thing he saw had perhaps, once upon a time, been such. Now it was a rotting horror, all exposed bone and gangrenous muscle, lumpen and lurking beneath a ruptured and peeling hide of armoured plates. Great curving horns surmounted its thick, fleshless skull and chains of mystical binding dangled from its gaping torso. It shifted its weight, and the vault seemed to shudder. A cloud of flies was dislodged from somewhere within it, and they filled the air, humming angrily. Its wings were tattered sails, shredded and flapping as it leaned forward on them, and its claws, still cruel looking despite their cracked and splintered state, carved gouges in the stone floor.

W'soran felt a burst of avarice as he gazed up at the abomination. 'It is… beautiful,' he said.

'I thought so,' Melkhior said.

'I will take it,' W'soran said as he turned to face his acolyte.

'What?'

'In recompense for your tardiness in supplying reinforcements,' W'soran said, rubbing his hands together in pleasure. 'Such a creature will more than make up for any military shortfall, I think, and quite nicely.'

'But master…'

'Think carefully before you reply, Melkhior,' W'soran said gently.

Before Melkhior could answer, a cloud of chittering bats suddenly swooped into the vault and circled him like a tornado of leather and teeth. The creatures swirled around him for a moment and then shot out back the way they had come. Melkhior snarled and turned. 'The orcs are back!'

W'soran hurried after his acolyte. 'This... Dork-creature you mentioned?'

'Yes, he's attacking the slave pens!' Melkhior said. He yowled out orders to his creations and they hurried to obey. W'soran gestured for his wights to follow them, and they hurried towards the lower levels of the citadel.

By the time they reached the slave pens, the battle was in full swing. Ghouls and skeletons clashed with orcs clad in scavenged gear and wielding improvised weapons. The orcs were not quite a horde – there were only perhaps a hundred or so, W'soran noted as he stepped out onto the overseer's balcony to look down into the pens. In the pens, the still-imprisoned orcs were rattling their cages and bellowing out encouragement. The few remaining human slaves had huddled as far away from the fighting as they could get.

Bats filled the cavern, diving at the attacking orcs and clinging to them like squirming, hairy shrouds. Groups of ghouls mobbed individual orcs, knocking them off their feet and the skeletal guards duelled with others. Melkhior leapt lightly from the balcony and dropped straight down into the melee, blade in hand, gruesome face split in a screech of rage.

He cleaved an orc in two as he landed and backhanded another hard enough to pulp the creature's skull. More of them rushed towards him with raucous howls. W'soran watched for a moment and then turned his attentions to the wider battle. He was in no hurry to join the fight; the orcs, for all their ferocity, were hardly a threat. Melkhior could handle them easily enough, and if he couldn't, well, it was of little concern to W'soran.

He scanned the battle, hunting. Dork was easy enough to spot, when you knew what to look for. Greenskin magic had a particular aura about it, like charged air after a storm, or cold water washing over stones. He could taste it on the air.

Dork was big, bigger than most orcs he'd seen. The mines built muscle, and the orc stood head and shoulders over his followers. He had the ocular pigmentation that marked him as a Red Eye, and wore a headdress made from the hides of cave lizards and armour scavenged from earlier battles. With an axe in one hand and a sword in the other, Dork smashed his way through the guards, bulling his way towards the slave pens. His intent was obvious. The orc needed an army. W'soran smiled.

The smile faltered when he saw the emerald lightning crawl across Dork's scarred flesh as he locked blades with a wight. Dork howled, his red eyes going green and blazing like torches, and the wight exploded, ripped apart by the brutal magics spiking out from the greenskin's twitching form. Dork stomped his foot and the cavern shuddered in sympathy.

'Well, aren't you full of yourself,' W'soran murmured, watching the shaman storm towards the pens. He leapt lightly from the balcony, his magics coiling about him like a breeze, carrying him safely to the cavern floor. As he landed, there was a thunderclap of dark magics and orcs were sent tumbling, their bodies wreathed in sorcerous fire. He didn't bother to draw his sword. Instead he wove complicated gestures and gave his magics free rein. Orcs died by fire and lightning; others were torn apart by living shadows, or swallowed by the rock of the cavern. Methodically, he carved his way through them until he reached Dork, who spun about, piggy eyes blazing with fervour.

'*Oi, Bluddrinka,*' Dork roared, clashing his weapons together.

'*Bossbluddrinka,*' W'soran corrected in the greenskin tongue. He spread his arms and bared his fangs. 'Come, beast... show me your power.'

Dork howled again, and his muscles seemed to swell. The hazy aura about him snapped into sharp focus, and W'soran was reminded of the vision he'd had of Ushoran, with Nagash's shadow superimposed over him. For a moment, the orc, as large as he was, appeared akin to a giant crammed into a body that was three sizes too small. The cavern shuddered and great chunks of rock fell as Dork charged forward, swinging his weapons.

W'soran eeled around the first blow and twitched aside from the second as Dork's aura sparked and snapped like an overfed fire and the green heat washed over him. He drew his blade in time to block another heavy blow, and batted aside the axe as it dug for his chest. The orc was fast – almost impossibly so. More green lightning sparked from Dork's frame, striking the walls and floor and W'soran as well. His flesh peeled and split where the crackling energy touched him and he hissed in consternation.

'*Crumpya,*' Dork roared. '*Chopya!*'

'I think not,' W'soran snarled. He shoved himself back, sliding momentarily out of the orc's reach. Dork was strong. Too strong, in fact. W'soran glared about, his mind calculating and discarding possibilities. He knew much of the greenskins, including... 'Ah,' he hissed. Death magic swirled about him in a black cloud as he began to draw power from every part of the cavern. Dork charged towards him, bellowing.

W'soran thrust out his arm, and a rippling bolt of black energy burst from his palm. It narrowly missed Dork, who roared in triumph and brought his weapons down on W'soran. The latter barely held back the descending blades with his scimitar, and he sank to one knee, momentarily overwhelmed by the raw, sorcerously enhanced strength of his opponent. Dork leered down at him, certain of his triumph. Then, when he saw the wide grin on his opponent's face, the orc hesitated.

'Yesss,' W'soran chuckled. 'You *are* a smart one.'

Behind Dork, the slave pens had fallen silent. Every single living thing, orc or otherwise, in the pens was dead, killed by the lethal magics that W'soran had hurled at them – hundreds of orcs, slain in a single moment. Dork's jaw sagged as his gaze flickered between the pens, hunting for any signs of life. Then he turned back, his eyes glowing so brightly that W'soran was forced to cover his own.

Dork howled. And every surviving orc, those who had

come with their new warboss to free their fellows, howled with him, their great jaws gaping as they gave vent to a communal scream of primal ferocity and berserk rage. The cavern began to shudder and shake. The ceiling ruptured and bats spiralled frantically as jagged chunks of stone crashed down, piercing the floor and releasing serpentine cracks that sped across the ground.

W'soran climbed to his feet. Nearby, a trio of orcs fell as their heads burst. As if that had been a signal, more orcs twitched and fell as their skulls popped. There was a growing pressure in the cavern, and W'soran's mystically attuned senses screamed a warning. The ground beneath his feet burst, the hard stone shifting like melting ice. He turned and ran. Dork remained where he stood, a focal point for the snarling rhythms of green lightning that threatened to collapse the entire cavern.

W'soran reached the wall upon which the observation balcony sat and scrambled up it, climbing like a malformed and arthritic spider. He caught sight of a black-clad form – Melkhior – doing the same. They reached the balcony at roughly the same time, and both vaulted through the archway into the corridor beyond as a heavy fang of rock sheared the balcony away from the wall. W'soran turned and laughed wildly as around them, Crookback Mountain shook with the rage of Dork of the Red Eye tribe.

'Did you see that, Melkhior? *Did you see it?*' he shouted, as the corridor groaned and the mountain's guts rumbled. Smoke and dust boiled out through the archway, and grit caked them as W'soran's wights, whom he'd left safely behind, helped them up. 'Fascinating, eh? Impressive, wasn't he? To have that much power in him must surely be a result of–'

'Impressive? *Impressive,*' Melkhior hissed. He snapped forward, like a striking adder, claws digging for W'soran's throat. 'You nearly destroyed everything, you fool!'

W'soran caught his wrists and jerked him around. With a twitch of his arms, he slammed his acolyte against the wall and pinned him in place, using one hand to hold his wrists and his other to cup his jaw. 'And so what?' W'soran asked. 'It is mine to destroy, Melkhior, just as you are. You are still mine, aren't you?' he continued, his voice dropping low. He squeezed Melkhior's jaw and felt bone crack and the muscle rip beneath his fingers. 'Yesss, I made you, my son, and I can unmake you. You are a tool, boy, to be used as I see fit, as is this citadel, and everything in it. And I will use you, to secure my victory.'

Without releasing Melkhior, he glanced back at the archway and the fallen rocks that now blocked it. 'You will dig that out. Dead, those orcs will likely make better slaves at any rate. Then you will bring the levels of production back up to my standards. I will be taking half of your remaining forces with me when I depart. Now, any parting words for your poor burdened master?'

He released Melkhior and threw him to the floor. Melkhior glared up at him, and rubbed his bloody jaw. 'If – if you take half of my forces, I will not be able to hold off the skaven, let alone supply you with your gold…'

'Oh, I'm certain you'll manage, my son. It would have been easier, had you a few of your fellows to help, but… well,' W'soran said with a shrug. 'One must make do with what one has, eh?'

'You… you are more powerful than I am. Let me go in your stead. With you here, the skaven will not dare attack, and I am more than capable of–'

'Of course you're capable, my boy,' W'soran said, looking down at him. 'That's why I left you here. You are much too useful for me to risk you on the battlefield. Why, if I lost you, who would guard my laboratory or my books? Though, it must be said, you're not very good at the former.'

Melkhior flinched. He made no effort to get up. 'I have always been loyal, master…'

'Loyalty is worthless if the source is useless,' W'soran said, turning away. 'You are useless, Melkhior, and you always have been. So greedy for my favour that you fail to see that I despise you. And I despise you, because you are wasteful, Melkhior. You break what is still useful, like a child throwing a tantrum.' He stopped, and glanced over his shoulder. 'The only reason that I don't kill you now, boy, is that you have made yourself indispensable, if in a thoroughly roundabout manner. I am running out of time, and simply by existing in this moment, you have become useful.'

He raised a talon, like a parody of the pedantic tutor he had once been, and said, finally, 'But use is finite. And though it would pain me, if yours should ever run out entirely, I will flay the foul hide off your crooked bones myself.' He turned and continued on, his wights following silently.

As he left Melkhior sitting in the darkness, W'soran called out, 'Use is finite, my son. Prove you still have yours!'

—< CHAPTER FIFTEEN >—

The City of Mourkain
(Year -850 Imperial Calendar)

'This is madness,' W'soran snapped, slapping aside the record books and scrolls that occupied the table. He shot to his feet as they fell to the floor. 'They'll never believe it, let alone forgive old grudges.'

'They will, because we have what they want,' Ushoran said mildly. He picked up a handful of the gold that W'soran's dead servants had clawed from the dark vaults beneath Mourkain. It had taken decades to find those vaults, but the legions of well-preserved dead entombed by mad, bad Kadon were now once more hard at work, building Ushoran a war-chest that outstripped even the wealth of long-lost Lahmia at its height. 'Gold is what interests the dawi, and only gold.'

'You forget honour,' Abhorash rumbled, standing nearby, hands clasped behind his back as he gazed down at the pile of maps that

Ushoran's cartographers had been hard at work crafting for the better part of two years. The edges of those maps were still hazy, but, if you squinted, and the light was good, the rough outline of an empire became somewhat visible.

It was only the three of them in the chamber of Kadon's pyramid that Ushoran had designated as his war-council. That was not unusual, though it had grown rarer as the years passed and they began to recall just how much they actually disliked each other. But initially, Ushoran had seemed to welcome the awkward camaraderie – indeed, he seemed almost desperate for it, and W'soran, despite himself, could not blame him. In the deeps of the mountains, a black voice tolled again and again, urging them on and whispering malevolently seductive promises. He recognised that voice, even if Ushoran did not, and it made him frequently question his reasons for acquiescing to Ushoran's request that he join him in the benighted land.

'I forget nothing. I merely disregard it in this instance. Mourkain – Strigos – has forfeited honour, to the dawi way of thinking. A change of leadership will not change that. All that is left is this shiny bit of promise,' Ushoran said, examining a nugget. 'And this, they want. They crave it, as we crave blood.' He tossed the nugget onto the table and sniffed. 'So we will extend the proper invitations and see what comes of it.'

'Idiocy,' W'soran said, leaning forward and balancing on his knuckles. 'Why beg what we could borrow, why borrow what we can take, eh?'

'Why take what will be freely given?' Ushoran asked. He glanced at Abhorash. 'What of the northern frontier?'

'The daemon worshippers come in great numbers, but they are...
fragile,' Abhorash said, his arms crossed, his face set. 'I can drive
them back, given time and men. Once a few of their champions
lose their heads, they'll scurry back to their wastes.'

'And what of the devils that accompany them, eh?' W'soran
sneered. 'Will you chop their heads off, champion?'

'I rather thought that you might help him with that, old monster,' Ushoran said, pulling a map towards himself. 'Unless, of
course, you have finally learned what you need to know from
Kadon's scribbling to acquire for me my crown?'

W'soran froze and he noticed that Abhorash did the same. Both
vampires traded a glance and then looked at the Lord of Masks.
For a moment, just an instant, something seemed to hunch over
Ushoran, something infinitely massive and terrible, and the
torches set into the walls hissed and flickered as if that same something were drawing the heat and light from them.

Oh yes, it had its claws deep in him, no doubt about it. The
question was, did it want him? Or was Ushoran merely... a
substitute?

Everything about the place seemed to press down upon him as
he stood there, as if it sought to force him to crawl before it. The
voice – his voice – was louder now, murmuring constantly, just
behind his thoughts. An aura of darkness clung to the stones and
his bones felt brittle and cold within their envelope of weak flesh.

Death coiled waiting in this place. But waiting for what – or
whom – he could not say.

W'soran licked his lips. 'Not – ah – as yet, Ushoran,' he said.

'Lord Ushoran,' Ushoran corrected. 'We must observe the

*proprieties, W'soran. I am a lord now… but I will be a king soon –
an undying one and a great one, as soon as you fulfil your part of
our bargain, old monster.' His eyes flickered, as if something lean
and hungry moved behind them, jaws agape and mind athirst.
'Get me my crown, W'soran, so that I might remake this world
into a better one.'*

The City of Mourkain
(Year -260 Imperial Calendar)

Mourkain was burning. The city was alight with a hundred
fires as its walls shuddered beneath the weight of the siege
that encompassed it. Smoke rose into the night sky in thick
plumes as the screams of dying men and the roar of battle
rose to mingle with it in the heights. Bats wheeled and
flapped across the face of the moon and the air was full of
wailing spectres and howling spirits.

W'soran hunched forward in his saddle and cackled as the
zombie-dragon smashed into the inner gates of Mourkain,
a cloud of noxious gas spewing from its bony jaws to engulf
the warriors who cringed back from it in horror. Its ancient
talons gouged the stone, sending rock tumbling down into
the river below. Its serpentine neck whipped back and forth,
and its pestilential breath spread across the wall and into the
gatehouse, killing men in their dozens.

The Strigoi warriors screamed and tore at their armour as
it corroded, and their flesh, even as it sloughed from their

bones. W'soran gestured and a rippling bolt of black sorcery tore through a watchtower, ripping the edifice from the wall and dropping it down into the gorge below to crash into the raging waters.

Satisfied, he flexed his will and the dragon pushed away from the wall with a rasping cry. It was not a natural sound and it affected those who heard it almost as badly as the zombie-dragon's breath had done. The monster flapped its tattered wings once, twice and then it was barrelling upwards through the smoke-choked night air.

Below him, the siege of Mourkain spread out in a gore-stained panorama. The city was surrounded by a heavy wooden palisade in concentric and ever-shrinking rings that jutted from the rocky slope. Smoke rose from within, striping the air with greasy trails. The decaying bodies of Draesca tribesmen had been impaled on great, greased stakes lining the approaches to the city.

Bone-giants battered at the palisade, killing men with every sweep of their great khopesh or spears. Ushabti crafted from bone and clay and rotting meat stalked through gaps the giants had already made, followed by hunting packs of ghouls and crypt horrors. The sky was filled with swarms of bats, both of the normal variety and the titan monstrosities that he had wrenched from their slumber in the depths. Squalling, screeching monstrous bats smashed into the watchtowers and high barricades, their quivering spear-blade noses sniffing out any defender whom they might devour.

Within the palisade, a great stone gateway rose, blocking

access to a wide bridge of thick wooden logs that led to a
second, smaller gate. Beneath the bridge, the river crashed
and snarled, and even at this distance he could feel the spray.
As W'soran cackled in glee, his wights led skeletal legions
towards the bridge as quickly as their dead legs could move.
The outer gates could be controlled from within the city
proper, as long as the ropes held. And if the ropes were cut,
the stone gates would remain closed and the bridge sealed
off. The Strigoi on the inner walls had been intent on doing
just that when he'd attacked. Now they had no time.

He looked beyond the wild river that separated the
palisades from the inner fortifications, towards the ancient
stones where what might have been the remnants of some
long-ago destroyed wall rose up, linked anew by newer stone
fortifications put in place long ago by W'soran's own servants. He found it to be the height of irony that those same
servants would now tear down all they had built.

It had taken almost three years for his forces to fight
their way through the lines of fortifications that marked
the Plain of Dust and surrounded Mourkain in its mountain fastness with a ring of stone and iron. Ushoran, ever
the keen student, had plucked inspiration from the four
compass points, mingling the military styles of Nehekhara,
Cathay and even the terrifying strongpoints devised by the
dwarfs – hard-to-reach isolated towers, firmly anchored to
the rock and packed with supplies and armaments for a
hundred men. For three gruelling years, W'soran had led his
nightmare legions past each defensive line, smashing them

one after the other. In that time, he had faced numberless enemy necromancers, northern mercenaries and dozens of Strigoi – Gashnag's peers, spouting childish incantations as they sought to match his mastery of the winds of death. None had done more than distract him. W'soran now wore a necklace of fangs to match his necklace of wyrdstone, and the still-aware, still-screaming heads of his vampire enemies hung from his standards like strange fruit. But none of them were the enemy he truly wished to face.

'Where are you?' he hissed. His free hand found the abn-i-khat amulets hanging from his throat and the urge to swallow them was suddenly overpowering. Soon, soon he would need them. Ushoran would not be able to resist this assault. Everything was going just as he had planned. His legions were without limit, his forces mightier even than those of Nagashizzar at its height, and soon, he would prove his mastery over the pitiful spark of Nagash that thought to impose its wretched will on the world.

'Master, is it? Who's the master now, eh? Who is the master, Nagash?' he snarled, spitting the words down at the black city below. The streets of Mourkain were like lines drawn on parchment, crossing one another over and over again. The city was a spiral of stone, with crude thatch huts and lean-tos giving way to more sturdy stone dwellings and finally the great buildings that seemed to form the heart of the city. The streets were choked with the smells, sights and sounds of a thriving, vibrant metropolis under siege.

The citizenry – those who weren't on the walls – fled,

seeking shelter away from the forefront of battle. There weren't so many of these; the Strigoi were a warrior race, even their women knew how to handle blades. Haphazard barricades were being thrown up at intersections and the dead who had entered the city were being thrown back, oft-times by other corpses, these animated by the magics of the Mortuary Cult. Dead men clashed in the streets in a gruesome gavotte, and the city itself seemed to shift in contentment.

Something had always been in this place, whether its name was Mourkain or not. It was a city in the same way that Lahmia had been, grown over centuries by generations, spreading first behind the river and then over it. As he swooped past the gates once more, he looked up and saw that its bulk was punctuated by hundreds of alcoves packed with skulls. Some of the skulls were brown with age, while others glistened white and clean. They were the skulls of Mourkain's enemies. As he passed by them, he gestured, and horrible fires blossomed in the depth of each eye-socket. Mourkain was a sump of dark magic, and it was easier here than most places to raise the dead, especially those who still burned with some small ember of hatred for Mourkain and the Strigoi.

The skulls, which were now mounted on new bodies composed of shadows and dark flame, squeezed from their alcoves and began to climb the walls. They slithered up over the walls and gate and fell upon the Strigoi defenders, burning and tearing at them. W'soran laughed wildly as his mount landed heavily on the gatehouse. He stood in his saddle and cast out a hand, ready to drag the dead defenders to their feet to join his ranks.

But... something prevented him. The bodies twitched and jerked, but did not rise. W'soran hissed angrily, and he twisted in his saddle, following the delicate skeins of interfering magic back to–

'Morath,' he snarled.

Morath of Mourkain, necromancer and nobleman, stood on the wall, surrounded by a flock of Mortuary Cultists, all garbed in black. Morath was much as W'soran remembered him, if a bit thinner. He had been handsome once, had Morath, but now he was like a knife that had been over-sharpened, all sharp angles and gestures, and his robes and furs flapped about him as he chanted hoarsely, incanting in W'soran's direction.

A flurry of flaming orbs streaked from the corona that sprang up around Morath's gestures. W'soran swiped at the air, snuffing the deadly comets before they reached him. Something akin to pleasure filled W'soran as he watched Morath begin to gesture anew after barely a moment's hesitation. 'Oh, Morath, you do me proud, my son,' W'soran called out.

'No son of yours, monster,' Morath shouted back. 'I am a son of Mourkain, and Mourkain alone!' He flung out both hands, and the gathering shadows cast by flame and moon swirled about W'soran and his mount; tendrils of purest darkness grabbed at the zombie-dragon, and the corpse-monster croaked a challenge. W'soran reached out and grasped one of the tendrils and let his will thrum through it. Morath gave a wail as control of his spell was torn from him, and he staggered.

W'soran examined the squirming, semi-ghostly tendril and smiled. 'Wonderful,' he said. 'You were ever the most impressive of my students, boy, and far superior to your fellows. It broke my poor heart when you refused my gift – think of what you might have accomplished without fear of death or infirmity, eh?'

'Think of what I would have lost,' Morath said, as his assistants helped him to his feet. 'What you offer is no gift, monster. It's a curse – better death than a carrion eternity.'

'Death – ah, well, that will be my last gift to you, then, I suppose…' W'soran said, with a shrug. Then he flung the writhing remnants of Morath's spell back at the group of sorcerers who opposed him. The shadow-thing spread and grew, like ink on water, billowing out and engulfing them. Several, Morath included, defended themselves immediately, bellowing desperate incantations to ward off the preternatural tendrils.

Those who avoided them were soon confronted by the skull-wraiths that W'soran had summoned. The bobbing skulls of Mourkain's enemies, riding their bodies of smoke and black flame, loped towards the sorcerers. Morath destroyed several with a burst of spellcraft, but others crashed into him, burning his flesh with their ghostly talons. Morath screamed and lightning snapped and snarled from him, shattering the champing, burning skulls.

Several of his acolytes pushed through their enemies to confront W'soran. But before they could so much as gesture, or bring the first syllables of a spell to their lips, a bestial shape blurred past them. A heavy blade went *snicker-snack* and their heads rolled free from their necks.

Ullo turned and gave his shark's grin. 'Three more heads for the pile, sorcerer!' he roared. W'soran smiled as the other vampire bounded towards Morath and his remaining students. Morath had succeeded in sending the shadow tendrils back where they had come from, but he was having a harder time with the skulls. Ullo crashed amongst the necromancers like a cat amongst pigeons, his broad blade looping out to lop off limbs or open bellies. Sorcery did a man little good when his guts were all over his feet. Soon enough, only Morath was standing, and he was forced to draw his sword and defend himself.

Ullo howled, and the two traded blows as W'soran watched in amusement. His mount screeched and belched gas over the Strigoi reinforcements approaching the gatehouse. Down below, a massive bone-giant tore the stone doors from their hinges, sending the ancient doors toppling down into the roaring waters below. The giant shoved its way through the gateway, followed by more of W'soran's forces – skeletal spearmen and archers took up positions inside the walls as armoured wights charged towards the reeling defenders, and cleared the walls of life with the help of fluttering masses of blood-bloated bats.

'Sorcerer! Watch out!' Ullo roared, flinging Morath aside. W'soran glanced at him, and then twisted around to see a descending thunderbolt clad in red. He screeched and drew his scimitar with only seconds to spare, barely halting the blow that would have split his skull.

Abhorash dropped to the parapet of the gatehouse, his fur cloak flaring around his crimson-armoured form. Though he had not seen the former champion of Lahmia in a century, he was as intimidating as W'soran recalled – sheathed in the serrated, sharply curved iron armour of Ushoran's personal guard, Abhorash was a giant amongst men. He wielded his great sword with its iron blade engraved with curling, savage sigils as if it were a feather, and he moved as if his armour weighed no more than a morning mist.

He sprang for W'soran again, his face contorted in a terrifying snarl within his dragon helm. With a thought, W'soran urged his mount into the air with a single snap of its wings, but too late. Abhorash's hand flashed out and his fingers sank into the gangrenous flesh of the zombie-dragon's flank.

Even as W'soran sought to put distance between them, Abhorash hauled himself up, eyes blazing. 'I knew you wouldn't stay out of it, you withered old fool,' Abhorash roared. 'I warned him that he was only courting betrayal by letting you live!'

'Who has betrayed who, eh, champion? You betrayed your queen and your new followers by serving a hag-ridden madman,' W'soran said, rising from his saddle, cloak whipping about him as his mount soared high into the air. 'What price your loyalty, Abhorash? What has he promised you?'

'I do not have to explain myself to such as you,' Abhorash growled.

'No, nor would I care to hear it, even if you deigned to do so, brute,' W'soran said. Then, so saying, he leapt from the dragon's back, and plummeted downwards. While he yearned to wipe the self-righteous sneer from Abhorash's face, the warrior was not his prey this day.

As W'soran hurtled away, the zombie-dragon twisted around. Abhorash, dislodged by the beast's undulations, fell, but not for long. The corpse-dragon, responding to W'soran's urging, coiled about the warrior like a striking serpent, its jaws agape and its talons crunching into the vampire's armour as it seized him the way an eagle might seize a rat. Its wings flapped once, carrying it higher, and dragged Abhorash into the dark sky.

W'soran dropped through the darkness. His spectral scarabs swarmed about him as he fell, wrapping him in a cocoon of ghostly light, and in the blink of an eye, he was no longer in the air, but standing in the courtyard beyond the walls of Mourkain. His sudden appearance startled Ullo and Arpad. The former grunted and asked, 'Abhorash?'

'Occupied,' W'soran said. As if on cue, the zombie-dragon screeched somewhere far above. He continued, 'Morath?'

'Gashnag organised a counter-charge. He and Morath are pulling back what's left of the usurper's troops. They're falling back to the next line of defences,' Arpad growled. 'They're not giving an inch unless we wash it in bone-chips and blood. And we still haven't taken the outer palisades!'

'Abhorash's Hand is to blame for that. That bastard Walak and his cursed brother are out there. It's all our men can do to keep them contained to the southern palisades,' Ullo snapped. 'But we hold the entrance to the city – if we can push on, and take the palace...'

'If we can take Ushoran, you mean?' W'soran asked. He stretched, and felt the raw power of Mourkain tug at him. It seemed to grow and shift at his notice, like the heat from a stoked forge. It was feeding on the death agonies of the hundreds who were dying even at that moment, swelling like a toad gorging itself on gnats.

In a way, this was what Nagash had wanted – for all life to be scoured away and the world to be wiped clean. Perhaps that was what Ushoran wanted now as well, and perhaps this moment was not by W'soran's design alone. The thought filled him with anger, that even now, even here, he was being used as a tool to scour life from the territories he claimed. In invading, in inciting slaughter, he was merely providing Ushoran with the raw materials he'd need for later conquests.

'Even after all these centuries, is that how you still see me?' W'soran muttered, casting a glare towards the distant palace. It was a massive structure, bristling with outcroppings and crude structural additions that seemed to serve no purpose save ornamental.

Though it had been designed to look like one, it was a pyramid in name only; the resemblance was superficial. It was a crude mockery of the great pyramids of Nehekhara, devised by barbaric minds and built by unskilled hands. Heavy dark stones had been piled atop one another much like the grim barrows which dotted the northern lands. It careened high above the city, and stable growths of structure flourished along its length. There were narrow windows and balconies and things that might have been towers. It crouched like a beast over the winding river which encircled and ran through Mourkain, and the rest of the city seemed to recoil from it, as if in fear.

He could feel the malignant will within it, beckoning him closer. Ushoran was as eager for this confrontation as he was. He had never denied himself an opportunity to prove his superiority over his followers, flaunting his might the way a foppish courtier might flaunt a fine cloak. 'I am coming, old friend,' W'soran growled. 'We go forward. If we must drown this city in death to take it, so be it!'

Ullo and Arpad shared a look and then both Strigoi grinned. 'You aren't half the coward Melkhior made you out to be, sorcerer,' Arpad said.

W'soran ignored the backhanded compliment. Overhead, the zombie-dragon shrieked again. The war machines he'd brought continued to fire from outside the city, hurling rocks and debris against the walls and into the city itself, and the street trembled beneath his feet. He could hear the clangour of weapons from around him, as his grave-legions fought against Mourkain's defenders. Over the tops of nearby roofs, he caught sight of a bone-giant, a heavy howdah on its broad shoulders. Skeletal archers fired down as the bone-giant stomped through the streets. His acolytes could keep the army functioning, while he turned his attentions to more important matters.

Even if they couldn't, it wouldn't matter. His army had done its job, and well. It had delivered him to the time and place he required and whether it survived or was destroyed now was of no consequence to him. Even Melkhior, squatting in his tenuous citadel, was of no more use, and good thing as well, for the flow of wealth and reinforcements had dried up swiftly.

The clopping of hooves caught his attention and he and the other vampires turned to see Voloch, new king of the Draesca and lord of the Grave-Host, and his wights approaching, accompanied by several renegade Strigoi, including the bulky brute known as Dhrox and the whipcord-thin lunatic known as Throttlehand. Voloch saluted with his double-bitted axe. Chown had succumbed to the helm's poisonous touch a year earlier, but Voloch was easily his match. Now Chown had joined his predecessor Shull amongst their descendant's bodyguard.

'We have breached the walls, oh Speaker for the Dead,' Voloch said. 'Our forces stream into Morgheim, but they face stiff resistance. We must break the enemy, and soon, for our forces are stretched thin.'

'Abhorash's Hand is scattered,' Throttlehand rasped, stroking his throat with an armoured claw. 'They're holding what they've got, but they can't mount an organised defence, not without the Great Red Dragon holding their hands.'

'Crush 'em,' Dhrox rumbled as he smacked his hairy paws together. His lumpen features were covered in dried gore and combined the worst aspects of bat and wolf. 'Smash 'em and suck the pulp.'

'I'd say Dhrox speaks for all of us,' Ullo growled.

'Good,' W'soran said. 'We will push straight through the city, like jamming a dagger into a heart. Let nothing stand in our way.'

They began moving forward, slowly at first, and then picking up speed. They flooded the streets, smashing aside barricades and driving back the men holding them. Swarms of bats flapped ahead of them, attacking the defenders, blinding and harrying them. Voloch's mounted wights thundered ahead of the slower skeletons and vaulted the barricades, followed by over-eager Strigoi like Dhrox. W'soran's eyes strayed continually to the pyramid. Ushoran had not shown himself, and W'soran knew that he was waiting in his throne room. Nagash too had refused to bestir himself, until the last moment.

The human defenders fell back, street by street, as the dead moved deeper into the city. Until, at last, the largest group of defenders made their stand in the great plaza before the pyramid. Ushoran's personal guard was there, and Gashnag, who rode at their head, and Morath, as well. Morath stood surrounded by the newly-risen dead – men and women, soldiers and otherwise, had been jerked from death's bower to defend their home. The zombies moved forward slowly, shuffling at Morath's gesture. W'soran noted with some amusement that Morath looked unhappy with the prospect of commanding the corpses of his people. 'Too much of the man in you, and not enough monster,' W'soran murmured. 'You'll learn though, if you survive.'

The two sides faced one another across the plaza. The space was immense, bounded on its sides by great columns covered in carved skulls and topped by massive braziers that still burned despite the siege, casting their light across the plaza. Spears were lowered and arrows notched as the two groups sized one another up.

But, before a single arrow could be fired, a terrifying scream rocked the city. W'soran looked up and his good eye widened as he saw his zombie-dragon twisting through the air, falling towards the city. He could feel the dark magic that animated it fading. Impossibly, improbably, Abhorash was beating it.

'By Strigu's bones,' Ullo murmured, looking up. 'He can't have won – he can't!'

'He has,' W'soran said flatly.

The zombie-dragon smashed into the plaza like a shrieking comet. Two of the columns exploded at the point of impact, showering the surrounding streets and the plaza with a hail of broken stone. As the smoke began to clear, both sides faced each other warily as they waited to see what pulled itself out of the crater now gouged into the street.

With aching slowness the writhing coils of the corpse-dragon stilled, as its false life fled at last. A tall shape rose up and iron sang down, ringing as it struck the rock of the street.

Then Abhorash stepped through the smoke, dragging the beast's head behind him by one splintered horn. His armour hung from him in tatters and his marble flesh was stained black and striped red, but the fire in his eyes burned undimmed. He had lost his helm, and some of his hair where the dragon's breath had scoured his flesh. He released the head, letting it flop to the ground, and reached up to strip the ragged remains of his cuirass and pauldrons from his torso, tossing them aside as if they were of no more consequence than the bloody wounds that were already congealing on his mighty frame.

W'soran cursed himself for a fool. He had suspected that Abhorash would triumph, but he had hoped that the fight would carry him far from Mourkain. Instead, it was as if some dark power had dropped one of the greatest obstacles to his plan directly into his path.

Others seemed to feel similarly. Arpad cursed, and before either Ullo or W'soran could stop him, he darted forward, moving like lightning. He sprang towards Abhorash and vaulted up, blade extended. Almost casually, Abhorash struck out, shattering his opponent's weapon and then, in a reversal so quick that not even the watching vampires could follow it, slashing upwards, catching Arpad as he descended. The latter didn't even have time to scream as his body was bisected, split in two from thigh to shoulder. The two halves fell to the ground wetly and Abhorash flicked his blade, cleaning it of blood. He met W'soran's shocked gaze and inclined his head. 'Take him alive,' he rumbled.

Fear flooded W'soran, washing away his earlier anger. He stepped back, and his spectral scarabs clicked and hummed softly as they swarmed about him, ready to yank him from peril.

He forced the fear down, driving it back into its hole. Nagash – no, *Ushoran*, not Nagash, Nagash was dead, crown or not – wanted him – fine. He was here, regardless. 'Ullo,' W'soran growled.

'He's mine,' Ullo snarled and bounded towards Abhorash. As if that had been the signal, the battle was joined as both sides surged forward. W'soran found himself locked in combat once more with Gashnag, and the Strigoi seemed to have no intention of allowing him to gain enough room to use his sorcery. Instead, Gashnag hemmed him in, his pale features split in a snarl.

'You heard the Dragon, sorcerer,' Gashnag said, slashing low. W'soran stepped back, knocking several men sprawling. 'Surrender yourself to us, and perhaps Lord Ushoran will spare you the worst of his planned torments!'

'W'soran – surrender? You must be mad,' W'soran barked. 'When I'm winning? When I'm finally on the precipice of victory?' He hissed an incantation and his scimitar became enveloped in obsidian flames. With a roar worthy of the Strigoi, he launched a flurry of attacks that drove Gashnag back. 'Surrender is for the weak – for the useless! I am not useless! I am not weak! I am the strongest! I am the master of all I survey – the master of life and death! Surrender – you should all surrender to me!' He battered the Strigoi backwards, driving into the ranks of the enemy, his swings lopping off limbs and shattering spears as he shoved Gashnag back, deeper into the ranks of men who kept him separated from his goal.

It had all been for this moment – every game, every death, all building to this point in time. Every scheme and plot had all been to buy him time and to arrange things so that the pieces would fall in his favour. He had forced Neferata's hand, and Ushoran's as well, forcing them into making the decisions he wanted. He had guided Mourkain, building the perfect cage for death's tiger. Let the shreds of Nagash's spirit thunder and rage, let him taunt and whisper. Ushoran knew as well as W'soran did that the game was done. The time for gods and monsters was past and now only two men – two minds – remained, to fight their final duel, a duel that W'soran of Mahrak would win.

He would not wear the crown, but instead shatter it and drain it. He would drink of its power, and with the strength of the Undying King added to his own, he would sink his fangs into the throat of the world and suck it white. He would do what Nagash had only dreamt of, and do it better. The world would bend and break beneath his heel and the sky itself would weep to see the agonies he inflicted.

He would be a god – a god of death and order, come to set the world to rights. He would become a god and put the world and all its peoples where they belonged... at his feet.

'You wanted me, my master?' he shrieked, slapping Gashnag's blade aside. 'You wanted to see your old student once more? Well, here I am! Here I stand!' Gashnag's blade shattered and the Strigoi staggered. W'soran, in his fury, had carved a red crater in the Strigoi ranks and men pressed back from the spider-limbed, splay-fanged apparition that howled and capered in their midst. W'soran tossed his blade aside and pounced on Gashnag, bearing him down. With a ripple of hidden strength, he hauled the Strigoi over his head. 'Here I stand, master! Here is your truest son! Not Neferata! Not Ushoran! Me! I am your heir, your servant – no, *I am your better!*'

Then, with a shriek, W'soran twisted Gashnag, shattering his spine and neck. He hurled the howling Strigoi aside and snatched up his scimitar. 'Here I am! Face me!' he screamed, gesticulating with his scimitar at the black pyramid. 'Face me, damn you! I have beaten you!'

NO. YOU HAVE NOT.

The words were like hammer blows on the surface of his mind. They nearly dropped him from his feet and his black heart, pumping sour blood, shuddered in its cage of bone. It was Ushoran's voice, but it almost wasn't.

COME, MY SERVANT. COME TO ME.

W'soran shivered as a cold wind cut through him, a cold such as he had not felt in centuries. It was the cold of a damp tomb, or of an open grave... the pure, inexorable cold of death. He hesitated... and almost lost his head as Abhorash's blade looped out and chopped into a nearby column.

W'soran snapped around and his scimitar carved a black trail across Abhorash's chest.

Abhorash stepped back and touched his chest. He examined the blood and smiled grimly. 'You are quicker than I remembered,' he said. He jerked his chin towards the pyramid. 'You heard him. He's waiting for you.'

'And I'm to believe that you'll just let me go to confront him?' W'soran snarled, straightening. He had always wondered whether the champion had heard the whispers of Nagash's shredded spirit as clearly as the rest of them.

'Yes,' Abhorash said. 'You might be the only one who can. Unlike you, I am not blinded by arrogance.'

'What's that supposed to mean?' W'soran spat as they circled each other. Abhorash seemed unconcerned, which infuriated W'soran. 'Why are you even still here? Do you willingly serve Ushoran, champion? What are you doing here?'

Abhorash was silent for a moment. Then he said, 'Repaying a debt.'

W'soran stared at him. Abhorash stepped aside. Behind him, there was a clear path to the pyramid. He could hear the voice of the crown in his head, urging him on, and what might have been Ushoran's voice as well, pleading with him. He shook his head and asked, 'Why?'

'If you have to ask, sorcerer, you wouldn't understand,' Abhorash said, turning away. 'I have a battle to win, W'soran. And you have your own. I would hurry.'

W'soran did. He hurried away from the battle, leaving his

men behind. No one tried to stop him from entering the pyramid. All of the guards were otherwise occupied, as he'd planned. But now, at the moment, he almost yearned for opposition, anything to delay what was coming next. What he feared was waiting for him.

He had visited the pyramid often enough in his time in Mourkain. But never before had it seemed so oppressive. The corridors were crafted from slabs of stone and, like the pyramids of home, they moved across from east to west, and then up south to north in a zigzag pattern. It was like following a well-worn path. He knew where it would come out as he recalled the routes he had taken decades before. With every step he took, the whispering in his head grew stronger. It was almost painful in its intensity, and he fought to ignore it.

The throne room crouched in the web of corridors that surrounded it, nestled like a cancer in the heart of the pyramid. Smoking, glowing braziers were scattered throughout the room, their light revealing the high balconies and great expanse of floor. At the other end of the room, a huge flat dais rose, and on it, a throne. The throne was made from the ribcage of some great beast and spread across the rear wall, and on that throne... Ushoran.

He sat slumped, as if bowed beneath an incredible weight, almost to the point of breaking. His shape rippled and contorted as he sat, as if at first assuming one form and then changing to the next in a blur of faces and shapes, both human and otherwise. He moved from monster to man and back again as he sat on his hard-won throne.

But it was not Ushoran alone who sat there; the great iron crown he wore seemed to pulse like the eyes of a predator as it sighted prey. A vast shadow unspooled from Ushoran's slumped form, spreading across the walls and floor, slithering towards W'soran, who, for a moment, forgot why he had come and what he desired, and wanted only to cower before the awful immensity which squatted in the throne room, looming over everything.

In his time beneath the crown's influence, Ushoran had grown strong. The Lord of Masks had become something else; something massive and world-breaking. And even as he realised that, W'soran knew that the process was not yet finished. That what Ushoran was now was but the merest shadow of what he would become in time. Like some dreadful seed, the true horror was yet to flower.

'No,' W'soran said, forcing himself to step forward. 'No, I won't let you... you won't take it from me. It's mine – this world, them – Ushoran, Neferata – they're all mine!' Even to his own ears, he sounded petulant. Like a child scolding an uncaring parent. The crown couldn't hear him. Nagash couldn't hear him, but he still lashed out, hoping to score points against the god that had failed him.

HELLO, W'SORAN.

Ushoran's mouth was open, but it was not his voice that reverberated from it. His hands reached up and clutched his temples, as if he were in pain. 'W'soran,' he gasped a moment later. 'You came...'

W'soran said nothing. He clutched the hilt of his scimitar so tightly that the bone of the handle cracked. Ushoran's eyes were tight with pain. 'I thought – I thought I could control it. I thought I was stronger than Kadon, but it is too strong for me. I need your help,' he said, between gritted teeth. 'It's taking all of my strength – all of me – to resist it, to keep it from killing every living thing in Mourkain and riding their corpses into battle with the world.' His eyes rolled madly in their sockets and his flesh trembled as if something was moving within him.

THERE IS TIME. IS THAT NOT SO, W'SORAN? WE HAVE TIME. TIME BEATS DOWN MOUNTAINS AND BREAKS WILLS… EVEN WILLS AS STRONG AS THOSE POSSESSED BY YOU AND YOUR ILK. THE STRENGTH IN SPITE IS FINITE.

Ushoran's voice – was it his voice? – echoed through the throne room, weighing down the air itself. W'soran's flesh crawled as the words brushed across his mind like greasy fingers. 'I thought it would be different,' Ushoran whispered. 'I thought I was a monster, that we were monsters, but we're nothing compared to *him*.' His eyed focused on W'soran. 'I can't take it off anymore. It won't let me.' W'soran's good eye widened as he saw Ushoran's claws dig into his own flesh, as if he sought to strip the meat from his scalp.

He screamed and hunched forward on his throne. His talons slammed down on the armrests, cracking them. He glared helplessly at W'soran and said, 'Help me, my friend… please…' He closed his eyes and shuddered, racked by pain.

'Ushoran, I–' W'soran began. Memories rose up in him; memories of Ushoran freeing him from his jar, of Ushoran saving him from Abhorash, of Ushoran rescuing him in the Marshes of Madness.

NO. THERE IS NO HELP. THERE IS NO USHORAN.
THERE IS ONLY DEATH.

Ushoran's eyes opened. But they weren't Ushoran's eyes. He rose, and there was another shape superimposed over his – a towering shape, wreathed in green fire.

'*YOU WANTED TO PROVE YOUR POWER, W'SORAN? COME THEN. SHOW YOUR OLD FRIEND WHAT YOU HAVE LEARNED,*' Ushoran said.

And W'soran did.

◀ CHAPTER SIXTEEN ▶

The City of Mourkain
(Year -327 Imperial Calendar)

'Neferata has failed,' W'soran said as he gathered up a number of scrolls and thrust them into Zoar's arms. 'More importantly, I have failed. We must find a new lair, my sons, and quickly, if we are to have any chance of success. Grab as many tomes as you can carry,' he barked, gesturing sharply to the others. 'Melkhior – where are the guards?'

W'soran's retreat was in an uproar. Burrowed deep in the heart of the mountain that Mourkain crouched on, his lair was unknown save to a few. Most thought he resided in the temple complex that belonged to the Mortuary Cult. His acolytes hurried about, grabbing up as much as they could of the carefully accumulated and jealously hoarded knowledge. Writing desks and scroll shelves had been upended and shattered. Melkhior watched it all from the doorway, his eyes glittering. 'The fire has them distracted,' he said.

'Good,' W'soran said. He'd just come from the temple that was the centre of Mourkain's Mortuary Cult. He'd set it aflame and slaughtered the priests. If he was being forced to flee, he was damned if he was going to leave any of his tools for Ushoran to use. Nagash had made that mistake, but W'soran was smarter than the Undying King. 'Grab everything we can't take – we'll pile it in the centre of the room and burn it. Nothing will be left behind.' Ushoran would not suspect him, not yet. That would buy them enough time to escape Mourkain, at least.

'Burn it?' Melkhior hissed, startled.

W'soran wheeled around to face his acolyte. 'Are you deaf? Yes, burn it!'

'But–' Melkhior began. Like many savages, Melkhior regarded the written word with an almost totemic fascination, as if the words themselves were holy, rather than the power that they unlocked. W'soran had yet to break some of his more stubborn Strigoi acolytes of that fascination, to show them that true power resided not in musty tomes but in how you put the knowledge they contained to use. And not only the Strigoi – a number of his acolytes had perished in the fall of Lahmia attempting to save useless volumes of mystic knowledge from the great temple library.

Knowledge was merely a tool, and tools could be refined and replaced. Spellcraft could be honed like a blade, stripped of useless components and ritual to make a leaner, deadlier thing. That was why he insisted that his acolytes craft their own personal grimoires, and that those grimoires be copied to his own library. His apprentices were tools he used to sift through the grit to find the precious minerals buried there. Every discovery they made added to his arsenal. Creatures like Melkhior weren't servants so much as they were walking spell-books, to be drained of knowledge and discarded when they had made their discoveries or refinements. Melkhior didn't yet understand that, and W'soran doubted he ever would.

'Tools that cannot be used are useless, fool,' W'soran snarled, leaning close to Melkhior. 'Useless to us, and – even worse – useful to our enemies. Ushoran already has that damnable crown, I'll not give him anything else. Burn it, all of it.'

'But... isn't this what you wanted? Isn't this what we've been working toward?' Melkhior asked, as W'soran shoved scrolls and loose pages into his arms. 'Ushoran is weak now, overcome by the power of the crown. We – you can take it!' There was a burr of greed to his words and W'soran shook his head.

'No,' W'soran barked. 'Now is not the time. We shall go east and see if we can find sanctuary with Vorag's rebels.' The Bloody-tooth had begun his revolt well before Ushoran had placed the crown on his head. Likely it was simply another addle-brained plan of Neferata's. Vorag had retreated to the eastern mountains with a bevy of cronies and their men, bellowing about a second Strigoi Empire.

So far Ushoran had ignored his rebellious vassal, but that wouldn't last. Vorag would leap at the opportunity to have a sorcerer of W'soran's calibre at his beck and call. Of course, that meant abandoning his place here. He shook his head, trying to gather together the tattered threads of his plans and schemes. A careful web had been shaken and stretched by the advent of Nagash's damned spark.

Flight was the only option available. If he stayed, the sheer malevolent force of the crown's presence would eventually crush his will, as it had Neferata's. She served her new master meekly, barely more than an automaton. If you fought, you were crushed. That was Nagash's way – he had no servants, no advisors, only tools. No dissent would be brooked in Ushoran's new Nagashizzar. Not even from the man wearing the crown.

He paused, remembering the look on Ushoran's face as the crown had set its hooks into him. W'soran remembered that half-moment of pleading, as Ushoran had realised just what he had awakened. Neither he nor Neferata had truly understood what the crown was. W'soran had tried to explain it to Ushoran, but he had been adamant. He had been convinced that the crown had held the power he required to carve an empire for his adopted people out of the mountains.

It had the power, all right. But it also had a will of its own, if no sentience, a terrible, night-black drive that hungered for the beautiful silence of Corpse Geometries. It had called them all out of the night, and brought them together to further that drive. It had chosen Ushoran as its mount, but it could have picked any of them, even W'soran himself. That it hadn't provoked both relief and an odd, savage spurt of anger. Once again, poor old W'soran had been tossed aside in favour of another. Once more, poor old W'soran had been judged wanting by unworthy minds.

'Blessing in disguise,' he growled.

'But why are we running? Surely your might is equal to his,' Melkhior said.

'Perhaps, but now is not the time to test that theory,' W'soran

snarled. 'Not with both Abhorash and Neferata under his thumb. No, no we must flee – we must find a place from which to observe and plot anew. We must–'

Suddenly, a series of howls echoed through the lair. W'soran stiffened. 'Damnation,' he hissed. He had stationed ghouls at the approaches to his lair, to keep watch just in case Ushoran wasn't quite as distracted as he appeared. Those howls meant that that was sadly the case.

It looked like they would be fighting their way out of Mourkain after all...

Crookback Mountain
(Year -262 Imperial Calendar)

In the end, it had been easy enough to escape.

Ushoran had let him flee. There had been no mocking laughter, no pursuit, merely satisfied silence, as if some long-argued point had been proven. He had fled the pyramid, ignoring the fate of his commanders, allies and acolytes, ignoring the battle that still raged. Abhorash had seen him, and had grown even paler, his stony face settling into an expression of resigned sadness that stung W'soran more than any blade or mockery.

He had fled the city, wreathed in ghostly scarabs, hurtling himself away from the malignant enormity that had almost claimed him. In the days that followed, some of his forces caught up with him. Barely a third of his army had remained, and that third had disintegrated by steady increments as he made his way back to the dubious sanctuary of Crookback Mountain.

Ullo was dead, he thought, though he couldn't be sure. Abhorash had killed him, or perhaps Walak or Morath, or maybe he too had fled. Dhrox and Throttlehand had led a fighting withdrawal, only grudgingly giving ground as they were forced out of the city. Voloch was dead, and his wights had borne his body out of the city, the Draesca trailing behind them. Voloch II, his oldest son, had already assumed the helm, and it was only the magics within it and him that had enabled the Draesca to escape the field. They had made for the west and the Vaults. Dhrox and Throttlehand had gone west as well, with their followers.

W'soran's acolytes were dead, torn apart by the vengeful Strigoi. It was only his concentration that kept his army together; and day by day, it slipped a bit more and he left a trail of rotting body-parts and bones in his force's wake. W'soran rode no steed, skeletal or otherwise, but instead stumbled through the hills and bowers, cloak pulled tight, his gaze directed within, rather than without. He did not notice as his forces collapsed or wandered away as his control of them slipped and faded. The great bats were gone, and the spirit-hosts had dissipated.

When he at last reached the passes that marked the entrance to his demesnes, he was accompanied only by what remained of his bodyguard – a dozen wights. The wights neither complained nor spoke, and it was not his will alone that kept them animated. The rites required to permanently anchor their spirits to their bodies had been an exhausting process, but one he soon found to have been worth the effort.

The forts that guarded the passes had never been repaired or garrisoned after Ushoran's attack. There had been no reason, and as he picked his way through the snow-encrusted ruins, he cursed himself for his lack of foresight. Not just in regard to the garrisons, about everything. He had been a blind fool. A starving wolf, swallowing tainted meat.

In that moment of confrontation, he had seen himself for the fool he was. He had stalled and prevaricated for centuries, avoiding that moment, comforting himself with reassurances that it was all according to plan. But there had been no plan. Not really, not truly. Not one worth the name. He had not been buying time – he had merely been putting off the inevitable.

He had thought himself a player in a grand game, when, in reality, he had been nothing more than a pawn, played off by one side against the other. He had been used to clear the field of obstacles – Vorag, the rebel Strigoi... Ushoran.

He had been made a tool.

W'soran raised his arms and howled as a frigid wind curled through the ruin. Dark magic crackled through him as his rage built, warring with fear and self-loathing for control of his mind. He had been wielded deftly and precisely, aimed to strike a blow. Even now, he could not say who had aimed him, and at whom the blow had been aimed. Had Neferata and Abhorash conspired to send him against Nagash? Or had Ushoran used him to accomplish some indefinable purge of his own people, and thus pave the way for his eventual victory? It didn't matter. All that mattered was that he had been used – he, who had fancied himself the master planner, the paramount schemer, had merely been a cog in someone else's scheme.

Panting with anger, he peered through the shattered gates of the fort. Beyond the pass, the jagged, curving fang of Crookback Mountain rose through the mist and snow in the distance, beckoning him on. The safety that it promised was only temporary at best, he knew. He had been allowed to flee, but he would not – could not – be allowed to live. The point had been proven, but he was still dangerous, he could still be a thorn, if he so chose.

No, they would not let him live. He had to flee. He had to seek sanctuary elsewhere, he had to find another protector... perhaps Vorag still lived, somewhere in the east. If he could reach the Bloodytooth, if he could pass the blame off onto other shoulders, he might – what?

'What?' he muttered. 'Renew the fight? Why? What is to be done? What now for you, W'soran of Mahrak? What now to strive for, eh?'

He snarled in frustration. Sorcerous bolts erupted from his hands, striking the remains of a bunkhouse and a sagging, half-shattered palisade. He howled again, unleashing his anger on the ruined mountain fortress as his wights watched silently. Steam billowed into the air as his magics melted the snow and blasted the rocks to slag.

'What now for poor betrayed W'soran, eh?' he roared. 'Will he return to his citadel to await the coming of his enemies? What would be the point?' He whirled and gesticulated to his wights. 'Answer me that, eh? The world has become a jar, and defeat is the stake that pierces my old heart!'

'So melodramatic, old monster,' a voice giggled. The words bounced from rock to rock and seemed to come from everywhere and nowhere. W'soran spun about, his good eye blazing.

'So,' he spat, 'I should have known. That is to be my end, is it? Used and discarded? Is there no grace left in the world, no honour or mercy?'

It was a woman's voice that had called out to him, and familiar, though he could not put a name to it. But he knew what it meant. Whether she had engineered his defeat or not, Neferata had obviously decided that it was time to take him off the board. Now that the titans had had their duel, the handmaiden had come to remove the detritus from the field.

'Funny words coming from a serpent like you,' another voice said, laughing. The snow was falling harder now, and the wind moaned as it rushed through the ruin. Shapes moved across the shattered palisade. High-pitched laughter scraped his ears.

'Maybe he lies even to himself, eh?' a third voice chuckled, too closely. W'soran twisted, expecting an attack. But none came. Quicksilver shapes moved around him, almost floating across the driving snow.

'Twist and turn as you might, old monster, but this is one trap you cannot escape,' the first woman said in a sing-song voice.

'Trap?' W'soran muttered. 'What trap – what are you talking about? Reveal yourselves!'

Something hissed, at his elbow. A pale shape lunged upwards, bursting from the snow, serrated blades angled for W'soran's heart. He reacted instinctively, catching the blades and bringing his fist down on his attacker's head with skull-crunching force.

The skaven flopped limply to the snow. It was clad in white sack-cloth and its pale fur was encrusted with ice. Its blood cut canyons in the snow as it twitched and expired. His good eye widened and he looked around, sensing more than seeing its companions approaching. He gaped as he realised that there were hundreds of the ratkin creeping through the snow towards him and that they had likely been watching him the entire time, readying themselves to attack.

The skaven had long memories. They had sent an army for him; not just the white-clad killers, but armoured, black-furred warriors, and heavy-limbed rat ogres as well. They moved through the ruin, eyes fixed on him. The rat ogres rattled their chains and bellowed in anticipation of the blood yet to be spilled. Hundreds of ratkin moved towards him with but a single goal. He wondered, as he faced them, if he should have been flattered.

Slings whirred and bullets of silver struck him, burning his skin and cracking bone. W'soran staggered, screaming.

'Kill them,' he shrieked, but his wights did not move. They stood as stiff and as still as statues, their eyes glowing dully. His magics snapped and coiled about them, stymied by an unseen presence, and he gawped, off-balance and unprepared. Another sling-bullet caught him on the back of the head and he collapsed onto his hands and knees, his body racked with pain.

This was how it ended, then. The whole of it, shaved down to this sharp point of time. This was to be how W'soran of Mahrak died... butchered by vermin within sight of his citadel. It was almost poetic. He grimaced. He'd never liked poetry.

The skaven crept closer, some drawing blades. Others stayed at a distance, crouching on the rocks or the ruined palisade, their slings ready. Then, a sharp, raspy voice barked a command and the skaven froze. W'soran looked up. A hunched, crooked figure drew closer, stalking through the snow, wrapped in heavy furs. Its eyes blazed a sickly shade of green within the hood it wore. Armoured talons held its mangy furs tight about it, and a scarred, hairless snout protruded from its hood. W'soran recognised those scars, and the carefully shaped eyes of abn-i-khat that glared unblinkingly down at him. 'Out of time, man-thing,' Iskar hissed.

W'soran was astonished that the creature was still alive. Its features within its hood were more bone and brass than flesh and the gauntlets it wore over its crippled paws were seemingly less for protection than to hold its aged limbs steady. 'The mountain is ours,' it continued, a worm-like tongue dancing over its teeth. 'All of this is ours.'

W'soran shoved himself to his feet. 'Is it, then?' He looked around. 'Is that what Neferata has come to now? Making bargains with vermin against her old allies?' he asked loudly.

Iskar laughed in a weird, high-pitched voice, the skaven's crippled body shuddering with its mirth. That laughter was met and matched by the falsetto giggles of the women. W'soran gnashed his teeth in anger.

'You make enemies the way some men make wagers,' a woman said, striding forward through the swirling snow. 'Foolishly and with no intention of paying debts.' She was clad in thick furs that did little to hide the scars that covered her arms. In one hand, she loosely clutched a spear, its wide blade edged in silver. Her voice was muffled by the mask of silver she wore beneath a headscarf of crimson wool. The mask's expression was beautiful, yet stern, but behind it, her eyes burned with raw hatred. 'Is it any wonder that your creditors come together, to force recompense?'

W'soran stared at her without replying. She gestured to her mask. 'Admiring your handiwork, monster?' she asked. 'I am as you made me.'

'Layla,' W'soran muttered. 'Ha.' A thin, crooked smile spread across his face as he looked her up and down. 'I thought you were destroyed. Then again, I assumed you were dead as well,' he added, shooting a look at Iskar. 'Ah, poor foolish W'soran, to be haunted by old mistakes...' he began, mock-wretchedly.

'You ruined her,' the second voice spat. W'soran turned to see the Lahmian called Khemalla striding through the ranks of skaven, followed by the crimson-haired Iona. Both Lahmians wore furs and carried swords. 'You broke her and flayed her and the sisterhood of the Silver Pinnacle will make you pay for every drop of blood you squeezed from her flesh. You will pay for her pain and for that of Lupa Stregga as well, old monster!'

'Ha!' W'soran barked. 'Come then, come and take your pound of flesh, hags and vermin.' He turned slowly, casting his one-eyed glare about him. He spread his arms. 'Here I stand, beaten and helpless. Poor W'soran is at your mercy.'

'Beaten, possibly, but helpless? I doubt that.'

W'soran gave a grunt and turned. A black cloaked shape was trudging towards the fort. The skaven made way for it, and W'soran didn't need to see its face to recognise it. The moment the wights had disobeyed his commands to attack, he'd known that only one other will could vie with his for control of the dead, even as fatigued as he was.

'Melkhior,' he growled. 'I wish I could say that this is a surprise, that I expected you to die like a proper acolyte, defending my citadel, but...'

'But I am, as ever, a disappointment,' Melkhior said, stopping a respectful distance away. 'I have endured variations of that observation for centuries, as well as other abuses by your hand.' He looked around, his grisly features splitting in a needle-fanged grin. 'I thought you were the mightiest creature in the world, when Ushoran first bid me serve you.

And I served you well – I fought for your praise, the way you taught me. I made myself indispensable. The others were weak and I disposed of them for you, and you called me wasteful. I followed you into exile, and you showered praise on that traitor Morath. I guarded you from assassins and treachery and I was repaid with distrust and insults. And now, at last, I gain my own back. Today, master, you die.'

W'soran didn't reply. Melkhior chuckled wetly and began to circle him. 'This was all my doing, you know.' He motioned to the skaven and the Lahmians. 'I was forced to resort to more oblique means of maintaining your citadel for you, old monster. Are you not proud of my ingenuity?'

'If you displayed any, I might be,' W'soran said.

Melkhior snorted. 'I made allies of enemies and all for the cheap price of... you. I bought myself time, just as you taught me. I bought myself peace.' He looked back at the distant shape of Crookback Mountain. 'What need have I of fortresses and mountains?'

'They were not yours to give,' W'soran said.

'Nor were they yours to keep – Vorag, remember? The true heir to Kadon's throne,' Melkhior said. He tapped his malformed skull. 'Your authority is based on lies, old monster. Plans within plans, webs within webs, but what happens when the web is torn, eh?' Melkhior stopped moving and pointed at W'soran. 'While you marched on Mourkain, I weaved my own webs. Better and stronger than yours – the skaven are quite willing to make a deal, if the terms are beneficial. And with the skaven as intermediaries, I made overtures to old friends...' He gestured to the Lahmians. 'And now, here, at the end of all things, your death is assured.' Melkhior grinned widely. 'I have beaten you. Me – *I beat you!*'

'Did you?' W'soran asked. 'I don't think so. In fact, I rather think that you have misjudged the situation. Is that not right, Lahmian?' He glanced at Iona, who frowned.

'Silence, monster,' she said.

'What are you talking about?' Melkhior snarled.

'Oh Melkhior, have I not told you time and again that Neferata is perfectly willing to subordinate her desires to her needs?' W'soran grinned. 'She needs me. She needs my power. Neferata is not wasteful, like you. She may bury me away, in the dark, but she will not kill me. She needed me to defend Lahmia, and she needs me now to help her defend her new kingdom. They are not here to kill me, you fool... they are here to kill *you.*'

Melkhior blinked. 'What?'

'She needs me, fool. She needs my power. But she doesn't need you, Melkhior. You are useless – worse, you are dangerous, in the service of the wrong master. They are here to kill you, to burn you even as I burned my scrolls and tomes the day we fled Mourkain.' W'soran clucked his tongue. 'Useless, foolish Melkhior – even in treachery, you are a disappointment.'

Melkhior shrank back with a hiss. He looked wildly about him. Grim-faced, the Lahmians approached him. The skaven watched, apparently content with this turn. Iskar's snout wrinkled in cruel amusement as he watched Melkhior retreat from the trio of women. The skaven looked at W'soran and tapped one of its eyes with a metal claw. 'Maybe she give you new-new eyes, man-thing,' Iskar chattered.

W'soran said nothing. He felt the skeins of control that extended from Melkhior to his wights weaken. 'Attack,' he murmured.

There were a dozen of the wights. Armoured and armed, they were an intimidating sight. Even motionless, the skaven were giving them a wide berth. Nonetheless, the ratkin were surprised when the wights sprang to the attack. The barrow-blades sliced out, and skaven squealed and died. Sling-bullets sang off the wights' armour to no effect, and the small blades the ratmen carried proved equally ineffective.

Iskar's ruined eyes widened slightly, and then bulged as W'soran pounced, snatching him up. 'What was it you once said to me... ah yes, there's always time, vermin. It's just a matter of using it effectively,' he hissed.

Metal talons raked across his face and he was forced to release the warlock-engineer. Iskar fell, but bounded to his feet with a hiss of pneumatic pumps. It flung aside its furs to reveal the armour that sheltered its ruined body. It was a crude thing of plates and pumps and like Iskar's gauntlets, seemed less for protection than to provide support. Nonetheless, the skaven seemed almost eager for battle. It revealed its blackened fangs in a snarl and raised its claws. 'Die-die, man-thing,' Iskar shrilled, flinging itself at W'soran.

The claws burned like fire as they carved into his arm. They were crafted with veins of wyrdstone running through them, and were more potent for it. Given the way his opponent was frothing, W'soran thought it likely that Iskar had consumed some of the stone as well. It was probably all that was keeping the elderly skaven alive, especially given his condition. The creature was held together by nothing but hate and magic.

The claws cut through his robes, opening his flesh with a sizzling hiss. W'soran caught Iskar by his throat and hefted him. The skaven thrashed and squealed, tearing at him frenziedly.

'You've lived too long, I think,' W'soran said. Then, with barely a flicker of effort, he reached up and crushed the skaven's skull. He hurled the twitching body aside and spun about as more silver sling-bullets slammed into him. Though the bulk of the skaven were occupied with the wights, there were still more than enough to be dangerous. He scrambled away, hunting for cover.

'Where are you going, old beast?'

The wedge of the spear-blade punched through his side, knocking him sprawling. W'soran screamed and tried to drag himself up as Layla approached. She had hurled the spear with enough force to bruise his spine, and his limbs weren't working correctly as he tried to pull himself away. He spat blood and hissed as she planted a foot on his back and took hold of the spear. 'You are correct, Lady Neferata does want you alive. But she said nothing about you being in one piece.'

She raised her spear, her eyes blazing behind the serene mask she wore. 'You ruined me, beast. Now I return the favour.'

With a surge of panicked strength, W'soran shoved himself up, dislodging her. She staggered back and W'soran rose to his feet, blood coating his tattered robes. He swatted aside the spear as she awkwardly thrust it at him and lunged for her.

His claws scraped across her mask, tearing it from her head. She screamed and clutched at her ruined face – the flesh had re-grown at last, leaving her now bestial features further marred by wide scars and blisters. She stumbled back, and he snatched up the spear. With a single thrust, he sent it tearing through her midsection and she fell, clutching at the blood-slick haft.

W'soran turned as a skaven blade skidded off his hip. Sorcerous fire writhed from his fingers, incinerating the ratkin and rippling outwards to catch half a dozen more in the halo of flame. He unleashed spell after spell into the swirling snow even as he backed away. Rat ogres roared and shoved towards him, urged on by their handlers, and he flayed the flesh from one with a savage gesture.

His back smashed into something and he glanced over his shoulder to see Melkhior. His acolyte was covered in wounds and panting like a dying bull. He held his blade extended towards the two feminine shapes loping towards them with deadly intent. 'Master, I–' he began.

'Shut up, Melkhior,' W'soran snarled. The wights had fallen, dragged down by sheer weight of numbers. The skaven approached, a living carpet of hairy killers skittering over the snow. The black-furred, armoured ratkin were closing in, shields raised and spears extended. Iskar had come prepared. There were more than enough of the ratkin to simply swarm him. One lucky strike and he was done for. Once again, there was only one option. Bitterness filled him, and he was tempted to ignore the obvious, to fight and kill until he was brought down.

It always came down to running. He'd fled Mahrak and Lahmia, Nagashizzar and Lashiek and Mourkain – a trail of cowardice, of spoiled dreams and thwarted desires, that was to be his legacy. Nagash had scarred the world, stamping his mark on the very skin of reality. But W'soran would be forgotten, crammed into another jar and only freed when there was no other choice. He would be nothing but a tool if he was caught, and forgotten if he fled. He was not a master of death, but merely its puppet. He was an engine, a tool.

'No,' he said, rejecting the thought. 'No. No, I am not a servant. Not any more.'

Through the blinding snow, he saw the shape of Layla rip the spear from her belly. He saw Iona and Khemalla approaching, the skaven gathering and, far beyond them, past the snow and mountains, the black shadow that hung over Mourkain. His enemies were all around him, even as they had been in Mahrak and Lahmia and Nagashizzar. Death – the true death – spread its wings over him, as it had so many times previously.

And just as he had those times, W'soran did not wish

to die. He would run. He would always run, because to do otherwise was to surrender and W'soran would never surrender, not to his inferiors, not to inevitability. 'No,' W'soran hissed. 'No, not today, not like this. I can't die. Not me. Never me, do you understand?' He hurled the words at his enemies. He wasn't a god, or even a king. He was just a man without any moves left, save one. 'I won't let you kill me!' he shrieked. 'The Master of Death does not die! Not here – not ever!'

The amulets of abn-i-khat still hung from his neck. He had not used them, had not dared. But there was nothing for it now, and anger overrode caution. The skaven at least would remember him, as they remembered Nagash, and the Lahmians as well, if only to curse his name. With a growl, he ripped the amulets from his neck and stuffed them into his mouth, his needle fangs grinding the soft stones to dust and releasing the hellish power they contained. There was no pain this time, only burning satisfaction. He was beaten, he was outnumbered, but when had it ever been otherwise? When had the world ever not sought to bury poor W'soran beneath its weight?

And when had he ever let it?

Green fire curling about him, he went to meet the enemy. Entire generations of skaven had been birthed and raised to what passed for maturity amongst their kind since the last time they had faced W'soran on the battlefield. But skaven memory was long, especially where fear was concerned. As he stepped forward, flames coiling about his thin arms and writhing in his dead eyes, the memory of fear was rekindled.

The skaven ranks began to retreat – pulling back from the apparition that faced them. W'soran's hiss reverberated across the pass, and snow and ice tumbled from the high crags to crash into the ruin. Then he howled and death flew from his fingers and mouth. Skaven died in droves, burnt, boiled or blasted aside. With a shriek that would have frightened even the great bats of the depths, W'soran ploughed into the skaven ranks, lashing out with whips of flame and blades of shadow. He did not bother to raise the dead; he had no need of them. He fought alone – he had always fought alone. Bodies tumbled and spun about him, sent hurtling into the air by his frenzied magics. The air was full of blood and fear-musk.

The abn-i-khat sang in his veins and burned in his blood as he washed the life from the mountain pass. They had taken his refuge from him, but he intended to see that they paid for it in full, measure for measure. So intent was he on this that he barely noticed what effect his slaughter was having on the pass in which the ruined fort crouched.

With a thunderous roar, several tons of ice, snow and rock plummeted from the upper reaches of the pass and speared down onto the ruin, shattering what was left of the palisades and bunk-houses. Skaven screamed as they were buried beneath the avalanche. W'soran stood, the power draining from him as he let the rock and ice crash around him.

He felt relief, but no fear. Was that what Ushoran had meant, so long ago on the coast of the Black Gulf? Was this what it felt like, when the fear was burned out of you?

His last sight, before the darkness consumed him, was of the shadow over Mourkain.

—❮ EPILOGUE ❯—

The Worlds Edge Mountains,
(Year -223 Imperial Calendar)

As the darkness cleared, taking his jumbled memories with it, W'soran's remaining hand snapped up and clamped against Melkhior's throat as the latter's jaws descended. Blood pumping from his torn throat, W'soran locked gazes with his treacherous acolyte. 'Webs within webs,' he gurgled. Melkhior's eyes widened as he realised his danger, but too late. He grabbed for W'soran's wrist, but couldn't break his grip.

In the end, W'soran had figured it out entirely by accident. It was ironic, and painfully so, but by that time, he hadn't cared. The secret of immortality had come so easily, in that white-hot moment of fear in Ushoran's palace, though he had not realised it until much later. And not simply that secret, but all of the mysteries which had plagued him had become clear in those disjointed moments as he had faced his enemy, and then fled.

It was about death. More, it was about the fear of death. There was a great power in fear, this he had always known. But through fear had come clarity. It was fear that had shown him the path to true immortality. The fear that had been his bane since childhood had shown him the way, at the last.

The answer had been in front of him the entire time. The body – the mortal flesh – was an anchor and in the case of himself, an anchor that could not be dislodged from its place without extraordinary effort. Vampires, liches and wights – every undead thing was a ghost haunting its own mortified flesh. And it was only when that spirit was in danger of being freed of its anchor that true immortality beckoned.

He had seen that for himself with the wraiths dragged from the mutilated flesh of necromancers. The spark of their power remained and blossomed into something beautiful once freed of its restrictive meat. Why should the same thing not be possible with W'soran himself? But try as hard as he might, the key to unlocking that power remained elusive. Until Mourkain, until he had felt the fear of destruction – the fear of the final darkness.

It was fear, the mortal fear of death, that motivated men like Morath, whether they admitted it to themselves or not. It made them learn, experiment, and evolve in ways that creatures like W'soran could not, frozen as they were in time like flies trapped in amber.

While W'soran lived, he could never truly attain the immortality – the power – he desired. Only in dying could he become the master of death. That was Nagash's secret – to transcend death and fear, one had to be consumed by them, like a disease burning itself out.

You have finally proven useful, my son, W'soran thought, *as I have always suspected you would.* His blood mingled with Melkhior's as they struggled and he read his acolyte's thoughts with the ease with which he might have read a book or scroll. Images flared and faded as he plunged through the shadowed recesses of Melkhior's mind.

He saw the aftermath of that final ambush near Crookback Mountain, and saw Melkhior being dragged from the icy tomb of the pass by Neferata's servants. By then, W'soran had been long gone and far away, having burned his way free of the snow and rock. They had taken Melkhior back to the Silver Pinnacle, where Melkhior had traded on his knowledge of his master to buy himself a few more years of life.

What did you promise them? Did you kneel at Neferata's feet and claim to be able to drain my secrets from my corpse? Did you swear that in devouring me, you would learn all that I knew and employ it for Neferata's benefit? If his throat hadn't been a gaping ruin, W'soran might have laughed. He almost admired Melkhior's sheer stubborn refusal to admit defeat. It was one of the few things they had in common.

Ah, but we both know that you had no intention of giving her what she wanted, did you, my son? Melkhior's thoughts whirred and flitted like frightened birds as W'soran spoke into his mind. *You spent years hunting me, hounding my trail, and for what? To give up what you learned to her? No, you have never been one for sharing, have you? She must have seen that. That is why she sent her hounds with you – to see that you returned. Did you think that you would fight them? That you could win? Or was the thought of servitude nothing next to your petulant desire to defeat me, and to prove yourself the master?*

He had had time to think, in his years of isolation. Not all of his acolytes had died – some had been smart enough to flee the battle at Mourkain or Melkhior's madness, and they had found him in the wilderness and he had begun again. But not because he intended to play the game, no, he knew better than that now.

This fortress, even himself – it was all bait.

Were you impressed with my acting skills? Did you even wonder why I desired the books now, when I had ever before been willing to sacrifice them for my safety? Of course you didn't, because you never understood that they are merely tools and of little conse-quence to one such as I. Bait, Melkhior, bait for the beast, bait for the trap, he thought, *bait for you, my most faithful son!*

He had learned his lessons. Before, he had been drawn in and spitted on his own hubris. He had made too many enemies, shown too much of his power. They knew him now, his foes. They had drawn him from his den, and seen his teeth and claws, and they would not rest until he was caged or dead.

He had been caged enough for one lifetime. That left death, the ultimate escape.

Webs within webs and plans within plans; flight had always been his preferred option, regardless of what he told himself. *Why do you always run*, that had been Ushoran's question.

And the answer was… *survival*.

To outlive and outlast his enemies was the only vengeance worth the name. Contests of strength were for warriors and brutes and W'soran was neither. He had been fooled, for a time, into thinking he was, even as Nagash had, but unlike Nagash, he knew better now. Power – true power – was not measured in heads on posts or kneeling foes, but simply in being the last man standing. To win ultimate victory, all one had to do was wait for a time. All one had to do was persist.

I am become death, he thought. *I am still your master, boy, and you are my tool, and you have not an iota of the will needed to deny me!* He dragged Melkhior close, so close that he could smell the other vampire's fear, and he lunged, driving his fangs into Melkhior's throat. *Goodbye, my son. In the end, at the last, you have proven your use as you always desired.*

Melkhior screamed. And W'soran died.

W'soran's jaws spasmed and then released their grip. He flopped to the ground. As the echoes of his scream faded, Melkhior opened his eyes and stared at his talons in something akin to wonder. They were strong, not withered or practically mummified, but fleshy and powerful looking.

'Ha,' he hissed. 'Death…'

'Melkhior,' the Lahmian said. He looked at her, putting a

name to the face – Khemalla. It took him a further moment
to recall that she was speaking to *him*.

'Yes, I am – well,' he rasped. He looked down at the shrivelled thing at his feet. 'He, however, is not.'

'He looked as if he were going to kill you,' Khemalla said,
sinking to her haunches beside the corpse. 'And then it
appeared as if he just... gave up.'

'He was tired of running,' Melkhior said.

'What?' Khemalla looked up at him.

'He was old. Far older than most things walking this world,
and he was tired. Why do you think he waited for us here?
We didn't ambush him... he knew we were coming. He just
didn't know when.' He looked down at the body. 'Good riddance to him.'

He turned and looked at the vault. Khemalla rose to her
feet. 'The Strigoi are still out there somewhere. We should
go.'

The Strigoi did not serve them, he recalled suddenly,
flipping through his memories and grabbing hold of the
right one. Though Neferata's hounds had sniffed out the
old wolf's lair first, they were not the only hunters on his
trail. Ushoran too – or perhaps Nagash – desired to control
W'soran, and to make use of his power.

Well, too late for that now.

'I think not,' Melkhior said. He looked at her. 'You and
your sisters can handle them easily enough. And I will need
time to... consume his secrets and make them my own, several days at least.'

Khemalla's eyes narrowed. 'Do not attempt to deceive us, sorcerer. One does not enter lightly into bargains with the Queen of Mysteries.'

'Poor, foolish Melkhior, deceive the mistress of the Silver Pinnacle? Perish the thought,' Melkhior said. 'I am not that old monster, woman. I wish peace, or at least a lack of enmity between myself and your sisterhood. I have no interest in games of power or empires.'

'But you will help us,' Khemalla said warily.

'Oh yes, yes, a bargain is a bargain,' Melkhior said. 'I will help your queen refine the teachings of Morath, and I will deliver unto her the pick of what resides in these vaults, as promised. And then, I will vanish, and leave your lot and Ushoran's to squabble over these pitiful mountains in peace.'

Khemalla stared at him for a moment, and then nodded tersely. She sheathed her blade and turned away. In the blink of an eye, she was gone; truly gone, and not simply hiding.

'Yes, a few days I think. That should be more than enough to see to things. And then... what? What then for poor – ah – Melkhior, eh,' he murmured, looking again at his hand.

He looked down at the shrivelled corpse, as if expecting an answer. When none was forthcoming, he knelt. He reached out a hand, as if to touch the slack features and the glazed eye, now forever unblinking. He reached up and traced the edge of his own eye. Then, in a quick motion, he scooped up the body and, cradling it to his chest, he turned to face the vault.

He spoke a single word. It hummed through the air and the stone of the walls and link by link, the chains began to rattle. They rose to the height of a man and in the wide space before the stone, motes of pale light appeared and blossomed into the same ragged phantoms as before. They screamed in silence, writhing beneath the weight of the chains as they began to move forward, straining against the wedge, pulling the chains. The wedge groaned in its housing and began to pull free of the hole as it had earlier. In moments, the vault was once more open and strange lights could be seen within.

And the Master of Death smiled.

ABOUT THE AUTHOR

Author of the novels *Knight of the Blazing Sun, Time of Legends: Neferata* and *Gotrek and Felix: Road of Skulls*, **Josh Reynolds** used to be a roadie for the Hong Kong Cavaliers, but now writes full time. His work has appeared in various anthologies, including *Age of Legend* and several issues of the electronic magazine *Hammer and Bolter*.